The Border Lords

T. JEFFERSON PARKER

The Border Lords

DUTTON

DUTTON
Published by Penguin Group (USA) Inc.
375 Hudson Street, New York, New York 10014, U.S.A.
Penguin Group (Canada), 90 Eglinton Avenue East, Suite 700, Toronto, Ontario M4P
2Y3, Canada (a division of Pearson Penguin Canada Inc.); Penguin Books Ltd, 80 Strand,
London WC2R 0RL, England; Penguin Ireland, 25 St Stephen's Green, Dublin 2, Ireland (a
division of Penguin Books Ltd); Penguin Group (Australia), 250 Camberwell Road, Cam-
berwell, Victoria 3124, Australia (a division of Pearson Australia Group Pty Ltd); Penguin
Books India Pvt Ltd, 11 Community Centre, Panchsheel Park, New Delhi–110 017, India;
Penguin Group (NZ), 67 Apollo Drive, Rosedale, North Shore 0632, New Zealand (a
division of Pearson New Zealand Ltd); Penguin Books (South Africa) (Pty) Ltd, 24 Sturdee
Avenue, Rosebank, Johannesburg 2196, South Africa

Penguin Books Ltd, Registered Offices: 80 Strand, London WC2R 0RL, England

Published by Dutton, a member of Penguin Group (USA) Inc.

First printing, January 2011
1   3   5   7   9   10   8   6   4   2

LIBRARY OF CONGRESS CATALOGING-IN-PUBLICATION DATA
has been applied for

ISBN 978-0-525-95200-8

Printed in the United States of America
Set in Sabon
Designed by Leonard Telesca

PUBLISHER'S NOTE
This book is a work of fiction. Names, characters, places, and incidents either are the product
of the author's imagination or are used fictitiously, and any resemblance to actual persons,
living or dead, business establishments, events, or locales is entirely coincidental.

For Rita
Bride, Partner, Sister in Arms

The Border Lords

Prologue

"**Charlie, Gravas here.** Reporting live from the Wild West."

"Good to hear from you, friend."

"My machine gun peddlers got a whiff of something. Me waiting there with my cash and meth like a dude with flowers and chocolates. They stood me up. How's my Seliah?"

"She sounded great like she always sounds."

"She doesn't tell you how hard this is for her."

"Neither do you."

"I feel strong, and clear in the eye. I want someone bigger than those machine gun punks anyway. I want someone with heft. I'm making some contacts out here. I'll get within spitting distance of Carlos Herredia if it kills me. Maybe I shouldn't put it that way."

"You're where you need to be. And when it's done you're out and rolling home."

"If Seliah needs something, she's going to call you."

"As always."

"I keep coming back to her, don't I?"

"You're supposed to come back to her."

"Gotta go now. Bad actors, incoming."

"Vaya con Dios."

"Yeah. I always go with God when I waddle around in hell."

1

Just before sunset the first bat fluttered from the cave and came toward him, wobbling and breeze-blown, like a black snowflake ahead of a storm. It rose and navigated between the trunks of the banana trees, then climbed into the magenta sky. Another flew, and then another.

The priest stood facing them, his feet together and his back straight and his hands folded before him. The reeking cave mouth yawned and the bats spilled out. He watched them come at him, then veer abruptly.

From the first few, he heard faint chirps but soon there were too many and all he could hear was their muffled flight. Then the air was heavy with them, a great dark blanket of membranous wings and small faces and tiny feet. One of them brushed his cheek and another glanced off his hair and another screeched at him in fear. Some of them dropped guano that tapped against his windbreaker but the priest stood motionless and let the flood of hair and skin rush past. *My music*, he thought. He considered the centuries and still the flood rushed.

When it was over he stepped inside. The smell was stronger. He lit a candle with a plastic lighter. Before he spoke he cleared his throat as he would before the homily.

"Yoo-hoo, little creatures of the night. Father Joe, here to see you."

His candle revealed the holdouts still hanging from the walls by their feet, wrapped like football fans, not in blankets but in their wings. Some of them squinted into the insult of the light; some shifted irritably like insomniacs, all snouts and elbows.

"Not quite feeling up to it tonight? The halt and the lame and the old and the sick. Feeling just a little off, are we?"

The priest strolled deeper into the darkness and the stench. A bat ran across his path, upright, wings raised overhead like a tiny man with an umbrella, looking back and up at him.

The priest stopped and held up the candle. A bat peered down from the wall and the man saw the glitter in its purblind eyes, the quivering, inquisitive expression on its face. The man cocked his head. The bat bared its teeth and screeched. The mouth was large for the face and the incisors were large for the mouth, and needle-like. The leafed nostrils were flared and its ears were enormous. The little animal began breathing faster, and it extended its wings and resettled them back around its body.

"Cold, my little friend?" The man saw the froth of saliva gathered at the chin, and when the bat sneezed the foam flew off.

The priest extended his free hand toward the animal. Again the bat bared its teeth and screeched but the priest didn't move, and a moment later the animal crawled down the wall a few feet closer to him. It was a cumbersome movement, with the thumb hooks grappling for purchase on the rock, and the minute toes spread for traction, and the sheer wings clumsy and useless. "Come closer, little *fliedermaus*. I'm not going to climb up there to get you!" The bat clambered closer and the priest stood on his toes and offered his finger and the bat climbed on.

The priest relaxed and lowered both arms and studied the animal in the light. Its eyes were bright in spite of their weakness. The man blew a puff of breath onto the animal, rippling its thin fur and revealing the almost-human shape of the rib cage. The bat cringed and screeched and bared its teeth again, and in this the priest saw humankind's embodiment of evil distilled into a single horrific face.

"Thank you," said the priest.

He dropped the candle to the cave floor where the guano devoured the flame and left him in darkness supreme. He gently cupped the bat between thumb and forefinger, then put it in his windbreaker pocket, zipping it halfway for security and oxygen. Then he carefully picked his way back out of the cave.

2

Charlie Hood sat in the ATF field station in Buenavista and watched the live-feed monitors. Hood was thirty-two, tall and loose, with an earnest face and calm eyes. He had been watching the screens for eight hours, doing his job for the ATF Blowdown task force. It was not pure excitement. He was on loan from the L.A. Sheriff's Department but by now he had spent fifteen months in this often infernal, often violent, often beautiful desert. He liked this place and he feared it. He palmed another handful of popcorn from its paper container without taking his eyes from the screen.

Buenavista was a California border town with a population of thirty thousand and an elevation of twelve feet. The monitors displayed live feeds from a "safe house" in one of Buenavista's nicer neighborhoods, three miles away. The Blowdown team called the house *the Den*. ATF had bought it on the cheap as a foreclosure, then wired it for sound and video. Hood's friend Sean Ozburn, an ATF agent operating deep undercover as a meth and gun dealer, had arranged to have it rented as a home for four young gunmen of the North Baja Cartel.

The assassins ranged in age from seventeen to twenty-two, and

ATF figured them good for thirty murders between them. Some in Mexico. Some stateside. Almost all business related, the business being recreational drugs. Sales of those drugs brought Mexico some fifty billion dollars a year—by far the single largest contributor to its economy.

Hood watched one of the pistoleros, Angel, standing in his kitchen while a pot of *carnitas* warmed on the stovetop. Hood knew it was *carnitas* because two nights ago he'd watched Angel prepare the pork for boiling. Now the pot was on the stove again and a tortilla was warming on one of the electric burners and there was a skillet of eggs going.

It was unusual for any of the young killers to be up this early but Angel was here in the kitchen and Johnnie and Ray were in the living room. Angel was the only one who ever cooked anything. He was a skinny little guy with a wisp of a mustache and an overbite. He stood still a moment and watched his own monitor, a little kitchen-size DVD player on which he watched nothing but American gangster movies. This morning it was *Scarface* again, in Spanish, Angel at times mumbling along with Pacino, mimicking his expressions. A machine pistol with a noise suppressor and an extended magazine lay on the counter by the DVD player.

These guns had first come to Blowdown's attention in Mexican crime scene photographs late last year. Nobody at Blowdown had ever actually seen one except possibly Hood, two summers ago, though he wasn't totally sure at the time *what* he was seeing. He knew for certain that brand-new semiautomatic handguns were being packed for shipment at a Southern California gun factory. This he had confirmed with his own eyes. Then these illegally made guns had slipped away from Blowdown, right under their collective noses—one thousand gleaming new handguns, gone. Hood suspected they were headed south to Mexico.

Now he wondered again if one of those apparently humble handguns could somehow be converted into a curve-clipped, silenced beauty like the one lying on Angel's kitchen counter. Hood would bet on it. If he was right, he knew for certain who had built the one thousand silenced machine pistols—a talented young gunmaker named Ron Pace. And if that was true, Hood also had very strong ideas about who had delivered them into the hands of Carlos Herredia's North Baja Cartel gunmen—a fellow LASD deputy named Bradley Jones. Hood was hot to get his hands on one of those guns. All of ATF was hot to get one. And Hood wanted to send Pace and Jones to the slammer where they belonged.

He ate and watched and opened another soda. Graveyard was hard on sleep and diet. He wondered if the assassins were up early because they had a job to do. Usually they slept until noon. His mind wandered back to Sean Ozburn again, and Hood wondered why Ozburn had gone silent. Almost fifteen months undercover, and once a day Sean would call one of the Blowdown team—usually Hood—even when he had nothing substantial to report. He called it *touching his life raft*. Fifteen months UC was a long run in anyone's book. Too long, according to many with experience. The calls had been Sean's established pattern and it had worked for him, and now he had broken it. Six days and no call.

So maybe Sean had been made, Hood thought. He wasn't sold on the whole idea of the bugged safe house, because of that possibility. One whiff of suspicion or one person who recognized Ozburn, and boom—he was dead, or worse. The Den was supposed to be an ATF jewel but they all knew its potential cost to their man undercover.

And the bugged safe house wasn't only a risk; it was frustrating, too. Hood understood that they didn't have enough evidence to arrest any of the four assassins. Most of their murders were committed across the border where ATF was essentially helpless. And the murders they were suspected of committing in the States were quiet and neat: no willing witnesses, no weapons left behind, no written warnings or mutilations or beheadings, just plenty of shots to the head and heart and that was that. Always .32 Automatic Colt Pistol rounds. Nobody heard. Nobody saw. Nobody knew anything. *All this manpower and technology, and not an arrest made*, thought Hood.

But the truth, and he knew it, was that ATF didn't want to roll up the Den and go to court just yet, because although the four young *sicarios* were only small-time killers, they were gold mines of information. Since this "safe house" had been activated four weeks ago, their conversations and phone calls had provided ATF hundreds of hours of talk and video, giving the Blowdown team a street-level view of the North Baja Cartel's blood-soaked battle for Southern California.

Behind Hood, three large, rolling whiteboards were backed against the far wall. Two of them were jammed with writing and one was beginning to fill—names, crimes, suspects, straw buyers, timelines, organizational charts, routes, possible tunnel locations, turf, family relations, feuds, debts—many grouped in circles and linked by solid lines or broken lines or some by strings of small question marks. Certainties were written in black. Suspicions were rendered in red, speculations in blue. It looked like graffiti. And all of it was gathered by ATF eavesdropping on the four baby-faced hit men. Blowdown wasn't after the likes of these boys. They were after the lieutenants and up, to the top of the food chain—the men who bought the guns and called the shots.

So, Hood thought, *the whiteboards are full of intel but the killers are free to roam about the cabin.*

He looked at monitor two and watched Johnnie and Ray playing Halo on the living room fifty-four-inch TV. Hood lifted an audio headset to his ear and winced: As usual the boys had the volume up loud. The hidden mikes were so good they could pick up both ends of a phone call, and this video combat game blaring through the home theater system sounded like Armageddon itself.

Johnnie and Ray were the two Americans, poor kids recruited from the rough Buenavista streets, kids with voracious desires and stunted notions of self-control. Hood knew their plan for happiness: Get a gun, get a job using it, get some decent clothes, get a better gun, get a car, get a big-screen television, get a truck, get a girl. Then, if you were still alive get a house, somewhere to put your girl and your stuff. They always bought the house last. It was the same for all the young pistoleros along the border. The cartels didn't care if they were American or Mexican. *Global economy*, thought Hood. Johnnie was the seventeen-year-old and he had earned a new Dodge Ram 1500 two weeks ago as a bonus for a hit in Tijuana. *Chunks flying out the back of his head*, as he'd bragged to Ray one evening, over and over. Johnnie had washed the gleaming black truck fourteen consecutive nights, up late, inside the garage of the Agate Street safe house so the neighbors wouldn't see him. He talked to the truck as he polished its coat.

Only Oscar was unaccounted for now. He claimed to have a girlfriend in Buenavista but no matter how much the other assassins teased him, Oscar had so far refused to bring her to his lair.

Hood heard two sharp knocks on the front door of the office, then the buzz from the ID reader. He glanced up at the security camera, then looked at the first light of the October morning just now touching the drawn blinds.

Dyman Morris came into the room with a tall cup of coffee and his war bag, and he set both on the desk, then sat two chairs down from Hood. He looked up at the screens. There were six of them.

Dyman smelled of soap and his dark skull was cleanly shaved. "Look at this. The baby killers are stirring."

"Maybe they've got something coming up."

"Still nothing from Sean?"

Hood shook his head and watched Angel flip his tortilla. "I left him another message. That's three in six days."

In the silence that followed, Hood thought of their comrade Jimmy Holdstock, kidnapped last year on U.S. soil and taken to Mexico. Hood knew that Dyman was thinking of Jimmy, too. Jimmy hadn't even been working UC like Sean. Jimmy wasn't setting up bugged safe houses for the North Baja Cartel like Sean. Jimmy was just a former divinity student, part of the Blowdown team checking ATF Firearm Transaction forms, keeping an eye on the licensed dealers, trying to stem the flow of the iron river—the guns heading south.

"What I don't get," said Hood, "is who tells these boys they can do this."

"Do what, Charlie."

"Kill people for money."

"The cartel recruiters tell them that."

"But what about the consequences?"

"You've seen the consequences, man—a new truck for a bonus, and free prostitutes, like last week. Remember when Ray got that ten grand for a job well done?"

"What I mean is, who tells them it's okay?"

"Who do they have to tell them different? Their parents either don't care or don't know what to do. These boys don't go to school. Probably haven't been inside a church their whole life. So who are they gonna listen to except each other, and the actors in the movies they watch, and the cartel dudes with all the cash?"

Hood thought about that. "Still seems like something's missing. Some kinda horse sense or something."

"You had advantages you didn't know you had. I had them, too. Bakersfield is like Beverly Hills compared to these border towns."

Hood, a Bakersfield boy, nodded. Morris of the South Bronx sipped his coffee.

By six thirty A.M. agents Janet Bly and Robert Velasquez had arrived. This was the transitional hour, when the graveyard watcher went off duty and the three-agent day team took over for another shift of interviewing firearms dealers, recruiting informants, shadowing suspected buyers and sellers, posing as straw men and illicit buyers, answering the phones and watching the young killers on live feed— all in a day's work for Blowdown.

"Well, look who's up bright and early today," said Bly. "Is that Angel with his *carnitas*?"

Hood nodded, looking at Angel's machine pistol again.

"Sean call in?" asked Janet.

Hood shook his head, saw the hardness in her face.

"Then maybe he called Mars or Soriana."

"He'd call us first if he was in trouble," said Hood, confident that his good friend Sean Ozburn would call Blowdown well before he'd call the ATF field station in San Diego. Ozburn was a soldier, loyal and focused.

But six days and no calls. So the ghost of Jimmy Holdstock— retired now with long-term disability from injuries suffered in the line of duty; in his case, torture—hovered there in the war room once again.

Then, as if that ghost had cast its long, dark shadow over the room, one of the monitors went white, then black, and the audio died.

Hood's attention had been drawn to it just a split second before it went blank.

"The hell," said Bly.

"Don't worry," said Velasquez, their techie. "It'll come back. I'm not sure what's . . ."

Thirty seconds later the other monitors suddenly all turned bright white, then black. And the audio feeds died with them.

Blowdown was on its feet now. Velasquez looked down at the main control panel, head cocked. The others stared at the dead screens. They had lost camera transmissions before but never all of them at once.

"This is what my son does when the satellite goes out during SpongeBob," said Morris. "He just stares at the TV like he can make it come back on."

"It'll come back," said Velasquez.

Hood dialed Buenavista police chief Gabe Reyes and asked for an unmarked unit to drive by the Agate Street safe house, and Reyes said the shift was changing right now but consider it done. *Ten long minutes*, thought Hood, ringing off.

"Cops are changing shifts," he said. "Ten minutes."

"We can't lose all six feeds," said Velasquez. "Even in a power outage, even if someone cuts the line. Those cameras have two hours of battery backup. You have to shut them down from here, or in the control panel on the side of the safe house. But I built that control panel, and I disguised it as a breaker box, and it's got a lock, and the only people who have keys are us. So what the—"

"I saw something on screen six," said Hood. "Just before it went out."

"I was watching Angel make his breakfast," said Bly.

"I was seeing if Johnnie's gravity hammer can kill brutes," said Morris.

"I saw something, too," said Velasquez. "Then it was gone."

"The Den is only three miles away," said Hood.

"Wait," said Bly, the senior agent.

Velasquez pushed various control buttons but nothing happened. "It's gotta be at our end. I'm going outside to check the cable."

"I'm with you," said Hood.

They emerged through the back door into the young light of morning, Hood first, his hand on the sidearm holstered on his hip. They walked quickly, looking up at the black coaxial cable fastened along the fascia board above the eaves. It entered the field station through a hole low on the eastern wall, and Hood could see the cable and the hole and the nest of gray steel wool crammed in to keep the rats and snakes out. Velasquez knelt down and tugged at the cable, then shrugged and stood.

They checked the circuit breaker panel and the relay boxes and the splitters and the transformers for the coax and the telephone landlines, and all of these Velasquez said were fine.

"The problem is at the Den," he said. "Unless some fine citizen plowed a car through a phone company switch box between here and there."

"What did you see on monitor six?"

"I don't know, Charlie. It happened too fast."

"It'll be on the tape."

"Monitor six is the side yard," said Velasquez.

"Where the control box is," said Hood.

They exchanged looks and went back inside.

The screens were still dead. Hood could tell by the forced calm of her voice that Bly was talking to Soriana out in San Diego. Bly was impulsive and Soriana was deliberate, and this tried her patience sorely.

She rang off and lowered her cell phone. "Soriana says give it five."

"I'd go right now," said Hood.

"I would, too," said Bly. She was a stout woman whose sweet round face the years with ATF had started to harden. "He's afraid the *narcos* will make us if we drive by looking like tourists. But we'll give it five, all right? Because he's the boss. Yes. Five *seconds*, that is. You guys ready?"

Dyman Morris, once a point guard for NYU, made it to the door first, swinging an armored vest off the coatrack like a kid going out to play in the cold.

A few minutes later Hood was guiding his Durango down Agate Street, looking at the little crowd of people standing outside the Den in the dawn's early light.

3

The neighbors greeted them with tales of gunshots and screams and a guy smoking off in a black Range Rover, so the Blowdown team went in through the wide-open front door.

Hood followed his autoloader into the kitchen where Angel lay nearly decapitated by a shotgun. The blasts had also torn the stove hood open and flung a storm of flesh and blood against the wall. The machine pistol was gone and the tortilla lay, shriveled, black and smoking, on the griddle.

In the living room Ray and Johnnie had taken multiple rounds and they lay in ribbons on the floor. Johnnie had gotten his gun up, or at least a gun lay next to him. It was one of the silenced .32 machine pistols that no one at ATF had ever seen until late last year. The Halo game had gone into sleep mode, its Gregorian chant soundtrack swelling across the room.

Hood and Morris moved through the house as a team. Hood had that nobody-alive-here feeling but his stomach and nerves were stretched tight. *Like Anbar, door-to-door*, he thought. Like a drug tunnel he'd once found himself trapped in by unhappy gunmen. They covered the empty house quickly, then backtracked to the living room where Hood shut off the video game and the chanting stopped.

He peeked through the blinds and looked outside at Bly and Velasquez. The two agents were helping the Buenavista cops seal the scene against the public. The agents looked cooperative enough right now, but Hood knew that in just a few minutes they would seal the scene against the Buenavista cops and bad feelings would arise. That's how it went down when the feds were in town.

Hood found another of the strange machine pistols in Ray's bedroom. He stood in front of a bedroom window and let the strong morning sunlight illuminate the weapon. The stainless steel planes threw off the light like the facets of a gemstone. He unscrewed the noise suppressor and retracted the telescoping handles and set aside the curving fifty-round magazine. Now the gun looked very much like the ones that he had seen being packed for shipment at the Pace Arms factory in Costa Mesa. He read the engraving on the frame: LOVE 32. That was it. No serial numbers, no manufacturer grip marks, nothing else.

"Who names a gun 'Love 32'?" Hood asked.

"Beats me, Charlie. But it's a sweet carry. Easy to conceal and basic, like a Mac, but it's got elegance. Reminds me of one of my kid's Transformer toys."

"Angel's was on the kitchen counter but it's not there now."

"I'll bet we can solve that one."

Blowdown had suspected for some time that the *sicarios* in the Den were using these silenced weapons on their jobs—several witnesses had reported that the guns were all but silent. Hood held the Love 32 in his hand and turned it once again into the morning light. This was what Ozburn had gone undercover for. Risked his life for. A gun. Hood shook his head.

A moment later all four met in the side yard. The side-yard camera, hidden within a functioning motion-detector light, had been yanked from the wall and thrown to the ground. The wires dangled from the wall base. Velasquez swung open the door to the faux circuit breaker box. It was partially hidden by a riot of wisteria vine that had crept from its trellis to the eave of the house. The key was still in the control panel lid and Velasquez turned to his team with a woeful look.

"It's been disabled," he said. "System off. By someone who had a key."

Within an hour Blowdown was sequestered with Soriana and Mars back in the Buenavista field office war room. Hood told the story while Velasquez compiled video recordings of the last minute for each of the six monitors.

The videos from the first five cameras showed nothing unusual. But monitor six—trained along the side-yard wall of the Den—did register a quick disturbance.

Hood's heart hovered, then fell.

"Oh, shit," said Bly.

"Freeze it," said Mars. "I can't make it out."

"No way I'm seeing this," said Morris.

Velasquez backed up the video and froze a frame midway through the brief movement: Sean Ozburn reaching up to camera six, a smile on his face, and his hand about to close over the lens.

Hood watched in disbelief but his disbelief couldn't change the truth.

There was Ozburn: tall and well muscled, with a head of long blond hair that reached his shoulders, a gunslinger's mustache. He wore his usual biker clothes and boots and a black bandana. Arms tattooed—Mom, Seliah, the Stars and Stripes, a soaring eagle. In the foreshortened wide-angle image, a combat shotgun dangled from his free hand, down near the bottom of the screen, small as a toy. No doubt who it was: badass Sean, meth and gun specialist with Aryan Brotherhood connections, La Eme connections, friend of the North Baja Cartel.

Supervising agent Frank Soriana, a stocky and often jolly man, looked at the Blowdown team as if they had all, including himself, just been sentenced to death.

Mars, his morose subordinate, stared down at the cheap carpet.

Velasquez played out the rest of the video in slo-mo and the team watched Sean's hand come up and cover the hidden camera; then the screen flashed bright white, followed by black.

He played it through in slow motion again.

"When's the last time you talked to him?" asked Soriana.

"Six days ago," said Hood.

"What about Seliah?"

"Two days ago. She wasn't any more worried about Sean than usual."

"Talk to her again. Tell her what's happened. Tell her we need to find him."

"Do that sooner than later," said Mars, not looking up from the floor.

Hood dreaded it. Seliah Ozburn was a friend.

"Robert," said Soriana. "Burn a video of Ozburn onto disc and another onto stick and delete every other copy. Every single one, including the master backup. I want the disc and the stick five minutes ago."

Velasquez moved toward the main control panel.

Soriana turned his back to the team and took a call. He listened a moment. "Tell CNN and the *Union Tribune* those are baseless rumors. Tell the *L.A. Times* and CBS the same thing. I don't care what Buenavista police told them."

Back still turned, Soriana rang off and punched in a number from his contacts. "Chief Reyes? Frank Soriana, ATF. Hey, look, we've got a situation here with your men making noises about ATF and the shoot-out in Buenavista. Can you tell your guys to leave ATF out of it? We don't need this, Gabe, not after last year. You hear me, don't you?" There was a long silence; then Soriana said, "Thank you, Chief. We appreciate that a lot. Call me when you know what the heck happened out there, okay?"

He snapped his cell phone closed and turned back to them.

"Silence to the world, people. If this gets out, Sean's a dead man and Blowdown is finished. But if we can keep a lid on it for a few days, Ozburn still has cover and we're still in business. It's our only chance."

"Chance to what, sir?" asked Hood.

"To find his ass and arrest him. You with us or not on this one, Charlie?"

"I am us."

"We don't have all the information," said Mars. "There's more here than we're seeing."

"I've already seen enough," said Soriana. "Find him. Tell me what you need to do the job. Do nothing else in this life until you find Sean. Dyman, Robert, get over to Ozburn's cover house ASAP. Maybe you'll find some clue as to what the hell got into him. Hood, Janet—talk to his wife. She'll know more than she thinks she does."

4

Seliah Ozburn climbed down from the lifeguard stand at the Orange County Aquatics Center in Irvine and walked toward Hood and Bly. The open swim had just ended and the kids were splashing and laughing and climbing out.

She wore a big straw hat and sunglasses and a long-sleeved T-shirt against the sun. Over the last year and a half she and Hood had become friends and she was an affectionate woman, but today she offered no hug in greeting, and no handshake or smile.

"Is he still okay? Why are you here if he's okay? You said he was fine."

"He's all right but there's a problem, Seliah," said Hood. "Can we talk?"

"I want some shade. There's a few minutes before the next group."

They sat facing one another in white resin chairs in a wedge of shade along the locker room wall. The fall afternoon was hot. Hood knew that Seliah lifeguarded year-round, and also taught swimming here at the complex, and was a senior summer lifeguard

21

up in Laguna Beach. She'd been a freestyler in college, third in the Pan American Games her senior year. She was fit and beautiful.

Hood told her about the video of Sean and what they found at the safe house a few minutes later. She said nothing. He said the video was definitive and the neighbors' descriptions fit Sean, right down to the tatts and the biker vest and a cut-down shotgun. She listened without interrupting, hat low, sunglasses on, unreadable.

"He wouldn't do that. He's a Christian. He protects his soul—doesn't ignore it. He's the most moral man I know and I do not accept this. Has he been framed?"

"We're pretty sure he did it," said Bly. "He's right on camera, and there are witnesses who described him in some detail."

"Did anyone see him murder anyone? Did anyone shoot video of *that*?"

"No, Seliah," said Hood.

"Then I'll wait for irrefutable evidence."

"What you should do is prepare yourself for the worst," said Hood.

"The worst is the cartels bag him and do to him what they did to Jimmy Holdstock. And if that happens to Sean, I'll never forgive you or the holy trinity of ATF. Sean would, but I won't."

"That's why we need to find him," said Hood. "Pretty much right now."

"You'll arrest him."

"We'll give him every chance to explain."

"Oh, shit on both of you. You've convicted him already. You're supposed to be his friends."

Seliah stood abruptly and her plastic chair tipped. Hood caught it with a finger and set it back upright. He had come to know Seliah as a calm and gentle person, even with a husband working under deep cover, and her anger now surprised him. She had always behaved as if her husband needed protection from his employers, an understandable stance among the spouses of people with dangerous jobs. But Hood had never seen her angry at ATF like she was now.

"We are your friends," said Bly. "And friends don't let friends commit triple murders."

Seliah sat down again, then pulled off the hat. Her shiny white, straight hair fell to her shoulders, cut on a glamorous diagonal. She took off her sunglasses and hung her head, and Hood watched the tears run off her nose. Hood set a hand on her shoulder and she shrugged it off.

"When did you see him last?" asked Hood.

"It's been two weeks," she said, holding Hood's gaze.

"You guys had no hall pass for that one."

"None whatsoever. It wasn't the first time. Those precious days kept us sane. Kept him alive."

Hood wasn't surprised. The UC agents were known for sneaking away sometimes—even from their handlers. "Where?"

"San Francisco."

"When did you talk to him last?" Bly asked.

Seliah didn't look up. "This morning."

"Did he say where he was?"

"He didn't *say* anything. He cancelled his cell service six days ago. Threw it away for all I know. It's all e-mail now. He sounded tired but okay."

Six days, thought Hood. She should have told them about the cell phone.

"Do you know where he is?" asked Bly.

"He can't tell me where he is because *I* can't know. He can hint when he'll be home. He can tell me he loves me but he can't call me by name because *I* might become a target. You office jockeys have no idea how awful undercover work is for a married man. There's a reason you prefer them single. I'm sorry. I'm sorry for what I just said. It's . . . This is hard. So damned hard."

"We understand," said Bly.

Seliah lifted her face and looked at them, and Hood saw not hours but weeks of torment in her red-rimmed blue eyes. Her pupils were screwed down tight against the light. She was twenty-eight years old. She'd aged since he saw her last. That was what—two months ago, when Sean had stolen a few precious days with her at home and they had elected to share some hours with his Blowdown brethren? She slid the sunglasses back on and tugged the straw hat back into place. Even in the shade her platinum hair shone.

"I don't love the sun anymore," she said. "And I can't stand the smell of chlorine. I've *lived* on sunshine and chlorine for twenty years and now . . . something's changed in me. More important, though, something changed in Sean, too."

"We want to know what it is," said Hood. "We want to help him. He's my friend, Seliah, and so are you."

She stood, strong-legged and broad-shouldered. "Come to my house this evening at six. I'll have some things to show you. Maybe you can make some sense out of them. I've tried and failed and now you're telling me my husband is a murderer."

5

At six ten Hood and Bly sat in the Ozburns' San Clemente living room. The home was up in the hills on the east side of the interstate. Hood looked down through the picture window at the terracotta rooftops of the city below, and the jut of pier, and the black Pacific stretching to the horizon, touched far out near its rim by the first orange sparkles of sunset.

Seliah brought in a laptop computer, moved a dog-eared paperback *Dracula* from the coffee table and set down the machine in its place. Then she went to the picture window and pulled the sunscreen down. The view vanished and a cool light radiated through the honeycombed cells of the blind.

When she turned to them her eyes were clear, and she looked to Hood like her old self. She wore a periwinkle shift and a matching barrette that held one plane of her hair away from her face. She had a lovely smile.

She sat on the couch between Hood and Bly and opened the laptop and squared it before her and logged on. A moment later she was in her e-mail program, scrolling down through the saved messages. Scores of them, scores more. *Fifteen months of life in there,*

Hood thought. She stopped and moved the cursor down and high-lighted one of them; then she sighed.

"Sean went undercover not long after Jimmy was kidnapped," said Seliah. "What happened to Jimmy hit Sean hard." She stood and walked to the blinded window and looked across the room to Hood and Bly.

"Six months undercover Sean started to suffer. He wasn't able to come home as often. I think he was down in Mexico a lot. For an undercover U.S. agent, that's like dipping your toes into the pools of hell. Right? His calls got fewer and he was less talkative. He was always tired because he was always scared. Who wouldn't be?"

This didn't track exactly with what Hood had experienced. Sean had called almost every day. He usually sounded evenhanded, cool, and often wickedly funny. But Hood had heard the pressure in Sean. He had sensed the wariness and the hard discipline that Ozburn used to maintain his cover and therefore his life. He was up on the high wire but he'd seemed balanced.

Hood now speculated that it might make sense that a man under heavy pressure would confide in his wife instead of in his team-mates. Or it might not.

Seliah pulled a chair up to the window and sat facing Hood and Bly. "Of course, I wondered about his new cartel friends. And the women. And what he needed to do to keep from being blown. That's always the question. How will they test him? What will they expect of him? So at the very least, temptation lifts its lovely face. Have you ever been in a tense situation with an attractive person of the opposite sex? A situation with pressure, maybe danger? With something at stake? Competition maybe? Sure you have. I have. It makes you feel brave and romantic and . . . downright urgent, doesn't it? It builds. And when the race is over you want to cel-ebrate. Oh, yes. You want release, don't you?"

"That does happen," said Bly. "We try to factor it in when we plan the operation."

"I *factored* it in, too. But the next six months were bad. Less contact. I'd see him every three or four weeks for a day, maybe two at the most. He was such a mess he couldn't eat or talk or make love. He couldn't even sleep. I could feel this story inside him, this life, these things, all needing to get out. But he couldn't even *begin* to let them out. He needed to decompress before coming up, but undercover isn't scuba diving. You don't get to stop and breathe at a certain depth on your way up. You don't have a buddy. You just shoot to the surface and bob there and hope somebody picks you up. Then, *boom!* You go back under. Down to the depths."

She stood suddenly, then seemed embarrassed. She sat again. Hood wondered at the calm Seliah he had come to know, and now this anxious new one. It looked like the undercover work had gotten to her, too. According to the ATF agent runners he had talked to, it usually did.

"Do you think he has another woman?" asked Bly.

"He has another life. So why not another woman to go along with it?"

"You should have told us he was in trouble, Seliah," said Hood. "That was always the agreement. You had the training, too. That was your part of this operation."

"Sean begged me not to tell you. He wanted to do something big and something good. He didn't want to be brought in. He wanted to set it right with Jimmy. So . . ."

She rose again to adjust a wall thermostat. Hood heard the air conditioner click on. Seliah went to the shaded window, then stepped away from the muted light and looked at them again.

"I looked into my heart, Charlie. It wasn't hard to see in. My heart has always been big and simple and obvious. My loyalty was to Sean. Not to ATF. Not to Blowdown. Not even to you, and you're the best friend we've had through this."

Hood's spirit withered when he heard the words *best friend*. What kind of a friend let this happen? What kind of friend failed to register such pain? True, Sean was a fine actor. And he'd acted well during their few hours together, here and there, over the last fifteen months. Seliah, too. They'd fooled Bly and Morris and Velasquez and Soriana and Mars. But doesn't a friend know? Doesn't a friend *see*?

"Three months ago, almost exactly one year in, he was close to breaking," said Seliah. "So we took off together. July, Costa Rica. It was somewhere we'd always wanted to go. Two weeks, just us, traveling around a beautiful country. We stayed in a cloud forest and on the beach and even up on the Arenal Volcano. We leased a little plane and tooled around it. No phones, no cartels, no ATF. Sean presented that trip to you as a much-needed break for me. You have no idea how exhausted and bitter he was. Everything came out."

"Bitter," said Hood.

"He thought the war on drugs was a sham and a scam. He thought the United States was arrogant and ignorant to throw away millions of dollars and quality guys like Jimmy Holdstock and sell it as a 'war.' He thought ATF was a pawn in that war, a bureau that wasn't given the right tools to do its job. He felt betrayed. He thought the Mexican government was even worse. The billions still come into Mexico year after year after year. What government would try to stop that? What government would shut down sixty percent of its own economy and turn legions of cartel gunmen, growers and traffickers into the unemployed? There would be another Mexican revolution. Guaranteed."

Seliah looked out the shaded window, then closed the drapes. A slat of evening light came through the center line. Hood watched her snug the drapes together and the light disappeared.

"We talked about a career change for him. Maybe teaching, which is something he'd always wanted to do. He's got a degree in economics. Of course he loves to fly, so we thought maybe he could do some charter work. Maybe firearms training, or consulting. It's complicated because he'd lose some retirement unless he stayed a fed, and he might have to take a pay cut in this economy. Still, we talked about it. That was a first for us, just the idea that there was life after ATF."

She sat down on the chair again.

"Then, one week into the trip to Costa Rica, something happened to Sean. Something good. We were on the volcano at Arenal, staying in a little hotel. You could see the volcano from our room, this big, smoking, gurgling mountain, rocks flying into the sky all the time. The whole thing's going to blow, just a matter of when. We woke up one morning, late, after partying in the hotel bar. My head was killing me but Sean said he felt better than he had in a long time. More like he used to feel. He'd had a real change of heart—he thought he was on the right track with ATF. He thought ATF was doing good things, even if he didn't agree on how it was being used. He seemed much more at peace. Much more grounded. He seemed almost . . . well, happy. I thought he might just be putting a good face on a bad hangover, but I was wrong. When he went back undercover a week later he was feeling clear and strong. I could see it. It wasn't an act."

"That brings us through July," said Bly. "So Sean has been better since the Costa Rica trip?"

Seliah sighed and stood again. She looked down at Hood with a resigned expression, then came over and sat down between them again. "Not exactly. He started sending e-mails about a month after we got back. He'd still call but it was mostly e-mails. I heard it in his messages before I heard it in his voice."

"Heard what, Seliah?" asked Hood.

"You tell me what."

She tapped the laptop screen to life and called up the e-mail she had highlighted. "This is one is . . . representative."

From: Sean Gravas [sGravas23@zephyr.net]
Sent: Wednesday, September 14, 2011 5:33 a.m.
To: Gravas, Seliah
Subject: good morning

My Dear Seliah,

Miss every bit of you, Sel. Want to kiss your LIPS again and again and . . . Weirdass dreams last night, now I can't sleep. So I'm writing you. Sometimes I think you're back in the bedroom here. Once I started making you a cup of coffee like I used to, trying to be your COFFEE BOY then I realized you were there and I was here.

But I'm doing all this for MONEY, right? Business is good and I'm making solid bucks but I'll come home to you someday and I won't LET you away from me. You will be my captive pleasure slave and I will be YOURS. I feel completely different now than before Costa Rica. Those two weeks in the jungle and on the volcano changed me. I believe that SOMETHING or SOMEONE is walking by my side, helping me accomplish what I want to do. I feel protected. I pray that GOD or JESUS will answer and direct me but I haven't heard back. I can't discuss details but a very large deal is about to go down and I'm a part of it. I'm the CENTER of it.

I wish I could tell you more about what I'm doing but that wouldn't be smart. There are cops and feds and bugs and wires and stoolies and creeps all over the place and loose lips sink ships so no details, sorry. Just starting to get light out. I ache for you. I mean that LITERALLY, my hamstrings ache and my lats ache and those glands under my jaws ache and talk about blue balls. I think it's all the LOVE I have for you trying to get OUT. Until I can hold you, these words are my butterflies and I hereby release them to bring my love to YOU.

Your,

Sean

"Do you know what the big deal was?" asked Bly.

Seliah cut Bly a sharp look and shook her head. She glanced at the screen and turned to Hood and blushed deeply.

Hood remembered that late August and early September was busy for Ozburn. He was often in San Ysidro, "purchasing" and setting up another safe house for Carlos Herredia's North Baja Cartel. He was in and out of Buenavista, too, getting the Agate Street house ready for activation. He was checking out properties in Yuma. Eager to establish U.S. strongholds, Herredia was renting stateside homes as fast as Ozburn could buy them.

Hood excused himself and let himself onto the deck. The sunset was an orange and indigo spectacle over Catalina Island. Soriana picked up before the ring.

"Frank," said Hood. "Oz sent Seliah some e-mails over the last few weeks. He's talking about something or someone being beside him, and a really big deal that he's at the center of, and some God and Jesus stuff."

"Shit."

"Any word out of San Ysidro or Yuma?"

"None."

"Sean sounds apocalyptic. Like a crusader, an angel of vengeance. Like he'll just keep on going."

"You think he'll hit San Ysidro or Yuma?"

"I think it would make some sense."

"We can't patrol San Ysidro and Yuma without giving away the game. We can't roll them up without busting Sean's cover and loosing the wrath of the North Baja Cartel on him. So what are you saying?"

"I'm saying that Ozburn sounds like he's out of his mind."

"I'd say this morning proves it."

"We're with Seliah now."

"Is she cooperating?"

"Mostly."

Back inside Hood caught inquisitive looks from both women. He apologized for the interruption and stood behind the couch again and looked over Seliah's shoulder.

"Then," she said. "Just a few days later, he writes this."

She highlighted another in-box letter and called it up.

From: Sean Gravas [sGravas23@zephyr.net]
Sent: Saturday, September 17, 2011 6:22 p.m.
To: Gravas, Seliah
Subject: strength!

Hey Sel,

I pressed three hundred sixty pounds in the workout room about an hour ago—that's the FIRST TIME I've ever done it! Weirdest thing. I haven't been doing anything different, just trying to eat right and hitting the iron pile three times a week when I can and like MAGIC, up go those three hundred pounds. My pecs feel

*heavy and dead right now, but wow, it was really cool. And I'm
not taking anything extra. It's not that. I think it's all my pent up
passion for you. Every part of me still aches. Next time I get
to hold you tight, LOOK OUT. But on the serious side, I think
that SOMETHING or SOMEONE, whoever is watching over
me these days, has put the bug in my head that I need massive
STRENGTH to accomplish my mission. I agree, even though I
still don't know WHAT that mission is! But I'll be ready! I pray all
the time for guidance. I wish GOD would communicate back.
Maybe HIS minutes don't roll over. Hardly any sleep again last
night. I hear everything at night and it's SO LOUD. I watched
a mouse walk across the floor and his nails sounded like my
dog CLYDE when I was a boy, running down the tile hallway.
The kitchen sink drips and it sounds like someone whacking
a cardboard box with a wiffle ball bat. All the sounds blend
together into a kind of music. I can actually HEAR melodies in
it, like a far off RADIO. Some of them are really cool tunes. They
blend and change and turn into other melodies. And I hear little
tiny voices, singing. Finally I slept a few hours and the dreams
were beyond weird. When I wake up I should be exhausted
but I'm not. Maybe that's tied in with the EXTRA strength, I
don't know. Bought a new pair of sunglasses today as the old
ones just weren't cutting the border glare down here. Seemed
like every bit of car chrome and every window and mirror were
flashing so bright at me, burning right into my eyes. Last night
the MOON was too bright! So I hope these polarized ones help.
Two hundred bucks but you get a FREE cleaning kit. Well,
guess I'll go see if I can pick up the front end of my Rover!*

Hugs from the circus strong man,

Sean

"He'd been taking performance drugs?" asked Hood.

"Years ago," she said quietly. "He experimented briefly but didn't like them."

"How often does he write?" asked Hood.

"Every day now. Sometimes two or three times."

"Does he have themes that repeat?" asked Bly.

"His mission—whatever it might be. That someone or something is protecting him, beside him, guiding him. Lack of sleep, terrible dreams when he does sleep. Hyperactivity. Sexual desire. Melancholy. Sensitive vision, sensitive hearing, sensitive skin. Sore muscles, sore joints. Thirst. Here, scroll through them. It's kind of personal but you can see for yourself."

Bly squared the laptop to her and chose from the in-box. Hood rose and stood behind the couch looking over her shoulder. Seliah turned and looked up at him and he saw the sheen of perspiration on her face and the fear in her blue eyes. The room was cool now from the air conditioner and still it hummed away.

From: Sean Gravas [sGravas23@zephyr.net]
Sent: Thursday, September 22, 2011 2:45 a.m.
To: Gravas, Seliah
Subject: Desire for YOU

Dear Seliah,

I miss you so much I can taste your BREATH and feel your skin and your hair as my fingers stroke through it, yes, the EXACT way your hair feels on the bottoms and sides of my fingers. I can lie in bed for hours and remember things we've done, slow motion, every moment replayed like I'm a machine or something and I feel like I'm on FIRE for you . . .

From: Sean Gravas [sGravas23@zephyr.net]
Sent: Saturday, September 24, 2011 5:15 p.m.
To: Gravas, Seliah
Subject: HEART

Hey Sel,

*Broke 310 on the bench today. Business is good; very good.
Miss you so much sometimes I want to cut my heart OUT just
to make it stop aching . . .*

From: Sean Gravas [sGravas23@zephyr.net]
Sent: Sunday, September 25, 2011 12:14 a.m.
To: Gravas, Seliah
Subject: REASON FOR BEING HERE

My Dearest Seliah,

*It's beginning to dawn on me what I'm here for, not here in
this desert but on the PLANET, and I can't tell you everything
but I must do two things and they are 1) perform GOOD ACTS
and 2) DEFEAT the forces of EVIL. This is not a Biblical thing
but a practical one. I'm beginning to see that there are actual
ways to improve the world we live in. I talk to Joe about this and
he agrees. Joe says it's better to take a journey than make a
plan. I'm becoming more clear on the NATURE of my mission.
I feel a lot of great energy building in me. I think that some of it
must be used to help the weak and some of it used to destroy
the BAD. More later . . .*

"Who's Joe?" asked Hood.
"An Irish priest. He was building a library near Arenal. Sean and

him hit it off. They talked and drank a lot. I told you we stayed up late partying one night. There were three Tucson reptile hunters and two American honeymooners, a bunch of German bird-watchers and French butterfly collectors, and Father Joe Leftwich."

"How often do you write back to Sean?" asked Hood.

"Four or five times a day," said Seliah. "Janet, scroll down to the 'weirdest thing ever' message. It'll be late last month."

From: Sean Gravas [sGravas23@zephyr.net]
Sent: Tuesday, September 27, 2011 7:19 p.m.
To: Gravas, Seliah
Subject: WEIRDEST thing ever

Dear Seliah,

I finished up work early today I was heading home and this truck on the road ahead of me hit a dog. Dog went FLYING. The driver didn't even stop but I did. It was a little black mongrel and she didn't look busted up but she was just lying there in the desert, breathing hard and BLEEDING from her ears. I took off my shirt and laid her on it and she didn't do anything but whimper. So I set her on the passenger seat up front of my Range Rover and figured I'd take her to the vet. I drove into town with one hand on her head just petting her real soft and talking to her. I even said a prayer for her, with my hand on her head. And I told her, you may not make it much longer in THIS LIFE but you'll have another one in HEAVEN if you've been a good dog. Like that. It took us a while to get there. Then, when I took my hand off her to make the turn into the vet parking lot, SHE SAT UP! I thought, well, okay, that's the last of her strength and now she'll lay down and die, but she shook her whole body like she'd just stepped out of a swimming pool, you know, nose-to-tail, and looked at me with one of those great, doggy, "what are we doing now?" expressions. I mean, there's BLOOD drops on the windows but she looks just fine. So anyway, was it a miracle? I think that's entirely possible. Do you? I hope you don't think I'm NUTS. I am nuts, for YOU! So now I've got this dog. I named her Daisy. Maybe she was just dazed by that truck, not really hurt bad at all. That must be it. I got some on video I'll send you. SEAN GRAVAS AND THE MIRACLE MUTT! I got her a basket and a pad and some food and I'll bring her home to YOU someday very, very soon. I MUST say that I'm feeling very strong and good today. In my HEART I feel MY great big JOURNEY is ready to continue. I'm ready. I'm more than ready.

Your Dog Savior,
Sean

Seliah stood again and snapped shut the curtains against the last of the sunset. She lifted her hair off her neck with one hand and fanned her face with the other.

As if on cue the laptop chimed and the in-box listings shifted down to make room for a new message.

"It's from Sean," said Bly.

"Read it to me," said Seliah.

" 'My Dear Seliah, I'm off into the wild blue yonder now. The mission is clear. Good acts and the defeat of evil. Blowdown will be in touch with you soon if they haven't been already. They will ask you to help them find me. Tell them what they want to hear, dear woman. But hold me in your heart. I will be with you soon. Sean.' "

Hood realized something that made his heart drop. There was a long moment of silence until Hood broke it.

"The wild blue yonder," he said. "Sean has a plane at Oceanside Airport, right? A yellow Piper Cub. *Bobbie* or *Betty* or something like that. The name is under the fuselage."

Seliah shook her head and held his look. "*Betty*. He moved her three weeks ago. He wouldn't tell me where."

"When were you going to tell me this?"

"Damn all of you."

Both Hood and Bly let the curse hang. Hood figured if Ozburn was in the wind, there would be few better ways to get around than in his own little aircraft. He'd stay away from commercial airports where he'd have to file flight plans. He'd find other ways. Oz could land a Piper Cub on a street, a dirt road, a level meadow, just plain old desert if it was flat and firm enough. Hood remembered Sean talking about his club, the Desert Flyers. He remembered that Ozburn had outfitted his plane with expensive lights but didn't bother with a radio or transponder. It was a private aircraft—made to be flown literally off the charts and under the radar.

"He cashed in his IRA last week," said Seliah. "Thirty grand after the penalties."

Hood thought he heard pride in her voice. "Will you help us find him?"

Seliah left the room. Hood heard her at the kitchen sink, running water. A moment later she was back, blotting her face with a wet paper towel folded into quarters. "I love him. I want to protect him. And now, after what you say he did this morning, I'll help you find him. But how?"

"Right now, just tell him the truth," said Hood. He turned the laptop to face her.

"Right now?"

"Right now."

"Are you going to tell me what to say?"

"Tell him the truth, Seliah. Tell him what you told us."

Seliah sat on the couch and set the damp paper towel by the computer. She looked at Hood, then at Bly, then down at the keyboard. She composed slowly, a phrase at a time. Five minutes later she turned the computer to Hood:

From: Seliah [seliahoz@zephyr.net]
Sent: Thursday, October 13, 2011 7:55 p.m.
To: Gravas, Sean
Subject: With You

My Dear Sean,

My heart is so heavy for you, sweet husband. Charlie and Janet told me what happened in the Buenavista safe house today. They want me to help them find you. I don't understand your mission but I want to be by your side. I want to be with you. Six years ago, when I promised you for better or worse, that was more than a promise. It was a statement of unchangeable truth. Please let me come to you. Please let me come to you. Your joy is mine as is your pain and we are one.

All My Love,
Seliah

Hood nodded and she sent the e-mail.

"I've betrayed him," said Seliah. A tear ran down her cheek and she dabbed it away with the paper towel.

"We need your computer password," said Hood. "We'll monitor his incoming messages every hour, and we'll forward his correspondence to you, immediately. And you'll have to do the same for us when you get the mail first. There's no other way for this to work. You have to trust us and we have to trust you."

Seliah stood and looked down on them. "You steal Sean's body and soul and now you even want his words."

"He needs your help," said Hood. "And so do we."

She gave them her password and the three of them sat on the couch and watched the laptop screen and waited for Ozburn to reply. After an hour and no message from her husband, Seliah asked them to leave. When Hood asked for the Piper registration number she wrote it hastily on a notepad, tore off the sheet and handed it to him. She stared at the floor as they walked out, then shut the door behind them.

6

When they were gone Seliah put on shorts and a tank top and running shoes and drove down to the pier and parked on the street near the ocean. The tourists were gone by now and the beach was nearly empty. There were lights on in the pier restaurants and a few diners in the sidewalk cafés beside the railroad tracks.

She stretched, then set off north along the tracks, running the edges for a while, then running down the middle of them with the gravel shifting underfoot and the moon leading her on. Her heart felt like a weight inside her, a great, cumbersome anchor that was trying to drag her down. She tried to outrun it but couldn't and it spoke her to anyway: *He murdered three men this morning. He murdered three men this morning. Did you, Sean? Gentle Sean, good Sean? Do I believe Charlie and Janet? Do I dare not to?*

After the first mile she checked her wristwatch and, just as she suspected, she was faster than two days ago—already fifteen seconds off her last time. Even carrying a heart that felt like an anchor.

She tried to concentrate on her stride and her breathing but all she could think about were the last four weeks. Four weeks and so many strange things for Sean and for herself. First there were Sean's aches and pains and his crazy sexual appetite. Then a few days later he suddenly gets much stronger in the weight room, and his body is still aching and he hears things he shouldn't be able to hear, and his eyes hurt so bad in light that he buys news sunglasses. What causes those things? Flu? Steroids? Drugs? The common cold? The plague? Sean had thought flu at first, but after a few days the symptoms were far stronger and stranger. Then the symptoms would vanish for a day or two. He took no steroids, no prescription drugs, no recreational ones. And he began sounding extreme, almost crazy, in some of his e-mails.

And the extra-weird part, thought Seliah, was that a couple of weeks after Sean got stronger in the weight room, *she* started getting faster on her runs! And two weeks after Sean started hearing things loudly, even hearing things he shouldn't be able to hear, Seliah start hearing them, too. Just like what happened to Sean, all those near and distant sounds would blend in her brain at night into mysterious, flowing melodies. Some were lovely. And two weeks after all Sean's sensitivity to light and cold, she got those symptoms, too. And she'd become easily angered and provoked. Thoughts of violence came barging into her usually gentle soul. She was either too hot or too cold, and neither seemed to have anything to do with the temperature of where she was. And the insomnia and the sex and the terrifying dreams. *My God,* she thought, *the sex was almost constant the last time we were together.* That was two weeks ago, when they snuck a weekend in Las Vegas—snuck it from Sean's criminal partners, from ATF, from the world. Undercover agents did it all the time. She was fairly sure that Charlie Hood suspected but he said nothing. *And Sean's crazy sex drive had all but killed me,* thought Seliah. *And now, now, two weeks later? I could do it again right now. I know I could. I'd love to, hour after hour after hour! And the brightness of the pool water in my eyes? And the roar of tiny noises at night and the pain in my legs and neck and back? All just as Sean had experienced*, she thought.

She lengthened her stride and felt the strength in her legs and the amazing endurance that was now hers. She wasn't even breathing that hard. She wondered if all of this shared sensory overload was some kind of sympathetic thing with Sean, like when a man feels his wife's labor pains. *Is there really such a thing? How can I feel what he feels? Am I just lonely and afraid? Am I just making all this up?* Dr. Clements had taken her temperature and looked into her ears and nose and throat and pronounced flu. Rest, plenty of fluids. Would twenty-four hours of sex and a couple of gallons of sports drinks spiked with vodka count? And of course Sean wouldn't see a doctor if he was well enough to walk through the office door. He had never been sick a day in his life. Until now.

She continued north between the tracks. She remembered the dream she was having early this morning, at about the time that her husband was *allegedly* gunning down three young men for reasons unknown. In the dream she had been ravenously thirsty, but water was revolting to her and sports drinks and sodas and juices and beer were all sickening to her body and soul. But she found one thing that really hit the spot, and she had drunk so much blood out of Sean that he was white and blue-lipped. But he offered his neck so she could have more! *What the hell has gotten into you, girl? Maybe time to cool it on the vampire books and movies and TV shows. Isn't there enough trouble in your life without feeding your inner devils?* But why were those bloody and ridiculous stories so . . . delicious? So compelling? A few short weeks ago she was dreaming of having babies. Wholesome dreams of beautiful daughters, beautiful sons. Hers and Sean's. *Soon,* she had thought—*it's almost time for that part of our lives.* When the undercover mission was finally accomplished they would be ready. Now this. Maybe the thirst for sex and the baby were part of the same larger desire, she thought. One led to the other.

She was pouring sweat now and the sounds were condensing around her: the shuffle of the waves on the beach and the plane droning overhead and the resounding clash of the rocks under her shoes, and she heard the Coaster train coming up behind her while it was still miles away, long before the approach lights began flashing and the train sounded its deafening whistle.

She glanced over her shoulder just once and stayed between the dully shining tracks, and she heard the warning blast again, much closer this time; then she heard it again. She heard the engineer screaming at her, or believed she did. Then she veered to her left and jumped down the embankment, leaping across the boulders toward the beach as the train howled past. She could feel the pull of its slipstream. The roar was almost unbearable to her. She hit the sand and sprinted to keep up with the Coaster, and for a moment it looked like she could stay even with it but the passenger windows began to outdistance her slowly, then quickly. She cut down near the water, laughing, and continued north.

When she got home she wrote an e-mail letter to her husband. It didn't have the rational, somber tone of her last one—the one *suggested* by Charlie and Janet. This one came straight from her heart. She told him of her passion, her loyalty, her love, her need of him. She pledged herself to him again, 'til *death do us part,* and she promised to find a way to help him on this strange and terrible thing he needed to do. *If you needed to stop three professional killers, okay, Sean. It changes nothing in us. And if we have to manipulate ATF and Blowdown and our formerly true friend Charlie Hood, then so be it. I am yours and you are mine and together we are greater than two. We can do anything.*

7

That evening Bradley Jones had sat through his first roll call as a sworn deputy of the Los Angeles Sheriff's Department. He was dark-haired and handsome, and seemed to be paying his usual half attention to things. He had turned twenty and a half years old the day before and was now eligible to work patrol. He was profoundly hungover from celebrating that milestone with his wife and some friends. This was his first shift working anywhere but the jail and he had an idea about how to make it special. Maybe even unforgettable. He stifled a yawn.

"Jones, you counting sheep?"

"Blessings, sir."

"We can send you back to the jail day shift if you can't stay up this late."

"I'm alert, sir."

"Look the part. Okay, here's tonight's headline: ten-year-old boy kidnapped right out of his own living room in Cudahy this afternoon; shots fired but nobody hit. His name is Stevie Carrasco and here's what he looks like."

The sergeant tapped his keyboard and a picture of the boy appeared on the briefing room monitor.

"This mug is already downloaded to the data terminals in the cars, so use the MDT if you think you see him. The kidnapping might be a gang thing because said ten-year-old is son of an Eme gangster with ties to some Mex cartel. And you know, these fuckin' cartel animals kidnap and murder each other's wives and kids like it's a sport. So . . ."

Bradley fixed the sergeant with a look of great interest, but he couldn't keep his mind on the man's words. He'd already gathered some of this story from one of his young deputy friends, Caroline Vega, who by luck happened to help take the kidnap report from Stevie's hysterical sister, who had called nine-one-one. Bradley believed in luck and in Caroline.

He also knew Stevie's father, Rocky. Rocky was a Florencia OG with Eme ties, a tattooed knot of a man with a reasonable outlook and a quick smile. He was also tied to the North Baja Cartel. Everyone knew that the North Baja Cartel was having a hard time maintaining supply lines in and around L.A. They were losing traction. Which led Bradley to wonder if MS-13 *sicarios* of the newly arrived Gulf Cartel had grabbed the kid to cripple a North Baja rival, bleed some cash out of him, and jack up the terror level so guys like Rocky might think twice about staying in L.A. Everybody wanted California real estate, thought Bradley. Especially the Mexican drug cartels. After all, it was the front door to the biggest drug market in the world.

In the motor yard they checked over the patrol unit, a late-model Crown Victoria Police Interceptor with almost two hundred thousand miles on it. Bradley, a motorhead, checked under the hood—fluids, belts, battery, radiator and brake lines—then used his own pressure gauge to check the tires. He washed the windshield twice, meticulously, nothing more annoying to him than poor view at night.

Jerry Clovis checked the MDT and radio, then leaned on another radio car and watched Jones do his work. Clovis was a thickly built middle-aged deputy, a family guy, easygoing and unambitious, the kind of man who made Bradley Jones want to take a long nap.

"Ready, Brad?"

"Nope. One minute."

Bradley tossed the squeegee back into the bucket, then walked down the row of black-and-whites until he was out of earshot. He called Rocky to see if he knew yet where Stevie was being held, and told Rocky it would behoove them all to find out fast. Then he called Theresa Brewer of FOX News and told her the ground rules again. Then he called Caroline to make sure she knew what to do and when. He walked back to the unit with a bounce in his step.

"Checking in with the wife?" asked Clovis as they boarded.

"Every chance I get."

"What's her name?"

"Erin."

" 'Atta boy. Take it easy. Keep it clean. That's been enough to get me through twenty-two years of this. Three more to go."

"Easy and clean, that's me."

"I see you have an ankle gun."

"It's an eight-shot Smith AirLite. Charlie Hood turned me on to them."

"Never had to draw my gun on duty. Not once."

"They'll kill that boy if they don't get their ransom fast enough. They might kill him anyway."

"Kill a kid over business," said Clovis. "Pure animals. Nothing's the same in this world anymore."

"Everything's the same as it always was."

"Can't say I really agree with that."

"And that's why I have two guns."

"Coffee?" asked Clovis.

"Let's just drive fast, make something happen, arrest somebody."

"Oh, man, you've got a lot to learn. First patrol shift, right?"

Bradley nodded, smiling. "I'm kidding, Jerry. Coffee would be good."

L.A. Sheriff's Department patrol area two includes the rough territory along the broken Los Angeles River, from Maywood down to Compton, which was where Bradley Jones and Jerry Clovis were now patrolling, fresh coffees in hand. These were no longer the days of Winchell's coffee but of specialty double espressos and low-fat lattes, which Clovis and Bradley drank respectively.

Clovis drove. Bradley looked out the very clean windshield at the city of South Gate, unassuming and unbeautiful in the smog-muted autumn light. They cruised Tweedy out to South Gate Park, looped it once slowly with an eye for drug peddlers, but it was quiet and the cover of darkness was still more than an hour away.

"You ever do anything heroic?" asked Bradley.

"I actually delivered a baby once."

"Fantastic. How did it go?"

"I didn't do much, really. Put her in back with a blanket from the trunk, then drove under siren, lights on full. Then when the screams got too loud, I got worried so I pulled over and held on to the lady's head while she screamed and pushed and thrashed around in the back. Then out it came. A girl. Bloody mess but she started bawling, too, and by the time we got to the hospital they were waiting for us and the mom was wrung out but smiling."

"Now, that's a good tale."

"Not sure how heroic it really was."

"You up for some heroics tonight?"

"Yeah, right, we'll bust a nickel-bag crack dealer in Compton."

"How about we rescue Stevie Carrasco?"

Clovis looked over at him. "Sure. Anytime."

"I'm going to find out where he is."

Clovis looked over at him again. "No, you aren't."

Bradley sighed. "Old men."

"You're joking again, right, Jones?"

"You in or out?"

"I can't believe we're having this conversation."

"Pretend we really are having it. Rescue Stevie Carrasco. Would you be in or out?"

Clovis said nothing for a long time. "Give me more details."

"Happy to: Carlos Herredia's North Baja Cartel has an old alliance with La Eme and Florencia Thirteen. A loose alliance. They've been here in L.A. awhile, low-profile, doing business, building market share. But the Gulf Cartel has moved in. Benjamin Armenta and his MS-13 gangstas mean business. They've taken out six Florence boys in four months but nobody has figured the *why*. That's because our brethren in law enforcement think the cartels are still safely confined south of the border. Well, guess what? Armenta and the Salvadorans have pretty much sewn up the east side and now they want South Central. Stevie's dad is Rocky Carrasco, an Eme favorite. The Salvadorans grabbed his kid. Rocky's already gotten a ransom demand for half a million in small dirty bills that smell like herb, crack, crank and Mexican brown H. With me?"

"How do you know this stuff?"

"Does it matter?"

"You're serious."

"I'm serious. What if you got a chance to do something good tonight? To use all your training, all your preparation, to do a good act. Delivering the baby? Absolutely fabulous, Jerry. But now you've got a chance to take it up a notch. Pull over, please."

Clovis pulled the prowler to the curb of Firestone Boulevard. The Los Angeles River dribbled before them, a trickle in a concrete channel.

"Let me tell you what I see in you," said Bradley. "I see a cautious man with the heart of a warrior. I see a man who knows right from wrong. I see a man who took an oath and meant it. Am I right?"

"Well, sure, okay."

"Jerry, sometime tonight I'm going to find out where Stevie is. And when I do I'm not calling in SWAT or hostage negotiation or backup. I'm calling in *me*. And that could mean you, too. I'm going to get that boy out alive. I'm going to make sure the world knows about it, too. Because I don't work for free. Are you in or out?"

"I'm in."

Bradley bored into Clovis's eyes but liked what he saw. "I can leave you out. You can sit it out."

"I'm in."

"Sweet, Jerry. Good. Okay, let's drive."

Clovis had just pulled back into traffic when Bradley's cell phone buzzed. Rocky told him no news yet, all his men were working it hard, they'd grabbed a Salvadoran who was bleeding a lot but talking not at all, and Rocky's wife was out of her *cabeza* with worry. Rocky said if they hurt Stevie, he'd kill every Salvadoran kid in L.A., every single last one of them.

"You be cool," Bradley said. "You get that address for me."

Rocky's call came in at nine thirty-eight P.M.

"The Salvadoran cracked when we started breaking off his teeth," he said. "They got Stevie in Maywood."

"How many of them?"

"Three Maras. Experienced guys."

"Talk to me."

"I'm on my way to drop the ransom at a church parking lot in Maywood. After they pick it up, the Salvadorans are gonna leave Stevie at Freeway Liquor in Bell Gardens."

"They think you're dumb enough to do that?"

"They have my solemn word I'm dumb enough. Bradley, man. You do this for me . . . You get Stevie outta there okay . . ."

"I'll get him."

"I can be there with some of my best friends. I've done this kinda shit before."

"Stevie will end up dead and you'll end up in prison again. I'm the one for this job. My partner and I. Now, is there a dog at that house?"

"I don't know."

"I need to know if there's a dog. I need to know if it's between other houses, or on a corner. Now, give me the address, man."

When he'd gotten the street and house number, Bradley hung up. *Perfect good luck*, he thought: The Maras had Stevie in unincorporated territory patrolled by LASD—no jurisdictional problems. He asked Clovis to pull over so he could make some calls in private.

He stood in a 7-Eleven parking lot and told Deputy Caroline Vega where and when to meet; then he told Theresa Brewer that they would be there in ten minutes. He went into the store and got an enormous energy drink and a pack of chocolate chip cookies and drank and ate them while looking at the covers of the car magazines in the stand. Too many fuel-efficient dinks, in Bradley's view, but the new M5 looked otherworldly. He thought of his mother, who had taught him to drive fast cars. He'd buy her that M5 if she were alive. Would have been thirty-five this year. He looked at his watch. According to plan, Rocky would call back in a minute or two, to confirm that his last call was of his own free will and not a setup.

The call came. No dog, corner house. Bradley popped the last cookie into his mouth and walked back to the prowler.

"We've got what we need," he said.

Clovis popped his holster strap. "This is good. I'm glad we're doing this."

"Be cool."

"From a twenty-year-old deputy on his first patrol."

"I'm twenty and a half, Jerry."

Clovis smiled and shook his head.

They met Theresa Brewer and a cameraman at a Shell station in Bell Gardens, around back near the restrooms and the air and water dispensers. She was a dimpled, green-eyed blonde and she greeted

Bradley with a smile. She wore light slacks and a green blouse and a black leather jacket. Her face was made up.

Bradley told her again that she was not to begin taping until he had the boy safely out of the house. Then they could shoot away. After the boy was secure in the back of an LASD patrol car, the deputies would be available for brief comments. She smiled again and he felt the energy drink bumping up against his nerves.

"Follow me," he said.

"I feel like my blood's been replaced with adrenaline."

"It's quite a thing, isn't it?"

"Good luck, Bradley."

Caroline Vega and Don Klotz were waiting for them at the Downey Road railroad tracks, five blocks east and five blocks north of Stevie Carrasco and his three MS-13 kidnappers. Bradley had dealt with a Mara Salvatrucha heavy once before. The man had unnerved him—an Aztec warrior with jug ears and a hooked nose and a tattooed face who looked like he'd be happy with a beating heart in his hands.

Clovis pulled up behind the other cruiser and cut the engine. Bradley stepped out and watched the FOX News van park behind them. The night was damp now and the sky over Los Angeles glowed dully and the power lines sizzled overhead. To his right was the concrete riverbed, a tiny wobble of water in its channeled center.

Bradley bumped fists with Vega, then introduced the two deputies to the two newspeople.

"Stay in the van," said Vega. "Don't shoot until we come out of the house with the boy."

"He's told us five times," said Brewer with a smile.

"At least five," said Erik, the videographer.

Vega fixed Theresa Brewer with a look. The deputy was dark-haired and dark-eyed and there was a predatory beauty in her face. She and Bradley had graduated from the Sheriff's Academy together, and she'd been on patrol six months now. "I hope it sunk in."

Klotz hooked his thumbs into his Sam Browne and looked at Brewer but said nothing.

"They're on our side, Caroline," said Bradley.

"Just making sure," said Vega.

Bradley cut Theresa and Erik away and walked them back to their van. It was a big Econoline with the FOX News logo on the flank. "Vega's wound a little tight tonight," he said.

"A little?" asked Theresa.

"Get in and wait here. I need to get the script straight with my people. Then we'll caravan to the house. Park . . ."

"I know, Bradley—we park three houses down, opposite side of the street, so we can see you coming out. Then traipse over and give you your fifteen minutes."

"I hope it lasts longer than that," said Bradley, smiling.

"Depends how good the footage is," said Theresa.

"If you hear shots, stay in the van and keep down. Don't just sit and gawk like tourists. There's no telling what kind of firepower they've got."

Theresa Brewer squeezed Bradley's hand, then climbed into the passenger seat of the van.

Bradley joined the other deputies and caught Caroline's hard glance. "Clovis, you and Klotz get a five-minute head start and the backyard," he said. "It's a corner house, so one of you can climb the fence on street side. No dog, but who knows what the neighbors might have back there. So be quiet, go slow, be careful. Caroline and I are going to knock and talk. Caroline will do the talking.

We're responding to a silent alarm in the neighborhood. We're not threatening or suspicious. If they let us in, we're golden. If they don't, we smell dope being smoked, and we go in."

"What makes you think they'll open the door?" asked Clovis.

"They won't know what to do. Two bored young uniforms checking out an alarm? One of them a hottie? A kidnapped kid stashed in the back somewhere? They'll have to just hope we leave. Anyone runs out the back, put them down and keep 'em down."

The front door was open but the screen door was closed. When he stepped onto the porch Bradley smelled frying onions and meat and boiling potatoes. Far back in the house a stout woman stood in the yellow light of a kitchen. Bradley was to Vega's left and he quietly popped the holster snap and rested his hand on the forty-caliber. He heard the leather squeak and felt the tapping of his own heart against his uniform shirt. He looked down at the screen door—old, bent, ajar. Caroline looked at him, her hand on her gun also, then rapped on the screen door with her knuckles, and the woman came down a short hallway toward them, both hands working a kitchen towel, shaking her head.

"No here. Nobody here."

"We have a report of a prowler in this neighborhood," said Vega. She said it again in Spanish. "Can we come in?"

"Nobody here." She had high cheekbones and a flat nose and black eyes. Her teeth were very white. She wore a shapeless gray smock and her hair was bunched into a shiny black ponytail. She was barefoot.

She closed the door and locked it. Bradley heard her walk away.

Vega rapped again. And again. The latch slid and the woman swung open the door and the dish towel was still in one hand.

"Nobody is here."

"There is a report of a prowler in this neighborhood," said Vega. "A prowler in this location. Can we come in, please?"

"No. *No persona.*" Then the woman rattled off a paragraph in Spanish. Bradley got the gist: *There is nobody here I'm cooking my dinner I am from El Salvador I have a green card I work in a factory in the garment district I am skilled and legal. I make the high fashions. You can go away and I will be very much okay.*

She closed the door in their faces again and locked it again. Bradley heard her move into the house.

"I wonder exactly who isn't here," said Bradley.

"I do, too."

"I smell the yerba, very strong."

"I smell it, too."

"Next time she opens that door I'm going to get my foot inside."

"I'll ask her one more time if we can come in."

"Be really careful, Caroline."

Vega rapped on the door and waited, then rapped again. It was quiet for a long moment; then Bradley heard the muffled thud of feet on the floor. The latch slid and the door opened and Bradley opened the screen and placed his foot against the door frame.

"No here, please. No here. Legal. Fashion."

"Do I have your permission to come in?" he asked.

"No *permiso.*"

"I smell marijuana. Do you smell it?"

"I smell marijuana," said Vega.

"No marijuana. No here, nothing . . . You go. You go."

Bradley eased his shoulder into the doorway and the woman backed up. Vega followed him in. The living room was small. To the right was a hallway leading back to the bedrooms and to the left was a dining room that opened to the kitchen by a pass-through and an open doorway. In the living room was a small brown sofa and a large TV cabinet with shelves of pottery and paper flowers and figurines carved of onyx and glass and wood. Bradley saw the dust on the glass figures and he saw the black stains inside the white clamshell inverted as an ashtray. He looked down the right hallway and saw that the bedroom doors were closed and there was no light coming around them. He stepped to the threshold of the dining room, and beyond the pass-through he saw the stove with the skillet heaped with onions and chilies cooking down, and the pot of peeled potatoes boiling, and the pan that held a pork roast recently removed from the oven, enough meat to feed several adults.

"You go!" She made as if to slap him with the dish towel but apparently realized the uselessness of it.

"Smells good," he said, smiling. He drew his gun and moved quickly back into the living room so he could see down the hallway to the bedrooms.

"You go! No one!"

"No one *what*, lady? No one *who*?"

The woman unleashed a string of curses and hit him with the dish towel very hard, and when the towel fell to the floor the potato peeler was planted high up into the left side of Bradley's chest. The first gunman came not from the hallway but up into the pass-through from the kitchen where he had been crouching, and Bradley shot him in the middle and the man collapsed just as the second *sicario* came down the hallway with a machine pistol blazing, trying to control the muzzle rise with his left hand, and Caroline shot him twice and the man stopped but kept firing and the muzzle of his machine gun rose up spitting bullets into the wall, then the ceiling, then into his own face. The gunfire was deafening in the small home and the air filled quickly with smoke. When the machine gunner fell, a very small man sprung up from behind him swinging his pistol on Caroline, and Bradley shot him in the temple and the man pitched forward with his face to the floor tile and his gun still clutched in one hand. The woman came from the kitchen with a sawed-off shotgun, and Bradley took two steps and launched himself. Midair he dropped his gun. He clamped both hands to the shotgun and rammed her chest with his face like he used to as a linebacker and he felt her feet leave the floor and his airborne momentum carry them backward into the little kitchen where they crashed into the refrigerator and sank to the floor. He wrenched away the gun and dumped it into the dining room and stood over her with a boot on her wrist, panting. He wiggled the potato peeler very slightly to see how deep in it was. He'd driven it in farther when he tackled the woman, and now it hardly moved. The pain was breathtaking and the blood poured forth through the groove of the peeler as from a tiny bayonet. He thought of his wife, Erin, and vowed that he would not be forced to say good-bye to her by a potato peeler.

He backed off the woman and handcuffed her to the refrigerator door. Then he took up his autoloader and followed Caroline Vega as she burst into the first bedroom, then the next. There on the floor they found him, his mouth gagged and taped and his eyes looking up at them in terror and his hands bound behind him with plastic ties.

"Hi, Stevie," said Bradley. " 'Sup? You're okay now, little man."

They cut the cuffs and unwrapped the tape and Stevie Carrasco cried without making a sound. *Tough as Rocky*, thought Bradley.

"That's bad, Bradley," said Vega, inspecting the potato peeler. "It's almost to the handle. Those sharp edges are cutting you up."

"Feels like a cherry bomb went off in there. Let's get him out of here."

"You don't move until I get paramedics." She called dispatch for medics and the coroner team.

Bradley stood the boy up and he and Caroline Vega walked him onto the front porch. It took just a few seconds for Theresa Brewer and Erik to arrive, Erik already shooting away with the shoulder camera and Theresa stepping in with her microphone raised. Clovis and Klotz came from the backyard. Bradley hefted the boy up into the crook of his right arm and smiled at Theresa. When he looked down, there was more blood than he thought there was. He handed the boy over to Caroline and tried to understand Theresa Brewer's question but it made no sense to him at all. He smiled at the camera again and sat down on the porch with his feet on the steps and sighed and listened to the approaching sirens. Theresa Brewer pressed the mike toward him, an uncertain expression on her face. He sensed the world letting go of him, and then it did.

9

Ozburn circled the landing strip south of Puertecitos for his lucky third time, then tipped *Betty* into her descent. He looked out at her yellow wing afloat in the blue morning sky. Poetry in motion, he thought with a smile.

Betty was a 1947 J3 Piper Cub and Oz had bought her nearly eight years ago, swept up every dollar he could find and borrowed the rest from his father. She'd run him $26,750, and he had felt guilty buying the gifts of flight and freedom for so little.

Betty had been a pampered little princess of a plane. She still was. She was delightful and loyal and calm. She was a prop-start, and to Ozburn there was nothing like that transfer of power from his body to hers when he threw her prop and the engine buzzed to life. Like she was taking his energy and his passion, and would soon turn them into flight. Her modified, updated engine put out seventy-five wild horses, could cruise at eighty miles an hour for almost two hundred eighty miles on a tank. She could take off from a nickel and land on a dime.

Her tires bit the gravel and bounced twice, then settled as Ozburn eased the tail to the ground. Ozburn loved tail-draggers, as had his father and grandfather. *You fly these planes, they don't fly you*, his father liked to say. Oz liked to see how quickly he could stop her, and, of course, how quickly he could get her into the air. He glanced down and smiled at the billowing tan cloud of dust rising alongside him. The *cardón* cactus that grew tall in this heat-blasted desert flashed past his windows in the evening light. The strip was a private runway owned by Carlos Herredia of the North Baja Cartel, nothing like the busy and clamorous *turista* facility up in San Felipe.

He taxied to the end of the runway where a small metal building squatted in the dirt. He steered to the side of the building where the tie-downs waited; then he shut down the aircraft and climbed out. He breathed in the warm October air and walked around to the passenger door and let Daisy out.

She leaped down, a thin-bodied, long-legged dog, all black except for a white splash on her chest. She had the high, upright ears topped with short out-flaps common in border mongrels, which gave her a daft expression. The understanding between man and dog was deep and felt to Ozburn like something remembered. Lately, he felt that a lot, that he was remembering things—feelings, ideas, even physical sensations—that he had known and forgotten. For instance, he loved the dog unconditionally but wondered how she'd taste roasted, though he had no intention of cooking her. Where had that thought come from? Daisy bounced high around him as he tied down the plane. A car came toward them from the west, dragging a cloud of dust, Joe Leftwich at the wheel.

An hour later Ozburn sat on the patio of a small restaurant built into the cliffside overlooking the Gulf of California. Daisy lay at his feet. Across from him sat Mateo, dispatched by Carlos Herredia to collect answers from Sean Gravas, whose safe house in Buenavista had proven extremely unsafe. But Ozburn had come here for reasons of his own.

Mateo looked at Ozburn as if he were made of dog shit. One of his gunmen leaned against a new Suburban in the parking area outside; two more loitered near the big beer cooler that stood near the entrance to the indoor dining room and cantina.

Sean explained in good Spanish that, first of all, he wasn't too happy about having his house shot up. He'd heard that there were brains in the kitchen and blood on the living room floor, and that was expensive stuff, that floor, real travertine for fuck's sake. Sorry about the boys, he added. Mateo asked him why such a thing happened in his house, on his property, and didn't happen somewhere else? Mateo spoke in a soft, accusatory rasp. Sean said it was pretty damned obvious why—someone had smelled out the safe house and sent better killers than Herredia's *sicarios*. In spite of their fancy and expensive Love 32s, the victims were very young for killers, yes? The Gulf Cartel was probably behind it. Gulf Cartel killers are not boys but highly trained military deserters. *Zetas*. They want Buenavista because TJ is now too hot again. Same with Juarez. Buenavista is three hours from L.A. The Gulf men could have gotten a tip about the house from neighbors. They could have recognized a Herredia hit boy and tailed him home. They could have an informant inside your organization, yes? Maybe it was the conveniently missing Oscar.

Mateo listened, his face hard and blank. He had the chiseled ranchero features and wiry body of the mountain-dwelling Sinaloans, from whom the current crop of cartel heavyweights so often came. Mateo was somewhere in his late forties—old in his profession. At the mention of a leak within his North Baja Cartel, Mateo's dark eyes took on a sleepy peacefulness that Sean recognized as prehomicidal. Pride ran deep in these men, he thought. Savages all.

Ozburn finished another Pacifico and banged the bottle on the tabletop for more. The German who ran the place looked at him and nodded.

"*Y carne para de perro!*" he called.

And meat for the dog.

The German brought two more beers and a tortilla topped with *machaca* scraps for Daisy. She stood wagging her tail and waited for Ozburn to set the tortilla on the floor before snorting up the food. The owner disappeared into the darker confines of the dining room and came back a moment later with dinner.

They talked of *fútbol* and the Mexican soap operas they both enjoyed, of Calderón and Obama. They drank three beers each and most of a bottle of good *reposado*. Mateo wore one of the short-sleeved plaid shirts of the mountain vaqueros, and a belt with a large oval slab of silver for a buckle, which made him look more like a cowboy than a *narco*. His hair was cut short and artlessly. But his boots were ostrich and he wore a Rolex with diamonds and a snazzy GPS unit clipped on his belt next to the gigantic buckle, and his sidearm was a gold-plated .45 with etchings of the *narco* saint Malverde on the grips.

When the dishes were cleared Mateo lit an American Camel and spoke in Spanish.

—Carlos is worried about his houses in San Ysidro and Yuma, Mateo hissed softly.

—*My* houses.

—He is worried that there was no message from the Zetas. No warning to abandon our hold on Buenavista. No mutilation. Why would the Gulf Cartel assassinate three of our *sicarios* and not take credit for it?

—Now I am supposed to answer for the Zetas?

—You answer me.

—I'll answer you: The Gulf Cartel has someone inside your organization. That's the only explanation. It's the trouble with any organization. That's why I wasn't so sure about this whole thing when you people first came after me.

Mateo's face was a dark, angular mask, too fixed to read. Ozburn knew that Mateo "El Gordo" Leya had just last week made the United States's Kingpins list, which put a government price on his head. This of course was a matter of pride among the higher *narcos. Maybe it's gone to his head*, thought Ozburn: Mateo did seem a bit more scornful than usual.

—We need to know that your houses are safe for our people.

—I need to know that your people are safe for my houses. I paid over two hundred grand each for those dumps!

—Carlos needs to know.

—Mateo, you guys figure it out. And I'll tell you both this: If my houses in San Ysidro or Yuma get hit, I'm out of this business. And you guys have one bigass problem.

—We are not the problem, Mateo said with a tone of finality. He sat back and gave Ozburn that sleepy look again.

Ozburn's anger spiked fast. He'd always had a temper, but for the last couple of months it had been growing steadily worse. The more he tried to contain it, the faster and harder it hit. And the more fun it was to just let it rip.

He looked out at the heaving, gray Pacific and waited for the anger to pass before he spoke again. He had bigger fish to fry than three dead *sicarios* and a re-grout job on the bloody travertine.

—I want to buy some of those Love 32s your people carry.

Mateo gave him a glassy smile.

—Only Carlos has the Love 32s, he said.

—You told me he'd think about selling me some. Tell him I'm ready. I want one hundred of them.

—Very expensive.

—I've got a lot of moncy.

—Only Carlos has those guns.

—I heard that he has them made right here in Mexico.

Mateo stared at him blankly.

—By an American gunmaker. Can you imagine that, Mateo? An American gunmaker operating a secret factory south of the border? A factory protected by the North Baja Cartel? I'm in the business of guns. I hear these things, Mateo. I don't make them up.

Ozburn grinned. In fact, he was making part of it up. He knew for a fact that Blowdown had come *that* close to busting Ron Pace, a young California gunmaker, last year. Sean had worked that operation. But Pace had gotten lucky and his thousand pistols had made their way south to Mexico and into the hands of Herredia's *sicarios*. He knew also that Pace and his pretty partner in crime had vanished from the U.S.A. So Ozburn wondered if Pace might be under the wing of Herredia, possibly even making guns for him. Guns were more valuable than gold in Mexico because you couldn't get them legally. The fact that Mateo would have this conversation about the possible sale of Love 32s told Ozburn that such a thing was very, very possible.

Mateo cracked a rare smile. His teeth were large and dilapidated and the bicuspids were rimmed with gold.

—They are made by the devil in hell, just for us.

—See, I was right.

—Maybe some truth.

—Tell Carlos I want to buy a hundred of them and I don't expect them to be free. I can move them and make some good bucks if the price is right. Because I'll tell you something, Mateo—at the rate your killers are getting themselves killed in my houses, I need a new profit center.

Mateo's smile brought another quick ripple of fury to Ozburn's brain. He'd benched three hundred seventy pounds in the gym a week ago and he wondered how it would feel to strangle bare-handed the sinewy Sinaloan. Good indeed. But he'd have to settle for less right at the moment.

So he leveled his pale blue eyes on Mateo and growled at him. It was a short, supple snarl. His lips were back and his teeth were sudsed with saliva.

Mateo smiled sleepily but looked toward his gunmen near the beer cooler. They ambled over. From under the table unfurled Daisy, her back bristling, her head down and teeth bared at them.

One of them swung his coat back to draw his sidearm, and Ozburn launched. He was six feet four and weighed two hundred forty pounds but he was fast as a thought. He had his autoloader pressed to the man's forehead before the *sicario* could get his gun up, and his free hand placed around the throat of the gunman beside him.

Ozburn growled again, this time at Daisy, and she dropped her tail and hung her head and slunk back under the table. Then Ozburn lowered his gun and took his hand off the man's neck.

—You guys sure get jumpy after a few beers. Sorry about the safe house shoot-up but that's your problem, amigos, not mine. I'm not taking the rap for that or anything else the North Baja Cartel brings upon itself. Tell Carlos I won't charge him a cleaning fee for my messed-up home. Tell Carlos anytime he wants to pull his boys out of San Ysidro and Yuma, that's fine with me. I'll get more rent on the open market, and no brains in my nice clean kitchens. And tell Carlos I want to buy a hundred of those Love 32s.

He growled again, just a quick one, just a snarl, then clicked his tongue, and Daisy bounded out from under the table and led the way to the waiting car and Leftwich.

Ozburn watched the rugged hills bounce past. He felt jacked up and itching for Seliah, no surprise there. Leftwich offered him the ancient, bat tered silver flask and Ozburn took a gulp of the powerful blend. Leftwich claimed to have invented it at seminary.

"How did it go, Sean?"

"Mateo's suspicious but he can't put me at the safe house. And he'll have to tell Herredia I want the guns."

"Perfect."

Ozburn felt the drink melt down into him. It tasted of smoky tequila with a soft undertone that reminded him of honeydew melon. Woody and clean and just a little sweet. It was always cool, which was odd, considering the flask rode in the priest's jacket pocket pretty much twenty-four/seven. Ozburn suspected cucumbers because of their unique thermal properties. Leftwich told him there were eight ingredients in it but wouldn't tell him what they were.

"My bones ache. My balls ache. I feel like biting people. I still hear mice walking two rooms away and I can hardly gag down a glass of clean water. Ever since I met you I've been falling apart, Joe."

Leftwich nipped, then offered the flask, and Sean drank again. "But coming together, too, wouldn't you say? Strong as a horse and your eyesight is keen and you're accomplishing something meaningful in your life. And I'll bet you and Seliah are making some very powerful love."

"You don't talk about her."

"I happen to be very fond of her."

"She wasn't too happy about you drinking me under the table in Costa Rica."

"*You* drank you under the table in Costa Rica."

Ozburn glanced at the padre. Joe wore his usual black shirt and the stiff white collar. He wondered how the man could stay comfortable in those clothes all day, every day, in the border heat and dust. "You coming to Mulege or not?"

"No, thank you, Sean. The Lord's work awaits me in L.A."

. . .

Five hours later Ozburn climbed the stairs to the Mulege apartment with one young gunman ahead of him and one behind. *The* narcos *seem to get younger every year*, he thought. He carried a briefcase that had already been inspected by the lead boy, who had also thoroughly searched him for weapons. Ozburn was giddy with anticipation as he took the next step on his dark journey. Just a few days ago he had sent word out through one of his best informants to Benjamin Armenta, word that there were to be new machine pistols for sale, machine pistols with very special powers. And the Gulf Cartel had responded quickly to the news.

The gunman knocked, and the door opened a moment later and Ozburn stepped inside. The apartment was poorly lit and smelled of cigarette smoke and chorizo and coffee. Ozburn thought it wasn't much of a place for a powerful crime clan. Hard times in the *narco* trade.

Seated at a small kitchen table was a large man wearing a white guayabera shirt, jeans, boots and sunglasses. His face was pitted.

"My name is Paco."

"Gravas."

The gunmen joined a third young man and now the three of them stood with their backs to the door. *Kids*, thought Ozburn. *Sixty years of life between them. This is their future.*

Paco motioned to him. Ozburn set the briefcase on the table and opened it and turned it to face the big man like a jeweler displaying a watch in a case. Paco appeared to be staring at the Love 32, though Ozburn couldn't see his eyes. Ozburn had already converted it to full automatic fire, inserted the fifty-shot magazine, extended the telescoping butt rods and screwed the noise suppressor onto the end of the barrel. *You only get to make one first impression*, he thought.

"This is the Love Thirty-two, Paco."

The man lifted the gun in his big dark hand. His finger looked tight within the trigger guard and Ozburn wondered why they had to send a bear to test-fire a handgun.

"You won't be disappointed. Those four boxes of ACP ammo are my gift to you. If you decide not to buy these guns, I trust that you'll get this one back to me. They run seventeen fifty a copy. Seventeen fifty."

"We are not thieves."

"No. You are some of the finest businessmen in all of Mexico."

Paco racked the gun and aimed it at Ozburn and pulled the trigger. "Armenta will judge."

"Fine with me. I'll await his decision. By the way, we can't make these things overnight. If he wants them soon, he'll have to let me know soon. And it's strictly American dollars, half up front and half when we're done. We don't deliver. You pick them up when and where we tell you to. You transport them. That's how it works in the gun biz."

"I know how it works."

"Nice meeting you."

Ozburn turned and walked out, his heart beating fast and an ache in his throat.

He flew back low, north across the sparkling Gulf of California, *Betty* casting her small, slow shadow upon the vast sea. He saw a pod of gray whales and watched them breach and blow. The coast was dotted with islands, some green and some stripped bare by goats. The secret of Mexican airspace was to stay low, under the radar. You didn't need to file a flight plan for short jaunts across the border. With no radio and no transponder, he was essentially invisible. If Mexican authorities got tough with him, he'd act like a dumbass gringo with no idea where he was or how he'd gotten there.

He used a private runway outside of Calexico. The owner was

an acquaintance and he'd given Ozburn permission. He still circled it his lucky three times, looking for signs of his ATF family, who were no doubt frantic to bring him in. But the strip was deserted and smooth, and Ozburn set *Betty* down short and sweet.

He got out Daisy's kibble and poured some into her bowl and set the bowl under the wing of the plane. While she ate he watched the distant cars on I-8 and listened to the roar of the blood in his ears.

They walked into town on dirt roads, Ozburn dead-reckoning his way in. Daisy acted as scout. Ozburn had his old Marine Corps duffel slung over his shoulder, pretty much everything on earth he might need in the coming days.

At the motel he asked for a room upstairs in back, paid cash for one night. He walked across the mostly empty parking lot toward his room. *Just a couple of weeks from now the snowbirds will be packing in here*, Ozburn thought. He fondly remembered his mother and father, who had mounted many a family vacation in their Winnebago—four kids, six bikes, a dune buggy and always a dog or two. From Dallas, it was a long drive anywhere.

In the motel room he checked his cell messages and downloaded the e-mails to his laptop.

He read them, then wrote Seliah:

From Sean Gravas [sGravas23@zephyr.net]
Sent: Friday, October 14, 2011 10:02 p.m.
To: Ozburn, Seliah
Subject: If

Dear Sel,

If I could touch you I would. If I could see you I would. If I could tell you where I am and what I'm doing—I WOULD. Be

STRONG for me and we will be together soon. Six years ago when I promised better or worse, it was a statement of fact, too. There is no power on EARTH or HEAVEN or HELL that can keep me from you when OUR TIME comes. Have faith in me as I have faith in you.

Sean

PS. Daisy says hello.
PSS. Hi, Charlie—I assume you have Sel's password now?

Ozburn paused, then sent the message. He knew the reference to Charlie was a breach of his cover story—if his North Baja Cartel "partners" were to get his laptop and read his outgoing mail, they might well wonder who the hell this Charlie was. *Over my dead body*, he thought. *And screw Herredia. Screw his North Baja Cartel. Yes, I will screw them royally.*

He stripped down and turned on the shower. The sight of the water coming from the head brought a painful ache to his throat. Weird. He wondered if it was a delayed reaction to Mateo's veiled threats and the gunman's move to shoot Daisy. But neither of those things had bothered him at the time, and *what a nice growl or two I gave them*, he thought. He had been fighting the urge to growl for more than a week now, and tonight he'd just let it come.

He stepped under the stream of falling water but he couldn't get the temperature right—first too hot, then too cold—then he realized it wasn't the temperature that was annoying him. It was the water itself. It was formless and threatening and suffocating. Eager to fill and penetrate. He shut the water off and lathered and shampooed, then turned it back on only long enough to rinse off. He shuddered as he dried, watching the liquid circle and slurp down the drain, his throat muscles on the verge of cramping. *Last night the headache just about killed me*, he thought. *Now this. And Seliah going through the same shit I was, a couple of weeks back. What's happening?*

He got his vitamins and supplements out of the duffel and laid them out on the bathroom counter—packets of multiples, extra B complex, glucosamine and chondroitin, protein capsules, omega oils—all the things he'd sworn by since his diving days in college. He'd never really been sick a day in his life and he was pretty sure this was why. Now it seemed logical that these natural things would reduce the aching in his body and maybe even calm the frightening tangents of his mind. He counted out his usual dosage and choked them down with some tap water.

He lay down on the bed and thought of Seliah, and after an hour the neck pain went away. He dozed. He awoke ferociously thirsty and he was able to drink. It was the most satisfying and delicious drink he had ever had.

He tried to sleep but he couldn't. He breathed deeply and dangled a hand off the bedside to stroke Daisy's smooth black head.

10

Hood rose early to call the rest of the Desert Flyers about Sean Ozburn and his missing Piper Cub. He'd struck out last night; then it had gotten late. Now he drank coffee while he woke up, and the morning news out of L.A. droned on from the kitchen TV. Standing out on his patio, he saw the sun climbing slowly over the distant mountains. Hood was a sunrise man and this part of the morning always made him thankful.

"Next, *Bradley Jones*, a young Los Angeles deputy on his *very first* patrol rescues a kidnapped boy and leaves *three men dead* in a Maywood shoot-out . . ."

Hood's coffee cup stopped midway to his mouth. He went back inside and set down the cup and turned up the volume. The anchorwoman continued talking as Bradley Jones appeared on-screen, bloodied and dazed, walking out onto the porch of a house holding a boy.

"Last night around ten *fifteen* two LASD patrol units responded to a silent alarm in unincorporated Maywood. Deputies Bradley Jones and Caroline Vega entered a residence and discovered a small boy, bound and gagged. A *violent* shoot-out followed. *Three* men were killed and Deputy Jones was seriously wounded. It was Jones's *first patrol* as a deputy. Now, you can see in this video that he is bleeding profusely. That's a *potato peeler* protruding from his chest. The deputy was attacked during the incident. An Amber Alert had been issued yesterday afternoon for the boy, and the Los Angeles Sheriff's Department says he was kidnapped by narcotics traffickers who asked an undisclosed ransom. There is speculation that this little boy may have tripped that alarm *himself*. Here's what the deputies had to say to FOX's Theresa Brewer."

Hood watched as Bradley talked to the reporter, handed the boy over to another LASD deputy, then sat down on the front porch and passed out. Then a fast-forward to Deputy Vega speaking to the reporter as she escorted the boy toward a cruiser. The news anchor went on to say that the dead men were yet to be identified and that Deputy Jones was in stable condition at County/USC Medical Center. The incident was being investigated by an LASD team.

Hood smiled and took up his coffee again. He laughed quietly. He shook his head. He had known Bradley since the boy was sixteen. Back then he was a brash, strong kid who looked like he needed a little guidance in life. Hood had encouraged him toward law enforcement. But Hood had also won the affections of Bradley's mother, Suzanne, and Bradley had never forgiven him for that. Or for arresting her. Or for being there when she died.

Suzanne's death had changed them both, but Bradley the most: He had sworn revenge on her young killer and taken it, Hood knew—though the murder remained unsolved. Bradley hadn't even been eighteen at the time.

And he had *still* gone into law enforcement, as Hood had encouraged him.

Now, on his first patrol, three men dead and a boy saved and Bradley a bloodied hero.

A hero to some and a scourge to others, thought Hood. So much like his famous ancestor, the outlaw Joaquin Murrieta. So much like his mother. Hood had loved her in spite of all that. And in spite of all this he bore a grudging admiration for the audacity, smarts and luck of her son.

He called a captain friend at LASD who said that Bradley had been released from County/USC.

Next he called more of the Desert Flyers and finally came up with George. George owned a "clean little landing strip" near Calexico, and Sean had asked him a couple of weeks ago if he could use it. George said yes because he liked Sean, and he liked the idea that the ATF might get some use out of his humble runway. Hood got three names and numbers from George, all DF members who owned private airstrips. All three told Hood they'd given Sean clearance—two, maybe three weeks ago. Hood had chosen the landing strip closest to Buenavista and hoped for luck.

Hood made the Calexico airstrip just before ten. No *Betty*. No planes at all. But he found fresh aircraft tire tracks and the kibble slopped around the imprint of a bowl left in the runway sand and the boot and dog prints leading down the dirt road toward town.

Now he followed the boot prints toward Calexico. Daisy's dainty prints were in the lead. The morning grew hot and by the time Hood came to the last of the tracks, he was standing on Cole Meadows Road looking south to the city.

The first motel he came to was the Mesa, where the manager recognized Hood's photograph of Sean Ozburn without hesitation.

"You missed him by two hours," said the manager. She was young and red-haired and reading a paperback vampire novel. When she had thoroughly examined Hood's U.S. Marshal's badge—a deputy was knighted a Federal Marshal when attached to a federal task force—she dug out a registration card. Hood recognized Ozburn's writing: Sean Newman, with an Oceanside address and a 760 prefix. She offered to let Hood have the card and even see the room if he wanted. The maids had not been in yet.

Hood stood in the upstairs room and saw the unmade bed and the small white towel bunched on the bathroom counter and the clear plastic cup by the faucet and the blow-dryer hanging from the wall. The ice container sat on the bathroom floor with an inch of Daisy's water still in it. The shower door was wet and there were small whiskers stuck along one latitude of the sink bowl. They looked like pepper.

"Did he do something?" asked the manager.

"We just want to talk to him."

"On TV that means yes."

"You're right—on TV it does."

"I didn't charge him for the dog."

"You're sure he walked here? No car?"

"I watched him come out of the desert and across the parking lot."

"You work some long hours, don't you?"

"I don't have much else to do. I just heard a car pull up. Close the door all the way when you leave, would you?"

Hood thanked her and watched her go, noting the older Chevy Astro Van parking in the shade by the motel office.

He studied the room and realized that looking for Sean wasn't the same as looking for a stranger. He knew the man. Knew his opinions, his values, his humor, his habits. Or did he? The Ozburn he'd known for almost a year and a half wouldn't have slaughtered three men without a clear reason. So, something was missing. A lot was missing.

Okay, Hood thought: Sean's clear reason. That he was embittered by his part in a seemingly unwinnable "war" on drugs and guns? Hard to believe. It had never bothered him before. Before what, though? Before going undercover and getting up close and personal with some very bad people. Before being yanked from his life and his wife and plunked down on a hostile planet. Before his nerves began to eat him alive and he found his crossroads on a volcano in Costa Rica and his salvation in a hard-drinking priest who led him back to his faith and his calling as an agent of the ATF. Thus setting the stage for the murders.

Sean had grown. Changed.

In many ways, Hood thought, this was the story of every undercover operation. The degrees of difficulty were variable, but they were rarely this extreme.

So why Ozburn? Hood knew him as tough and funny and typically non-philosophical about his job. It was his work and he believed in it and that was enough. You're out at fifty-five—maybe travel or fix up the house or goof off with the grandkids. Sean wasn't a seeker; he was quietly Christian. He was neither cynical nor subversive. He wasn't overly proud of himself. He wasn't driven by material goods or women not his wife or by alcohol or drugs. So why? Why murder the three?

It's beginning to dawn on me why I'm here, not in this desert but on the PLANET . . . perform GOOD ACTS and DEFEAT the forces of EVIL. This is not a Biblical thing but a practical one . . .

Hood sat on the bed and looked around the room again. He wondered if Sean's reasons might be less obvious. Maybe his reasons come from the fissures and faults hidden in his heart, the secrets kept even from himself, the seams not quite true. So that when the whole system was sunk to depth, it would come under such pressure that something might give.

If Ozburn had secrets, he was careful with them, Hood thought. He kept them for himself and for his wife.

. . . miss you so much sometimes I want to cut my heart OUT just to make it stop aching . . .

Which left him with Seliah and her anger at Blowdown and her puzzlement over her own husband.

And Ozburn's family back in Texas, and his friends outside of work, if there were any.

And with four private airstrips Ozburn could fly in and out of whenever he wanted, though Hood knew that bold Sean could set his little plane down in a million unforeseeable places.

All four of the runways were located outside of municipal borders, which meant they were patrolled by county sheriffs, which meant that Hood as an LASD deputy might get some cooperation from his brethren in other Southern California counties. Might. He began with an acquaintance at Riverside SD.

"Sergeant Trask."

"What do you want me to do about it?"

"Charlie Hood. I thought that was your twang-ass Bakersfield voice. How are you?"

Hood stood and started yapping while he took one last look around the room, then closed the door behind him.

By the time he made Buenavista he had arranged for three different sheriff's departments to make occasional patrols of the four strips. He gave them a description and numbers for the Piper. With its classic Cub-yellow paint job and the name *Betty* painted beneath the fuselage, it would be hard to miss. The deputies couldn't promise anything but they'd try. Hood thanked each and offered his help in return, anytime.

Find the plane, he thought, *find the man*.

He had just pulled into the IHOP parking lot for lunch when

Bly called. "At nine o'clock this morning, Sean had himself and his dog baptized by a Mexican priest in Nogales. Sean makes a speech about . . . Well, I don't know what it's about. He sent a video of the whole thing to Seliah. And some other weird videos, too. What in hell's going on here, Charlie? What in hell?"

11

Father Jaime Arriaga of the Church of Santo Tomás in Nogales was young and thin and had a twinkle in his eyes. Hood sat in his office. Arriaga's English was as good as Hood's Spanish and they alternated easily between the two.

He told Hood he'd watched a yellow airplane land on the dirt road that ran through the desert around the church. This was a curiosity. Arriaga had watched as a very tall man with long blond hair had come walking across the desert toward Santo Tomás. He was dressed like a motorcycle gangster. A black dog trotted along ahead of him.

When the man walked into his office, Arriaga saw that he had a machine gun of some kind slung over his shoulder. He introduced himself. He said he wanted to be baptized and he wanted his dog to be baptized also. Arriaga said that the man did not seem to mean disrespect to our Lord by having his dog baptized along with him.

"But you don't just baptize someone into the Catholic Church," said Hood. "Do you? Don't they have to go through certain steps, learn certain things?"

"Yes," said Father Arriaga. "But he brandished the machine gun instead."

"Describe it."

Father Arriaga laughed deeply. Tears of mirth rimmed his clear brown eyes. "I baptize a dog and you ask me to describe a gun! Oh, you have made my day a better one, Mr. Hood. I'm sorry. I mean no offense to you."

Hood laughed, too. "None taken. His wife sent this to me."

He set his smartphone on the priest's desk. They watched the tiny screen as the miniaturized priest sprinkled water onto Sean Ozburn's forehead and intoned the baptism with solemnity and feeling. Daisy sat beside her master, looking up. Sean had one of the Love 32s in his left hand, held loosely like an umbrella or a bundle of flowers for a loved one. The strap dangled almost to the floor.

. . . in nómine Patris, et Fílii, et Spíritus Sancti . . .

When it was Daisy's turn the priest's voice became good-humoredly dubious and he managed to get through the ritual. Daisy lapped the water from his hand, then off the pavered floor. The priest's voice echoed in the empty church and the lapping of the dog was pronounced. A stained-glass window threw a burnished orange light that to Hood lent the proceeding a dignity he had not anticipated.

"When I saw the weapon I had decided that my fear of the gun was greater than my fear of blasphemy," said Arriaga. "I am a man, and weak. But the Lord knows my heart and I know He will judge me with mercy and fairness. Please don't ask me to describe what the dog was thinking."

Hood smiled again and watched Sean Ozburn face the camera and speak.

"I, Sean Gravas, have seen all manner of good and evil. And I have seen things that are not good or evil, strange things without values we can assign. At the end of my understanding begins my understanding. At the end of my life begins my life. If every man and woman on earth would do one small good thing each day for someone else, the world would be better. This is my small good thing for today. Just as man is not less than God but only separate from Him, so is Daisy not less than me but separate and distinct from me."

With this, Ozburn stepped closer to the camera and leaned down and put his face into the lens and growled. It was brief and wild. Then he smiled and reached out and took the camera and aimed it down at the altar boy who had been holding it, and Hood saw fear on the boy's face.

Please leave us now, said the priest. His voice was tremulous and thin and it seemed brittle coming from the tiny speaker in the empty church. *Leave this house to God and His children, Mr. Gravas.*

Hood reclaimed his phone and slid it closed. He followed Arriaga down a hallway and into the vestibule, then into the chapel. They stood on the proscenium where the baptism had taken place. The basin was no longer there but the same warm light came through the stained-glass windows. He smelled incense and burnt candle wax and the smell of decades. Hood felt goodness surrounding him here, a notion that only good things were allowed within this tiny part of the world. He wondered if he was only imagining goodness.

"What did you talk about besides baptism?"

"He wanted to know if God communicates directly with some people."

"What did you say?"

"I said that this is possible but rare. Mr. Gravas said he has felt the presence of something he cannot understand in his life. This something moves him to emotions and actions. He compared it to an ocean swell that invisibly moves toward land and when it hits the land becomes waves. He said he felt like the waves, propelled by an unknown swell. He suspected that the swell was God. Sean was uncertain about the baptism of the dog. He believed God wanted him to do it, but he wasn't sure."

Hood considered. He was never a churchgoer and he had never given much thought to God or the devil until fifteen months ago, when he'd met a man who claimed to *be* a mid-level devil. Mike Finnegan. Mike had talked knowledgeably about doing things he could not have done. He knew things about Blowdown personnel and cartel players that flabbergasted Hood. At times, observing Finnegan, Hood believed he was seeing something outside his experience. Later, of course, Mike had repudiated his devilish claims and chided Hood for even half believing him. And Hood had chided himself.

"So just how rare is it, that God talks directly to us?" he asked the priest.

"I honestly don't know. He has never spoken one word to me. That I could actually hear, I mean. I do feel presences. I feel the presence of the Lord when I walk into this church. I have felt evil in certain men."

"Sean?"

The priest thought. "Perhaps. But I felt in him the presence of God, too."

"That's contradictory," said Hood. "That's unhelpful."

"Good and evil are not always separate," said Arriaga. "They are often together. They are parts of us—present, changing, unequal."

"A doctor would say that Sean has delusions of grandeur," he said.

"There are many ways to see a thing," said the priest. "And many words to describe the seeing of it. Sean can hear God and perhaps even a devil inside him. A doctor can hear madness. Either way, Sean is a man driven by things he does not understand.

His growl? There was something primitive in it. It was genuine and pure and true. I fear for him and for those around him. And, although his growl frightened little Israel, and although he forced me to commit a venial sin by baptizing his dog, Mr. Gravas was most generous to us."

Hood waited.

"Mr. Gravas offered five thousand American dollars to us. I very gratefully accepted. You cannot imagine what good five thousand dollars will do in this parish. We can help feed the hungry and clothe the poor. We can buy desks for the school. And textbooks. The roof needs patching and the parking lot needs a coat of slurry to keep down the dust. It would take us a year to get that in the collection plate. Our faithful are poor. For us, this is a small miracle."

Hood listened, unsurprised. Sean and Seliah had always been generous—a sponsored child in Somalia, the ASPCA, Big Brothers— even with the beggars who would hit Hood and Ozburn up on the streets of Buenavista.

Arriaga sighed. "Let us pray for him. And for you to find him before any tragedy takes place."

Arriaga prayed aloud. Hood closed his eyes and thought of the three assassins blown to smithereens two mornings ago by Ozburn; then he opened his eyes, barely, just enough to see the light coming through the stained-glass window and the dust motes rising up through this light, and the glow of the old oak pews and the floor pavers cracked and crumbling from years of faithful trample, and the tall wooden cross with pale Jesus hung in agony upon it.

From the shade of the church portico Arriaga pointed to where the plane had landed, and Hood traipsed off through a few hundred yards of hard flat desert to stand on the wide washboard road. He saw Sean's prints and Daisy's prints and the fat tire marks that *Betty* had left.

12

Ozburn circled three times, then put down *Betty* at a strip two miles south of the fishing village of Puerto Nuevo. This tiny hamlet was just a few miles south of Tijuana, and the small runway that Ozburn now taxied away from was one of Carlos Herredia's exploratory outposts within the territory of the Tijuana Cartel. Mateo had told him about it during one of their meetings. Later he had given Ozburn a key to the simple hangar and permission to use it at his own risk.

Ozburn left the plane at idle and climbed out and let Daisy free. She bounced about, delighted by terra firma. While he fished the hangar key from his jeans pocket, he watched a white Suburban trundle slowly along a not-quite-distant hillside, then come to a stop. He strapped the Love 32 over his right shoulder and tightened it flush to his body and put on his Chargers windbreaker. He talked to Daisy and glanced over at the Suburban often as he worked.

The hangar was metal, with large doors that slid on runners and echoed hollowly in the quiet evening. When the doors were open he got back into the plane and taxied in, then cut the engine and shut down the machine and climbed back out. There were no windows in the hangar but Herredia's assemblers had cut small observation slits on all sides, covered by sliding panels. He pulled one open, looked out at the unmoved Suburban. He opened *Betty*'s luggage compartment and from his duffel he took his satellite phone and used this to call a taxi, *pronto, amigo!* He looked out at the SUV again, then slid the cover shut. Then he hooked the heavy phone to his belt and slung the duffel over his shoulder.

Back outside he closed and locked the hangar doors, then stood in the eastern shade of the building where he could see the vehicle. It puzzled him. If it was a Herredia gunship, the men inside would know of Ozburn and let him be. It wasn't like he was difficult to identify.

But if it was a Tijuana Cartel SUV, then as soon as those men realized that this blond gringo and his black dog were no friends of theirs, they would come forward with the intention of rubbing them off the face of the earth. As far as Ozburn could figure, there would be no better time or place to do that than here and now—evening shadows, miles from town. So he thought maybe it was Herredia's people, checking in on their hard-earned property.

The taxi arrived and off they went. Halfway to town the Suburban came up behind them, lying back a hundred yards, and Ozburn saw it through the dusty taxicab window: late model, Baja plates, blacked-out windows, satellite antenna bristling from the roof. He sat back and patted Daisy's head, the blue XXXL windbreaker easily covering his bulky torso, the Chargers' lightning-bolt logo emblazoned across his chest.

By the time the taxi traded the highway for the rutted road into Puerto Nuevo, the Suburban was gone. Ozburn made the driver wait outside the Restaurant Chela. Tourists chose their lobsters from tanks outside each restaurant. Young Mexican boys and girls walked the streets selling gum and trinkets. An old woman carried a load of folded blankets over one shoulder, an avalanche of colors piled high. A young American couple walked hand in hand across the pitted street, the man slender and the woman curvaceous and curly-haired, both dressed beautifully and both lost to each other in ways that Ozburn recognized from his first years with Seliah, the kind of love that is much bigger than the two people involved, and in some way more fragile. After five minutes outside the restaurant the driver became nervous and asked that he be paid. Ozburn caught the man's eyes in the rearview and growled at him softly. The driver nodded emphatically, then jumped out of the car and onto the wide, uneven sidewalk linking restaurant to restaurant, and disappeared around a corner.

Ozburn waited another five minutes, petting Daisy's head. No Suburban. Five minutes more. He saw the cabbie peering at him from up the street. He dropped way too many bills into the driver's seat, grabbed his duffel and got out. Daisy sprung after him and he strode up the narrow street, a large man with flowing blond hair and a Chargers windbreaker buttoned against the Pacific cool and a light-footed black dog in the lead.

He sat on the upstairs deck of Josefina's restaurant in Puerto Nuevo, Daisy at his feet. It was late and the street outside was nearly empty of the tourists.

The young couple he'd seen crossing the street earlier happened to share the deck with him. They spent most of the time looking into each other's eyes, speaking softly, sipping their wine. Ozburn could see the woman's face and she was flush with love. Her eyes shone and her earrings sparkled and her laughter rippled toward him like a stream.

Ozburn smiled; then her laughter was joined by the sounds of the restaurant owners back in the kitchen, and by a *corrido* on a distant radio, and the surge of the ocean against the rough rock shore, and even by the voice of a man that Ozburn could see on the street, nearly two blocks away, standing in a pay phone booth while he talked excitedly to someone about a car he was hoping to buy. Ozburn knew he shouldn't be able to hear the man, but what was new? Usually it was at night that the sounds became unbearably loud, and this night was shaping up to be one of his worst. He closed his eyes briefly and the sounds converged toward melody.

He finished his dinner and some beers and was now enjoying a clear, bright tequila. The lovers touched their wineglasses with a sharp ping and the man set his hand on her leg. *Ummm*, she said, to no one in the world but her lover, and Ozburn. The man in the phone booth swore and slammed down the receiver. Daisy ate her scraps loudly. The white Suburban wobbled up the street toward the restaurant, tires grating sharply on the gravel, fan belt screeching, the AC condenser groaning. The woman laughed like a stream again.

Ozburn leaned back from the light cast by the Josefina's sign and watched the SUV pass. He ordered another tequila and his check. The lovers paid and left in an uproar of chair legs on tile, a draft of perfume, her laughter as they pounded down the wooden stairs. Ozburn leaned very slightly over the balcony rail and looked left, in the direction of the Suburban. The driver had U-turned and parked facing him, lights out. He sat back in the darkness. A moment later a second Suburban came toward him from his right. It was wine-colored in the faint light coming through the screen door of a cantina, where it parked. Dust rose into the headlights; then the headlights went out.

Ozburn called a taxi and paid for dinner and Daisy lead the way down the stairs, toenails clicking. He took three steps toward the second Suburban, then hooked hard right down an alley. Daisy scrambled to keep up with him. He walked fast, his boots heavy, the duffel in his left hand, straddling the trickle of wastewater that crawled toward the sea and sounded to Ozburn like a child thrashing in a swimming pool. He heard cars on unseen streets, a hundred televisions in a hundred unseen rooms. The invisible ocean battered the rocks with rhythmic fury. He unsnapped his windbreaker and loosened the strap of the Love 32 so that one jerk on the quickrelease would let the weapon swing free.

At the last building the alley fed into a dirt road and Ozburn stopped and listened. Daisy sat and looked at him. From within the concurrent floods of sounds he concentrated very hard to isolate the tap-tap of footsteps—rapid footsteps—on the sidewalk. They came from his left, the direction of the white Suburban. Then another set, more sharp reports of running men, and these came from the opposite way.

He walked around the rear of this last building, the moonlight full upon him, and peered around its corner, looking up and down the main street. He saw that because of the slope of the small village and its few streets and its proximity to the ocean, he now stood in a place unavoidable to anyone looking for him. Unavoidable to anyone who knew the simple layout of this village. And absolutely unavoidable to two teams of hunters who had him caught between them like these had. Perfect. He released the gun and punched off the safety and felt in the windbreaker pocket for the spare magazines. He gave the sound suppressor a good turn for luck. He patted Daisy's head.

Then he waited, listening. Riots of sound. Symphonies. Looking up beyond the lights of Puerto Nuevo, Ozburn saw the harvest moon tinged with orange. And the flicker of the North Star. Ozburn thought that this was not the same North Star that had guided the ancients. Their North Star had changed its position millennia ago. And he knew that this new North Star would change its position, too, someday, long after humankind had died out. On it would shine, a lighthouse for a shipless sea.

The footsteps closed from either side of him. Louder now, and faster. The beautiful lovers came down the street arm in arm, heads tilted toward each other, the woman's laughter coming again to Ozburn like a rippling stream. They turned up the dirt road toward him. Ozburn glanced the other way and saw the shining car that was surely theirs. The footsteps to his right became three men, who spilled from an alley into the dirt road, and when they saw the lovers they halted and hunched like surprised coyotes; then, gun barrels flashing in the light of the harvest moon, they rushed the lovers and tore them away from each other. The woman yelped and the man tried to speak rationally but the cursing of the gunmen was louder. And again like animals they seemed to sense Ozburn's position and they marched their hostages toward him, the young woman and man pushed before them as shields. Ozburn heard the second group to his left, closing faster, and when they turned from the alley into the road they were three men also, pistoleros, with their weapons drawn. Daisy growled and Ozburn kicked her smartly.

They slipped through the back door of a lobster restaurant. Like many of the buildings here, the ground floor was where the owners of the restaurants lived with their families. Ozburn came into a small mudroom with hats and jackets and the slickers of the fishermen hanging on the walls, and pairs of rubber boots lined neatly along another wall, and there were plastic buckets and hand nets and fishing poles and reels, and the reek of fish and shellfish and sea.

He walked down a short dark hallway, Daisy close behind him, passing two bedrooms and a bathroom and into a small kitchen, then into a larger room that wavered in television light and where on a couch sat three youngsters and an older girl of maybe twelve and they were all clearly terrified of man and beast. The smallest one broke away and ran up the stairs. Ozburn could hear the banging of pans and voices up in the restaurant kitchen, where the parents were shutting down the restaurant for another night. The other two little ones fled upstairs next and Ozburn heard the fearful cacophony of their voices and their parents' voices. He told the girl not to be afraid. Daisy panted at the girl and wagged her tail. Ozburn stepped across the room for the front door and looked up the stairway to see a stout, aproned woman brandishing a tortilla press charging down the steps, followed by a man with an aluminum baseball bat.

He hustled through the front door, duffel first, and let Daisy out, then slammed it shut and walked quickly up the sidewalk toward the cantina and the wine-colored Suburban. He ducked into an alley and ran the alley to its end and here he stopped and listened and closed his eyes, and he was able to hear, through the roar of the village and the deafening panting of Daisy and the tremendous pounding of his own heart, the beautiful young woman sobbing and the young man pleading and offering money. He heard the *sicarios*, too, infuriated by Ozburn's disappearance. He set down the duffel very softly. They were not ten feet from him, just around the dark corner. He motioned Daisy to stay.

Ozburn swung around the corner and quietly placed a full-auto burst into the man without a hostage. Then another into the man who had forced the woman to her knees. His blood struck her face. Her young lover saw his moment and elbowed his captor sharply in the nose and Ozburn blew the gunman back into the dirt road. All of this happened in near silence—faint puffs followed by meaty slaps. He stepped into the chaos and the thank-yous of the woman, and the young man offered him a fist to knock. Ozburn ignored them and shot the men once each in the head, then shushed the lovers with a finger to his lips and shooed them toward their shiny car. He hurried them along like children, pushing them with the end of the duffel bag. When they were almost there he whistled sharply for Daisy and they ran back into the alley from which they had come. He stopped just around the corner. He popped out the partially spent magazine and traded it for a full one. Daisy looked up at him admiringly.

He heard the second group of men conversing one alley over, voices puzzled. He had the advantage because they were the hunters and it was their job to act. But they had heard nothing other than the crying and the pleading of the lovers and this had confounded them, and Ozburn knew it and waited. He knelt in the dark behind a modified fifty-five-gallon fuel drum that would be used as an outdoor heater in the cooler winter months to come. It smelled of wood smoke and ashes. He patted Daisy's head as he listened to the engine of the shiny car turn over and the tires chirp and the car speed toward the highway. The voices of the gunmen were close now as they came down the dirt road toward their three fallen comrades.

"Miguelito! Jorge?"

"*Capitán? Capitán?*"

Where the alley ended, the moonlight began, and into this the two men stepped. Ozburn crouched, peering at them around the flank of the drum. One of them glanced into the darkness but did not see him. When the third man joined his fellows on the open ground, Ozburn rose from behind his cover and cut them down in a long, steady, back-and-forth burst. He braced the gun against the muzzle rise with his left hand. There was the clatter of the weapon and the whack of the bullets into the men and the pinging of the brass on the alley dirt, and blood and arms and blood and hands and blood and gasps thrown up into the night. In a moment Ozburn had stepped past them and into the dark alley, where he traded out for a fresh magazine, then secured his weapon close to his chest again and snapped the windbreaker shut.

He walked to the main street and saw the people loping excitedly for the alleys that would lead them to the dead men. These people looked as if they were participants in some game they didn't quite understand but were told would be fun. He realized they had little idea what had happened or what they might find in the dirt road behind the buildings of their village. They were hopeful. They were innocent. They were who he was doing this for.

Ozburn walked the other way, stopped and set the duffel down and bought a pack of Chiclets from a vendor with a tray of confections and cigarettes slung over the back of his neck. He continued down the nearly empty street and back to Josefina's, where the taxi was waiting for him, as requested. Same driver, and a brief smile for the big payday of hours ago. Ozburn heard frantic yelling from the direction of the massacre. He held the door open while Daisy jumped in and then he climbed in beside her.

Twenty minutes later he was in the air, Daisy beside him, the few and scattered lights of Puerto Nuevo opening before him as the little airplane roared into the sky. What sound, what tremendous, singular sound! Ozburn buzzed above the village and he could see the tiny figures down in the dirt road in a ring of light, and they seemed to be coming and going with a purpose indiscernible.

He guided *Betty* over the black Pacific and climbed the breeze as up a soft-runged ladder, higher and higher until he banked north by northeast and headed toward the border. Flying east, he could see jovial Ensenada to his left and the great, violent sprawl of Tijuana beyond it.

Ozburn listened to the musical whine of the Piper engine, finally giving himself over to the sound. Melodies within melodies. He looked down at the lights of coastal Baja diminishing into the un-lighted blackness of the desert. At night his vision seemed to come alive. He saw none of the steady glare and the sharp reflections of daylight. He felt tears running down his face, tears of relief, tears sent by God to clear his eyes for the work ahead. He felt the re-turn of the pains that had beset him for the last four weeks. They came upon him suddenly, like pigeons returning to their roost. Sub-stantial, undeniable pain—the arches of his feet, joints, muscles, glands, teeth, even skin. And the ferocious ache for sexual release. He breathed twice, deeply, then held in the third breath for a count of three. Twice more. Better. Maybe.

He steered north toward Lake Arrowhead in California.

He circled three times, then landed *Betty* in a meadow between stands of lodgepole pine and spruce. He taxied under a metal cover and tied down the plane. His feet and knees quaked in pain but the air was cool and clean and smelled of conifers. He walked to the Red Squirrel Lodge, where he had stayed with Seliah last spring for a wonderful weekend. They had neat little cabins with Wi-Fi and a free breakfast.

He asked for cabin eight because that was where he had stayed with her. When he let himself in and turned on the light their sto-len hours came surging back on him like a rogue wave. He stead-ied himself on the door frame. Daisy flew past him and jumped on the couch. Ozburn went back to the porch and got the duffel and lugged it inside. He found his health supplements and vitamins and shook out a stronger dose than usual. Unwilling to drink or even look at a glass of water, he saved up his spit and swallowed them down. He was amazed how much saliva he could produce in just a few seconds. He chased the pills with a good, big shot of tequila.

He kicked off his boots and set the Love 32 beside him on the bed while the e-mails downloaded to his laptop.

There it was:

From: Seliah [seliahoz@zephyr.net]
Sent: Saturday, October 15, 2011 5:45 p.m.
To: Gravas, Sean
Subject: our plan

My Dear Sean,

Okay, I give up. I have to be with you. I have no choice. My body and soul demand you and I was not given this life to play some extended game with the man I love. I would go to the ends of the earth for you, Sean, to the gates of heaven or even hell. You cannot know the ache I am for you. More on that later.

I realize that you can't write me without all of ATF intercepting your words, often before I even get them. But I can make plans with you, dear one, and they don't know unless I tell them.

So here goes.

First, here's a way for you to know if my email to you has been ordered or doctored by your criminal enemies or not.

If my salutation reads "Dear Sean," you will know that the email has been compromised by them.

If my salutation reads "My Dear Sean," then you will know that I've written it in private and no one will see it, ever, but you.

As a back-up, if my closing ever reads "Your Loving Wife," then you will know that the email is somehow compromised.

Simple.

So here is my plan. Meet me in the main bar at Rancho Las Palmas in Palm Desert tomorrow evening at seven o'clock. If I'm wearing sunglasses propped up in my hair get out of there as quickly and casually as you can— I have been followed or otherwise found out. I'll have our suite waiting for us.

If you agree to this plan, mention Daisy in your next email to me but mis-spell her name as: Daisey. I expect to see that name mis-spelled, Sean. Oh, please mis-spell it!

Sean, we had such a good time at that hotel a couple of years back, before all of this. I will see you there and love you there as you have never been loved before. After that, you and Betty will have to make room for one more. (I assume you're with her!) I'll pack very lightly. I'll have just enough with me to follow you to the end of the earth. Sean, we tried. We tried to follow the rules and walk the straight and narrow and do the right thing and all that blind obedience they drill into your brain from the time you can focus your eyes. All it did was make us crazy. Enough. It's all a crock. We're lighting out for the territory ahead, Sean. Strange new worlds. Infinity and beyond. You and me and Daisy. I hereby close this book I'm writing, and begin another.

*In love and passion and the absolute knowledge that we will
be together again.*

*Your Forever-Insane-For-You-Lover, who is about to send then
delete this message,
Seliah*

PS—When can I get baptized?

Ozburn read the e-mail three times. Sometimes it was hard to concentrate through the noise and the aches.

The plan seemed so good.

So simple and workable.

So much like something Blowdown would think up.

He forced himself off the bed and dug out kibble for Daisy and got her some water. He went outside and stood for a while as the moon hung in the treetops and the pine trees hissed in the wind.

Fifteen minutes later Ozburn got another e-mail from Seliah. It was seven pages long, impassioned, anguished, mostly logical. He could hear her voice. He read it three times, too.

Sounds like something I'd write to her, he thought. He addressed another note to her but he couldn't figure out what to say. He walked outside and looked at the mountains again. Daisy came with him, then seemed to forget why. She sat and watched Ozburn stare out.

He went back into the cabin and paced the little room for a few minutes, trying to unknot his thoughts. He wanted so badly to see her but he knew it was dangerous. Maybe perilous. He smelled Blowdown behind this, smelled them strongly. He decided his answer would have to be *no*.

But after walking a few more lengths of the cabin, he realized that with a simple *yes* he would be holding her close to him this time tomorrow, showering her with all the splendid gifts he had waiting for her. And after that, they would be on his mission together, husband and wife, for better or worse, for life. Seliah, *Betty* and Daisy. All he loved. How could he refuse her? And himself? After all this?

Finally he hit the reply command and wrote back.

Dear Seliah,

I just had a walk outside. Beautiful night. I love October. I love you. Daisey says hello and together we say GOODNIGHT. I wish you were here so we could tuck each other in.

> *Hugs and more,*
> *Sean*

13

Hugely distracted by her evening plans, Seliah worked half of the following day at the Aquatics Center. Sundays were busy when it was hot. It was three and a half hours of near-blinding sunlight, and three and a half hours staring at the water, which made her nervous and nauseous. The water that had always been so beautiful to her, pliant and sensual, was now an alien thing. She hoped she wouldn't have to touch it. The sight of it made her throat ache. A cold coming on? Maybe.

Then, just as she had feared, little Amy Leitman staged a mid-pool panic. The girl screamed and gasped histrionically, threw herself around. Fourth time since July. Seliah knew that she was expected to strip off her hat and shirt and sunglasses and jump in and pull the girl to the side. Amy wouldn't touch the life buoy. She was an attention-starved fifth child and she openly worshipped Seliah and thrived on this ritual.

Seliah cursed under her breath, stripped down, and dove in and felt the terrible water close around her. She was only moderately claustrophobic but her sudden envelopment in the liquid felt like being buried alive. It *was*! She came up and drew a deep breath and looked through her stinging eyes at Amy, who was thrashing dutifully just a few meters away.

When Seliah was upon her she turned the girl and hooked her strong arm around Amy's chin from behind and drew her elbow firm. She sidestroked across the pool, trailing Amy out behind her. After just a stroke or two, the girl stopped struggling and let Seliah pull her through the water. Seliah could see the little girl's face turned to the sky, eyes big, and her mouth drawn back in a grimace of alarm so fake it would have been funny if Seliah's heart was not pounding viciously against her rib cage and her lungs weren't working so hard and getting so little air. Her skin felt as if it were crawling with something—fleas, flies, worms?

She came to the stainless steel ladder and manually clamped both of the girl's hands to the curving handles. Then gave her fingers a good hard squeeze.

Amy spit up some pool water, but not much. "You . . . saved . . . me. Seliah. *Seliah*."

"Yeah, yeah, yeah, Amy. Climb the goddamned ladder."

"You hurt my hands."

"Get out."

Seliah hoisted herself to the deck and stood. She reached down and took Amy's hand and pulled her from the pool. Amy stood trembling on the deck and spit up another small load of water, then started crying.

"You don't like me anymore."

"No, I don't."

"I want Mom."

"She won't be her for half an hour. Cry all you want."

Amy looked up at her, bawling. Seliah registered the heartbreak in the girl's face but was unmoved by it. By then a small crowd had gathered. Some of the open-swim kids had seen this before but many had not, and some of the moms came over to comfort Amy, and the dads to size things up.

Seliah looked at the gathered faces, then down again at Amy, whose blubbering was gaining momentum, and she walked back to her stand and gathered up her things and walked toward the exit.

The Aquatics Center director intercepted Seliah at the gate. He was a former butterfly All American with wide shoulders and an easy manner.

"Sel? You okay? What's up?"

She stopped and looked at him. "I quit, Dave. As of right now."

"Well, wait a minute . . . Why?"

"I can't stand the sight of this place."

"What happened out there?"

"Amy again."

"You were always good to Amy."

"Not anymore. Mail the check."

"I thought you liked it here."

"I can no longer stand it here, Dave."

"Did something happen?"

"I changed."

Dave crossed his arms and nodded. "Okay. But if you change again, I'll hire you right back. I mean, I think I will. What's . . . what's wrong with you, Seliah? I noticed this at least a week ago. You're not yourself."

"I'm too much myself. See you around, Dave."

"You okay?"

She shook her head and pushed through the gate and strode toward the parking lot and didn't look back.

At home she found a yearningly sweet e-mail from Sean waiting for her. She forwarded it to Charlie, then answered it with a slightly longer one—how strange to not even mention the secret that was devouring both of their minds right now! It felt almost good. She thought she might be starting to get the feel of being undercover—its heady deceptions and secretive powers. No wonder Sean had gone half-crazy. Full crazy?

She packed, lightly, as she had told Sean she would. Three days of clothes, the ruby choker and earrings he had given her, toiletries, a floral nightie he liked.

Charlie wrote back a moment later, asking after her, his usual polite and understated self. *This must be hard for you, Seliah. Please know that I am here for you as a friend. I know we both want what is best for him.* She imagined having sex with Charlie, something long and exhausting, animal-like, then rebuked herself for it, then forgave herself because she could barely control her own actions that way, let alone the thoughts that swarmed up from inside her. She'd given up on controlling those two weeks ago! Not much she could do when she saw the cute mailman in his little blue shorts; or her hot, hunk, bachelor neighbor who had a different chick every week; or the barista at her favorite coffee place, who couldn't take his black eyes off her. She had varied her routine to avoid them. She had stayed home all day to remove temptation. But that was worse, because all she had thought about was Sean, hundreds of miles away, and the Flexi-Dong, a nominally fleshlike device she'd bought online, which was right there under her bed. Enough.

She endured a long shower and felt better when she stepped out and dried herself. In the mirror she saw a beautiful woman in her prime, shapely and fit, with a pinched expression on her face. But it was uncomfortable to look at her own reflection—it seemed . . . ghastly. *What next*, she wondered. She flung back her hair and blasted away at the roots with the blow-dryer and forced a smile. She thought of Sean. Pictured him walking into the bar at Rancho Las Palmas. Better.

She gassed the Mustang and circled the block a few times look-ing for Charlie or Janet or some other cagey little ATF agent try-ing to follow her. Nothing. She widened her circle up and down El Camino Real and saw no one, then made a series of arbitrary turns and U-turns that finally led her to Interstate 5. It was four fifteen P.M. She punched the Mustang V-8 down the on-ramp and hit the freeway at eighty miles an hour.

She sat at the R Bar, nursing a Bordeaux in an oversize goblet. She'd taken a circuitous route to the resort hotel, then walked the grounds casually for nearly half an hour to make sure she hadn't been followed.

When Sean walked in, her breath caught in her throat. It took most of her self-control to remain seated as she watched him walk toward her. He'd traded out the biker gear for something more soulful—tight black leather pants and soft black boots and a cotton jacquard Robert Graham shirt open over a black tee. His leather messenger's pouch was slung across his right shoulder and hung down low on his left. A weapon, she knew. When he got closer she saw his cross and iron cross and the SEL on stainless steel chains around his neck. His hair was just washed and it flowed nearly to his back. It looked like it had grown two inches in the two weeks since she'd last seen him. The gunslinger mustache couldn't hide his smile.

He sat down beside her and set his sunglasses on the bar top. "I'm Sean."

"I'm Seliah. Let me buy you a glass of wine."

"I'd like that."

"You look very good, Sean."

"So do you, Seliah."

"You look like all of heaven squeezed into a man."

"You I won't even try to describe."

They leaned toward each other and kissed briefly. Seliah felt the rush of blood in her eardrums.

"Please once more," she said.

They touched lips again and she inhaled his smells into her when it was over. She saw the bartender glance at them.

"Where's Daisy?"

"In the Rover. In the shade. She can't wait to meet you."

The bartender brought the wine and Seliah paid for the round with cash. They pivoted their stools to face each other and she could see his whole front side now, his blue eyes and the wrinkles at the edges of them, his lightly freckled cheeks and his good strong chin and neck, the funny slope of the right shoulder he'd had his whole life, even in the boyhood pictures she'd seen. They drank the wine quickly and Seliah could see the wildness coming into her husband's expression, the same thing she'd seen in him two weeks ago. She understood it now. Or at least she knew how it felt to experience it. It was hers now, too, whatever it was. She heard the bartender talking quietly with a customer at the far end of the bar, the air conditioner humming, a mockingbird trilling from a lemon tree outside the building, heard the splashes of the swimmers in the distant pool and even the faraway pop . . . pop . . . pop of tennis balls being hit on a court she couldn't see. The sounds blended and separated and merged again as a new sound, melodic and nimble.

"We need to be alone," he said, taking her hand.

The suite was cool and spacious and the evening sunset pushed orange light through the blinds and fixed it in a soft glow. Daisy nosed her way through the rooms. Seliah used the bathroom but when she was done she couldn't stand to look at her own reflection in the mirror.

In the bedroom Sean was naked to the waist, hanging a spare blanket over the dresser mirror.

"It's weird, Sel. I can't look at myself anymore. Am I that bad?"

"You're beautiful. But I don't like myself, either. You look at me and I'll look at you. How's that?"

At sunrise the next morning Seliah lay awake on the sheets beside her husband. He was naked and snoring softly and his hair was a damp, tangled mass on the pillow. *Still wet from the shower*, she thought. She stared at the ceiling. Her thighs ached and her butt ached and her jaws ached and her mons was sore and her insides were tender. All night. Hours straight. Just a few bathroom breaks and short naps and a shower and a few minutes for drinks and snacks from the minibar, then they'd fall to the bed and he'd be inside her again for another insistent hour and another tremendous climax that would leave him not spent but crazily starved for more.

Seliah timed her husband's breathing against the beat of her heart. For the first few minutes last night she had felt something like she had always felt with him—desire and an urgency slowly building inside. He always loved finding her rhythm and following it and he had found it last night, too. Again and again. After an hour, and five strong orgasms that left her legs trembling and her heart racing, she had felt that familiar sensation of pain and hypersensitivity that had always signaled her full satisfaction and *no more now, please*, but Sean had gently spread her arms out wide and interlocked his fingers with hers and used his weight and strength to demand more. And she had given more—eight, ten; what did numbers matter? They were pained things, twisting and nerve-sharp, and she gave herself over to where the pain might lead. She had looked over at the bedside clock. It was ten oh five.

After that Sean had made a wobbling raid on the minibar. He brought Seliah a bag of pretzels and a bottle of water and a little bottle of vodka, then took some candy and water and a bottle of gin to his bedside. Daisy begged most of the pretzels from her. Seliah could hardly drink the water but the vodka was good. She sat cross-legged on the floor with a bedsheet over her shoulders and wondered what wonderful/terrible thing was happening to them. At least they were together now, and things seemed possible and at moments, even good. Sean sat on the edge of the bed with a bath towel over his lap, breathing deeply and watching her with the wildness in his eyes. *Black eyes*, she had thought, *eyes I want to climb inside of.* While he ate and drank and told her about a nice young couple he'd helped down in Puerto Nuevo, Seliah knelt and brushed away the towel and took his unrested cock in her mouth. After a while she took it out and stroked it, saliva-drenched, in her strong good hand. She thought he could burst. Delicious. Then back into her mouth until her neck and jaws couldn't take any more; then she rose and pushed him back onto the bed and rode him. Later her arms and legs gave out and she lay all of her weight on him but he buoyed her easily and it was like riding a mountain of muscle. She laid her head on his chest and he stroked her hair.

A few minutes later she had eased into a strange dreamlike state in which she felt physical sensation somehow after the fact, and she felt emotions not quite when she thought she should feel them, her whole being tilted off its axis. It wasn't a bad thing. She drifted in and out, aware of everything but focused on nothing. Vivid memories of girlhood, the Rockies and the rivers and her beautiful Boulder home, brother Scott and brother Jake, all of the several Labs they'd always had as family dogs coming back to her in singular detail. Friends. Relatives. Trips. School. College and swim team. On and on. It felt like a hallucination of some kind, but it was a factual hallucination—nothing invented, nothing changed. *Like floating on a cloud of your own life*, she had thought, *on the cloud of your history*.

Suddenly she had free-fallen back to this earth, this room, this bed, and she renewed her full devotion to the man surrounding her, straining deep into her with a need for something she badly wanted him to find. *My gift to you, husband. From me. Here. Oh. My. God.* She had pulled his face down and kissed him as she came, as her pain inverted and blossomed into a pleasure that she had never had before, one so large and consuming that she knew she was getting only a small part of it. Sean, too. He growled and began to quake and he shuddered and shuddered more and he was like a man discharging electricity. How long could it go on? Finally he collapsed onto her and Seliah stroked his hot wet hair and said, *I love you so much, so much*, and she saw the clock said eleven twenty-two and then he was in her again, driving powerfully, yearning and unsated, searching for her rhythm once more. Seliah searched, too. Gradually she found it and led him to it, a spark of pleasure waiting for her at the end of each long, slow stroke. *Our love*, she thought. *Our journey.*

"Give me a child, Sean."

"Soon. When I'm finally home with you. He will be perfect. She will be perfect."

Seliah was regular with her pills but out of motherlike speculation she had noted the moments of possible conception. Which one was best? The twelve forty-eight? The two oh five? The three twelve? The four forty?

Now she looked over at him sleeping and she ran her hand over the sheet and felt his hardness and took her hand away. What was this? What had happened? She touched herself, and beneath the surface pain she felt the ache of unsatisfied desire.

She slipped from the bed and into the bathroom. She brushed her teeth without water and looked at her reflection and wondered why it had been impossible to behold the night before. It didn't seem so bad now. She ran a cool shower. The sight of water unsettled her. It took some willpower to let it have her but she was exhausted and finally she tilted her head back and let the jets beat against her scalp and run down her straight white hair. Her eyes were closed but she could sense the bathroom door being opened and shut, and feel a cool gust of air as Sean came into the shower behind her and ran his hands down the length of her hair as the water rushed down. She moved back into him. He told her about how great it was to fly *Betty* again, and how much he looked forward to taking her up, and they could make a nice little spot for Daisy behind the seats, though she would probably be a little bit miffed when Seliah deposed her. He wondered if they could get her an aviator's scarf. He was thinking maybe Colorado was in their future, back closer to her roots. Seliah heard him take the shampoo off the rack and she felt the cool puddle that dropped to the crown of her head; then she felt his big strong fingers spreading it over her hair. When it was spread he began kneading it in, working up the lather. It smelled of grapefruit, lovely and light. He massaged her hair and scalp and neck and shoulders. Indescribable pleasure in this. He bent her head back for a long, cool rinse, rubbing firmly at her temples, then gently tilted her face forward to rinse the other way. He parted her legs and slowly entered, cupping his hands under her butt and lifting her to her tiptoes. She braced herself on the shower wall, the tile cool on her palms and her cheek, and let the water come down.

"Don't stop."

"Can't."

"Don't ever."

An hour later they finished together, an ecstasy she could hardly stand, but not quite get enough of. She turned to him, her legs trembling, and saw the smile on his big face and the love in his eyes. She saw no wildness in them, just love and gratitude and relief. He held her for a long time under the cool water; then he soaped her and washed her.

"What if we make something grow in here?" she said, patting her tummy and whispering into his ear past the water.

"When I'm home. When this is over."

"But we're not right, Sean. We have to be right to be parents. And we are clearly not."

"No."

"I love you. I love doing all this. But I should be able to control it, like normal people. See? Even when I'm talking about controlling it, I can't." She kissed his ear, running her tongue along its contours.

"I can't control it, either. Maybe we're really *not* normal people, Seliah."

"Then what are we? There must be an explanation. Should we try another doctor?"

"I'll go online."

"I've *been* online. According to them we might have flu, PTSD, fibral neuralgia, lead poisoning, toxic levels of mercury, rabies or syphilis. Or maybe HIV, schizophrenia, hysteria, drug interactions, environmental toxins. And it's possible we're being poisoned by someone and don't know it. Online won't cut it, honey."

"Okay. It has to be a flu. Or a reaction to something. Last week I had headaches. They were terrible."

"You didn't tell me."

"I can't tell you everything. I think, yes. We should go to a doctor."

"We can do it together."

"Okay. Good."

"And we'll go to another doctor for the baby. We'll make sure the baby is perfect."

"He'll be just a cell or two, won't he?"

"You can't be too careful in the first trimester."

When he had finished washing himself and gotten out, Seliah was still there, the water that she had loved for so much of her life splashing over her body. It was good again. Water was good. Maybe all she had needed all along was her husband. This was the beginning of their new life. She lifted her mouth and drank from the stream.

She took a few extra minutes to comb out her hair and put on some makeup that fit her mood. Even though she would be a mother soon, and it was early morning and the fierce desert sun was already outlining the curtains with bright slashes of light, she was still hungry for something dark and primitive, so she painted her eyes and brushed her lashes thick and hollowed her cheeks and painted her lips dark plum. In the mirror she saw a platinum-haired, blue-eyed predator. She smiled at herself. Little white fangs in a blood-drenched mouth. She growled, then giggled. Her pussy was tingling and wet and when she brushed it with her finger she felt the air cool on its outer fold. She left the towel tied up under her armpits and stepped out.

They spent nearly all of Monday in bed, curtains drawn, AC blasting, both televisions turned to sports and muted, with breaks for room service and brief naps. They ate ravenously and drank fruit juices by the quart.

They broke a few times so that Sean could e-mail her sweet, lovesick messages. They didn't want ATF suspecting they were both AWOL. Seliah e-mailed him lovesick words in return, playing along just in case someone at ATF had found a way into her hard drive. They laughed and tried composing such letters while having sex in exotic positions. Their e-mails heated up. They joked about Charlie and Janet reading them and struggling to keep their clothes on. More laughter, then more sex.

Daisy slept at various stations within the suite, following the narrow slats of sun that got past the curtains.

In the long twilight Seliah put on her running clothes and loped out into the cooling desert where she ran along flowering gardens and country club ponds and a golf course closed this month for re-seeding the fairways. There were towering palms and plaster walls hung richly in bougainvillea. Even in the waning light the bracts vibrated with color. Every green and living thing was framed by the clean beige desert sand. She glided past man-made waterfalls and fountains and ponds and creeks, water gushing everywhere. Every inch of her was sore but the motion helped her gather the pain into one big neat package and will it all away. *Maybe we could move here*, she thought: *Raise the baby here in the good, clean desert heat. Sell the San Clemente house. The prices here are cheaper.*

When she got back to the suite Sean was gone. All of his things were gone. Daisy, too. It was like they'd never been here, like the whole thing was some fever dream she'd had and she would wake up soon in her San Clemente bed, trying to remember all the good moments of the last twelve hours.

All that was left of him was the light scent of his shampoo and shave cream, and a handwritten note on the Rancho Las Palmas stationery:

> *Dear Seliah,*
>
> *I've thought it through and there's no way I can complete this mission with you. The risk would be unacceptable and my options would be limited by you. Please, please understand. Now that we have been together again there's nothing I want more than you and you and YOU. Go back home. Get Dave to give you your job back. Tell him you were having a bad day. See a new doctor. Find out about us. And wait for me. Wait for me. We will be together soon and we will be together forever. Walking through that door without you will be the hardest thing I've done in my life.*
>
> LOVE ETERNAL,
>
> Sean
>
> *PS—Daisy misses you already. I had a talk with her but I don't know if it did any good.*

Seliah took the note and sat on the bed and looked around at the darkened room. The curtains were tightly drawn and the blanket still covered the dresser mirror. She gathered a handful of bedsheet and wiped the tears from her face. She could smell him in it, his wildness, his unsated needs. She stood and ripped the bedsheet with her teeth, then tore it to shreds with her hands. Seliah sprung up and pulled down the blanket and saw herself in the mirror but again she couldn't stand the sight of herself. She picked a vase off a side table and threw it hard into the middle of the mirror and saw a circle of glass splash into shards and spatter to the tile floor.

"Fuck you, Sean. *Fuck* you."

14

Bradley did *Larry King Live* the next evening with a fresh haircut and his left arm in a sling. He sat up straight for the interview and he looked sharp in one of his tailored LASD summer weight shirts. He tried to sound objective as he answered the questions and gave his account, downplaying his role as hero, giving large credit to Deputies Vega, Clovis and Klotz.

"They saved my life," he said.

Then King cleared his throat and sat forward. "Three dead, Bradley. A deputy-involved shooting. There's an ongoing investigation and it's possible that you and Deputy Vega will face disciplinary actions or even criminal charges. Talk to me about that, will you?"

"I can't, Larry. It's department policy. All I can say is that the LASD Internal Affairs teams are professional and thorough and they'll do the right thing."

"Are you worried?"

"No, I'm not."

"You know, there's been no neighborhood backlash thus far. No cries of misuse of force. Do you think there's a sense that these alleged Gulf Cartel kidnappers got what was coming to them, taking a little boy who is an American citizen?"

"People love Stevie Carrasco."

"You know we wanted to have him on, but we had to respect the privacy of his family. That's number one, in a case like this. What can you tell us about him? How did he behave that night? Do you know yet if he was the one to actually set off the silent alarm?"

Bradley nodded and furrowed his brow. He had invented the alarm story for Theresa Brewer, to explain their appearance at the kidnappers' house. And she had passed it along to FOX News, which later solidified the tale for scores of thousands of viewers. Bradley figured when LASD dispatch checked the tapes and found no such alarm call, they'd blame FOX for the error. And he also figured that this seemed like a good moment to wash his hands of it.

"Larry, I don't know who set off what. So far as Stevie goes, he's brave, cool and tough as nails. He didn't shed a tear. But his old man did when he got Stevie back, is what I heard."

"I'm sure you know that his father is a convicted felon. A former member of the violent prison gang La Eme?"

"I've never met him. I'd guess that even gangsters can love their children."

"How's your chest wound, Deputy Jones?"

"Oh, yes, gangsters love their children!" said Rocky Carrasco. "You're quite a philosopher for being a dumbass cop!"

He smiled as Bradley walked into his El Monte lair an hour later. They bumped fists semi-elaborately. Bradley went to the fridge and got a cold Pacifico and plopped down on the leather sofa in front of the big-screen TVs. There were three of them, each tuned to picture-in-picture mode, which, when coupled with Rocky's digital recorder, gave him all the Mexican football matches and *Pimp My Ride* and *Wild Planet* and *Simpsons* he could handle. Rocky pulled a remote from the waistband of his baggy Lakers shorts and muted all three monitors.

Bradley had shed his uniform and sling and now wore plaid shorts and a white Lacoste tennis shirt and flip-flops and a narrow-brimmed hat. He raised his left arm gingerly to the sofa pillows. The little bayonet of a potato peeler had gone in two full inches, the doctors had told him, and it had sliced through a goodly portion of pectoral muscle but stopped short of the major blood vessels that lay deeper. They'd cleaned it out but left it unstitched so the wound could drain and heal. They'd given him twenty thick, sterile adhesive pads and pumped him full of antibiotics and told him to take a week off from any demanding physical work.

Which was fine with Bradley because he had plenty of non-physical work to do tonight.

Rocky sat at the other end of the sofa. He was a small knot of a man, muscular, covered in tatts and the scars left by various enemies. Shirtless, and wearing the oversize basketball shorts, Rocky appeared gnomelike. His skin was pale from years at Pelican Bay and years of indoor living. As the linchpin of Carlos Herredia's L.A. franchise Rocky liked privacy and anonymity. He rarely left this compound. He was the opposite of the showy gangsta and he claimed that his quiet life would allow him to live a hundred years, as his father had. The old patriarch had been gone a year now.

"I hear El Tigre might have a deal for you," said Rocky. "A proposal."

"Carlos always has something cooking."

"You're gonna like it. Mateo told me not to tell you so I'm not telling you."

"No."

"He says it's a good thing. I say it's kinda like this Larry King deal, but bigger."

"What could be bigger than Larry King?"

Rocky laughed. "You will be seeing what I mean."

Bradley checked his watch. "How'd we do this week?"

"Three hundred fifty plus some."

"Down again."

"I don't get it," said Rocky. "In a bad economy people need to get wasted even more. You know they're getting their kicks somewhere, man."

"Maybe from the Mara Salvatrucha—Armenta's hired cutthroats. I hear his product is terrific. Well, let's get this thing done, Rock. I have a long drive."

"Yeah, man. You rest. I got cut four times in a fight and they took me to a horse doctor 'cause nobody knew a real doctor that wouldn't call the cops. It was one shit feeling when I woke up the next day. I killed the boy, too. Stupid. We knew each other. Fuckin' Mexicans. I'll get the stuff ready."

"Thanks, Rocky."

"Hey, amigo. Just in case I didn't make it clear to you, I'm thankful for what you did for me. For Stevie. I'm thankful to you and God Himself."

"I'm proud to have you as a friend, Rocky."

"You're gonna have me for a friend for another fifty years, man."

Rocky walked over to his game room. He grabbed the cue ball on his way past the pool table and backhanded it sharply into a corner pocket. In the corner was a large wall safe. A moment later Rocky swung open the door and stepped inside.

Bradley went to a window and looked out at the compound. Rocky owned two adjacent homes on Gallo Avenue, which Bradley found amusing because *gallo* meant *rooster* in Spanish and it was slang for marijuana, of which Rocky moved tons throughout his So Cal network every year. Not to mention the heroin, cocaine and meth. The homes were old and two-story, and the lots were large. Rocky owned two more homes one street over and directly behind the Gallo Avenue houses, and these faced the opposite direction, so that after Rocky removed the fences, all four spacious backyards formed one big space. Rocky had walled off the front yards as close to the street as municipal setback codes would allow, giving the four-plex a fortresslike attitude. He and his wife and six children lived in the house in which Bradley now stood, while his brothers and sister and their families occupied the other three homes, along with countless children, stepchildren, relatives and friends. Rocky's father, the hundred-year-old George Carrasco, had lived out his last quiet years shuffling from home to home, sipping tequila mixed with vitamin water, bearing gossip and news and describing the visions for which he was known.

Bradley looked down on the central backyard. In the bright security floodlights he could see the little Mexican village/playground that Rocky and his family had established: the *palapas* and concrete tables and benches, the big freezers with the Pacifico and Corona and Modelo ads on them, the grills made from split fifty-five-gallon drums. There were dozens of tall palms and bird of paradise and plantain, and big pots of *mandevilla* and plumeria plants now dying back for the season, and succulents overflowing their pots and barrels. There were brightly painted plywood shanties for the kids to play in, a hoop and half-court for basketball, and a foreshortened football field with its one goal and a wall of upended pallets forming one out-of-bounds line. There was a chicken coop and a screened-off garden and an aboveground kiddie pool and bikes and scooters and skateboards and pit bulls lounging everywhere Bradley looked.

He joined Rocky in the game room, where four large suitcases filled with cash now waited on the pool table. The cash had been separated by denomination and rubber-banded into blocks that a man could just get a hand around. Rocky had set the digital scales up on the bar counter. Bradley could smell the vacuum sealer warming up down by the jukebox.

Two hours later they had weighed the cash and pressed it into tight bundles and sent them through the sealer. There were too many bills to count by hand, so they went by weight instead: exactly one pound of twenties contained four hundred eighty bills worth $9,600; a pound of fives was worth $2,400; a pound of hundreds, worth $48,000. The sealing machine was made for game meat but the thick plastic discouraged the ICE dogs from smelling the one-pound bundles. Bradley pictured a German shepherd with a forty-eight-thousand-dollar brick in its mouth, and this did not amuse him.

He picked up one of the bundles and read the denomination through the plastic. All of this money was only about half the California profits for Carlos Herredia's North Baja Cartel, he knew— four hundred grand plus for the week. Another hundred grand had gone into the pockets of Rocky's hundreds of young pushers who worked the So Cal streets, and into the pockets of dozens of middlemen, and more to the lieutenants and captains he knew. And of course another fifty went to Rocky himself, some of which was shared with his Eme equals, most of whom could only dream of it from their prison cells. And this did not include the fabulously lucrative markets of the Bay Area and San Diego, also serviced by the North Baja Cartel, and by others. Bradley looked at the bundles and shook his head.

"What a fucked-up country we are, Rocky."

"Yes, but we make a good living fucking it up."

"If we were smart, we'd just make it legal. You know, legal to have some for yourself. Legal to grow some or make some for yourself. Let the junkies kill themselves off. Let the crack and meth heads do the same. So people get stoned more. So what? It's no worse than booze. Then there's no market for us. We have to find other things to do."

"Americans won't give themselves freedom like that. It would make them feel bad about themselves. It would hurt their self-esteem. And jobs would go away."

"No. It won't happen."

"No. I'll live to be a hundred and it won't happen."

They put the money into one rolling suitcase and filled two others with new clothing, the store tags still on. Then two of Rocky's men carried all three suitcases downstairs. They re-packed the cash into a cutout under the rear cargo space, then set the carpet back in place and slid in the two decoy suitcases. Around and on top of them they packed in store bags of loose clothing—jeans and shoes and shirts and underwear, all new, all in children's sizes. Store receipts, too.

Bradley got in. He strapped on the seat belt and glanced at his personal luggage on the seat beside him. On top of it lay a letter from the Los Angeles Catholic Diocese, beautifully forged by a friend, introducing him as a delegate of the Sacred Heart Charity of Santa Monica and tasked with delivering weekly gifts of clothing to the poor of Mexico. Beside this letter was a clipboard thick with invoices and charitable-donation receipts and IRS forms, and page after page of Mexican charities and churches to be receiving the gifts, and maps showing how to find these places. It was a blizzard of forged documents and scavenged forms but it was also his history—some of the dates went back almost three years.

"*Vaya con Dios*, Bradley. You listen close to Herredia. I think you're gonna like his idea."

He drove away from Rocky's compound. There were armed escorts in the truck behind him and in the SUV ahead of him and they accompanied him onto the freeway, then vanished.

Bradley drove the speed limit and thought of his wife, Erin. He looked at the picture of her that he had taped to the dashboard and his spirit lifted. It was a promotional shot for Erin and the Inmates. They had her turned out pretty well, he thought—the hair and the makeup and the clothes and the whole 'tude of the shot. But there was so much more to Erin than simply her beauty. There was her heart, her soul, her life, her music. What heart, what music. Bradley glanced at the picture again.

Since meeting her nearly four years ago, not an hour of his life had passed without him thinking of her. He had long wondered if this was not love at all but some kind of obsession. He had read about love, and talked about love with his friends and teachers and his mother and a minister he once liked, yet he had never heard nor read of a love like his. He absolutely craved being near her. Same room. Same space. He didn't have to be touching her, didn't need her attention. But she had to be close. And if she wasn't there, he would imagine her, daydream her, mutter to her. He would picture himself as seen by her.

He wondered if he was wired differently from other people. But wasn't everyone? Didn't they spend half their time and energy hiding the odd wires, the frayed connections, the suspect splices? Maybe nobody talked or wrote honestly about love. He wished he could write a poem about it. Poetry was big enough to handle love. The poets got closest to making sense of love, in his opinion. Neruda did. He thought of Neruda. A line came to him and he spoke it out loud in Spanish, then in English. Bradley wished he could steal a good poem the way he had stolen other things—an Escalade, say, or fifty thousand rounds of factory .32 ACP ammunition. But some things could not be stolen.

He took a deep breath and spoke a voice-dial command into his headset.

"You," said Erin.

"It's so good to hear your voice. Talk to me. Say anything you want. Just talk and don't stop."

"Okay. I can do that . . ."

He listened. She talked to him for miles, his heart brimming with love at the sound of her, his mind firing with images, but every mile that led him farther away caused its own specific pain, too. The lights along I-5 stretched south toward the border, as if pointing the way to his fortune. But they were taking him away from Erin, and for this he cursed them.

Two hours later he was at the border crossing in San Ysidro. It was Tuesday night and the traffic was light. Bradley rolled down the window and dangled his arm into the cool night. He wondered if he should show his badge. He tried to use it sparingly, but an aggressive ICE agent was always worth badging. He could see the agent questioning the next driver. The agent was an expressionless black man with big arms. He waved the Volvo through with hardly a word and Bradley thought: *Piece of cake.*

He had yet to show the forged letter at the border—the Americans rarely asked more than his destination and time of stay. And the Mexicans, under Herredia's firm influence, had yet to pull him over into secondary. The only thing they didn't want coming into their country was guns, anyway.

But, in Bradley's opinion, it was important to give the border guards different looks: Sometimes he hid the money under pounds of fishing gear instead of charity donations. Sometimes he drove his black Dodge Ram; sometimes the classic Cyclone GT he'd restored. Sometimes he used forged plates. Sometimes he made the run in the early morning; sometimes at rush hour.

"Destination?"

"Ensenada, then Mulege."

"Business or pleasure?"

"I have charitable donations from the Los Angeles Diocese. Mostly clothing. Nowhere near ten thousand dollars' worth. I make this trip four times a year."

"What's in the luggage?"

"More clothing."

"To churches? Schools?"

Bradley tapped the clipboard. "Mostly churches. Some orphanages. It's all here."

"May I see that?"

Bradley handed him the clipboard. The big man leafed through the first few pages, then placed a dark thumb under the bottom sheet and riffled through the stack like a deck of cards. Bradley sensed the sheer volume of the useless information dimming the agent's curiosity. He handed back the clipboard.

"Good deeds. Have a safe trip."

"Thank you."

Bradley left his window down and lit a cigarette as he joined the traffic moving south through Tijuana. He smiled to himself, checked his new haircut in the rearview. It was short but casual, kind of a jarhead meets Brad Pitt thing, he thought. This part of the trip always found him happy. He put on a new demo CD by Erin and the Inmates. God, could she sing. And write music. *Gifts*, he thought. *But I have work. Work is for those who don't have gifts.*

And Bradley was happy to have the work. These weekly runs from El Monte to Herredia's compound, El Dorado, were the real cornerstone of his fortune. He made roughly fifteen thousand dollars per week, tax free, in cash, fifty-two times a year, year in and year out. Eight hundred grand in the last twelve months. All this for roughly eight hours of work per week—it was four hours down and four back, depending on the northbound wait at the border. Sometimes he'd stay overnight and party with El Tigre, but most weeks he would hurry home to Erin. *That* was the longest four hours he had ever experienced. It wasn't like he could break the speed limit with fifteen grand vacuum-packed and hidden in the car, but seventy miles per hour was torture to Bradley with four hundred Porsche horses under his foot and Erin waiting for him just a few miles away. The danger, the cash, the speed limit, the lack of sleep and the absence of Erin all conspired to make Bradley something close to crazy. They made the most emotional love on those strangely beautiful mornings.

So, coupled with his base LASD paycheck of $1,280 per week and the decent health benefits and retirement plan, not to mention Erin's increasingly handsome income from her performances and recording and publishing, Bradley was amassing a fortune that hardly even showed. Erin had no idea of it, though to explain some large purchases, Bradley had intimated a substantial inheritance from his mother. He felt shame in this, one of his two large dishonesties with Erin. But he couldn't tell her the truth without turning her into a criminal accomplice. His second sin was using Erin as part of an alibi to cover killing a man he hated. He had badly needed that alibi. He had not felt good about it and he still didn't. She suspected what he had done but she had not confronted him. Charlie Hood knew he'd killed the man but he couldn't prove it. The cops couldn't prove it, either. *Screw them*, he thought: *I did what needed to be done.*

He pictured his secret vault, beneath the big barn on their property. It contained his most important secrets—his history, his fortune, even the poems he had slaved at over the last five years. *Maybe someday I can show her our fortune*, he thought, driving through the black Baja night toward El Dorado. *It's really her fortune, isn't it? She's the reason for all this, isn't she? It's for her. For the children we'll have someday. For their children. So they won't ever have to be the weak of the world. So they won't have to work their hands to the bone for someone else. So they can* live a little.

He imagined showing Erin the safes with the cash he'd earned, and the jewelry and watches he'd been stealing since he was eleven years old. He imagined showing her Joaquin, El Famoso, his ancestor. He'd love to watch her run her beautiful fair fingers through all the diamonds and gold and pearls, even the cold, grimy loot. *All for you, my love. All for you!*

15

Herredia's compound awaited him, as always, at the end of a labyrinth of tortured roads and guarded gates and surreal walls that seemed to separate nothing from nothing and were patrolled by men in Federal Judicial Police uniforms. Bradley knew that some of them were real FJP officers, others less so.

He also knew that he had never been brought to El Dorado exactly the same way twice. For the last half hour of driving he was accompanied by two SUVs bristling with men and guns, one behind him and one ahead. Tonight a helicopter hovered low, like a Christmas star to lead them on. Then Bradley saw the pastures and the cattle frosted by moonlight and the airstrip and the nine-hole course upon which Herredia merrily hacked and cheated on his scores, and then Bradley saw the compound softly lit and nestled into a valley ahead.

Bradley dined with Herredia and old Felipe in the stately hacienda-style dining room, the rough-hewn table piled with grass-fed beef and quail shot the day before and a dish of white asparagus roasted with goat cheese, and platters of fresh cold jicama and cucumbers and carrots served with lime juice. Herredia was a big man, thick-bodied and curly-haired, often sunburned. He was a man of extremes, Bradley had found, capable of generosity as well as mayhem.

Herredia told them tales of his latest fishing expedition, a ten-day raid on Isla Cerralvo near La Paz. One night after fishing he'd gone to one of La Ventana's fabled cockfights and drunkenly bet two thousand U.S. dollars on an unfavored rooster. But he had won the bet and bought freedom for his heroic *gallo*, then gotten half the village drunk for the next forty-eight hours.

Bradley listened. Herredia was a good storyteller, although his stories featured only one hero—himself.

Later they retired to the poolside cabana for cigars and brandy. Three pretty, well-dressed gringas joined them and the blond one talked to Bradley at length about G-20's smart inclusion of developing economies, and the apparent fact that Iran's latest "secret" uranium-enrichment site didn't have half the centrifuge capacity that even the smallest nuclear power plant would need to operate, which, of course, left it good for one thing: weapons. Then she pried off her espadrilles and tossed her dress and undies onto a chaise longue and dropped into the pool and waved him to come in.

Bradley excused himself and took a walk out to the pasture, tailed at a polite distance by three real or fake FJP officers. He looked at the stars and thought of Erin. He tried to bounce a message off the moon to her but doubted that it got through.

Later Herredia offered Bradley good brandy and a Cuban cigar and they sat on the ends of the chaise longues leaning forward like men unable to relax. The women swam and drank. Felipe sat in a chair across the pool with the moths buzzing the tiki torch above him and his shotgun across his lap.

"What did Rocky tell you?" asked Herredia.

"Nothing."

"But Rocky cannot say nothing."

"A little, sir. He said you had an idea for me."

"Yes. Yes. Listen. Another story from El Tigre. There is a man, an American citizen. He is a partner of mine in the United States. I had to trust him but I never trusted him. He did little things for me. He bought some product at a high price. Okay, I figure he's a fool. He loans money to a friend of mine and lets the man not pay back. Okay, he's a *puto* who wants buy big friends. He flies a plane. He uses his plane to move some product for me. He makes me a good deal. Fine, fine, fine. He has money. He buys homes in the U.S. and rents them to my men. This is good for us both. Real estate is down. Rent is cheap. The houses are nice. My men take good care of them. They have big screens and good air-conditioning. They are in good neighborhoods. Then suddenly my men are dead. Slaughtered. They were no more than boys. Murdered, right there in the safe house. The safe house! I suspect that Armenta was informed. He's trying to run me out of California, as you know. This man, then, his name is Sean Gravas. He rents to me but informs to the Gulf Cartel, correct? He's a traitor. Imagine his arrogance. He allows my men to be murdered."

"That's a terrible thing, Carlos. The safe houses were a good idea. I'm surprised that there might be a leak in your organization."

Herredia's eyes flashed. "The leak was Sean Gravas. But his betrayal and murder of my men was not enough. Now he wants to buy guns from me."

"The Love Thirty-twos?"

"*Es verdad!* He wants one hundred Love Thirty-twos. I guess that he wants them for Armenta. I think that Armenta saw one and now he wants to have them for himself."

Bradley considered. He drew on the good Cubano and swirled the brandy in his snifter. "You could sell Gravas the guns and then kill him and take them back."

Herredia glowered at him. He had thick eyebrows that moved tellingly—up toward each other in the middle and he looked soulful; down and he looked stoked for violence. Now the eyebrows were down. "I could rape his wife and behead his children while he watches, too. I could detach his face and have it sewn onto a soccer ball and kick it down the street. But I am not that kind of man."

"I meant no insult."

"It is gringo arrogance to insult the Mexican. Call him an animal. A beast."

"I've never said nor believed that. With all due respect, Señor Herredia, I descend from one of the greatest Mexicans of them all."

"Murrieta," Herredia said quietly. He smiled.

"You've seen the proof of this, sir."

"It was an unforgettable moment."

"Tell me your plan."

Now Herredia's eyebrows went to neutral. "I have a better idea what to do with Sean Gravas. I want to give him to you. As a gift. He is an American partner of the Gulf Cartel. He has crossed an important line. And I want you to give him to the Los Angeles County Sheriff's Department. He can spend his life in prison. Here. See the man. When he meets with Mateo, my secret spy took his picture!"

Herredia produced a cell phone, touched the screen with his big suntanned fingers, then let Bradley scroll through six pictures of Sean Gravas. He was big and tattooed and looked every inch a gun and meth man. Bradley felt his heart do a little jig. An American cartel partner would be a splashy prize, he thought. An American who housed killers on U.S. soil and arranged murders and used his own plane to fly dope and money around? An American buying one hundred machine pistols from one Mexican drug cartel to sell to *another*? A trophy that would be *his* to award to a deserving law enforcer. Charlie Hood would die for a chance to impress his Blowdown handlers with Sean Gravas and atone for some of the one thousand Love 32s they let slip by last year. But maybe Hood wasn't the right deputy to gift in such a spectacular way . . .

"What do you want in return?"

Herredia raised his eyebrows in a show of innocence, and spoke softly. "I ask for nothing."

Bradley smiled inwardly. He nodded and sipped the brandy. "I would arrange for Gravas to be arrested in the act of buying the Love Thirty-twos from your men, correct?"

Herredia nodded and sipped his brandy thoughtfully.

"So we keep the guns."

"Yes."

"And the money."

"Yes. Of course."

"What about your men? We couldn't let them just walk away."

"They will be men without value. American boys purchased for money to do a job. Take them. They will know nothing."

Bradley knew that one hundred new Love 32s, made by his friend Ron Pace and outfitted with the sound suppressors and extra-capacity magazines, would cost Herredia right at one hundred thousand dollars. Who knew what price Sean Gravas could get from Benjamin Armenta and his murderous Gulf Cartel.

Bradley felt another bump of excitement. The whole idea was crazy in a way that appealed to him. Outlandish, yet Herredia could easily afford to punish a traitorous partner, sacrifice more than a hundred grand cash and forfeit a hundred new machine pistols— considering the hundreds of thousands of dollars that he received from Bradley every week at El Dorado. *And*, Bradley thought, *if you considered that other couriers were bringing Herredia like amounts of drug profits from elsewhere in the United States, the cash and guns were just drops in Herredia's bucket.* And he had many buckets. Bradley wondered what Herredia wanted in return.

He thought about the idea for a moment before he spoke. "How can I know about this deal between Gravas and the North Baja Cartel? I'm a simple patrol deputy."

"Because you are a good cop. And you are lucky, too. You say you have knowledge that an American criminal, Sean Gravas, may be buying guns. You don't know details yet. But you believe your informants have good information. Of course. And as it will turn out, your informants are truthful. You will be congratulated. You will come under no suspicion at all."

"Why not?"

Herredia smiled. "Because American policemen do not do such things."

Bradley smiled, too. For a man with blunt lusts for money and power, and a sixth-grade education, Herredia sometimes had an incisive worldview. He was right. An American cop might sell a little confiscated dope on the side. Might let a working girl stay free to work, for an occasional favor. But no one would suspect a young deputy of helping one Mexican drug cartel destroy another.

Bradley knew that some of his fellow LASD deputies would wonder how he could be so lucky. The same deputy who had rescued a kidnapped boy on his very *first* LASD patrol? He'd need answers for questions like that. And there were other problems.

"What if he's ATF or DEA?" Bradley asked. "They'll spring their trap and take the money and guns with or without your help or mine. And if any of your people are unlucky enough to be caught, too, they'll lean heavily, Carlos. American prison terms are not light. That's how the feds work their way up to people like you."

Herredia drew on his cigar and looked down at the coal. "Then I have only sacrificed a few weapons and a small amount of money that was not yet mine."

"Sacrificed for me? Why? I don't understand why you would do that." He was dying to understand. What did Herredia really want from this? It was much more than a simple favor. It had to be.

"This Mr. Gravas does strange things," said Herredia. "He growls viciously at people. He claims to have performed a miracle of healing upon a dog. He now flies around with this dog in the plane beside him. He has this dog baptized. Or so he claims to my men. He is seen in Puerto Nuevo the night that six gunmen are slaughtered yet no one sees or hears a thing. He's too crazy to be with DEA or ATF."

"What if it's just part of his cover?"

"Then he is *corrupt* DEA or ATF. Murderous. This makes him even more valuable. My friends in the Baja State Police will share evidence with your friends in the news media. A very good story, yes? The flying gringo is buying guns for the Gulf Cartel. Where else can this man get one hundred fifty thousand American dollars in cash? There will be abundant testimony. And I will give up evidence of his ownership of the safe house where the *sicarios* died. And more evidence that he knew his renters were bad men. The ATF and DEA do not rent housing to Mexican killers on American soil. We can be sure of that."

Bradley thought this over. "No, I wouldn't think so."

"Then you accept the gift?"

Bradley imagined the benefits of having provided the tip that had taken down an American working for a Mexican drug cartel, and led to a small fortune in arms and money—all of which would be retained by the LASD under asset forfeiture laws. Working behind the curtain, choosing the right people to take down Sean Gravas, he could earn goodwill that would trickle down to him for years into the future. *An investment*, he thought. *Something you do now to earn dividends later.*

"The first ten guns will be delivered to Gravas next week in Ensenada," said Herredia. "This makes it easy for both of us. The other ninety will be in L.A. They can be built almost instantly, now that Ron Pace can build them without interference from American police or ATF."

Bradley pictured the new Pace Arms factory hidden in Tijuana, partially financed by Herredia, and fully protected by him. Ron Pace had pumped out thirteen hundred more beautiful new Love 32s earlier in the year and it had taken him all of eleven days. *Eleven.*

"And you think Armenta will pay fifteen hundred per gun?"

"He'll pay whatever Gravas asks. The Zetas are abandoning him here in Mexico. If he doesn't rearm quickly, I'll bury him. He knows this. It's why he is attacking my men in California. Do you accept my gift?"

Bradley weighed the consequences. At age eleven, he had dreamed of jumping off the Oceanside Pier at night with his eyes closed. In the dream he was too afraid and he couldn't do it. But the next night he'd badgered his mother into driving him to the pier. He lied about his reasons. He had a beach towel and a heavy winter jacket with him. It was summer but the breeze was cool and the water, Bradley had read in the *Union-Tribune*, was sixty-one degrees. As they walked toward the end of the pier, he had explained to her what he had dreamed and what he was doing now and she said almost nothing. This surprised him. When they reached the end he told her he loved her and he closed his eyes and jumped. The pier was higher than in the dream, and the fall was longer than he had imagined, and the impact harder. He had swum back to the beach and climbed out of the cold Pacific and his mother had met him on the sand at the foot of the pier with the towel and jacket. He was numb with cold. She had hugged him tight and he had felt her large warmth trying to get into him. Shivering, his heart pounding, he had asked his mother to hold the beach towel around him, then stripped naked and pulled the big winter parka over himself. She had gathered up his wet clothes and put her free arm around him and together they hustled back to the car.

"Yes," he said. "I'll accept that gift."

Herredia's weathered fisherman's face broke into a smile. "I want this transaction to happen without delay. It will bring us to deeper friendship, Bradley. I will deliver the prize to you and your Los Angeles Sheriff's Department."

"This is good, Carlos."

"*No existen balas capaces de matar nuestros sueños.*"

"There are no bullets that can kill our dreams. It was true before and it's true now. Thank you, Carlos. You continue to smile on me."

"Malverde smiles on both of us."

"Malverde kind of gives me the creeps, sir. Now, tell me what you want in return."

16

Herredia laughed and Bradley drew on the cigar and felt the smoke soothe his nerves and thought of Erin and waited for El Tigre to tell him what he wanted in return for Sean Gravas. Herredia refreshed the brandy in their snifters.

"What is it you want, sir?"

"I have a thought. It makes my heart heavy. It wakes me from beautiful dreams beside beautiful women. It is this: My people in L.A. are under siege by Armenta. Twenty of my men dead this year in Southern California. Two every month. Then suddenly three more in Buenavista, when Sean Gravas betrays my men to Benjamin. Do I know each boy they have murdered? No. But these are my soldiers. These are my representatives and they are being treated very poorly. My earnings are down, as we saw again tonight. Six months down, Bradley. Six! Armenta's Maras are overrunning Los Angeles."

Herredia drank more brandy and re-lit his cigar. From the bar Bradley heard the women laugh, and some American rock and roll came on. The centrifuge blonde smiled at him directly. Then the women began to dance. Felipe sat upright in his chair across the pool, still as a statue.

"I need friends in L.A.," said Herredia. "I need help from the law enforcers to whom I am generous. I need Armenta's network prosecuted like the murderers and rapists that they are. I need my good men free to do the business that keeps both the lawless and the law enforcers employed. This to me seems like a humble and realistic request."

Bradley was an optimist and he began to catch the whiff of possibility. He considered Herredia, accepted the lighter from him and re-lit his cigar.

"It would take several lawmen."

"You must know many men who would do this."

"I don't know a single one, sir. We're talking about the United States of America. Not Mexico."

"Your country is very backward."

"Well, call it what you want. But American cops are American cops. They swear to uphold the law and most of them take that pledge seriously. Unlike your cops, ours make a decent wage. They raise families and they don't get murdered for doing their jobs. Not like down here."

Look at Hood, he thought. No way Charlie would bend for something like this, no matter how big a fish Sean Gravas might be to Hood's ATF handlers, no matter how much of that hundred thousand dollars might find its way into his pocket. Coleman Draper would have signed on, but Coleman was dead. Caroline Vega would approve of this arrangement if she could dip her beak into the cash, but as a yearling she was virtually powerless within the LASD.

But what about Jack Cleary, he thought, *the sergeant?* He was resourceful, self-serving as a dog, and fundamentally unprincipled. Bradley had befriended him, even invited him to his wedding, because he had the feeling that he would be able to use Cleary someday. Cleary could be persuaded. Cleary spent too much time losing at the Caesar's sports book. Cleary was assigned to narcotics now. That was good luck. As an old-fashioned, tough-on-crime detective, Cleary might have the street clout to mess up Armenta's L.A. network, one man at a time. Might.

He looked up at the moon and thought of Erin again. *Everything I do, I do for you*, he thought.

"I'm sorry, sir. I wish I could help you in L.A. But I can't."

"Why not?"

"Because law enforcement in the United States cannot be bought by cartel gangsters."

"But I have bought you!"

Bradley nodded, already doing some math in his head. "But I'm not enough. I would need more me's. I would need friends to help me protect your interests in L.A. But I can't ask my friends to risk their jobs and their lives for nothing, Carlos. You must see this."

"One hundred fifty thousand dollars and one hundred new automatic weapons is not nothing."

"With all respect, sir—the guns would get melted down and then most of the cash would be forfeited to the State of California. You are asking protection in return for impressive gifts that are not useful."

Herredia glowered. He looked down at the snifter in his big suntanned hands and Bradley wondered if it was about to burst. "But *could* you do it? Could you and your friends ruin my enemies and leave my business alone?"

Bradley sensed the possibilities here, good and authentic possibilities. Outlandish as they might seem, they could be made real. They were simply jobs that could be done with the right attitude and the right people. "Of course."

"How?"

Bradley nodded and stood and strolled around the pool. His

mind was racing and his heart was going hard. The blonde snapped his butt with a towel and Bradley yanked it away and dropped it to the pool deck without missing a step. By the time he came back to Herredia the words were jumping out of his mouth.

"First of all, when I pass along the Gravas story to my superiors, I make sure they know he's in business with the Gulf Cartel and their L.A. Maras. Right from the get-go, the Gulf Cartel is the target. Next, I'd hit the street-level Maras. Bust them left and right—drugs, loitering, jay-walking. It's not like they're hard to find. I've got some TV contacts who might like some fright-night stories on the Maras and the Gulf Cartel working in L.A. Fear is television bread and butter. And L.A. is already afraid of the Gulf Cartel—the kidnappers of Stevie Carrasco were Mara Salvatrucha doing Gulf dirty work, right? The Maras are perfect for TV, because they got those ugly-ass tatts up and down them. They're graphic. Perfect bad guys. Everyone will start screaming about the menace Benjamin Armenta. That's how it works. But you? You would be quietly doing your business the whole time. You might even feel neglected because Benjamin gets all the attention. I like that. Yeah. How's that for a business plan, Carlos?"

"You think like a college-educated *narco*."

"That's a nice compliment. But you know, Carlos, just like you, I'd need to generate logical and profitable returns. This isn't a small undertaking. It's a large one."

"How large?"

Bradley's mind was spinning now, but it spun around a very clear and calm center: ambition. "Ten thousand a week."

Herredia's brow furrowed and his face darkened. It looked now as it had looked that sunny day last year when Herredia had test-fired his first Love 32. For targets he used five men chained to a dock at a remote private beach. Rivals. Captives. Bradley had watched them twist and grasp helplessly as Carlos cut them to ribbons. Blood in the air. Blood in the water and on the sand.

"I will pay you five."

"Carlos, your people are getting wasted in L.A. Your earnings are down twenty percent in six months from Rocky's network alone. That's seventy grand a week. In six months you've lost almost two million dollars! Don Carlos, *con permiso*, but we're talking about ten thousand dollars to reverse this damage."

Herredia stood and looked down at Bradley.

Bradley stood not in defiance but respect.

"You have a deal," said Herredia. "And I will have American lawmen to look after my interests in Los Angeles."

Shit, thought Bradley, *that was easy*. Ten grand a week for running down some Mara thugs and letting Theresa Brewer in on a good bust or two. Cleary would love this. Cut him in for two grand. Caroline, too, another couple thousand. Bradley drew on his cigar, thinking that he might be able to pull this off.

Bradley sat down again. He felt suddenly very excited. His head was still spinning and he already felt $520,000 a year richer. Adrenaline was better than alcohol. *A majestically good feeling*, he thought. He thought of Erin.

Herredia looked at Bradley with a twinkle in his black eyes. "Now we have new business to celebrate. Tonight we drink and enjoy the women."

"Not tonight, sir."

"You will be missing magnificent tits and ass."

"I'll be missing nothing."

"Bradley, sometimes you are such a hard man. And sometimes you are such a soft boy. You won't take the whore tonight because you love your wife. You won't even stay the night here. You will drive home to be with this one and only woman you can love."

"True."

Herredia smiled and wrenched Bradley up in his big arms, pounding his great paws against Bradley's back, laughing.

Bradley gasped in pain but he didn't flinch or push Herredia away.

"Oh, Bradley Jones. You son of the son of El Famoso. You stay with me and you will be bigger than him someday. Your name will be like thunder across the world! And when they cut off your head people will pay not one dollar to see it but hundreds! Thousands! There will be a TV show about you!"

"I'm in no hurry for such a show, Carlos."

"No. We have many things to accomplish before we meet the devil. Let's go get your money. I will pay you the ten thousand for the next month of protection. Then you can go home and have your woman and I can have mine."

Erin was waiting for him on the porch of their Valley Center home. She was wrapped against the chill in a Navajo patterned robe and in the porch light her hair was a shining wall of red from around which her fair face looked at him. He could tell by her posture and expression that something was wrong. He slammed to a stop and killed the engine and ran up the wooden steps to her. She stood and he took her in his arms and held her close. His chest throbbed where the potato peeler had been.

Only after a long time did Bradley step back to see her. Tears ran freely down her face but she made no sound.

"What is it, Erin? Talk to me."

"Nothing, Bradley. Nothing happened. I'm okay. Nothing happened."

"Then what? *What?*"

She stepped in close and hugged him again but this time it was harder. Bradley felt the urgency in it.

"I got off the House of Blues gig at one. And I got kinda lost in West Hollywood even though I've been there a million times. I finally got to the freeway and I went the wrong *way*. And when I got off to turn around I couldn't get on southbound because of construction so I pulled into a gas station and the guy looked at me like . . . like I don't know what. And, honey, right then I was so sure that something had happened to you. I felt it so strong and clear. Like I'd been kicked in the chest by a horse. And you know this, hon, I can't call you when you leave me at night like that. Once a week I can't call you and you don't call me pretty much all night. And I was scared, Brad. I was so scared and I needed to talk to you and I couldn't. And I really need to know what you're doing out there one night every week. You have a girl, Brad? You have a poker game? You have something you can't tell me? What's the deal with you, man?"

He held her firmly and stroked her back and pressed the side of his face and neck into hers. He smelled the dizzying aroma of her perfume. His heart opened and his brain tried to close it down fast but it was too late.

"I drive a load of cash from L.A. to Mexico every week. The customs people are paid off and I make good money for my time. There's no risk. It pays ten times what I make in a week from the Sheriffs. *Ten*. It helped pay for this ranch and the cars we drive and the clothes we wear."

This time Erin stepped back to look at him. Her face was always lovely and always readable. He saw it coming but did nothing to stop it, not even squint. Her open hand cracked into his cheek once. Then the other. Then the first again. She cried softly and her eyes bored into him. "That morning last winter when you were gone,

Brad. When I told Charlie you were with me and the guys. And the gangsta that shot your mom got murdered up in L.A. Did you do that, honey? You can tell me. I'd understand if you did it. But you have to tell me the truth if we hope to make this marriage work."

But even Bradley's overflowing heart was no match for the peril he sensed here, and he did not hesitate in his answer.

"I didn't do that, Erin. I was helping out a friend. I swear this to you and the many children I hope to have with you."

"You would swear on them?"

"I do swear on them."

She stepped back into his arms and squeezed him gently. He could feel the tapping of her heart against his chest. "Stop the Mexico runs. We can live on less."

"No. I'll do anything you want but not that."

"Why?"

"So I can become."

"Become what?"

"A man able to protect what he loves."

"You didn't protect me last night."

"I can change that. There will never be another night like it."

She moved away again and looked at him and he saw the uncertainty in her eyes.

He went to his knees. "When you look at me it's like walking into a beautiful room," he said. "The most beautiful room on earth. It's the only place I ever want to be."

A tear rolled down her pale face and she wiped it away. She bit her lip and stepped forward and helped him up.

17

Wednesday morning Hood sat in the Buenavista ATF station watching Sean Ozburn's videos again on the now-useless safe house monitor number four. Oz was using a Flip now, so the latest videos sent to Seliah were of better quality than the first few. Playing any of them on the good monitor made them even clearer, and more haunting.

Hood watched the miracle healing of Daisy. It was like seeing it for the first time. Ozburn began this segment with an establishing shot and Hood now recognized El Centro. Then came a jumbled, poorly focused episode: a black, bleeding dog lying on the side of the road, a little crowd forming, Sean scooping up the animal in one big tattooed arm while holding the cell camera high in the other hand for an aerial shot as he crunched along the sun-cooked street toward his car.

Hood noted that the actual miracle healing wasn't caught on video because Ozburn was presumably steering with one hand and healing with the other. But Oz narrated his actions as the unmanned camera filmed the headliner of the Range Rover.

And now I place my right hand over her head. There is blood coming from her mouth and nose. She is not conscious but she is breathing. Now I pray to you, God in heaven, that your power move through me and heal this simple blameless animal, you for whom the creation of heaven and earth was pretty much a snap . . . Yes . . . I feel your power moving through me into the beast and I feel her life returning and her name will be called Daisy . . . Wow . . . Oh, WOW, check this out!

Phone back in hand, Ozburn focused on the dog, bouncing along with the rhythm of the vehicle, panting gently, looking up at Sean with affection and loyalty.

Man, this is so cool.

Next came a sermon delivered by Sean at an outdoor service of some kind. Hood couldn't place the landscape: rolling hills, grassland, some oak and madrone and manzanita. Someone else was working the camera. Ozburn stood before twenty or thirty people sitting on fallen logs and a crumbling adobe brick wall. The cameraman panned the people. They were a mix of ages, half of them brown and the other half white. There was a big fire ring made of river rock but there was no fire. An orange cooler sat on a slouching picnic table, and beside it was a glass jar with a few coins in it.

An aged evangelist introduced Sean Gravas as a "man come newly to our Lord," but Hood saw annoyance in his craggy face. The evangelist held a Bible in one hand and wore a white shirt buttoned to the top with no tie, and a beaten black coat, and his crucifix was large and made of silver and turquoise.

When Sean stood and faced the assembly and the camera, Hood could see that he wasn't right. Sweat poured down his face and he looked to be in pain. He was dressed in his sleeveless biker vest and the black jeans and harness boots and he wore a black bandana pirate style. Over his left shoulder was slung a Love 32 with the curving fifty-shot magazine and the noise suppressor screwed into place.

He held a white-covered book in both hands but he didn't open it. He kept looking skyward, as if he was waiting for something to appear, something perhaps not good. Daisy stood at his feet and looked up at him with a similar expression.

Here in this rude theater we sense God. His breath is the wind that touches our skin and gives life to our dust. His eyes are the creeping and flying and swimming things that see us better than we see them. His ears are the canyons that amplify our sounds and songs and prayers. Lord if we offend Thee, strike us down, and if we please Thee, raise us up and place our bodies upon the blade of Your truth that we may be pierced with Your spirit . . .

Sean sweated and talked on. Blood and life eternal. The lamb and the sword.

Hood's heart broke some as he watched and listened. Sean was a good man. And something had gotten into him. Something had changed him. Sean had all but lost his once-kind and strong and generous self. Who was this inhabiting his body? Who in hell? Where was Sean?

Then came the baptism of Daisy by Father Arriaga.

Then came a long lecture on the evils of whoredom. Hood watched Sean throttle a young man, then drive him through a window of what appeared to be a bordello bedroom. A prostitute flailed at him with a red stiletto shoe and cursed in Spanish. Ozburn growled at her and she ran out. He went bar to bar and club to club in what Hood recognized as Tijuana, lecturing whoever was too afraid to scuttle away.

Then came video that Hood had never seen before: a beautiful Mexican girl lying on a bed, wide-eyed and sobbing, a woman holding a bag of something against her neck.

Hood checked the time and date: It had been sent to Seliah just an hour ago. Ozburn narrated:

In the village of Agua Blanca a girl was dressing for school. She put on her hat but a huge scorpion fell from the hat to her neck and drove its deadly stinger into her flesh. Then it fell to the floor. Her mother trapped the scorpion under a glass bowl, then ran into the streets to find the curandera. *The village had no ice so the* curandera *filled a plastic bag with peeled cucumbers, dandelions and cool well water. She viewed the scorpion and said it was the deadly variety, the only scorpion that can kill a healthy girl. The girl's neck swelled up at the sting. I'm here in Agua Blanca on a personal matter but it can wait. Now I see that I was brought here by someone or something, for another purpose. My purpose here is to save this girl. Her name is Silvia.*

Ozburn turned his camera to the floor and got a close-up of the upended glass mixing bowl. The scorpion nearly spanned its diameter, head and pinchers facing the camera, stinger cocked up and ready for action. Daisy nosed the bowl and the scorpion swiveled on her; then she sprang away.

Hood knew from his boyhood that the *curandera* was right: There was only one deadly species of scorpion in the West. But she was wrong, too: The one that had stung the girl was a much larger and darker, and less potent, creature than the slender, pale, lethal other.

Hood watched Sean try to convince the mother to take the recorder. Ozburn said he wanted to say a healing prayer while touching the girl. Finally the mother took the camera and shot video of the *curandera*, a wizened woman with a troubled face and sharp teeth and a scapular festooned with the heads and tails of very large rattlesnakes. She drank from a can of orange soda.

Ozburn sat on the bed beside the girl, his machine pistol slung over one shoulder. He held the plastic bag to the girl's neck. In this part of the video Hood couldn't see Ozburn's face. All he saw was his broad back and big shoulders, and the blond hair and the fearful face of the girl. Beside the bed were a pitcher and a bowl and a rustic vanity with a mirror. Someone had draped one of the girl's dresses over the mirror and it looked to Hood like an observer, a ghost.

The mother spoke in rapid Spanish and the camera wobbled dramatically. Hood heard the *curandera* answer in a strangely low and disapproving voice. Though it was much clearer than the audio of his cell phone, Hood still couldn't understand her words.

Father of all days defend this girl from the venom of evil so that she may live to be an angel . . . Mother of all nights defend this girl from the poison of the devil so that she may live to be an angel . . .

He said the sentences again and again.

Offscreen the *curandera* spoke in the background, and although again Hood could not make out her words, her voice was low and trembled with foreboding.

Offscreen the mother answered her in an anxious tone.

No! said Sean. *No water for her.* No agua!

The *curandera* hissed something and Sean turned and ordered her to shut her foul old mouth. His eyes were crazy black, and Hood saw almost nothing in them of the man he had known. He was sweating badly. Daisy looked away from him.

Hood was surprised by the enormity of the change in Sean, as revealed by the good video monitor. Only a small fraction of it had registered over the tiny screen on his cell phone.

Ozburn turned back to the girl and set the plastic bag on the bed and pressed one of his great rough hands to the girl's forehead. He kept repeating the two sentences. Gradually the girl's eyes closed. He prayed on, the same words, the same cadence, his voice growing softer and slower until Hood could barely hear it. And still he prayed.

A minute or two later Ozburn removed his hand from the girl's head. Her eyes were still closed and her face was peaceful. Her chest rose and fell in the rhythm of sleep. Offscreen the *curandera* muttered something accusatory.

Ozburn reached back and claimed the recorder. He turned it on the girl, zooming in close to the wound on her neck. The swelling had gone down and the skin was reddened. Hood could see the mark the stinger had left, much like a bee sting. Ozburn put the cooling sack of cucumbers back over it.

Ozburn panned the room and settled the camera on the *curandera*. She spoke to him in Spanish now and for the first time Hood could both hear and understand her words.

—Why did you come to Agua Blanca?

—People talk of you. I'm suffering and I want you to make it stop.

—Your suffering will stop when it is finished.

—Tell me what it is.

—It lives in the caves of your blood.

The *curandera* moved to the vanity and pulled the dress from the mirror.

—*Bruja*, said Ozburn, swinging the camera away from his reflection.

Witch, thought Hood.

The *curandera* reached up and grasped one of the snake heads on her scapular. The camera came in on it. Hood saw the glazed eyes with their vertical pupils, the enlarged nose scales, and the pits through which these vipers could sense the body heat of their prey. He was impressed by its size, though the many others were easily as big. He'd seen his share of rattlesnakes in and around Bakersfield but rarely had they been more than five feet long, as these snakes had once been. Most of the rattles separating the heads were blunt rectangles, at least two inches long. The *curandera* held it up to the camera, a matter-of-fact expression on her dark, wrinkled face.

—You two look a lot alike, lady. You must have a hundred of those heads.

—Come with me, white devil. I will show you how your suffering will end.

—Let's do it, *bruja.*

Hood's scalp crawled as the picture faded to black.

A moment later the girl appeared, sitting up in bed with a bowl of soup in her lap and a spoon in her hand. She looked at the camera shyly, then blushed.

Ozburn narrated:

Two hours later. Silvia slept for almost two hours and woke up hungry. I will still not allow her to drink water in my presence. As you can see, the wound is nothing now but a very small mark. The Lord has acted again through me and in my humble amazement I am content and Silvia is cured.

The camera zoomed in close. Even the once-reddish patch at the sting site was gone. All that was left was the small pinprick of the stinger.

Then Ozburn swung the camera down and walked into the next room where the scorpion was still trapped under the glass bowl. He reached down and lifted it and the scorpion raised its pinchers and tail and scuttled backward. Ozburn's harness boot crushed it into the dirt floor. Daisy sniffed the boot toe.

—*Curandera! Apúrate!*

Hood made Agua Blanca by afternoon. It sat along a potholed asphalt road, ten miles below Tecate. The buildings were rectangles of blue and yellow and pink and green, and the speed bump gave Hood and his SUV a sharp bounce.

He bought two orange soft drinks at the mini-super Ayala and asked about the *curandera*. The clerk told Hood that she lived at the far end of town, on a dirt road that began at a green ice cream stand and a white pharmacy. He said to drive west one hundred meters and look for the driveway marked by a hubcap and some flowers. He said the *curandera* had saved a girl from scorpions.

Hood stopped at the ice cream stand and got two deluxe Popsicles, one coconut and one orange. He turned right and crunched down the wide dirt road. Half a mile later he saw the hubcap with the spray of plastic flowers long blanched of color by the sun. The driveway was not quite wide enough for his Durango so the manzanita branches streaked its flanks. The house was a pale green cinderblock rectangle with a water tank on the roof.

She stood in the doorway as if she had been expecting him. He climbed down from the vehicle with the drink bottles in one hand

and the Popsicles in the other and swung the door shut with an elbow. They spoke in Spanish.

—Good evening. I'm Deputy Hood.

She peered at him, face darkly lined, eyes fierce but steady. She was short and wiry and wore a black dress to her ankles and red slip-on sneakers. Her scapular today was made not of rattlesnake parts but of dried peyote buttons interspersed with plastic Telmex calling cards with action pictures of famous soccer players on them.

Hood held out the Popsicles and she took the orange one and a soda. He explained that he wanted to see what she had shown to Sean Gravas, the man who had filmed her healing of the stung girl, Silvia. She motioned him into her home. The floor was swept recently, broom marks on concrete, and there was a propane oven and a three-burner stove and a sink and a poured concrete counter. She opened her bottle and handed the opener to Hood.

—He is a white devil.

—He is a sick man.

—Silvia is strong.

—Sean is weak. I want you to take me where you took him.

—It is ten minutes to drive.

It was a thirty-minute drive. The dirt road that wound up past the *curandera*'s house soon narrowed to a twist of ruts. Hood straddled them in the big SUV. The sun was lowering now and there was a pink tint to the mesquite and madrone, backlit by the sun. They cast blue shadows on the tan desert sand. The *curandera* threw her Popsicle stick and wrapper out the window and a minute later the soda can.

Finally the road ended in a fan of uphill paths that looked more traveled by flash floods than by humans or animals. The *curandera* put her hand on the door pull and Hood parked and shut off the engine. He came around to her side and she started up a trail through the dry brown brush. Hood got his Glock from the toolbox in the back and clipped the holster to his belt, then locked up the vehicle and caught up with her.

She led the way, walking briskly. Lizards hugged the rocks for the last warmth of sunlight. They climbed for a few minutes, then walked downhill into a stand of scrub oak and greasewood. Hood smelled the spring and saw the foundation of a small house that had been destroyed, now just a black smudge upon the earth. There was a rock chimney. Beyond the foundation scattered sticks and rusted swatches of chicken wire lay half-buried in sand.

She led him past the house and coop and a well and along the copse of greasewood trees. The ground around them was piled high with the dead needles into which spiders had tunneled. Their webs caught the sunlight, and just inside the mouths of the tunnels the spiders waited pale and still. She ducked under a branch and brushed between two trees, and Hood followed. The greasewood grew close together and Hood smelled the mint smell of them and felt their oil on his hands as he pushed aside the branches to follow her. A trail opened and after a minute they came to a clearing. Here the trees had not grown or were removed long ago.

In the middle of the clearing was a rude rock pyramid four feet high, made of desert stones held together with cement. It looked to have been hastily made—thick seams of cement and an erratic shape. There were two staunch iron rings set into the concrete, one low and one high. A length of heavy chain ran from each ring to the ground and ended in a manacle drilled for a lock. Hood looked down at one, the large, rusted iron bracelet an exaggerated and seemingly ancient version of modern-day handcuffs. There was another pile of stones thirty feet away, at the edge of the greasewoods, and these were piled loose and dusted with dead brown needles.

—Juan Batista lived here, she said. Crazy. Eyes like the devil. Eyes like Sean Gravas. That is how I know.

The *curandera* walked to the manacles and placed the longer one over her small hand. Her dark fist moved easily in and out so she raised it, and the huge rusted cuff slid to the crook of her elbow. The short lower manacle she placed around her ankle, and over each one she made a locking motion with an invisible key. Then she threw the key into the greasewood and sat down in the dirt and looked at Hood.

—He locked himself up and threw away the key?

—Yes. Seven days in the sun and he died. Many weeks later they pulled his hand and foot from the manacles and buried him where those stones are.

—Why did he do this?

—He lived with his young wife and gathered firewood. He got a fever. He began to tremble and scream. He panted but could not drink. He drooled all down his shirt and pants. He growled like a wolf. He became strong as a *chupacabra*. He bit and raped his wife for four days. He repented and locked himself here to die. To save her life.

—What made him go crazy?

—He was not crazy. He went with the devil.

—Was he an evil man?

—No. He always loved God.

—If he loved God, why did he go to the devil?

—The devil came to him.

—How?

—In the caves of his blood.

—I don't understand.

—You cannot understand. You cannot see. You cannot hear. This is his power over us. But when he comes into you, when it happens, then it cannot be hidden. All see and all know. This is our power over him. This is why he leaves us quickly.

She squinted at Hood. The sun was low and in her face, burnishing it copper around the sharp teeth and the wise but feral eyes.

—When did you know that Sean had the devil inside him?

—The smell. The eyes. He would not look at his own reflection. He would not allow Silvia to drink water. These are signs.

Hood looked at the crude stanchion, then at the loose pile of stones that marked Juan Batista's grave. The sky was orange and black now in the west and Hood suddenly felt alone and afraid. *Like Oz must feel*, he thought. He felt uncertain, too, as he knew Sean must. And Hood also felt compelled to finish his mission and find his friend. Just as Ozburn, he thought, must feel the need to complete this journey of murder and attempted miracle that he had conceived.

Hood thought again of Mike Finnegan, the man who had claimed to be a minor devil, and Mike's insistence that no devil could possess a human, that a devil's work was to influence, to direct, to cajole. Finnegan had said that men were free to choose. Finnegan had said that devils *wanted* men to be free to choose, to make their own laws, define good and evil for themselves.

—What did he say when he saw this? he asked.

—He said nothing as I told him about Juan Batista. Then he touched the manacles. He put them on and stared at them. He prayed. He became furious and the prayer became a scream and the scream became a howl. I walked home a hidden way.

They drove back toward the village in darkness. Hood couldn't shake the fear and the aloneness. He felt that he was connected to Sean. Felt that he owed Sean for enduring this terrible curse so that he wouldn't have to. *The least I owe him is respect*, Hood thought, *and some attempt to understand what he's going through.*

—Did Gravas drive into Agua Blanca?

—There was no vehicle at Silvia's house.

—Where is your nearest airport?

—Tecate.

—There must be something closer.

—There is a strip outside of Agua Blanca. Follow the main road back to Tecate and turn where you see the sign to the gringo resort. When you see the large white boulders turn right.

Hood saw the boulders ahead in his brights. He slowed and made the turn and bounced onto a rough dirt road. The wind had come up and the dust swirled in his headlights. A few hundred yards in, he followed an arrow spray-painted on a big rock, and this road ended at an old lake bed that stretched as far as Hood could see in his high beams. It was flat and cracked, with wisps of tan, dry grass waving between the tiles of dried mud.

He drove the Durango out onto the bed until he found the tire marks left by a small plane. He followed them until they ended in a semicircle. He stopped and got out and looked where someone had tied down the airplane. There were old stakes with lengths of bailing wire for securing the tires. There were footprints lightly stamped into the hardened mud. Dog prints, too, or possibly coyote, but Hood suspected otherwise.

"Hello, Daisy."

Hood got the flashlight from the SUV console and walked an enlarging circle around the tie-down stakes. The wind sent little puffs of sand from along the edges of the mud segments and the dry grass went flat, then rose again, bent. Hood heard the crunch of his boots and the urgent hiss of the wind in his ears; then the wind would stop as if it had gone forever. He found a damp spot and a pile of dog turds.

He traced the circle, larger and larger. The wind came up stronger. All his thoughts turned black and ugly and very clear: his father gone crazy with Alzheimer's; the heartbreaking slaughter he'd tried to investigate in Anbar as a hated Naval Criminal Investigator; a woman he loved, bleeding to death in his arms because of things he did and did not do; the hero Luna he'd seen murdered by his own countryman; the young soldiers decapitated by cartel killers near Batopilas. Hood knew this could be the life of any grown son, cop, lover, soldier, and he had signed on for these things willingly and knowingly, but there was no consolation in this, not with the darkness and the wind and the crude altar where Juan Batista had offered himself and Sean Ozburn's terrible madness flashing through all this blackness like a tracer round.

Hood continued. When he looked he could see his footprints just touching the dried earth, one after another, circle within circle within circle growing smaller until they began where cute yellow *Betty* had sat. The wind tried to take him off course but Hood was a dogged man and simple in his stubbornness.

He put one foot in front of the other and looked at nothing else, as he had often done in his life, a practical code of behavior, just him and his feet and where they were taking him.

He advanced outward onto the lake bed and the dirt became softer. He saw another set of human footprints, not a circle but a faint straight line leading into the darkness. There were dog prints also.

Hood followed these to the edge of the lake bed. Here they stopped or were lost in the creosote bushes that were eking out their livings. There was sagebrush and prickly pear, too. He turned his light before him and saw something unusual on the ground. He nearly stepped on it. He picked it up and shone the light on it. Paper. Hundreds of pages crushed into a rough ball. He recognized from boyhood the sheerness of it, and the small biblical typeface. Genesis. Exodus. Leviticus. Numbers. Deuteronomy. He pushed them into the pocket of his windbreaker.

Hood scanned the brush with his light. Pages everywhere, some wadded tightly, others flapping alone, some still bound and fanned by the wind. Hood could hear the soft hiss of sand blowing against the paper. He went from one to the next, collecting and examining each in his light. One blew loose in the wind but he snatched it back. Chronicles, Ezra, Proverbs, Jeremiah. He stuffed all of them into the pocket, too. Samuel, Kings. Some were torn down, and some across, and some had been ripped into small pieces that flickered against the bushes in his light beam and blew from his hands when he tried to gather them.

In the midst of these torn and scattered books Hood found a white leather binding. In his flashlight beam he saw the words HOLY BIBLE embossed in gold. Below that, in smaller letters, was written, "Sean William Ozburn." There were no pages left in it, just glue and tattered edges along the inside spine. Hood recognized it as the cover of the book that Ozburn had held in his hands while he preached to the strange congregation in the grasslands of a country he couldn't identify. In his video to Seliah, he had never opened it.

Hood held the emptied cover and looked around him at the pages shivering in the wind. He pictured Ozburn standing out here at the end of the world, just him and his crumbling faith and his dog. Hood could see him well and he understood what Oz was feeling: *He has healed Silvia and seen the* curandera *and heard the story of Batista. He has seen Batista's end and in this he has seen his own end. He is afraid. He doesn't know what is happening.*

He walks out here to the edge of the lake bed with his Bible. He tries to read from the truth that has always sustained him. But he can't read, Hood knows: Sean can't read because he can't believe, and he can't believe because he feels only pain and madness. He tries to pray but he can't even do that. He became furious and the prayer became a scream and the scream became a howl. So, starting logically, in the beginning, when God created the heavens and the earth, Sean yanks out the foundation of his belief and throws it into the desert for the wind.

19

The next day Hood drove up to the Valley Center ranch where three years ago he had interviewed Bradley Jones's mother, Suzanne. It was Hood's first assignment as a prospective LASD homicide detective and he'd made a fool of himself that morning with her.

Now Bradley's voice came over the intercom as Hood waited at the gate. A moment later it slid open and a pack of dogs boiled around Hood's old IROC Camaro as he drove in. The meadow grasses had gone to tawny brown that shimmered in the crisp October light. He looked out to the ranch house and the big barn and the casitas up on the hillside.

He drove past the barnyard where Bradley and Erin had gotten married last year. There had been a stage for musicians and an absinthe bar and a dance floor and the bullring in which Bradley had nearly gotten himself killed. Hood remembered how lovely his companion, Beth, had been that day, and he remembered the musicians who played, and the tents set up in the meadow for the guests, and Beth taking him into their tent that night. Oh, what a night that was.

Hood parked up by the ranch house, in the same spot he'd

parked four years ago. Instead of Suzanne watching him from the porch deck, it was her son. Hood got out.

"That car is still your best quality," said Bradley.

"It's not for sale."

"I could steal it."

"How's the wounded hero? I saw you faint on TV."

"That was my sensitive side showing through."

"Musta hurt," said Hood.

"The thought crossed my mind that I'd die of that damned little thing and never get to see Erin again."

"That would be a high price to pay, Bradley. Though it's a hard fact that you don't deserve her."

"I've told her a million times but it doesn't change her mind. Come on up. We can sit in the breakfast room where you tried to seduce my mother."

"That's not exactly what happened." Hood pictured Suzanne in her wrinkled periwinkle nightshirt, the sun on her hair and her eyes on him.

"I was there, don't forget."

"Let's walk," said Hood. "I like this day."

Bradley went inside and came out with two bottles of beer. He launched one down at Hood, who made a good catch. They walked out into the barnyard and stood in the shade of the oak tree. Hood watched a pair of young red-shouldered hawks wheel above in the pale blue sky, keening sharply.

"Congratulations on freeing the boy," said Hood.

"We stumbled into him. Pure luck."

"You've got a lot of that."

"The kid had the brains to set off a silent alarm wired to us."

"I hear they're having trouble finding a record of it."

"Yeah, well, lots of things get lost at HQ. Or maybe the media got it wrong and there never was an alarm."

"Well, then, how did you choose that house?"

"Dispatch chose it, Charlie." Bradley moved away from Hood and faced him. "Now what?"

"Just wondering."

"You're like a prying old woman sometimes, Charlie. Tell me something interesting about Blowdown."

Hood told him they were sticking it to the gunrunners—they'd recovered sixty-two firearms in a buy last week. And ATF had spent a lot of time and money getting Spanish versions of their computer gun tracing programs into the hands of law enforcement officers and prosecutors all over Mexico.

"I saw the gold-plated Uzis that DEA and the Mexican army found in the La Familia bust," said Bradley. "Saw the pictures, I mean. What, ten or twenty of them? And fifty gold-plated pistols?"

Hood absorbed the insult with a nod and a smile. "They need them to do battle with the thousand Love Thirty-twos some enterprising gringos sold to the North Baja Cartel."

Bradley laughed derisively and shook his head. "You're incorrigible. I can't wait to be your boss someday."

"I saw you and Pace, and I saw the guns."

"What you *thought* were guns turned out to be new jeans we'd bought for poor kids south of the border. The reporters even got that right. That was egg on ATF's face, Charlie. And not even you can hold me accountable for Ron Pace."

"The Pace Arms building in Costa Mesa is empty now. Ron still owns it but the penthouse is abandoned. Where did he go?"

"I don't know. I'd tell you if I did, because we're on the same side, Hood. I'm a deputy sheriff now, remember?"

For the next few minutes they traded deputy gossip—the union negotiations, the new LASD pursuit policies, county health care cuts, who'd get the current sheriff's backing when he decided to step down. Hood enjoyed this. It was like having a younger brother. He was the youngest of the five by a lot, always looking up at the rest—last to arrive, last to know, last to be included—his boyhood a series of good-byes as his siblings grew and left. He was closer to them now as adults than they'd been as children. Slightly.

Back in the house they barged in on Erin in her studio. She was putting new strings on a Gibson Hummingbird and when she saw Hood she smiled and rose and kissed him on the cheek.

"Erin? Charlie's here to make his usual baseless accusations, but I thought you'd want to see him."

She cut a hard glance at her husband then smiled at Hood. "What did he do now?"

"I congratulated him on rescuing the boy and he got very defensive about his astonishing good luck."

"Well, he's a lucky one," she said quietly. The smile was gone and Hood saw wear on her face.

Bradley sat down and took up the Gibson and took the high E string from its envelope and worked it into place.

Hood looked at Erin while she told him about the upcoming Erin and the Inmates tour. She was a trim redhead, pretty in an open and forthright way. Blue eyes and a smile that made you smile. Raised mainly in Texas, four years older than Bradley. But her easy good humor didn't prepare Hood for the stark emotions of her lyrics or the fragile beauty of her music. She seemed wiser than her years and this impressed and intrigued Hood. He was eight years older and somehow looked up to her. So it angered him to think that Bradley Jones was leading a double life just as his mother had led, and was less than truthful with this woman. And it angered him to suspect with good reason that Bradley had used her as an alibi for a murder. He sometimes wished that he had met her first, one of the several moot wishes of his thirty-two years.

". . . then there's the Broken Spoke in Austin, the West End in Dallas and we've got two shows in Houston but I'm not sure where, then on to New Orleans and Miami and on up the East Coast. We've got twenty-eight shows in thirty days. No rest for this little band."

"I'll catch the Belly Up show in Solana Beach."

"You better. Bring that pretty doctor with you in case you need medical attention."

"Looked like she could cure about any ailment you might have, Hood," said Bradley.

Bradley tightened up the E string and attempted to tune the guitar by ear while Erin squinted, pained by the sound of his crude aural approximations. Then he picked the opening nine notes of the "Dueling Banjos" and offered a brain-damaged smile.

"Honey? You're more than a little flat there and it's making my scalp crawl." Hood heard the edge in her voice.

"No. I've got perfect pitch." Bradley pouted and clunkily strummed the first chords of "Knockin' on Heaven's Door."

Erin put her hand over the hole of the guitar and the chords died against her fingers. "Come on, men, let's get a beer and set on the porch."

They sat three across on a picnic bench in the shade of the porch. Dogs lay strewn about, panting. Erin absently picked the Hummingbird and told Hood about getting a guitar made by a fella back in Texas, would take him almost four months to do it but he hadn't even started yet. He made them for Clapton and Sting and James Taylor and pretty near all the stars. Only reason he'd make hers was one of her brothers knew him. Hood listened and looked out at the rolling hills and the green oaks with their branches overgrown to the ground and their afternoon shadows flat and blue on the tan grass.

"Have you seen Mike Finnegan lately?" Hood asked.

"He and Owens pop up at the L.A. clubs sometimes," said Erin. "Weird people. It's been months. Why?"

"He keeps popping into my mind. I'd like to talk to him."

"About what?" asked Bradley.

"Why do you care?"

"*'Why do you care?'* You're sounding like that prying old woman again, Charlie."

"Knock it off, you drooling primates," said Erin. "We don't have any way to get hold of Mike, do we, honey? I know I don't."

"I don't, either," said Bradley. Then he stood and stepped around a big husky and hopped the porch railing to the ground. The dogs all rose and stampeded down the steps after him, the terriers barking.

"Charlie, throw me your keys. I want a look under the hood of this thing."

Bradley caught the keys just before a leaping Labrador retriever could close its mouth on them.

Hood sat back down on the bench. He thought of the strange conversation he'd had with Mike Finnegan, about a year and a half ago, in Imperial Mercy Hospital down in Buenavista. He was in a full-body cast and his broken jaw was wired, but his words were clear:

. . . *Charlie, you are just the kind of person I would love to form a relationship with. It likely wouldn't happen—you're much too strong-willed and law-abiding for the likes of me. Unless, of course, there was something you wanted very, very badly. Something I could help you with . . .*

"Anyway, the next time you see Mike, give him my numbers."

She looked at Hood with a small smile. "Not so you can find Owens?"

"Not Owens. Mike."

"She's one spooky beauty."

"That she is."

"Damaged goods, Charlie. Stay away from her. That's my decision."

"There you go again, giving me advice I didn't ask for."

"I gave advice to all my brothers, older and younger. When I love someone I feel the need to run their lives."

Bradley had the hood of the Camaro up and he stood looking down at the engine as if it were a chessboard. He wiggled the fan belt and a battery cable and swung the dipstick out over the gravel so it wouldn't drip on the car. "You don't love Hood. You love me."

"There are different kinds of love, Bradley."

"You run natural or synthetic in this car, Charlie?"

"Synthetic."

"Why did I even ask? She doesn't love you."

"She just said she did."

"I do love you, Charlie. No matter what he says."

Bradley held up the stick to the light. "About due for a change, Hood. Looks like you got at least four thousand on this stuff."

"Thirty-two hundred is what's on it."

Bradley swung a drip onto the gravel, then slid the stick back in. He banged the hood closed and wiped his hands together, then on his jeans. "I couldn't love a man who doesn't keep his engine oil clean."

He unhooked the cell phone from his belt and walked out into the barnyard.

There was a long silence. "How are you?" asked Hood.

"I'm okay. It's all good."

"I worry when I hear that sentence."

"Bradley's trying to do a good job at the deputy work. He . . . takes it seriously. Looks forward to it."

"I'm glad to hear that."

"I mean, we all make our mistakes, right?"

Hood said nothing but she offered no explanation.

"You still don't trust him, do you, Charlie? But you like him. You see something of yourself in him. And something of his mother."

"I owe him. I hurt his chances in life when I took up with Suzanne."

"You don't get to take any blame for what happened to her, Charlie. Suzanne was hell-bent and she got unlucky."

He nodded.

"Something's changing," she said. "I don't know what it is but I'm changing."

Hood considered this. Her words were an eerie echo of Sean and Seliah Ozburn's. "Explain that if you'd like."

"I can't. I have nothing firm to report."

"Good change or bad?"

"It feels like both. Maybe it's two different changes."

"I'll be your ears anytime, Erin."

"I'm seeing that he's like his mother. More and more."

Hood tried to find the right words but he couldn't. "If you know something—"

"God, Charlie, I married him and I love him."

"Love him all you want. But don't take a fall for him."

"You're trespassing."

"I didn't see the sign."

"I don't think you miss much. You just blunder in anyway."

"Man, that's the truth, Erin."

Hood watched a flock of gnatcatchers swoop in unison into the oak tree. They vanished into the leaves but he saw the flicker of tails and wingtips. He set his empty bottle on the deck and stood. She rose and hugged him with one arm, the other hand clamped to the neck of the Gibson.

"If I run across Mike Finnegan, I'll tell him you want to talk."

"I'd appreciate that."

"I really don't like or trust that man."

"Don't ever change."

"I just told you I was changing."

"Well, okay. But not too much."

"See ya, Charlie."

Hood waved to Bradley and got into his Camaro. He swung a turn and rolled down the dirt driveway, glasspacks rumbling and the dogs setting up a dust storm behind him.

20

Two nights after the great crash of his faith, Ozburn landed *Betty* at a private strip near Indio, California. The runway had been offered by one of the Desert Flyers. He called a cab that took him to one of the motels along Interstate 10. He had his mane tucked up under a cowboy hat, and he wore a Mexican poncho over his shoulders. As always now, he wore his sunglasses against the brightness of the light, even after dark. It felt right to change his look. ATF was certainly out there, tracking him like a pack of silent hounds.

He got an upstairs king with free Wi-Fi. He swung his duffel onto the bed and pulled out a fresh bottle of tequila and poured half a plastic cupful. He drank it in a gulp, to an ovation of warmth and excitement inside. He counted out his vitamins and supplements and washed those down with another gulp.

While Daisy sniffed around the room, Ozburn drew the curtains tight against the night and hung bath towels over the bathroom mirror. He could look at his reflection only very briefly before revulsion made him look away. He closed his eyes against this apparition and he felt the urge to pray. *But who do you pray to when you have pulled your faith out by the roots and flung it into the dust forever?*

At eight P.M. the room phone rang as planned, and Ozburn told the caller his room number. He made sure both of the Love 32s were fully loaded and off safe and he slung one over each arm and moved a chair to the middle of the room facing the door and waited for the knock.

Half an hour later he heard it and said, "Come in."

Big Paco lumbered into the room with the same briefcase in which Ozburn had delivered the first Love 32 to him. He was not as tall as Ozburn would have thought but he was certainly as big. His sport coat must have been fitted by a skilled tailor. He wore his sunglasses as before and his pitted face caught the light unhappily. Paco shot out a stout leg and the door slammed shut. Ozburn stood.

"Tequila?"

"Yes, please."

Ozburn poured drinks into plastic bathroom glasses while Paco set the briefcase on the bed and opened it. Ozburn handed him a drink and Paco handed him a small digital postage scale. Ozburn set the scale on the tabletop and turned it on and reset it. When the weight settled to zero he set the stacks of hundred-dollar bills on it and read the readout: one pound, eight ounces. Ozburn tapped his calculator. Seventy two thousand dollars. Then he weighed the twenties and the fives. There were eighty-seven thousand, five hundred dollars—one-half of the total.

"The first ten are almost ready," said Ozburn.

"The sample gun is very good. Is quiet. We are ready for the first ten."

Paco placed the money back in the briefcase and shut it. He slipped the scale into the pocket of his sport jacket. They touched plastic cups.

"I want to trust you," said Paco.

"As I trust you."

"But you now have eighty-seven thousand and five hundred of our dollars and we have nothing. You know that the Gulf Cartel can't be in the business of loaning money to strangers."

"You have my word and you will have the guns. Someone has to trust someone for things like this to work, Paco."

"We have something even better than trust. Come see."

Ozburn followed Paco outside to the parking spaces where a new Escalade waited. The windows were darkened but Ozburn saw movement inside. Then a rear door opened and a man in a green military uniform stepped out. He had a machine gun strapped over his shoulder. He looked at Paco and Oz, then reached back into the vehicle and brought Silvia out by the hand.

There was no sign of her having been severely stung by the scorpion but the girl was plainly terrified.

"We have friends in Agua Blanca."

"There's no reason to bring her into this."

"We want no reason to hurt her. She is our guarantee that our money and our good friend Sean Gravas will not disappear. She guarantees that the guns will be delivered to us."

"You people have no rules anymore."

"You saved her life. Now her life depends on you, again."

Ozburn turned and walked back into his room.

Time to call an old friend, he thought. He unwrapped one of his several new preloaded phones. He drank more tequila, then lay back on the bed and called Charlie Hood.

"Charlie, Gravas here."

"It's good to hear your voice."

"Do I sound like me?"

"You do."

"I looked in the mirror a second ago and I thought, man, what happened to you?"

"Something did happen to you and we can find out what it is."

"If I'll come in and surrender. Not yet."

"Seliah's falling apart without you. If you can't come back for you, come back for her."

"Charlie. You dear old friend. You square. You cop. You Boy Scout."

"That's what you were, too."

"But it doesn't apply to this."

"What *is* this? Define your mission."

Ozburn thought for a moment. "Perform good acts and defeat evil."

"That's not good enough, Sean. Try again. Why did you gun down the safe house assassins?"

"Disgust. We provide a home for them, so they can murder? No. No more living off the fat of the American land for those killers. Herredia is the mother rattlesnake and they are all his living children."

"It was an experiment. We were working them. We were getting some good intel out of it."

"All our plots and plans. All our manpower and money. It's all useless, Charlie. It's a jobs program for people like us. It's make-work. Like digging a hole and filling it up again. Over and over. Don't you ever feel the need for clean and clear action? For defined and attainable goals? Something simple with the pure ring of accomplishment in it? Don't you just want to take a really high-quality, well-built gun, and feel the balance and weight of it in your hand, and kill somebody who deserves it?"

"I've felt that."

"These Love Thirty-twos are awesome, Charlie. You put your hands on one yet?"

"The one you left in the Buenavista house. I haven't fired it."

Ozburn looked down at his filthy jeans and his dusty boots and the big gnarled hand resting across his dirty poncho. "It builds up, Charlie. Over the years. I guess the undercover did me in. I couldn't take it anymore. Then Sel took me down to Costa Rica and somehow I got better. Then I got a whole lot worse. I'm not sure I'm me anymore. That make sense?"

"I don't doubt you, Sean. I know who you are."

"You don't doubt me or yourself, because you're simple."

"If you say so."

"Simple is good. It must be like having a flashlight with batteries that never wear out. You can depend on it and it will show you whatever you want to see, whenever you want to see it. I was like that, but now I'm not. When I shine the light I see dark."

"I'll come get you. Right now. We can figure a way to make things work, Sean."

"I've got something better."

"Explain."

"The Love Thirty-twos? They're being made in TJ now, in a secret factory run by Ron Pace and protected by Carlos Herredia."

"Pace Arms is operating out of *Mexico*?"

"That's the word. And if you think it through, it makes sense. Global economy, man. So, how would you like to nail some Gulf Cartel men with a hundred of those guns and one hundred and fifty thousand dollars? Right there in L.A.?"

"Quite a bit."

"Good, because Sean Gravas is the dealer. With a little help from me, the guns, the men and the money will all be yours. It'll be the biggest deal I ever did for ATF."

"You murdered three men, Sean. That kind of puts you on the outs at ATF."

"Murders? Why? They land me right where I need to be, don't they? According to the new cartel rules?"

Hood said nothing for a long beat. Ozburn chuckled. "I'm still ATF, Charlie. In my little wooden heart. You don't think I'm out here just having fun, do you? I'm on to something big. I'm going to accomplish it. And when I deliver the guns to my buyers, you can be there. I'll surrender to you. But not before. I'm not coming in until I have something to show for all this."

"When?"

"I'll be in touch."

Ozburn hung up and dropped the cell phone to the bed. He sat at the table and set up his laptop and wrote.

Dear Seliah,

I MISS you terribly, like a phantom limb, like a piece of my heart. We'll be together soon in a better place and we'll begin again.

I've lost something. FAITH. The words to express faith. Everything I thought was TRUE. But you know something? I feel okay with that. I feel that I am enough and that my days here on EARTH are to be of value.

I'm so TIRED right now, body and mind.

I hunger for your touch.

Sean

He took the bottle and cup outside to the small deck and sat on a plastic chair and watched the cars on the interstate. Daisy sat beside him. He felt the spasm of his throat muscles. The supplements and tequila seemed to be somewhat of a palliative but when the spasms became cramps, there was little he could do but fold to his knees and press his forehead to the ground and shudder with pain. He drank. He thought of Hood. He thought of Seliah.

Then he imagined he was looking down on himself sitting on this tiny deck beside the raging interstate in this great, dry, Southwestern desert, and he tried to account for his presence here, tried to establish a reasonable explanation for it, to see it in some perspective. But as he worked chronologically forward through his adult life he could get no further than Costa Rica and the Arenal Volcano and the resort in the trees where they had stayed. And what had he found there? Well, some cool frogs and birds. A boy and his pet monkey. Other tourists. Father Joe, who became a friend. Some nice hours with his wife. Arenal Volcano smoking and rumbling in the distance. So what was it? Why, when he looked back to that time—three months ago now, if that—was everything a strange, descending, darkening blur? *Fuck if I know*, he thought. *I wish I did. I wish I did.* He half filled the cup and drank again. The bottle was half-gone.

Suddenly he was on his back on the deck. He could see the pinpoints of stars high up above the lights, and these stars were racing back and forth across his vision and Ozburn realized his head was snapping violently side to side. He couldn't move his arms. He felt his fingers trying to dig into the deck and his boot heels thumping on it. He could hear the guttural rumble of his breathing and the crunching of his head as it rocked side to side while the stars raced back and forth in opposite sprints. Then it was over and he lay panting but more or less still. His heart pounded and his fingertips burned and his legs were rubbery but he was still at last and the stars were fixed again as they were supposed to be. His sunglasses had flown off. He lay there for a long time. He saw Daisy's head blot out the stars and felt her tongue on his cheek.

He worked his way up and got his sunglasses on and went back to his plastic chair. Daisy wriggled up close and rooted her cold wet nose under one of his hands. The tequila bottle had been knocked over but it was capped and unbroken.

Ozburn stared at the cars on the highway, blinking. They streamed in and out of his vision.

"Our what, who art in what, hallowed be thy what . . ."

But he couldn't finish the prayer, gutted and useless as it was. He sighed and rested his elbows on his knees and lowered his face to his hands. The only thing he could think of that was any comfort at all was to remind himself what he was doing here. What he was trying to accomplish. Because, unsure as he was of the paths and the powers that had led him to this place, he was still clear on what he needed to do.

Perform good acts and defeat evil.

He repeated this short sentence over and over until he felt his mind begin to calm and his muscles begin to relax. He went back to his laptop but he couldn't bring himself to write Seliah again.

Later he called out for a large pizza and family salad and ate it all, repeating the sentence in his mind as he ate. He finished the tequila and climbed into the shower in the darkened bathroom and washed himself with his eyes closed because the sight of water revolted him and against the revulsion he muttered the sentence again and again and again. Then he lay down on the bed and with the sentence still ringing through his head he took the long, dark fall into sleep.

21

Hood and Janet Bly walked into Seliah Ozburn's darkened home just after nine the next morning. She stood back to let them pass and smiled briefly at Hood, then looked down as he came by her.

They sat in the living room and Hood saw that the sun blinds were down and the curtains were pulled closed also. The air conditioner started up. Seliah sat on the couch with her laptop on the coffee table before her. She looked tan and fit as always. She wore a simple black shift and her straight platinum hair was newly trimmed. Her nails were painted red.

"I've been thinking about this since we decided to do it," she said. "I thought it would be easy but I don't know what to say to him. Maybe I'm afraid he won't want to see me. Maybe I don't want to betray him."

"It's the only way to save his life," said Bly. "We're trying to get him back alive from wherever it is he's gone. He's clearly losing his reason."

"I know. I see that."

"But he's passionate about one thing—you," said Bly. "Can you be passionate back?"

Seliah looked at Bly and nodded and lowered her hands to the keyboard. "Let me see. How about this? 'Dear Sean, let's meet in Las Vegas and hump 'til we're cross-eyed. Hugs, Sel.'"

A silent moment.

"Not bad," said Bly. "Maybe something a little more romantic."

"What do *you* know about romance, you dried-up cunt?"

Bly stood. "I'll get some fresh air. Call me if she stops hissing."

Seliah looked up at Hood with anger in her eyes. "You can't make me do this."

The front door slammed.

Hood sat in a chair across the coffee table from her. Seliah hugged herself against the chill from the air conditioner. Then her cheeks flushed and Hood saw the sheen of moisture appear on her forehead and shoulders. She was still glaring at him. Slowly the glare softened and she took a deep breath and let out a wavering sigh.

"I've vanished, Charlie," she said softly. "I don't know where I went."

"Sean's there."

"I don't know where he's gone, either."

"Think."

"Think what, Charlie? All I do is think about what went wrong."

"Any progress?"

"Costa Rica. That was the beginning."

"On the volcano."

"The Arenal Volcano."

"In the hotel in the jungle."

"Yeah. There. I'm so ashamed of what I said to Janet. I don't do that. I'm just not me anymore."

"Forget what you said, Seliah."

"I have thoughts I can't control."

"All of us do."

"But I have actions I can't control."

"Have you seen a doctor?"

"Flu. Stress. High blood pressure. Depression. Take your pick."

"Tell me about the volcano. Where this all started."

She closed her eyes and nodded and a small smile appeared on her lips. Her skin glowed damply and the AC fan stirred her hair. "The frogs were so loud at night you could hardly sleep. The hotel rooms were built up onto the branches of the trees. The rooms all had screens instead of windows. Like a big tree house in the jungle. There were geckos and macaws and toucans and a green boa constrictor. They got more bugs and beetles than you could believe, ones with horns and pinchers and stripes and dots. Ones that make noises, ones that smell good and ones that stink. I always liked that kind of stuff. Nature's pure weirdness. Nature's extravagance. Sean, too. Down in the lobby the hotel owner's son had a tiny baby monkey in a birdcage. Sean held it. It was about the size of a pear, eyes like silver buttons. And Sean stared at that little thing for a while and he looked up at me smiling and he said, 'Sel, can you even believe this thing? Who designed it? Whose *idea* was this?' And of course Sean tried to give him twenty bucks for it and I said, 'Hey handsome, come up to the bar with me and I'll buy you a drink and we'll talk about this monkey. Because *I* can give you something you'd like even more.' That was when it hit me. When I knew I was ready for a baby. Took me twenty-eight long years to get to that point but, well, there I was. So. I talked him out of the monkey."

She opened her eyes. "Father Joe—I told you about him—well, he told me that the Lord would bless our union with many children."

"That must be nice to know."

"We'll have them, Charlie. I'm going to have them."

"I know you are."

"And Father Joe told me he got strong feelings from certain people and that Sean and I were two of them. People who would have some effect on the world around them. He sought those people out, he said. He'd invite himself right into their lives because he enjoyed their company. He said it was unusual for both people in a marriage to strike him that way. And I said, 'You're not going to follow us home and take up residence in the spare room, are you?' And we all got a laugh about that. Man, oh, man, did we do some drinking that night. Father Joe—you're going to love this—he had this secret potion he wouldn't tell us the ingredients of. And he'll only let you drink it straight from either his silver flask, or this old cocktail shaker with the top that fits tight. That's because he doesn't even want you to know what it *looks* like. And Sean's all, 'Go ahead, Sel—try it. You'll love it.' And I'm not brave about things like that, so I'm all, 'Okay, I'll try it *once*.' And, weird thing is, it tastes really good. Kind of like wood smoke with a little mint in it. Like if you could make a liquid out of cedarwood. Cold. Went down a little too easy. We drank beer and tequila, too, so maybe it was just the combo, but I've never been quite that messed up in my life. In college I'd drink so much that the next day in the pool I'd exhale underwater and smell it. Really. So I can hold my liquor, Charlie. But that night with Father Joe. Wow."

"What happened?"

"What do you mean?"

"Tell me about that night and you and Sean and Joe."

"Nothing really happened."

"It's just that you've already told me so much about it. I can see the Arenal Volcano smoking in the background, and the rooms with screens instead of windows up in the trees, and all the birds and bugs and geckos. I can see you and Oz and the priest and his silver cocktail shaker with his secret elixir. That's quite an opening scene, Seliah. I'm hooked."

She smiled and Hood thought it was the first true smile he'd seen from her since this nightmare had started. He also thought that for the events of the last ten days to have had their beginnings on the volcano, then something damn well had to have happened. She wanted to tell him. She'd led him up close to the rim of that volcano. But she didn't know exactly what had occurred, or she didn't remember it clearly or she had buried the memory of it.

Hood heard the front door open and close. Bly stood in the entryway to the living room.

"Potty mouth still here?" she asked.

Seliah stood up and ran to Bly and took her hands. She bowed her head. "Please forgive me for that ugly lie. *Please.*"

"Forgiven, Seliah."

"I'm so sorry."

Bly hugged Seliah and Hood heard her whispering into Seliah's ear until Seliah said something he couldn't understand; then she whispered into Janet's ear and the women didn't let go of each other for a full minute. Unincluded, Hood timed it on his watch, wondering at the durability of women.

When they broke the embrace Hood saw the tears on Seliah's face and the long clear ribbon of mucous hanging from her chin. She glanced at him with a hunted expression, hurriedly swiped it onto her hand and hustled into the bathroom.

She was back a few minutes later, her face clean and a fresh coat of lipstick on. She sat on the couch behind the laptop. "Okay. I can do this. I'm going to give it a try."

Her fingers found the keyboard. "'Dear Sean,'" she said. "That's a good start, now, isn't it?"

Half an hour later Seliah had composed an invitation to her husband. Hood stood behind the women and read over their shoulders. Seliah had proposed a weekend in San Francisco, at the Monaco, where they'd stayed before. "'Just three days from now we can have a bit of heaven, sweet man.'" She assured Sean that this was a private e-mail, an absolute and total secret from Blowdown. It was classy and sexy and perfect, Hood thought. He felt bad about it.

"I'd say yes to this," he said. "I'd get there early."

"He'll say yes, too," said Seliah. "There's no way he can refuse me."

"Maybe not the first time," said Bly. "But eventually he'll say yes and we'll . . . have him and he'll be safe with us."

Another moment of silence.

"You've done the right thing, Seliah," said Hood. "And you're going to get him back."

Seliah typed, "Your Loving Wife, Seliah," then tapped the "send" bar with a red nail. She sighed and sat back.

Hood put a hand on Seliah's shoulder and she reached up and set her hand on his. He was surprised how hot it was, like she was burning with fever. "Let's go out to dinner tonight," she said. "The three of us. Dutch and nothing fancy."

"I've got a date, believe it or not," said Bly. "With a real, live man."

"You're a lucky woman, Janet. Charlie? Me and you?"

"Sure."

"Come by six thirty, would you? Sean will have accepted my invite by then. We can catch the sunset at the Fisherman's. And I can finish that Costa Rica story. I'll tell you everything that happened."

. . .

Hood drove toward Buenavista.

"What's wrong with her?" asked Bly.

"I don't know."

"How can you sweat when it's fifty-five degrees inside? Did you hear the way she hissed at me? In her bathroom she's got a beach towel hung across the mirror. So I peek in the bedroom and she's got the dresser mirror turned around to face the wall. Every curtain and blind in the house, drawn tight. Vampire books and videos all over the place—did you see them? What's *that* all about?"

"Sean acts the same way," said Hood. "In the videos. He hisses obscenities. He sweats. He hung that dress over the mirror in the scorpion girl's house."

"There's a warning in that e-mail," said Bly. "They've worked something out. You watch. If he accepts, they'll scoot off somewhere else and we'll look like the Three Stooges. Do you trust her, Charlie?"

"No."

"Be careful tonight, Deputy."

"Always. You, too."

Bly cracked a small smile. "I am not what she said I am."

22

Hood knocked on Seliah's door and waited. He heard music inside. He turned to look at the sun lowering toward Catalina Island.

"Come on in, Charlie."

She wore baggy hiker's pants and a Susan Komen T-shirt and an Angels cap and red slip-on sneakers. She followed him into the living room where the curtains were still drawn tight and the laptop sat where it had been before.

"He turned me down. Bly got to it first and forwarded. She must have called you."

"Yes. You knew that would happen, Seliah."

Hood sat and read Ozburn's message.

. . . I love you more than life, Seliah, but I smell Blowdown on you. This letter doesn't even sound like you. Don't let them manipulate. Don't let them break you down. Go away if you have to . . .

"Do I need to write him back right now?"

"No. Later is better."

She slung a little silk bag over her shoulder. "Ready?"

Hood drove them down the hill to the restaurant at the foot of the pier. They got a table outside and a bucket of clams and beers.

Seliah drank hers quickly, then ordered a bottle of petite sirah. Hood couldn't read her face through the sunglasses and the hat. She was subdued and deliberate. She told him she'd run ten miles after he and Bly had left, and she felt a little spacey.

"So, we went to Costa Rica to help Sean," she said. "The undercover assignment was killing him. He was bitter and disillusioned with his work. He missed me and his home and our runs on the beach. So we got to San José and rented a cute little Piper and tooled all around the western coast for a couple of days. Expensive, but, Charlie, there's nothing like the earth from above. Then we got checked into our tree house hotel on the volcano and we made great love and ate good food and enjoyed the creatures and the staff and the other tourists. It was called the Arenal Volcano View eco-resort and you could see the volcano from every single room, the bar, the dining room and the observation deck. You could hear it rumble. In the middle of the night people would rush out onto their decks if it got loud enough and they thought it would blow. Everybody but us had at least two cameras going—a video and a regular. We just had my little digital but we got some good shots.

"There were all sorts of characters running around that place, getting the volcano rush. One night Sean and Leftwich stayed up late talking. The next day the three of us took a nice long hike up the volcano. It was beautiful and dramatic and Sean and Joe had to hike way the heck up near the rim and, of course, I had to keep up with them. We got close. Every few minutes the volcano would rumble and spit up rocks the size of passenger cars and tons of black-red magma would come pouring out. Just like you picture in hell. Awesome to behold. Of course if it blew, even just a little, we'd have been cooked where we stood. That was part of the rush. Leftwich told us he'd never seen Arenal so angry as that day. He was messing with us, but it was fun.

"We got back that afternoon and started drinking. By dinnertime we were fairly bombed. Joe had his magic potion that somehow stayed cold on its own, and we had cocktails, too, then ordered bottles of wine with dinner and brandies after. I remember the conversation getting heavy between Sean and Joe. The consequences of sin. Good and evil. God and the devil. Man and Jesus. The blackness of human nature and God's love. Sean was really letting it hang out about his work. No details, nothing about which agency he was with or where he was stationed, but all the bitterness and anger, Charlie, it was ready to blow up, just like Arenal. I went to the room. My head was spinning. I read a page and crashed. I woke up at two in the morning, the light still on, about a billion bugs stuck to the screen outside.

"Sean wasn't beside me so I got on some clothes and went down to the bar but the bar was closed. I saw a light inside Joe's room so I walked down there. I stepped up close to the screen to look in. There were lots of bugs and moths and freaky-looking things on the screen so I crept up slow so they wouldn't fly up into my face. And when I looked in, there was a ceiling fan, making the room flicker. Sean was flat on his back on the bed, still wearing his tropical shirt and shorts and flip-flops. He was actually snoring. And Father Joe was sitting at the foot of the bed in a chair, leaning forward toward Sean. His back was to me. It looked like he was reaching out with his hands. His head was bowed. I thought he was praying but I wasn't sure. So I moved a couple of big steps to my right, and I'm really quiet about this because something tells me not to disturb him. The bugs flitter and flutter a little. And from there, I could see that Father Joe wasn't praying at all. His hands were out and he was . . . well, touching Sean's toe. Or possibly toes."

"Touching his toe or toes."

"Correct. And he was talking very quietly. Conversationally. I couldn't hear the words. Weirdest thing, Charlie. A drunk, muttering priest with my husband in his bed. Playing with his toes. It made me . . . mad. I thought maybe he was one of those molester priests."

Seliah finished her first glass of wine and poured another. She smiled and offered the bottle but his glass was still almost full.

Hood watched her pour, saw the orange of sunset on her cheek and the sheen of perspiration. There was a cool breeze coming onshore and he felt a chill through his denim jacket.

"I feel hot," she said, smiling. "It takes me hours to cool down after ten miles."

"I'm enjoying the story. So you're looking through the screen at Sean and the priest—"

"And all of a sudden the moths and bugs got spooked and flew and their wings were noisy and flapping. I could see their wing dust floating in the light. Then Leftwich turned around and I saw something fall from his hands to the floor. It landed in the bedspread. The spread was bunched on the floor because it was way too hot to sleep with it over you. Joe popped right up and opened the door for me. Big smile on his face. A bunch more bugs went flying. I went inside and asked him what he was doing and he said he was praying and watching Sean sleep. He said he was about to come get me. He said they'd had a great conversation. But he'd rarely seen a man of such moral fiber and spiritual goodness so dispirited by his work. He said Sean had reserves of strength and goodness that were rare. He hoped that he had helped a light go on in Sean's mind—the idea that his work against drugs and guns was vital to the freedoms that we Americans enjoy at home. *Vital*, he said. He said he tried to paint the world in simpler terms than Sean's complex, shaded, compromised world. He said it was one of the hardest things he'd ever done but he finally convinced Sean to think of himself as good.

Good. A good man. And I said, 'Well, that's all fine and dandy, Joe, and pardon my French, but what the fuck were you doing with his *toes?*' He chuckled and his face lit up and he said he was shooing away a fly. 'Some of them can draw blood,' he said, 'make a nasty little sore—the owner's son lost a toe to an infected bite, ask him about the flies here. He'll show you his half toe.'"

"And what were you doing while this priest was going through all that?"

"Looking for what fell into the bedspread."

"I knew it. I like your curiosity and your practical side, Seliah. Tell me what it looked like. What was the first thing you thought of when you saw this thing fall into the spread?"

"I barely saw it. It happened so quickly and I was upset and the light was bad. It was something heavy and small, inside something larger and loose. Like . . . like a golf ball wrapped in a washcloth. But we couldn't find it. Joe saw it, too, and came over to help me look. We lifted up the bedspread and shook it real good but nothing was there. Nothing under the bed, either. Joe just kept talking away. I could smell the booze on his breath, though to be truthful it could have been the booze on my own. Sean just lay there snoring through the whole thing. That's when Joe told me he thought Sean and I were special, that we'd do great things on earth. I said getting Sean to his own room would be a good start. I finally woke him up, which wasn't easy. He walked to our room and crashed down on the bed and fell asleep again. I tried to get his shirt off but he was just too heavy and dead asleep. I took off his flip-flops. He'd dinged a toe on the walk over, so I got an alcohol wipe and cleaned it up. Just a drop of blood, not even that. Or maybe it was one of the flies Joe was shooing."

"Did you see the blood before you got him home?"

"No."

"But the light in Joe's room was on, right?"

"Yeah, but weak, like I said. And the ceiling fan, chopping it into spokes. But the blood was nothing, Charlie, less than a drop. That isn't the point. The point is the whole way Leftwich pried into Sean's life. And kind of . . . what . . . pointed Sean in a new direction. Changed him. He woke up a new man. I'm not saying the new direction wasn't good. I know the priest meant well. But he drinks Sean under the table with his secret concoction and watches him sleep and plays with his toes. The whole thing just basically gave me the creeps."

"What did the priest look like?"

"Short side, muscular. Black hair and blue eyes. From Dublin. Had the accent. The drunker he got, the stronger the accent. He had . . . what—charisma? Force of character? Sean hasn't been the same man since he crashed out that night. He woke up filled with optimism about his work, and us, and having a family someday soon. That was all good. But after it wore off, then all the things that he wrote in the e-mails started up. All the pain and the aches and the insomnia and hyperactivity. All his crazy talk about being chosen to do a mission, that someone or something was guiding him. All the . . . Just everything. Then, what you say he did down in Buenavista. That was not my husband. That could not have been Sean."

"It was but it wasn't."

Seliah swirled the wine and drank. "And I have to admit, Charlie, I've been feeling the same way. The same . . . *wrongness*. The same *strangeness*. I can't . . ."

"What?"

"Explain it any better to you."

"You don't have to."

"Like what I said to Janet. I don't say things like that. I don't *think* things like that."

Seliah finished the wine and ordered another bottle. They ate the clams and ordered dinner. The sun set in a red-black sky and fell out of sight. Seliah took off her sunglasses and Hood saw that even in this soft darkness her pupils were closed down hard against the light. She excused herself, slinging her little bag over her shoulder and navigating between the tables. An older woman at the adjacent table gave Hood a disapproving look. Seliah was back a few minutes later. She ate quickly—her swordfish, all of the bread, dessert—and drank most of the second bottle of wine.

"We'll get through this, Seliah. We'll get him back."

"Then what?"

"I don't know what."

"If what you say happened really happened, then I won't see him for a good long while."

"It's up to us. When we know the whole story, things will make sense."

"I believe that, Charlie. I believe things will make sense and that Sean and I have a future."

Hood reached out and put his hand on hers and felt the startling heat.

Later he drove her home and walked her to the door.

"Let's see what Sean wrote," she said.

"Good."

23

nside she leaned over the laptop and tapped the keyboard. "Excuse me, Charlie."

He heard the bedroom door shut. He sat and watched the in-box fill on the computer screen. A few minutes later she came out wearing a long, cobalt, satin bathrobe. The sash was tight to her waist and the lapels framed her breasts. Her eyes were darkened by new makeup and her lipstick was fresh. She gave him an embarrassed glance.

"Glass of wine?" she asked.

"I'm fine, Seliah. You go ahead."

She was back a moment later with an oversize goblet half-full. She smiled and sat down close to him on the couch. Hood was unhappily aroused. She reached across him and deleted a few messages, then opened the one from Sean. She took a long drink of the wine, then put the glass on the coffee table and set her hand on Hood's knee.

From: Sean Gravas [sGravas23@zephyr.net]
Sent: Wednesday, October 19, 2011 9:19 p.m.

To: Gravas, Seliah
Subject: end of faith

Dear Seliah,

Tearing up my Bible was a terrible thing. I'm still exhausted by it. It must sound like some kind of symbolic destruction but it wasn't. It was REAL and genuine destruction. I felt a piece of my soul leaving with each page I yanked out. When I saw what happened to Juan Batista I felt personally fooled and betrayed. He was a good man. So was I. AM. I'm moving toward the ACCOMPLISHMENT of the MISSION. Or at least toward the opportunity to accomplish it. If I sound doubtful now instead of optimistic it is only because I AM. I once thought that God led us to the brink of things, to the very edge of the cliff, and helped us do what was best. But now I see that WE lead ourselves to our own cliffs and heights and WE decide what is best.

We are free to be brave and free to be terrified and I am BOTH.

All of this GREAT JOURNEY will lead me back to you. When I'm finished we'll be together. We'll resume our life and begin our FAMILY. We will be THREE then more.

I ache for your touch. I want to be welcomed back into the vast universe of your heart and the warm mystery of your flesh.

Your Shooting Star,
Sean

Hood felt Seliah's hand tighten on his knee. Surprisingly strong. He heard the rough rumble of her breathing, then a catlike purr from deep inside her. She looked at him and the tears rolled down her cheeks. Her pupils were tiny and there were small beads of perspiration along her upper lip. She turned back to the screen and stared at it, breathing slowly. Hood felt her hand trembling on him. Time passed but the trembling did not. Then Seliah placed her free hand over the hand on Hood's knee, pulled it away and stood.

She was in the bathroom a long time. Then the bedroom. She came out wearing a red silk tank that covered her to mid-thigh and that was apparently all. Her body was damp and lotioned. Her makeup was fresh, her blue eyes set in darkness. Her platinum curtain of hair swayed as she flicked off the living room lights and sat down next to him again, the smell of her surrounding him. He could hear the deep rumble down in her chest again—a catlike purr or the rattle of mucous—he couldn't tell. She leaned into him and put her nose to his ear. Rattle. Purr.

Utterly flummoxed, Hood stood and walked into the dimly lit kitchen and looked back at her. She stared at him for a long moment, almost dreamily, then strode over. She lifted his hand to her lips and watched his eyes while she kissed it. Then she stepped into him and put her arms around him and raised her mouth to his. Hood felt the heat of her breath and the weight of her body and his own swift reaction. He unwrapped her arms and held her at arm's length and tried to read her face in the half-light. Gradually Seliah's dreamy expression became a small smile and she tried to embrace him again but Hood held her away. She was very strong and Hood stumbled and she let him overcorrect and it seemed that she was playing with him. She pulled him in closer without effort, as if he were a toy, and looked at him with an expression unreadable to him. He moved her away and felt the unlikely strength of her arms. She bit at him, her teeth clicking together. She laughed. The laugh ended and the smile departed, and Seliah looked down at herself.

She easily broke free of his grip and ran from the kitchen into the bedroom and slammed the door.

Hood stood there in the kitchen with his heart pounding, wondering what to do. His standard default options seemed pointless. He felt as if he'd been led to the edge of chaos and was being asked to jump into it. The water in the master bath went on. He went to the bedroom door and listened.

Then back to the living room. He sat in front of the laptop and rubbed his hands down his face. He looked at her wineglass, empty. She'd had a beer and a bottle and a half of wine with dinner. Another big glass here. But alcohol didn't account for this, just another explanation rendered pointless by Seliah Ozburn.

When she had been gone ten minutes Hood went again to the bedroom door and listened. The water was no longer running.

"Seliah? Seliah?"

The knob turned in his hand and Hood pushed open the door. The room was dark but the light was on in the master bath. She was talking to herself.

"*Hang in there, Seliah,*" she said softly.

"Seliah. I'm coming in."

"Go home. I don't want you here. *Hang in there, girl; be steady now.*"

"Are you all right?"

"I'm all right. Go away."

"I want to see that you're okay."

"*Hang in there, Seliah.* Get away from me! *You're good. You're gonna be just fine, hon. That's it . . . Hang in there.*"

He walked to the threshold of the bath. In the hard light Seliah sat on the tile floor near the toilet. She was wearing the red tank and nothing else. She tracked his eyes and lifted the shirt off her thighs and sneered at him. She had handcuffed one wrist to the toilet seat hinge. Saliva hung from her chin. With her free hand she swept it away and wiped it on the tile.

He drooled all down his shirt and pants. He growled like a wolf. He became strong as a chupacabra. *He bit and raped his wife for four days. He repented and locked himself here to die. To save her life.*

Hood took a step in and sat on his haunches on the floor a few feet away from her and looked only at her eyes.

"Let's get you to a doctor."

"Why?"

"Look at you."

Her sneer had dropped away. "A pretty girl drinks a little too much and wants to kiss you, so you call a doctor? Maybe the doctor should be for you."

"I want a good doctor to take a look at you."

"Oh, all right."

"That was easy, Sel."

She raised her rump and with her free hand pulled the tank to cover her more and held it there. She sighed. "I know you're right. You can't believe how tired I am."

"I mean tonight. Now."

"Okay, Charlie. I know you're a true friend. I was trying to protect you. See? I flushed the key. These cuffs are Sean's. I don't know why the Juan Batista story affected me so strongly. I feel very drunk."

He was not crazy. He went with the devil.

Was he an evil man?

No. He always loved God.

If he loved God, why did he go to the devil?

The devil came to him. In the caves of his blood.

"I'm going to call for the paramedics, Seliah. They can help."

"Are you going to leave me locked up until they get here?"

"Yeah."

"Good thinking. But you better stay here and keep an eye on me because I could chew off my arm and escape. Come, sit right here."

She let go of her blouse and patted her palm on the tile beside her.

"I'm good here, Seliah."

She laughed. "Charlie, if you get in range, I'm going to yank you close and kiss your cute little mouth right off. Then I'll eat you alive. *Stop that, Seliah! Hang in there, girl.*"

Her smile collapsed and she wiped her chin again and the tears came down her face in rivers.

Hood sat on the bed and called Soriana, who said he could circumvent the ER. He'd also get some of Seliah's background information to the examining physician ahead of time. She sobbed and talked to herself, then went quiet. When Hood went back into the bathroom she was asleep with her head on the toilet lid and a hand towel folded over for a pillow. He could have used his ATF handcuff key to set her free but he left her sleeping as she was.

The doctor was Tim Brennan, a general practitioner affiliated with San Clemente Hospital. He was young and cheerful for being called from home to work at ten thirty p.m. He let them into a small examination room.

Seliah was calm. After the paramedics arrived, Hood had taken off her cuffs and she'd gotten into a simple white tee and the hiker's pants and athletic shoes of earlier in the day. Now she sat uncomfortably upon the exam table, looking close to exhaustion. Brennan asked a thousand questions and made notes on a yellow legal pad with a thick wood-bodied pen. Hood stayed for the interview and sat in an empty waiting room down the hallway while she was examined. The TV was on but Hood muted it and thought about Seliah while images of her terrible beauty flashed out of order through his brain.

Brennan found him there and sat down in the chair beside him. Hood glanced at the closed door of the examination room. "I want to keep her tonight. She's okay with that. She's very tired and fairly intoxicated. I've given her a light sedative. I took some blood and a urine sample and now she can get some rest. Tomorrow we'll probably have a vastly improved young woman. I've got a few questions for you, Deputy Hood. I got most of this from Agent Mars over the phone, but the husband, Sean, he's been living away from home for how long?"

"Fifteen months."

"Isn't that long for an undercover assignment?"

"A year is usually tops but this one was . . . Well, it was especially important."

"ATF tries to control guns going south into Mexico?"

Hood nodded.

"So Sean Ozburn, working undercover, is active in infiltrating the criminal drug cartels, posing as a gun seller or buyer or what have you?"

"That's what we do."

"Has anything happened recently to Sean that could be a precipitator to Seliahs behavior? Some disaster or very negative event?"

Soriana's job, not mine, thought Hood. "No."

"Is there any chance you could bring him back from his assignment, or whatever you call it? Just let him come home and help take care of his wife?"

"He can't return right now. Soon, we hope."

"I understand. Seliah probably started feeling the stress well over a year ago—before her husband even left. And that stress has continued to build for a very long period of time. Still, she has a clear grasp of the world around her, and of herself. We'll determine which of her symptoms are real and which ones might be imagined, or stress-related. We have tests for just about everything, as you know. My job right now is to find out if what she says is going on really *is* going on. She's got a respiratory tract infection for certain, and a low fever. She says she's had dramatic mood swings and emotional outbursts, in addition to the physical symptoms. Speaking generally, I think she's a strong woman with a bad chest flu who has reached the end of that strength."

"It's more than flu and stress."

"Very possibly, but don't underestimate the flu virus. Seliah has an odd group of symptoms. Influenza is most likely, Deputy. She could also be hypo- or hyperthyroid. An autoimmune disease comes to mind. So does drug abuse—meth, cocaine, prescription—they'll show up in the blood tests. And again, we treat a lot of the worried—well. This could all be rooted in stress and anxiety. Very anxious people often exhibit these unusual symptoms, ones that don't fit together and don't make sense."

Hood said nothing for a long moment. "Sean had the same symptoms a month ago."

"One more reason to think virus."

"They both got strong. Physically strong. Anger. Some violence."

"Oh? She didn't mention that."

"Sean was more prone to it. But even Seliah—more hostile and aggressive than I've ever seen her."

Brennan looked at his watch. "Is there anything you want to tell me?"

"I've gotten to know her over the last year and a half or so. Through Sean. She's changed dramatically in the last few days."

Brennan nodded. "Changed how?"

"She was an athlete, spiritually concerned, a squared-away woman," said Hood. "She was positive and poised. She loved her husband and liked her job and wanted to start a family. A little over one hour ago she was coming on to me sexually, aggressively. When I didn't take her up on it, she handcuffed herself to the toilet and started talking to herself. She was drooling. Did she tell you what happened tonight?"

Brennan looked skeptically at Hood. "She said nothing about sexual aggression or increased saliva production. She didn't drool, either, although I heard mucous in her respiratory tract with the stethoscope. There's certainly an infection. She did tell me about dinner with you and drinking way more than she usually does. Has this happened before?"

Hood sighed and looked down. "No."

"Are you having an affair, you and Seliah?"

"No, Doctor."

"It's not my business but it could be a factor. Don't you think that loneliness and alcohol and a strong attraction to a friend could explain the sexual advances?"

Hood shook his head and looked to the closed door of the examination room. "I don't think you know how sick she is."

"No, I truly don't. But I'm going to find out how sick she is, Deputy Hood. And how well she is. I'm going to do everything in my power to make her better."

He took a card from his wallet and wrote on the back. He was handing Hood his card when the exam room door opened and Seliah's head poked out. "You didn't forget about me, did you, guys?"

. . .

On his way back to Buenavista Hood called Soriana, who listened to Hood's story and request without interruption. Twenty minutes later he called back to say that with the ATF budget down to a trickle he couldn't approve international travel to interview a relatively minor background witness. He apologized and said the priest could be back in Ireland for all they knew. State could send someone out from the consulate, he said, and talk to the priest, though that would probably take some time.

Hood said he understood and he'd need a few days off. Soriana wished him luck. Hood booked the LAX–to–San José flight for the next morning on his own credit card. It was fabulously expensive this late in the game, and his modest frequent-flier miles did not apply to the non-reclining middle seat.

At home he packed up four days' worth of clothes and toiletries and his laptop. A lady friend, Beth Petty, had left him a message to say she missed him and looked forward to their "next couple of seconds together, whatever century that might be in." She was an ER doctor at Imperial Mercy Hospital here in Buenavista, and between their two demanding careers, hours together were rare. She was beautiful and unfettered and Hood missed her pointedly. She was often in his thoughts. Sometimes he would pretend she was watching him doing whatever he was doing and this made him proud and want to do it even better. His dreams were comfortable with her. When he read Sean Ozburn's hot letters to Seliah, they made him think of Beth. He checked his watch: She was working the graveyard shift at Imperial Mercy.

He looked at a framed picture on his kitchen counter of them together at a Bradley and Erin's wedding. Beth was wearing a beige knit dress with glints of mother-of-pearl worked into it, and her dirty-blond hair was up and her eyes were chocolate brown. She had on a sapphire necklace and earrings. Beth and Hood were relaxed and leaning into each other. She was almost as tall as him. She was smiling. To Hood she had been heart-stopping that day, and she was heart-stopping in his memory and in the picture, too.

He double-checked to make sure he had his passport and the U.S. Marshal's badge that would allow him to carry on his gun and a spare magazine. He wrote Beth a blunt note as was his style, and found a very nice piece of quartz outside. The desert around Buenavista was filled with rocks that during the day would twinkle like lights across his field of sight, all the way to the great curving end of his vision—miles of sparks and jewels. He and Beth went on excursions to collect them, sometimes tracking a particular bright beacon across the rough desert, then lugging it and others in Hood's SUV for use on his walkways and in Beth's abundant cactus and succulent garden.

At his kitchen sink Hood rinsed and sponged the rock until the clear crystal facets shone. They were pink. He shut down the house, left on a couple of lights and hit the road for L.A. It was two in the morning, which would put him at the terminal on time for the 7:10 flight. He was exhausted.

But he swung by Imperial Mercy anyway and plucked a few humble gazanias from the planter outside and left them with the note and rock at Dr. Petty's station in the ER. She was nowhere to be seen. Hood waited a few minutes in hope of glimpsing her for just a moment, but she did not appear. He saw that Beth's world was badly in need of her at this hour as he waded back out through the ocean of the sick and injured and the halt and lame, the terrified and stupefied and, rising among them like swollen islands, the destitute pregnant, solid evidence that life goes on.

24

Hood set down his bags and looked out at the volcano. It was green and verdant around the base, tapering into a bare lava cone that ended in a ragged maw. Wisps of smoke rose into the blue sky while orange-tinted lava crawled down the blackened tip.

The Arenal Volcano View lobby had been busy when Hood checked in. There were German birders, serious and well organized. The quetzal, Hood gathered, never found in zoos, was the hot bird. The trogon ran close second. There were French butterfly fanciers and two California frog and toad hunters on their way to Monteverde to find the golden toad in its only habitat on earth.

While checking in, Hood had met the owner, Felix, and his son Eduardo, the boy with the monkey and the half middle toe visible through the sandal on his right foot. The primate was a local squirrel monkey whose father had been killed by a car. Eduardo had found the baby clinging to its father's back, miraculously unhurt. It was now nearly eight inches tall, Hood estimated, and had a wide-eyed, can-do expression. It roamed a decorative wrought-iron birdcage in the lobby when it wasn't mounted on Eduardo's shoulder. Eduardo had named him Pepino.

Now through his screened window Hood watched the volcano for a few more minutes but he didn't unpack his bags. Instead he went back down and convinced Felix to let him see the registration forms for July. He showed his U.S. Marshal's badge but said he was on a mission of friendship. He sat in the fan-cooled lobby and drank a cold beer and easily spotted Father Joe Leftwich's signature. July eighteenth, seven nights, room twenty-four. He found Ozburn's Sean Gravas on July twentieth for four nights, room seven.

Hood handed the forms back to the owner and asked if he could move into room twenty-four. Pepino eyed him with a bright curiosity, cracked a seed in his teeth and dropped the shells to the cage bottom. His hands were tiny, perfect, black. The owner checked his computer and said he would be happy to make the room change for Hood.

"Thank you very much, señor," said Hood.

"It is not a problem."

"Do you know Father Leftwich?"

Felix worked the registration slips back into the rectangular cardboard box. He looked at Hood dubiously. "Yes, of course. Why?"

"I'd like to meet him. We have mutual friends."

"He left here in July."

"Where did he go?"

"He said nothing to us. We were relieved that he finally left here."

"Why?"

"He enjoyed provoking trouble. He inflamed our Germans with stories about Hitler. And the French with comments about Vichy. Once, he caused a fight between Spanish and Mexican businessmen, right in our dining room. There were two large beautiful Americans who bought him far too much alcohol and they shouted and argued and laughed very loudly for two straight nights. This hotel is for ecotourism, not fighting and drinking."

"Was he belligerent?"

"No. Always polite. Always happy. Never having the appearance of the drunken man. It was always the people around him who suffered most."

Eduardo ran into the lobby and swung open the cage, and Pepino crawled up his arm to his back. The monkey looked wide-eyed at Hood.

"Nobody understood Father Joe," said Eduardo. "He is a good man and interested in everything."

"But you are eleven years old," said his father. "So you don't see how he makes people angry."

The boy shrugged and the monkey picked at something on the back of its tiny paw. "You and Itixa are superstitious about him because he's a man of God."

"I am not superstitious, Eduardo," Felix said with a smile. "I am realistic about unhappy guests. This is our business. This is what pays us for your food and clothes and your TV."

"And for yours."

"Of course." The owner looked at Hood. "My father built this lodge. I am very proud of it. Because he is young, Eduardo thinks all things will come easy to him forever."

"Have you seen the library that Father Joe was building?" asked Hood.

"No. It is between here and Tabacón."

"I have!" said Eduardo. "The Quakers are building it. Father Joe helped them. But that isn't why he came to Costa Rica."

"Why did he come here?" asked Hood.

"To cause trouble in my dining room and bar," said the father.

"No! To study wild things!"

He looked at his father, then at Hood, and ran out. Pepino spread his arms and clung to the boy's shoulders, turning back for a bug-eyed look at Hood. He looked like a tiny man on a big motorcycle.

"He's a good boy," said Hood, smiling.

"He's a good boy," said the owner.

"I wonder what wild things Father Joe was studying."

"If you can catch Eduardo, I'm sure he will tell you."

Hood moved his bags into room twenty-four and unpacked. He still had the great volcano view. He ran a hand over the bedspread, then got down on his hands and knees and looked under the bed. There was dust and two dead flies and that was all. His cell phone had worked when he landed in San José but now there was no service. He turned it off and put it in a dresser drawer beside a Bible.

That evening he tried to eat alone in the dining room but the German birders asked him to sit with them. Hood spent the next hour eating his dinner and looking at the various cameras that were pressed upon him. The trogons and toucans were stunningly beautiful but no one had seen a quetzal as yet. The Germans were chipper and all of them spoke English precisely. They were off to try for quetzal again the next day.

After dinner Hood found Eduardo in the lobby, cleaning up Pepino's cage. The monkey clung to the boy's back and stared at Hood.

"Can you show me Father Joe's library tomorrow?"

"There is no school tomorrow, Detective. Yes. My studies will be done by four."

"I'll pay you as a guide."

"I guide for free but thank you."

"Can we see his wild things, too?"

"We can see them after the library. We need the dark for those."

Hood sat on his observation deck and drank bottled water mixed with bourbon from his duty-free bottle. He saw the great black hump of Arenal against the lighter black of the sky, watched the red crawl of the lava. Insects clung to the screen behind him and the frogs built a wall of sound in the jungle beyond. He turned and looked through the room at the bed where Sean Ozburn had snored and at the foot of that bed where Father Joe had sat and spoken quietly to Sean and then at the screened window through which Seliah had watched and mistaken this strange behavior for prayer. The moths and beetles fluttered on the screen, and the ceiling fan sectioned the room with moving shadows as Seliah had remembered. *And I said, "Well, that's all fine and dandy, Joe, and pardon my French, but what the fuck were you doing with his toes?"*

The late afternoon was cool and the volcano was shrouded in clouds and silent. Eduardo led the way down the road with Pepino on his back.

"Father Joe was a good man," said Eduardo. "He knew everything about nature. I've lived here my whole life and he was only visiting but he knew more. He could name all of the different types of scales on the head of any snake. He knew all the Latin names of the animals of Costa Rica. He was a true expert on birds. He said his favorite Costa Rican animal was the sloth, because it is one of the seven deadly sins and the one he enjoyed the most. This was a joke because he was a priest. He was always joking about things. It's true that he caused trouble in the dining room. He liked to stir up people and see what they did."

"Your father didn't like him much. Was it only Father Joe's dining room behavior?"

"No, that's not the only reason. My father *says* it's the reason, but it has more to do with superstition than science."

"Explain that, Eduardo."

"Detective, superstition is belief without proof. Science is belief with proof. Older people like you and my father come from the age of superstition. But the young know better. We believe in science and technology. For example, my father hates his computer even though he learned to use it. Father Joe was very young in his heart. He showed me many shortcuts on the computer. He knew it very well. And other things. For example, he told me that the theory of evolution and natural selection is absolutely true. He said creation is also true. He said that what God created was the place where life could begin and evolve. It was a place with a few basic elements but that is enough. So, creation and evolution actually go together."

"Okay, then what superstition does your father have about Father Leftwich?"

"He thinks he's evil."

"Why?"

"He doesn't have a reason. That's why it is superstition."

Hood thought about this. Pepino looked back at him, bright-eyed, head bobbing.

Eduardo set off down a trail that ran east from the road. The jungle was high and dense around them but the trail was good. It was cooler here in the shade and the vegetation was so varied and diverse that Hood quickly exhausted his knowledge of the splendid living things around him.

"If you ask my father, he will have reasons," said Eduardo. "For example, my father thinks he has a sense about people. He calls it intuition. Which sounds very much like superstition, doesn't it? His intuition is that Father Joe is not a real priest at all. Another intuition is that Father Joe has committed crimes. What kind of crimes? My father can't say what kind. Then there's Itixa. Itixa is in charge of all of the resort housekeeping. She is full of superstitious Mayan blood. She whispers and gossips without stopping. She claims to see the dead and talk to them. She believes in werewolves, and in *asema*, which are vampires. When she believes there is an *asema* nearby, she makes the cook add extra garlic to all meals. The *asema* hates garlic, she believes. She drinks a bitter herb tea so that her blood will not taste good to a vampire. She told my father some things about Father Joe but my father didn't tell them to me. He only told me to stay away from the priest. And when I asked Itixa what she said to my father, she would not tell me. She said some things are not for a child to see and know. She is all superstition and no science. She drinks more beer than a whole football team. She is afraid to touch a cell phone because she felt one vibrate once and believes they are alive."

Hood stayed close behind Eduardo as the boy hustled along the trail. Through the occasional breaks in the tight vegetation, he could see Arenal looming in the clouds ahead of them.

The trail opened to a clearing dotted with grazing cattle and small, neat homes ringing the perimeter. The homes were painted yellow and blue and green and pink, and smoke rose from the chimneys of some of them. Hood saw corrals and a large American-style barn, and there were chickens and pigs in pens and horses and cattle roaming free. The northern field was thick with brown cornstalks dying back after harvest, and the southern field with coffee.

"This way," said Eduardo.

Near the cornfield they came upon four men framing the outside walls upon a concrete foundation. They were big-boned Caucasian men, strong and diligent. They waved or nodded at Eduardo and

Pepino, who now sat ramrod straight on Eduardo's shoulder. Hood guessed the new library at twelve hundred square feet.

"The libraries are important," said Eduardo. "Many towns and villages have no high school. And many poor students don't have the time or the travel money to make a two-hour trip to a faraway high school every day, and then another two-hour trip home. The village libraries are the only place where these children can find things to read. You have to read your book right there in the library. You can't take them home with you. Or there wouldn't be enough books. Father Joe brought books in his minivan. Boxes and boxes of them in Spanish and English. They are children's books on science and history and nature. Many pictures. I helped him carry some of the boxes into the barn. When the library is finished they will have hundreds of books that he brought. I told him he should have brought computers, too, and he said he would try to do that the next time he comes here."

"Where did he go?"

"He didn't tell me. He just wasn't here one day. I was sad. He was the one who gave me advice on what to feed Pepino, and how warm to keep him, and he told me that squirrel monkeys love their fathers very much and I would become Pepino's father if I was gentle and slow with him. He taught me that a diet heavy in bananas would make him die. I asked him if Pepino's species could evolve into human beings someday and Father Joe said no, because monkeys and humans have common ancestors but many years ago monkeys evolved one way and humans another way."

Hood heard melancholy in the boy's voice. Pepino looked up at him and pursed his lips.

"So, that will be our library someday," Eduardo said quietly.

"Will you use it?"

"No. My family has enough money to send me to high school.

Because of ecotourism. I'm an all-A student. I want to be a film director or astronomer."

Hood walked over to the workers and asked the Quakers if they knew Father Joe Leftwich and where he had gone. The younger ones looked to the oldest one and he set down his hammer and measured out his words. Yes and no, he said. Father Leftwich had been here and worked very hard with them; he had brought good books from Ireland, where he lived; then he had simply not appeared for work one day and that was that. He was gone. *Such are the blessings of the Lord*, he said, *offered and withdrawn according to a plan we cannot know*.

Hood nodded and returned to Eduardo, who was looking up at the volcano. Some of the higher clouds had cleared and now the great black cone rose majestically into a blue sky from a downy base. Smoke rose steadily.

"Ready for the wild things, Detective?"

25

They continued past the village and around the corn. The trail narrowed and climbed and Hood saw that the creeping vines were prolific here, winding up the trunks of the larger trees. They stopped and waited while a deadly fer-de-lance crossed the trail.

Pepino stood with his hair on end and screeched down at the serpent.

"*Terciopelo*," said Eduardo. "The velvet snake. Very deadly and aggressive. It's good that he can't hear Pepino but all snakes are deaf. Father Joe told me that snakes evolved not into lizards but from them. He thought it odd that a more recently evolved creature would not have legs or ears."

Hood watched the big spangled viper inch its way into the jungle. It looked deadly. He had read that there were nineteen species of venomous snakes in Costa Rica. The fer-de-lance killed more people than any of the others. They could get eight feet long. This one looked to be five feet. The moment its tail disappeared into the foliage Pepino stopped screeching and sat down again.

"Is that the wild thing that Father Joe was studying?"

"No. But soon."

The trail rose and the evening fell and Eduardo led him into a gorge. Its walls were red rock and gently sloping. They sidestepped down the viney flank and Hood steadied himself on the jungle branches until Eduardo told him the eyelash vipers hid in the bushes and their bites were unbearably painful though almost never fatal. They continued down to the bottom of the gorge and walked along a stream until they came to a small clearing ringed by banana and plantain and palms. Here it was nearly dark and Hood was glad he'd brought his penlight for the walk home.

Eduardo pointed up through the trees. At first Hood saw nothing but the vegetation and red rock of the gorge wall. Then he made out the ragged mouth of a cave. The opening was partially hidden by vines and the blackness of it was an invitation and a threat.

"Be careful for snakes and tarantulas," said Eduardo. With this, he slipped through a stand of palm trees and began climbing up the gorge face. Hood followed. The rock was studded with ledges and toeholds and not difficult to climb. Hood pulled himself over the top and stood up on the wide rock shelf. Eduardo pointed to the cave mouth that hung open before them.

"Father Joe asked me where to find the bats," said Eduardo. "We have many bats. Some boys from school showed me this place a long time ago. If we stand right here, they'll fly past us. Father Joe and I did this several times."

A few minutes later a small bat flitted from the cave mouth and came toward them. It flew just over their heads and Hood turned to watch it climb through the banana trees and disappear into the purple dusk.

"Bats," he said.

"Many hundreds," said Eduardo. "Look. More."

Another came climbing unsteadily, then two more; then Hood heard a strange burst of flesh and fur and high-pitched squeals and the sky turned black with them. It was a river of wings and small faces and it flowed over them, and Eduardo giggled softly and Hood could smell the guano and the meaty reek of their bodies and when he glanced at Pepino, the monkey had buried its face in the back of Eduardo's neck.

"Vampire bats," said Eduardo. "Father Joe wanted to see vampire bats. Not fruit bats. Not pygmy or long-eared bats. Only the vampire. They were named after the vampire myths of Europe, not the reverse. There are of course no vampires here in Costa Rica, or anywhere else. That is superstition. But these bats live on the blood of animals and sometimes people. This is science."

Hood watched the black onrush. He felt the air moved by their wings and one of them swooped low and grazed his face and Hood leaned away from it but into another that flapped past with a sharp chirp not six inches from his ear. Tiny eyes glimmered and flashed within the black, membranous flow.

Then the flow ended and a few stragglers bounced out into the air and Hood turned to watch the black bulk of them melt into the sky toward the farms and villages.

"They will feed tonight on the blood of living animals," said Eduardo. "Mostly cattle and horses. Their saliva contains an enzyme that makes their bite impossible to feel. This is how they fool the host. They scrape the flesh and lap the blood. They do not suck the blood. If I become a director, my first film will be a documentary on the vampire bat. It will deal with both superstition and science. These animals have faces that terrify people. They even frighten me. So, am I superstitious? I don't think so. They frighten Pepino. But how can a monkey be superstitious? Maybe it is scientific to be afraid of vampire bats. But then, how can a monkey be scientific?"

"Well, it's scientific to let the fer-de-lance cross the path without disturbing it."

"Yes! Proof of science. Father Joe would have liked you. He said science and superstition are different answers to the same questions."

"Have you been inside the cave?"

"Never. Father Joe told me about the Ebola virus and other fatal viruses. Probably ones that don't have a name yet. He said to never go inside the cave."

"What did Father Joe do here?"

"He observed. He wrote in a small notebook. He took photographs. He captured some bats with a butterfly net and we inspected them. One evening on the way home we found Itixa on the road and it was obvious that she had followed us. She was perspiring and stuck with leaves and twigs and trying to stay ahead of us. I believe she told my father what we did. And the next day he told me not to go anywhere with Father Joe. He said that Father Joe was not trustworthy and not what he pretended to be. That night our meal had very much garlic. And all meals after that until Father Joe went away."

Hood stepped to the opening and shined his penlight inside. The breath of the mouth was rank and cool and he could see the white mounds of guano on the floor and the malingering vampire bats still fastened upside down to the rock ceiling.

"Do you remember the Americans? Sean and Seliah Gravas?"

"She was beautiful like a goddess."

"They liked Father Joe."

"They ate and hiked and got drunk together."

"Did you talk to Sean and Seliah?"

"Mr. Gravas liked Pepino very much. He offered me twenty dollars for him but of course I refused. Mrs. Gravas was amused by Pepino's expressions and she told her husband that he needed a monkey of his own. Those two people had love. You could tell.

When Mr. Gravas was drunk he became very emotional about his work. He never said what he was. What was he, Detective Hood?"

"A businessman. He buys and sells guns."

In the near darkness Hood could see Eduardo give him a long look. "That makes sense. Because he seemed convinced that he was not doing good in the world. Yes. That does make sense."

"Seliah told me that one morning at your resort, Sean woke up and felt good about his work. He had a new, positive attitude."

"I didn't know that."

"Seliah believes that Father Joe had somehow swayed Sean into this new way of thinking."

"But that's something my father would say. Superstition."

"Well, certainly a strong-willed person can influence another person."

"Yes."

"But then, a few weeks after they got home to California, Sean began feeling bad. His body hurt and his mind wouldn't slow down and he couldn't sleep. He began doing strange things. Then foolish things."

"Such as what?"

"He had his dog baptized."

"That is blasphemy, but it is funny, too."

"Seliah told me that one night when Sean was sleeping, Father Joe sat at the foot of the bed and spoke to him in his sleep. And touched his bare toes."

"Why would he do that?"

"I don't know. Were you around that night? Did you see anything like that?"

"No. I go to bed at nine o'clock during the summer."

"Did he ever do anything like that to you?"

"No, never."

"Father Joe told Seliah he was not touching Sean's toes at all. He said he was keeping away the biting flies. The same kind that bit you and infected your toe. Seliah found blood on Sean's toe that night after Father Joe had spoken to him and touched him—or didn't touch him—in his sleep."

"Detective, it is scientific to keep away those flies. This is something that Father Joe would do. Mrs. Gravas must not have reasoned accurately. If she saw blood on his toe, isn't this evidence of the biting fly?"

Hood looked at Eduardo in the early dark. The boy's eyes were chips of light and so were the monkey's eyes but lower and closer together.

"What do you think happened down here between Sean and Seliah and Joe Leftwich?"

"I think they became friends."

"Did Joe ever talk to you about the night that he shooed the fly from Mr. Gravas?"

"I knew nothing about it until now."

"Did he ever talk to you about Sean and Seliah?"

Eduardo thought for a moment. "He told me he thought they were people who might do important acts."

"Acts."

"That was the word he used."

"What do you think?"

"I have no way of seeing such things."

"And if you did, would it be science or superstition?"

Eduardo thought again. "I think one can turn into the other. Father Joe said this."

"What did Father Joe say about you?"

Eduardo laughed softly. "He said I was the future of the world."

"He's right."

They stood in silence for a moment. "I want to talk to Itixa."

"She will talk to you. Believe me." Eduardo told Hood the best time and place to find the woman.

"Thanks for bringing me up here," said Hood. "I've got a light to help us get home."

"Keep it on the path in front of us. Some of the snakes are nocturnal and they like the streams. Snakes shine at night. Even more than wet branches. Watch for what shines."

Before dinner Hood sat on his observation deck and watched the volcano. The night had cleared and he could see it clearly in the distance. The lava moved down from the mouth in red fingers, and a cloud of steam wafted up. Arenal rumbled every few minutes and twice Hood saw large molten boulders rocket into the sky, then slam down to the earth where they showered sparks and rolled down the mountain in loudly cracking crisscross patterns until coming to rest in bursts of rising embers. The happy-hour crowd in the Volcano View bar sent up a cheer.

At dinner the bar and restaurant were raucous. The Germans saw two quetzal and documented them thoroughly. The French had had a terrific butterfly day and the California frog and toad hunters had done well with five species of tree frogs, two with deadly poison in their skin and glands.

Hood watched Itixa come down a torch-lit pathway toward the rear door of the kitchen. She came out a few minutes later through the same door with a plate of food covered in tin foil. Hood waited below the oil torch and when she saw him he spoke in Spanish.

—Good evening, Itixa. My name is Charlie Hood.

She stopped and looked at him. "English. Quakers teach me."

"I apologize for interrupting your dinner. But I want to talk to you about Father Joe Leftwich and the Gravas couple—Sean and Seliah."

"Why?"

"Some bad things have happened to Mr. and Mrs. Gravas. And they all seemed to begin here at this lodge with Father Joe."

She was short and stout and had a belly. Her black-gray hair was pulled back in a tight ponytail and she wore a loose maroon dress with birds and butterflies embroidered around the neck. Her cheekbones were high and her chin narrow and her face an etched lattice. She searched his eyes matter-of-factly.

"Come, I tell you."

Hood followed her up the dirt pathway. It bore rake tracks and either side was bordered by tropical plants and flowers. Her casita sat behind a small grass clearing with a blue table and three blue chairs. She set her plate on the table and tapped the back of a chair, then disappeared into her home.

Hood sat and smelled the food. Tonight's entree was roast beef with garlic and baby onions and he was hungry again. He saw a bat flicker at the edge of the torchlight, then wheel back into the darkness. He looked out to Arenal and the trickle of hot red lava lacing its way down the cone and thought of the saliva swaying on Seliah's chin and he wondered if she had spent another night in the hospital.

Itixa came back with two open beers and she handed one to Hood, then sat. From a pocket of her dress she produced flatware wrapped in a white paper napkin.

"I eat. Tell me of bad things of Mr. and Mrs. Gravas."

Hood told her what he could about their strange ailments and erratic behavior. He told her that Sean had left his job and his home and left Seliah, too. As he spoke he watched her expression become worried, then calculating, then touched with fear.

"A man when he lies have a look," she said. "Hard to see. Father Joe have the look. I stay away him and he stay away me. Mr. Gravas have look. Mrs. Gravas no look."

"What lie did Joe tell?"

"He was the lie."

She ate and Hood sipped the beer.

"*Asema*," she said quietly.

"Joe was an *asema*?"

She studied him, chewing. "In the day, a man or a woman. At night, the *asema* take off his skin and become a ball of light. Blue light. Drink blood of people. If they like the blood, they drink until the person die. *Asema* hate garlic and some herbs. You find the *asema* skin and put many salt and pepper and skin will shrink. *Asema* cannot get skin back on so it dies. Sun kill *asema* also."

"What does this have to do with Father Joe?"

"Listen. Eduardo goes to the library they build. Eduardo think Father Joe is good. Always talk and laugh. Eduardo tell me Father Joe want to see the bats. Bats are evil, this I know. I follow because I fear for Eduardo. They see the bats fly. They are the blood-drinking bats, the bats of damnation. The bite of this bat will create *asema*. I see Father Joe push Eduardo into the cave. It was in my dream. When they leave the cave I run fast but they see me. Later I tell Eduardo *I don't care you see me! I protect you! I tell your father everything I see!* He calls me superstitious witch."

"And his father told him to stay away from Father Joe," said Hood, remembering that this was when Itixa upped the garlic for all Volcano View meals until Father Joe left.

He watched Itixa swipe the last of a tortilla across the last of the juice on her plate. She finished her beer and got two more from her casita. They were open and cold.

"You told him there are some things a child does not need to see or know."

She looked at Hood and in the torchlight he could see the worry on her face. "I tell Felix. For his son."

"Please tell me."

She looked past Hood and out at the jungle, then leaned toward Hood and spoke quietly. Her eyes caught the torchlight and they were black and shiny as obsidian. "On the night they all drink too much I am there for beer. I like beer. I see Mrs. Gravas embrace Mr. Gravas. I see her shake the hand of Father Joe. Then she go walking, not . . . not a walk that is straight. She go to her room. I come back very late for only one more beer. Bar is closed but I hear voices of the men in Father Joe's room. Is loud. Both talking. In the morning I clean the rooms. Everyone gone. In Joe's room I empty the basket into the bag. Something is moving in the bag. I put down the basket and open the bag and look in. There is a bat. It is wrapped in tissue. It makes very bad face. Hate is this face. It is a vampire bat. Bloody mouth and bloody chin and bloody teeth. One wing is broken. It is almost escaping the tissue."

Hood felt his heart downshift. "A bat like the ones in the cave?"

"Yes. That make the *asema*."

"What did you do with it?"

"Shake bat out of the bag. Step on the bat five time. Use towel. Flush down toilet. Wash floor with bleach and rub with garlic. Say words that have power over evil."

Hood figured Joe Leftwich had put the bat in the wastebasket. *Creatures get into these rooms all the time,* he thought—geckos and mice and moths and mantids and cockroaches. Joe had probably found it in his room and tried to dispatch it, then wrapped the animal in tissue and thrown it away, thinking it was dead. Or, in the poor light of the tree-house room, superstitious Itixa might have seen something else altogether. A mouse?

"How big was the bat?" he asked.

Itixa held up her hands about a foot apart. "The wings." Then moved them to what Hood guessed was four inches. "Body. There was blood on the tissue in the basket. There was blood on the bedspread on the floor. There was blood on the sheets at the foot of the bed. Small blood. Drops of blood. Mr. Gravas's blood. *Asema* Joe drink his blood. He share it with the bat."

And in his mind's eye Hood saw what dropped from Joe Leftwich's hands as the priest turned to greet Seliah as he turned away from Sean Ozburn's sleeping body, and this thing fell into the folds of the bedspread.

Something small and heavy wrapped in something loose, like a golf ball wrapped in a washcloth.

A bat, thought Hood.

Superstition meets science.

"Excuse me."

He used the resort satellite phone in the dining room to call the number that Brennan had written on the back of his card. When the doctor answered, Hood could hear the baseball play-offs on Brennan's TV.

"There's a good possibility that Sean Ozburn was bitten by a vampire bat in Costa Rica on or around July twentieth," said Hood. "That's about five weeks before he started feeling strange and bad. And about nine weeks before Seliah started feeling the same way."

The television went silent. "Deputy, can you repeat that, please?"

Hood repeated and there was a brief silence.

"This changes everything," said Brennan.

"What do you know about rabies?"

"Maybe *one* out of ten thousand physicians in this country has even seen a case of human rabies. I'm not one of them. But I do know this—by the time symptoms show, it's almost always fatal. And it's transmittable by sexual activity, even kissing."

"Didn't a girl survive it just recently?"

"They used the Milwaukee Protocol," said Brennan. "It very likely saved her life. Very controversial. Potentially very damaging on its own. How did the bite occur? Where was it on his body?"

Hood told the truth, not the whole truth, and something other than the truth. He looked out at Arenal. A shower of red embers puffed into the air and he heard the distant clacking of the thrown boulders knocking their way down the mountain.

"The Milwaukee Protocol," said Hood.

"The Medical College of Wisconsin. Dr. Rodney Willoughby and colleagues. I followed that case. The protocol had a potentially huge effect on the way other infectious diseases are treated."

Hood felt his anger ignite, something bright and violent but controlled. Father Joe Leftwich with a little bat in his hands. Sean Ozburn. Seliah.

"I'll put Wisconsin and CDC on alert," said Brennan. "They can get the serum antibody test done faster than I can. Other tests will be necessary to confirm the virus. If she's symptomatic with rabies, then she only has a short time to live. I mean days. Maybe a week."

"How is Seliah doing since you admitted her?"

A silence and a sigh. "She checked herself out about two hours after you left. We've called her cell and home and left messages. No return calls. Before I do anything else I'm going to call the Health

Department. They'll get the Sheriffs to bring her in if she's not co-operative."

Hood remembered Seliah's surprising strength, her erratic and erotic aggression, her derangement. "If she's not cooperative, look out."

"I've read about their strength," said Brennan. "And the aggression. Rabid dogs get violent, too. Foxes, bats, all of them."

Hood punched off and called Soriana, told him the facts. Told him they needed to round up Seliah Ozburn and get her to Milwaukee yesterday.

"I'll have people to her place in less than an hour."

"Frank, if she's got this thing, she's very dangerous."

"I understand that. We'll subdue her."

"What's the word on Sean?"

Soriana said nothing for a long moment. Hood looked through the dining room and saw Itixa padding her way to the bar.

"About two o'clock today Sean wasted two young men in our San Ysidro house. Came up back side again, walked right by the exterior camera and smiled up at us. Didn't bother to take out the surveillence system this time. He just barged right in and shot them. No shotgun anymore. He used a couple of those Love Thirty-twos you guys came up with. One in each hand. Eighty shots fired in probably about five seconds. Carnage. We got the whole thing. It's his death sentence."

"One of them."

"We could use you here, Charlie."

He was out on the nine twenty to L.A. the next morning.

Seven hours later Hood, Bly, Morris and Velasquez were in the Ozburn home in San Clemente. Seliah's car was not in the garage; the laptop was gone; there were a few clothes on hangers left strewn on the unmade bed. Hood and Bly poked around in the closet but couldn't find the red slip-on sneaks or the Angels cap she'd worn to the restaurant a few evenings before. Or the cobalt blue robe for that matter. The mirrors were still covered or turned to the walls.

"What's with the mirrors?" asked Morris.

"We've all been wondering that," said Bly.

"Creepy, man."

Morris and Velasquez tried to coax something useful from an older desktop computer in the spare room, without luck.

Hood had already been told what to expect here, but he wanted to see it for himself. He'd also learned that Seliah had changed the password for her laptop computer. No surprise there. He looked around the living room again, the curtains closed tight over the sun blinds and the house dark but uncharacteristically warm. Hood checked the thermostat and it was turned off. Seliah was gone as gone could be.

His phone buzzed. "Deputy Hood, Dr. Brennan. We couriered the blood sample up to L.A. yesterday evening. Seliah is positive for the rabies antibody. They'll run other tests to confirm, but she almost certainly has the rabies virus in her, too. We have to assume she does."

"Have you talked to the Medical College of Wisconsin?"

"UCI Medical Center can do the protocol right here in Orange County. Rodney Willoughby is willing to personally consult. In fact, he insists on it. But UCI can't do the protocol without the patient."

"We're working on it."

"She might have just a few days to live."

Hood rang off and gave the other agents the news. Not one of them spoke. They stood looking down or at the thin line of sunlight coming through the window.

"I'm going to try again," he said. He dialed Seliah's cell number and got the recording so he left another message about what he had discovered in Costa Rica, and what Brennan was testing for. Then he sent her an e-mail, his third in the last two hours.

Dear Seliah,

The test came back positive for the antibody. They can do the Milwaukee Protocol up in Orange County. But it has to happen fast. As in right now. Please call me. Please answer this. Please come back from wherever you've gone, and bring Sean, and we'll get you both to the hospital and treatment. You can win this, Seliah. You and Sean don't have to suffer.

Love,
Charlie

A minute later she wrote back from her new e-mail address. "She's back," said Hood. "She's back!"

From: Seliah [wildblueyonder@zephyr.net]
Sent: Monday, October 24, 2011 3:24 p.m.
To: Hood, Charlie
Subject: this situation

Dear Charlie,

I can't believe what has happened. I'm not sure I do believe it. But I'm not coming back for treatment without Sean. I'm going to work on him because if what you say is true then his infection is two or three weeks ahead of mine. Apologies for my quirky behavior last Wednesday. I didn't appreciate you committing me to the hospital until now and I retract anything ugly I may have said. If rabies is what I have, I can tell you it brings some wicked evil thoughts into a brain. They are like nothing I've ever had. Stand by.

Seliah

26

Bradley was led into Narcotics Bureau Commander Miranda Dez's office in the LASD headquarters. A sergeant held open the door for him, then closed it when Bradley had stepped inside. Bradley wore his uniform and no sling, although he was not scheduled back to work for two more days. He carried a trim briefcase that Erin had given him one Christmas, with his initials embossed on the smooth black leather.

Commander Dez came around her desk and shook Bradley's hand. She looked as good as a woman could in such a uniform. Her hand was warm and firm. "Have a seat. Must be nice to have that sling off."

"Yes, it is." Bradley sat and set the briefcase on the floor. "The wound is healing up pretty well. Back to work in a couple of days."

"We've never met, have we?"

"No. I've seen you in the cafeteria, and once at the court-house."

She smiled. "I should have personally congratulated you on the Stevie Carrasco rescue."

"I don't feel like I did anything special. The whole thing felt like I was on autopilot."

"I was involved in a shooting once. Afterward I couldn't remember specifics. Couldn't remember how many shots were fired, how many people were there. I couldn't even remember the knife that was pulled on me. So, good job, Deputy Jones. You made us all proud."

Miranda Dez was pretty and firmly built and when she smiled Bradley was reminded of his mother. When she didn't smile he was reminded of her also. And when she spoke, walked, sat, talked. It was uncanny. It wasn't so much that they looked alike. *Similar*, he thought, *not alike*. But the first time he saw her, in the HQ cafeteria, tray in hand, talking to one of her captains, Bradley had to watch her.

"Are you enjoying your work here?"

"Yes, I am. The best thing about it is the people I work with. I feel like I fit in."

She smiled. "I know that feeling. Kind of like a big family. I know that's been said before, but it's true."

Bradley nodded and looked at her. His mother had had a lovely face. Commander Dez's face was lovely in the same way—slender, serious, eyes dark, ghosts contained. Then the smile, subtle and promising as a break of dawn. She drove a red Corvette and his mother had always loved red Corvettes, although she'd never owned one.

"What about you?" he asked.

"Me?"

"Are you enjoying your work here?"

"I live for this job. I don't know what that says about the rest of my life. I do have some outside interests."

"Children."

"A boy and a girl."

"Anything else?"

Bradley saw the little flash of darkness cross her face. He figured it meant either *no* or *none of your business*. "I'm sorry," he said. "Clearly not my business."

"I make jewelry out of old typewriter buttons."

"Oh?"

"It's lighthearted stuff. And I ride mountain bikes."

Bradley smiled now.

"Why do you want to know that?" asked the commander.

"Every once in a while I meet someone and I want to know everything about them. It's not necessarily a good quality. It puts some people on the spot. You are one of those lucky individuals."

"Why?"

Bradley studied her quietly. "There is no why."

Commander Dez sat back, glanced at her monitor, then looked at Bradley. "You asked for this appointment. What can I do for you?"

"I got a tip from one of my confidential informants a couple of days ago. He's a Mexican national, comes and goes when he wants. He's got Gulf Cartel connections south of the border and Mara connections here. He's been reliable on the little stuff and now he's on to something bigger. He says an American named Sean Gravas is going to buy a hundred new machine pistols. They're American-made. The deal is being brokered by a cartel heavy. *Silenced* machine pistols. It's going to happen somewhere in L.A."

"When?"

"Soon."

"Who's Sean Gravas?"

"A crazy dude with a yellow airplane. Fabio in Harley gear. Guns, meth, Aryan Brother."

Commander Dez looked at Bradley. "A hundred new silenced machine guns?"

"Pistols."

"I didn't think anybody made a silenced full-auto pistol."

"They're a new thing."

"A whole new gun?"

"That's what I'm hearing. Made in America," he lied. "Fifteen hundred apiece."

Dez looked at her computer monitor. Bradley watched her. He remembered watching his mother as she read to him, way back when he was three or four, remembered the warmth of her body and the timbre of her voice and her smooth, strong, emotional face registering the moods of the tale. Her beautiful face. Mysterious and thrilling. With a smile like the dawn. He wanted to own it. Even back then. He had vowed to own it. And when it was taken from him just a few short years ago, he had vowed to avenge her, and this he had done.

"Fabio in Harley gear," she said. "That's funny. Tell me more about the guns you say he has."

"Apparently the silencer works very well. You can put fifty rounds into a body and all you hear is the clothes and meat tearing."

She gave him a hard look.

"And according to my man, a hundred of them are about to change hands in L.A."

Dez pushed away the mouse and sat back and looked at Bradley. "Why didn't you go to your sergeant with this?"

"He's patrol and you're narcotics."

"Guns aren't narcotics."

Bradley shrugged and let his gaze settle on her face again. "Here's what I think, Commander. I like my guy. I take care of him and he takes care of me. If he's right, then Sean Gravas is going to buy a hundred machine guns from Gulf Cartel enforcers, somewhere in Los Angeles County. If we make the bust, then, well, that's a good thing. More than good, Commander Dez. Spectacular is what it would be. A hundred automatic weapons that won't hit our streets. A hundred and fifty grand forfeited to us. Picture *that*. Picture a hundred of those shiny new puppies laid out before you, and your photo in the *L.A. Times* and out on all the wires. I think that you should bitch-slap the Gulf Cartel and their Mara errand boys who are polluting this city. You should be the one to step up and take some credit. It's about time our citizens realize that the Gulf Cartel is right here in L.A. pushing their drugs to our children."

She broke out laughing. It took a while to end. "You're more than a little funny, Bradley. You should be in media relations."

He shrugged again. He was secretly proud of the way he'd already blamed this thing on the Gulf Cartel. He knew that there was no practical way for American readers and viewers to distinguish Gulf Cartel cutthroats from any others, nor did they really care. A *narco* was a *narco*.

"No," he said. "I would not do well in media relations. I have too much respect for the truth, and better things to do with my time. But I have a confession to make."

Bradley leaned forward and held her gaze and spoke in a softer voice. "I've seen you more than once in the cafeteria. Half a dozen times at least. And each time, I could hardly take my eyes off you."

"Oh, brother."

"I don't mean it like that. Listen. Why couldn't I take my eyes off you? I thought that we had something in common. So I did just a little poking around. That shooting you were involved in left three people dead—two creeps and the other narc you were undercover with. You killed them both and got knifed pretty badly for your trouble. You were half bled out but still breathing for your partner when the medics got there. He didn't make it to the hospital. It took you a month to get back to your brand-new desk job. You know what all that says to me? It says you're a kick-ass lady and you put it right on the line. So you deserve the best. You say you live for this job? Then take it up a level. We need all the heroes we can get. Just look around you."

Her stare was flat and penetrating.

"I've always had luck, Miranda. And I believe in sharing it with people I feel strongly about."

She shook back her thick brown hair and smiled, a cagey and knowing thing. "I get what you're about, Bradley Jones. And don't call me Miranda."

"Yes, Commander."

She sat back and studied him. "How old are you?"

"Twenty and a half."

"I see you're married."

Bradley nodded and said his wife's name out loud and felt the predictable flutter in his chest.

"Children?"

"Someday."

"Do you plan on staying with us?"

"Absolutely."

"Why did your mother claim to be a descendant of Joaquin Murrieta?"

"My mother had an active imagination."

"Was it an excuse for what she did?"

"She was proud of what she did."

"I felt sorry for her."

"Why?"

"She seemed compelled to act. Almost against her will."

"That's a popular theory."

"Is it only a theory?"

"I'll tell you something I've never told anyone at this department. She lived for her job just like you live for yours. And I don't mean just the teaching job. I mean the other one, too. I found this out later. Reading her journals."

"But why? It was dangerous and hurtful and it got her killed."

"It was dangerous, exciting, and a turn-on. And lucrative, too. She never hurt anyone. Not one person. She saved an old man's life with CPR on one of her robberies. She gave money to the poor—real money, not a hundred here or a hundred there but scores of thousands of dollars. Yes, it got her killed. Something always gets us killed, sooner or later."

"I'll take the later, Bradley. I hope you do, too. We're off to a decent start—we might be the only two LASD deputies stabbed in the line of duty before the age of twenty-one."

"We are. I researched it."

"I'll never forget those videos your mother sent to the networks. That mask with the crystal on it. The derringer. Her voice. Trying to explain herself. One of the strangest things I've seen. You remind me of her. Not looks. 'Tude."

"I loved her and I miss her." Bradley lifted the briefcase to his lap and felt his cheeks flush. "She loved red Corvettes."

Dez eyed him. "Thanks for the tip, Deputy Jones."

"Yes, ma'am."

"Don't call me that, either."

"I'm left with Commander Dez."

"That is who I am."

"I like the sound of Sheriff Dez better."

"I'll remember that when I run for office."

"Also remember that you can't buy the kind of publicity that a high-profile bust will get you."

"I hear Allison Murrieta again."

"That's a nice compliment, Commander Dez. I'll give you information as I get it. I'll do everything I can to make sure it's good stuff."

"But what if your man is just telling tales to pay for his next fix?"

"If that's the case, you can blame it all on me. But it won't be the case. He's good for this. But I do ask one thing of you, my commander."

Bradley smiled and waited a beat.

"Let's hear it."

"Leave my name off of this as much as you reasonably can. We new hires are competitive. Everyone wants to outdo the others—except for the clock punchers. I had great good luck stumbling into the Stevie deal, I'll admit that. But if I'm shown to have even more great good luck in find out about Gravas, well, my peers are going to hate me and my superiors are going to wonder."

"Maybe I'm wondering."

"I was born lucky. I've got more luck than I want. Gravas is for you and I want no part of him."

"What do you want?"

"For you to be a friend and mentor."

"You really puzzle me, Bradley Jones."

"I puzzle my own wife."

She studied him for a long moment, then wrote a number on the back of her card and handed it across the desk to him. Bradley stood and took up his briefcase and walked out, holding the card between his fingers like a cigarette.

27

Erin and the Inmates took the Bordello Bar stage that night in L.A. for a sold-out show, Erin trim and fair-skinned in lavender leather and ankle-high lavender boots with stainless zippers. Sitting at a table near the back, Bradley felt his breath catch as she led the Inmates on. The crowd went off.

Mike Finnegan sat on one side of him and his alleged daughter, Owens, on the other. Bradley had met them at one of Erin's performances back before they were married. At first Mike and Owens seemed to be groupies of some sort but they had turned out to be more than that. Exactly *what*, Bradley was not sure. They had made a few calls that had helped him send a large shipment of Love 32s through Charlie Hood's fingers and into the hands of Carlos Herredia. Mike knew way more than he should about various criminal enterprises in the American West and in Mexico, but he also knew more than he should about law enforcement, history, ornithology, astronomy, viticulture, the wholesaling of bathroom products, underground comics from the sixties, black-powder gunsmithing and gold mining. It was fairly obvious that Mike was not Owens's father but Bradley saw no reason to spoil their fun, or whatever it was they were having.

Erin strapped on a white and gold Les Paul and the crowd went off again.

"God, she gets more beautiful every month," said Owens.

Mike flinched. "Yes, she truly does."

Bradley clapped and yelped loudly for his wife. Her hair was red and lush and held up on the left side by a clip that a fan had made for her, a cute little porcupine with big eyes and quills that were laser pointers that shot a moving pattern of red dots to various points throughout the small and very crowded bar. Her hair caught the stage lights with a vengeance, he thought, the sparks and pops of loose electricity.

"Red, red and more red," said Finnegan.

"Like your hair is supposed to be," said Owens.

"Change is good. Where does it say that a man can't change the color of his hair?"

"Beware of little men with big ideas," Owens said to Bradley. Finnegan grinned and threw up his stubby little hands and waved over the waitress for another round.

Bradley sat back and sipped Dickel on the rocks and gave himself over to Erin and her music. He'd fallen in love with her doing just this, nightclubbing on the Sunset Strip with a fake ID, age sixteen. July third, he thought. Hot and humid for summer. He'd jacked a Porsche Carrera—just to drive that night, not to sell—and he was trying to tamp down the adrenaline with vodka. A skosh tipsy. Her band was called the Cheater Slicks then, and her hair was longer and she wore jeans with holes in them and ropers and a skimpy green silk halter. By the end of the first song of the first set he was unquestionably in love with her. He went back the next two nights and tried to catch her eye but failed. Near the end of the third night Bradley bribed the bouncer to get backstage and there, she had really *seen* him for the first time. He said something to the effect that looking at her was like walking into a beautiful room. And this was their beginning.

The Inmates were a guitar, keyboard, bass and drums, and their rock was rough and electric. There were shards of metal in it, shades of country, bits of barrelhouse. But Erin's voice was clear and articulate so it sounded to Bradley at times as if she was trying to sing her way out of the music, like she was something pure stuck on something wild, an angel lashed to a Harley.

In the relative quiet between the second and third songs, Finnegan leaned in close to Bradley. "Tell me, how is Felipe?"

"Felipe who?"

"You know, the puckered man with the eternal shotgun. You'd be surprised how forthcoming he can be with a little *perico* in the offing."

Parakeet, thought Bradley, *narco* slang for cocaine, because it makes you chatter like a parakeet.

"He's just developing a taste for the stuff after thirty sober years of drug trafficking," said Finnegan. "And how is El Dorado?"

"You're babbling, Mike. You're making no sense to me."

Finnegan grinned at him. Bradley had long ago given up trying to figure the man's sources for information. He seemed to know a lot of people and things, but he obviously read lots of books and periodicals and knew his way around the Internet. Bradley had decided that Finnegan actually knew far fewer people than he claimed, that he was a researcher, not a player. He seemed to crave participation but rarely participated. An observer. He was certainly a man who forgot nothing. Oddly, Bradley carried some distant memory of having met Mike long before that night in the Viper Room, a few years back, when Mike had first introduced himself and Owens. But he couldn't remember when, or where.

Finnegan smiled at him, eyes aflicker with mischief. "I'm sorry, Bradley. I must have you mixed up with someone else."

"Listen to the music, man."

"She is in fabulous voice tonight. It becomes stronger with every season. Summer was better than spring and now fall is better yet. Climates of vocal change. I can hear them in her."

"Shut up, Mike. Have another drink."

"And you must, too. These are on us tonight. After all, we sailed in here without a flag and boarded your table like pirates."

Owens considered Bradley with her cool gray eyes, then turned her attention back to the stage. She was an actor, beautiful, dark-haired, quiet. Bradley found her inexplicable as her father but much more exotic. He had seen her in two commercials—one for a cell phone and one for a home improvement store. As she looked away Bradley's gaze was drawn to Owens's wrists, each underside ringed with scars. She often wore bracelets to help hide them. Tonight she wore long sleeves.

"I wonder if Sean Gravas will smell it out," said Finnegan. "The setup."

Bradley swallowed his bourbon and water hard, an ice piece going down in the reflex.

"Wrong pipe, Bradley?"

"I don't know what you're talking about," said Bradley. "That's above my pay scale."

Finnegan looked at him dubiously now. "Yes. I *must* have you mixed you up with someone else."

Bradley felt the anger shoot through him. He was prone to it and had spent most of his short life trying to keep it down. True,

Finnegan had helped him with the Love 32s, but now all Bradley could see was a small, annoying man who thought he knew things, a meddler, a dilettante. Bradley's instincts told him to keep Finnegan and Erin far apart, on either side of himself, that they were elemental opposites of some kind and only catastrophe could come from mixing them. But here he was, jovial and generous with the cash, buying rounds and offering Bradley help on a project he could not possibly know much about.

He was relieved to see Caroline Vega and Jack Cleary come in, and he waved them over.

"I guess you do, Mike. And I've got some friends coming in and we've got some things to talk about."

Bradley regretted his words before they were out. Now Finnegan would focus all of his ferocious senses on Vega and Cleary, and would come away from this night knowing far more about them than he should. He'd assimilate them, digest them. Add them to his friends list. Like he did everyone else.

"I'm sorry you're angry, Bradley. But remember that Gravas is increasingly irrational."

"I'll remember that."

"I might be able to help."

"See you, Mike."

"Yes, sir. Owens, hon? We've been foreclosed upon."

But by the time Erin had announced that the Inmates were taking a short break, and Finnegan had collected his change and stuffed his fat wallet back into his jeans, and Owens had put on her jacket and slung her purse over her shoulder, Caroline and Cleary had arrived.

"Mike, this is Caroline Vega," Bradley said curtly.

"Hi, Caroline," said Mike. "We met at the street festival last year in West Hollywood. You had the LASD booth and the sun in your face and I had the lovely daughter and the great big frozen lemonades."

"I haven't forgotten you or that lemonade or your daughter, Mike. You're leaving?"

"Just buried in work tonight. And Owens is shooting early tomorrow so I should get her home."

Owens and Caroline shook hands and Bradley saw them exchange looks of recognition. Bradley had to introduce Jack Cleary also, and, in a pleasant surprise, Cleary and Finnegan had never met. Cleary, large and well muscled, looked down on the little man as if he were something stuck to his shoe.

"Well, carry on, kids," Mike said with a smile. He clapped Bradley on the shoulder and began to work his way out of the crowded room.

Bradley saw Erin catch up with the little man and say something in his ear. Finnegan bobbed his head and smiled, looking pleased. He kissed Erin's hand in good-bye, which pissed off Bradley. He watched her work her way through the crowd toward him, in a state of wonder, for the millionth time, that Erin McKenna belonged to him and he to her. He stood and wiped off the back of her hand with a drink napkin, then pulled out his chair so she could sit.

Late in the show Bradley huddled close with Caroline and Cleary, and told them he had a confession to make. He confessed to believing that there was more to life than risking it by chasing small-time bad guys for not much of a salary and crummy hours. *Witness the potato peeler*, he said, tapping his sore breast. To address this imbalance in this tough economy, he proposed an arrangement wherein the three of them would target the MS-13 street dealers and enforcers now overrunning L.A. as paid employees of Benjamin Armenta's besieged Gulf Cartel. Cleary, a Narcotics Bureau sergeant, would gradually get Vega and Bradley into his unit and they could work a lot of the busts as a team. Why? Because Armenta and his Mara errand boys were scourges on the city. Because they made Rocky Carrasco's outfit look like Boy Scouts and the city was better off without them. *Kidnap Stevie? They're worse than animals*, Jones explained. When he was almost done with his pitch, Bradley's heart was pounding and he felt flushed and exposed. He knocked back his drink and stared at them.

Both Vega and Cleary stared back. He sensed that this idea appealed to Vega's young sense of adventure but Cleary looked uninterested.

Bradley heard Erin singing in the background, a ballad she'd written called "Blue Rodeo," but not even the pretty melody and high emotions of the lyrics could penetrate the heavy silence at the table. He held the gazes of Cleary and Vega one at a time, back and forth, thinking, *Screw you two wimps if you can't see an opportunity and take it.*

Then, into the silence scratched only by the music of his wife, Bradley dropped his final bomb:

"Two grand a week for each of you."

Now he felt not just exposed but utterly naked—stripped down to his bare chassis—no extras, no options.

"Say that again," said Cleary.

"Please do," said Caroline.

Bradley said it again. Neither of the other deputies said anything for a long moment. Bradley stared at his wife onstage, ignoring them.

"Two thousand a week? To fuck over the Mara Salvatrucha, Brad? Well, that's pretty much what I do anyway. I'm in."

"Good, Jack. Good." Whew. Wow. One down, he thought. "You, Caroline?"

"Finally, a little something to go with four twelves a week and a skimpy paycheck. I can build on a couple grand a week. I'm way in."

Bradley looked at each of them in turn and they touched their glasses. He felt as if something had been loosed inside him, a torrent of relief and richness and possibility. He felt as if he were riding a bull, and he was staying on; he was winning.

He went back to watching Erin and the Inmates. Bradley's heart slowed to its usual rate and he felt all of his exposed parts retracting back into the new shell that was now not his alone but comprised of the three of them. The power of three. And another six grand into his own pocket every week. Three hundred twelve thousand a year. Bradley caught their sideways glances over the next hour, but neither Vega nor Cleary asked him the obvious question of who was paying large sums of cash each week to mess with the Maras. They must have figured that Bradley got lucky with Rocky Carrasco's boy, and maybe Rocky and Bradley talked later, and maybe they talked about how the old days were better, before the Gulf Cartel invasion of L.A.

This pleased him, because he wanted his team to be self-starters who could figure the score in their heads without fuss. People who understood the power of silence. People who knew an opportunity when they saw one. And had the drive and the skills to take care of business.

It was early morning, nearly four, when Bradley and Erin got home to Valley Center. The drive was long but worth it. The ranch had grown to eighty acres now, and the house had been recently remodeled and the outbuildings updated and Bradley had installed a secret bunker beneath the barn and he was the only one on earth who knew it was there.

Bradley drove onto the property first, winding up the dirt road between the Indian land and punching his gate opener as he watched the headlights of Erin's X5 settle into the dust behind him. Then he drove through a gentle swale and along a fence that blossomed with climbing white roses and he passed the barnyard with the enormous oak tree in its center. The dogs had surrounded him by now, an eclectic pack of purebreds and mongrels led by a huge husky named Call in honor of Jack London. Call loped alongside Bradley's Cayenne, looking up at the driver, and the larger dogs stretched some to keep up and the little terriers spent more time in the air than on the ground, flying, arch-backed and ears flapping, yapping furiously but slowly falling behind. There were twelve of them total. They roamed the acres with proprietary arrogance for everything but human beings, who, they had been clearly taught, ran the show. Bradley sped past the barn and looked ahead to the cottages scattered back on the hillside where lived Clayton the forger, Stone the car thief and Preston the fraudster, crooks all but nice young men, paying their rents on time and pooling their skills and resources—sometimes with and sometimes without Bradley—and generally doing okay for themselves in a tough economy. They had straight jobs, too, and under Bradley's influence they had developed good instincts for the bigger paydays, the easier, the better.

They pulled up in front of the house and Bradley got Erin's gig bag and purse and carried them up the stairs to the porch and into the house. He put his arms around her and kissed her lightly.

"I gave Mike the message from Charlie."

"I saw you. Why are we talking about Hood?" He kissed her again.

"I'm so wrecked tonight, baby," she said.

"I was hoping to wreck you further."

"You're an animal with no morals or conscience."

"When you're around."

"I want a long hot shower."

"You take it. I'll slop the dogs and be waiting for you."

"I've got a little something for you, Brad. When you come to bed."

"Umm-*hmmm*."

In the flickering fluorescent tube lights of the barn Bradley fed his twelve associates. They ate seventy dollars' worth of food and fish oil each week. Call began first and the others made not even a feint at his bowl. One of the Jack Russells lay flat on the floor opposite Call, her muzzle to the concrete and her eyes aimed upward at the big dog while he methodically ate. Bradley turned off the lights and left the big sliding barn door half-open so the pack could come and go. While they ate crunching and snorting he stood out by the big oak tree and again counted this place as a gift and remembered his mother, who had first fallen in love with it, and thought of Erin upstairs in the shower by now, exhausted after nearly three hours of performance, and he saw again that he had been blessed hugely in this life not once, but twice.

When he came upstairs Erin was waiting for him in the big sleigh bed. A bedside lamp was on, and that was all. She was propped up on pillows and she had the spread snugged up to her chin. Most of her hair was in a tight ponytail, except for the sides, which were swept up and back. To Bradley, a car guy, they looked like the exhaust pipes on a dragster.

"What's with the do?" he asked.

"What I feel."

He smiled and began to undress.

"Stop," she said. She growled at him. Bradley hopped to a stop with one boot in his hands and a question on his face.

She growled again and threw back the bedspread and brandished her fists at him. Three long white claws protruded from each hand where her fingers should have been and Bradley thought of Wolverine, a favorite character of theirs, and he saw as she slashed at him that she was holding the claws firm, and now that he looked closer he saw the funny little windows on them and realized what they were. She growled, then beamed at him.

"Yes?" he asked.

"Yes. Six tests. I just couldn't stop once the good news started."

"God and again."

"We're going have a baby, baby."

He launched onto the bed and braced his landing and Erin screamed and released the pregnancy testers and they fell back into the sheets.

28

Ozburn stood in Mateo's room at the Solmar Hotel near Ensenada and looked down at the ten Love 32s arranged in two rows of five on the bed. Each lay upon an oil-dotted red shop rag. Mateo had screwed on the noise suppressors and extended the telescoping butts and fitted an empty fifty-shot magazine into each weapon. They had a stainless steel finish that shone dully in the hotel room light. Their presence was dramatic, Ozburn thought: tiny machine pistols, perfect and deadly, born live and ready to bite. A carton of ammunition sat on the floor beside the bed.

Daisy stood beside him, trim and alert. Mateo, his face weathered and his eyelids heavy, stood over a small desk with the empty ice bucket and an ashtray on it, weighing the money.

—This is half, he said. Seventy-five thousand.

—I'm surprised you can count that high. Here's for the ammunition.

Ozburn pulled a wad of twenties from the back pocket of his jeans and tossed it onto the bed. The ammo was still in the factory box, .32 ACP, ten cartons of fifty. He pulled open the box and removed one carton and flipped it open. The new loads were pack-aged bullets up, their copper domes like bald men seated in church pews.

—Maybe you sell these to the Gulf Cartel, said Mateo, his voice a soft rasp as always. So they can kill us in L.A.

—Maybe that's what I'll do.

—I told Carlos don't sell them to you. I told him, where else will Gravas get the money to buy one hundred of the Loves? He needs the money of an organization but he is not part of an organization. Or is he? Is he just one of Benjamin Armenta's *pendejos*?

—Careful, now. I've been in a good mood for almost five minutes.

—You have no weapons but a useless dog. I have three men waiting to kill you if I tell them to. I think you killed our *sicarios* in Buenavista and San Ysidro. It happened in your houses. El Tigre blames Armenta but I blame you.

—Kill my own renters? Mateo, my friend, you are free to imag-ine anything you want.

Ozburn, angry now, watched Mateo weigh the money again. Ozburn's desire for violence had become sudden and strong. And like many of the unusual feelings he'd experienced in the last few weeks, this new desire actually felt very old and inbred in him, as if remembered from another age. The Sinaloan was wearing his swanky GPS unit clipped to his belt up near the outlandish buckle. Ozburn realized how easy it would be to strangle the man, load a few rounds into one of the gleaming new weapons and cancel the door guard, then take the GPS unit and scroll his way into the waypoints. Where, of course, he would certainly find El Dorado. Then he could load up a couple of Love 32s and whack the body-guards waiting for Mateo out at the Denali. *Take five minutes*, he thought. He'd have the money and the weapons and he could either fly or drive out to Herredia's compound and blow him into the next world. Perform good acts. Defeat evil.

—I'd love to do that, he said.

—Do what?

But then, as Father Joe had pointed out, a dead Carlos Herredia would only make room for another one of his type to fill the void. That was law enforcement strategy, to cut off the head of the snake and foment bloodshed between possible replacements. But Herredia's organization was well run and El Tigre was much feared outside of it and much loved within in. No, thought Ozburn, the change of guard would take place practically overnight. So the best way to defeat El Tigre and his organization was to use his own guns against him: Complete the sale to Armenta's people and sit back and enjoy the fireworks show in L.A. That way, *both* teams were beating up on each other and the good guys could do better things with their time. Start not with the head of the snake but with the tail. Such a war would go on for months. *Ruin his business*, said Joe, *and the man will follow. The final goal is not to kill him but to make him wish he were dead.* Wasn't that the greatest punishment a human could receive? To be made to regret his own life?

Ozburn went to the window and looked out at the gray-green Pacific. Even with his sunglasses on the scene was punishingly bright. Surfers rode a small rolling break and two boys sat their horses bareback and swayed slowly down the beach. Ozburn could see the door guard's boots dark in the long sunlit sliver between the door and the paver tiles. The guard and Mateo had checked him for guns and knives before allowing him into the room, which Ozburn had found funny, considering he was carrying seventy-five thousand dollars to give to Mateo for his boss. It was half the money for the hundred guns, the other half due upon delivery of the finished product.

—You smell sick.

—I've been feeling really good, Mateo. Good enough to fight a bull.

—Gringos don't have the balls to fight bulls.

—A man can learn plenty of things in his life. There's no reason I can't fight a bull.

—You should fight your dog. That would be a fair fight.

Ozburn looked at Daisy, then at Mateo. He growled lightly and saw the sleepiness return to the man's expression. Mateo pulled a handgun from the rear waistband of his Wranglers, slid it back into the pants right up front where he could get to fast. Ozburn laughed at him.

—When will the other ninety weapons be finished?

—Friday. Four days from today. Delivery will be in Los Angeles.

Strange, thought Ozburn. *But a lucky break for me and the Blowdown team. I'll take luck. I have no problem with luck.* The North Baja Cartel's skill at crossing the border must be highly developed by now. What were ninety guns, considering how many tons of dope they smuggled north?

—Why Los Angeles?

Mateo smiled joylessly.

—Because it is safer. Because there are not thousands of soldiers and *federales* searching for us in California. I joke to El Tigre. I said you would like it in California because you would be near to Armenta's Maras in L.A. Easy for you to sell the Loves to our enemies.

—You have a wild imagination, Mateo.

—I have no imagination at all. Four days. Friday. You need to be in Buenavista at the Gran Sueño Hotel and we will call you and tell you what is next.

—I'll need to see them.

—I'll need to see the money. The remaining half.

—Next time, I deal with Herredia, not you.

—He will never deal with you.

Ozburn packed the guns and ammunition in his duffel and whistled up Daisy and they walked down the colonnade through slats of shadow and light to the far side of the parking lot where his car was waiting. It was a loaner from Father Joe, just a humble Crown Victoria, but the registration was up-to-date and the air conditioner blew cold and Daisy could lie down on the bench seat beside him and rest her muzzle on his thigh and there was plenty of room for both of them.

He drove back toward the Estero Beach Hotel feeling in control of himself and of the things around him. Things were finally lining up. He'd cleaned out the Augean stables—both the Buenavista and San Ysidro safe houses—five fewer murderers living in the United States as guests of the ATF. He'd talked to Hood and brought Blowdown in on the act. He was surprised that Hood had given up on him so quickly, that Charlie just wanted to bring him in and charge him with the safe house killings. Shortsighted. Ye of little faith, thought Oz. Moreover, he'd gotten half the money from Paco and passed it—minus his two hundred fifty per unit—to Mateo. He'd just received his first ten weapons. He had overcome the temptation to whack Mateo and Herredia and some bodyguards, taking a longer view of his mission. He'd been feeling better the last few days, too, likely due to increased vitamins and supplements and plenty of rest. It was nice to be less prone to cramps and spasms and even convulsions. And he loved his otherworldy physical strength.

Ozburn sped along. Then he spotted some vendors and their

wares outside a beachfront hotel, and pulled over. He needed something. Daisy waited in the car while he examined the crafts and curios, asking questions about manufacture and price. There were paintings, ironwood carvings, pottery, silver and turquoise, bootleg CDs, wristwatches, lacquered-wood posters of Jesus, the Virgin Mary, Elvis, Mick. He settled on a bouquet of large paper flowers and a beautifully glazed and fired vase to hold them. The flowers were purple and orange and red and yellow and the vase was black with molten red runners, like something melting down it, *like Arenal,* he thought.

A young woman was selling Chiclets and cigarettes. Her small son had a baby opossum tethered by the neck with a string of old shoelaces to a big iron birdcage containing a red macaw. The opossum looked at Ozburn as he approached, and when he knelt down in front of the animal it hissed at him. There were small bubbles on its chin whiskers and Ozburn could hear it wheezing and see the straining in its flanks.

—Is hurt, said the boy.

—Yes. I will hold it.

—He bite.

—No, he will not.

Ozburn gently lifted the animal and cupped it in his big hands and bent his face forward to it, his nose just inches from the pink, dribbling snout.

—Dogs almost kill.

—He's terrified. Does he eat?

—Rice and churros.

He got his Flip from the car and showed the woman how to work it. When she began shooting video, Ozburn closed his hands over the tiny opossum and looked at its face staring up at him through the bars of his thumbs. It was swinish and ratlike at once and Ozburn marveled at its strange design, the hybridized oddness that somehow worked in this world. He felt his great strength flowing down into and consolidating in his hands. He let the strength gather and then he tensed his muscles until they trembled and he continued to watch the opossum as it watched him.

—You hurt him.

—I cure him.

Ozburn glanced at the camera. Then his fingers began to shake and the veins on the backs of his hands stood out and it looked like he was being electrocuted and that whatever was in his grip was being electrocuted also. He pressed his hands together more tightly. He could feel the astonishing lightness of the thing and the tactile throb of life that was inside it: ribs flaring, heart tapping away, muscles rippling.

—I used to pray to God when I healed. Now I don't pray to anybody or anything. I don't need them.

—God is good, said the boy.

—I make the life inside me flow outside of me and enter the injured being.

Ozburn looked down at his shivering hands and saw the opossum looking up at him. He summoned a last surge of life all the way from his heart to his hands and he felt it flowing from his fingertips and into the animal. He growled softly and the boy stepped back from him. When he opened his hands the animal was on its side, limp, mouth open, tongue out. The tail spilled deadly over Ozburn's palm.

—Good.

—Dead.

The boy's eyes filled with tears.

—Watch.

He set the opossum down on the ground, then sat back on his

haunches and waited. The boy did likewise. Ozburn looked out at the fine October day, cool and sunny and the air smelling of ocean and sagebrush. He smiled at the woman shooting the video. He couldn't wait to share this with Seliah. He thought of Seliah and traced an *S* in the sand with his finger and wondered what he could do for her, the suffering love of his life.

Then the opossum's eyes opened and its tongue retracted and it lifted its head. The boy smiled and blushed at his own gullibility. The animal gathered itself and stood up wobbly but found its balance. Its tail rewound into a neat, loose coil. Ozburn brought a tissue from the pocket of his leather biker's vest and wiped the foam off the animal's chin. It tried to walk toward Ozburn but its leash ran out. It strained for a moment, then looked up at Ozburn with its weak, small eyes. It was no longer wheezing or laboring to breathe. He pet it a few times, then stood.

—When it is strong you should let it go. It is a wild animal and won't do well with you.

—Many dogs.

—He fooled you. He can fool them.

Ozburn bought some gum from the woman and gathered up the bouquet and vase and his camera and drove south.

He let himself into suite twenty-four to find Seliah sitting at the small dinette, her back to the sliding glass door of the patio. Daisy bounced to her and put her nose on Seliah's thigh. Ozburn set down the duffel. The curtains were drawn against the afternoon sun but a slant of light caught her shoulder and one side of her face. She wore the cobalt blue satin robe he'd bought her last Christmas and her hair was combed straight and lustrous against it. Her computer was open before her and Ozburn saw the minor play of the monitor light on her beautiful pale face.

"Seliah. These are for you."

Ozburn stepped into the cool room and set the vase of flowers on the kitchen counter. He could see that Seliah's pupils were constricted against all light. She had not touched Daisy. He was in for another argument.

Four days ago she had e-mailed him that Charlie Hood had handcuffed her and forced her to go to a hospital in San Clemente. She was vague on why. She had "escaped" the hospital and quickly packed a few things at home, then driven to Las Vegas. From here she had sent him a series of crazy e-mails about Father Joe and a bat and a maid and the rabies virus. Ozburn realized that she was hysterical and it would be perilous to bring her into his mission. But he loved her. And she was plainly terrified by what Hood had done to her. Ozburn saw no choice but to bring her close to him, where he could protect her.

She arrived distraught, hyperemotional, random. He'd never seen her like that. They had spent much of that time making love. In the quiet moments between, while they devoured room service meals, Seliah had tried to make him believe they were both suffering from advanced rabies infection. She had a Wikipedia entry that described rabies symptoms, and she had the articles about the miracle of the Milwaukee Protocol. She had e-mails from Charlie and Dr. Brennan about the positive antibody test. She had an outlandish story about Father Joe and a bat, told, of course, by Hood. The whole conspiracy theory was interesting on a hypothetical level but Ozburn didn't believe one word of it. He saw no reason why Father Joe would purposefully infect him. What would he or anyone else gain from such a thing? The idea was illogical and preposterous and it angered him that she couldn't see this and it maddened him that Hood had handcuffed her and towed her off to a hospital like some violent lunatic.

But over the last two days Ozburn had also wondered, mostly

idly: What if Charlie and Seliah were telling the truth? This idea made him want to bounce Joe Leftwich off the nearest wall and get some answers out of him. What *was* that in his trash? If it was a bat, why hadn't he maybe just *mentioned* that he'd found one in his room the same night Sean had passed out on his bed?

"Charlie keeps sending me e-mails that the protocol can work," she said.

His heart fell and his anger rose. How many times had they been through this? "Charlie isn't a doctor."

"Dr. Brennan is a doctor and he's made arrangements for us up in Orange County. We can beat this virus, Sean. We can be the first adults to survive it. Ever."

"There's no virus, Sel. I've told you that."

"It was a bat. A vampire bat. Joe was holding it to your foot. I saw it with my own eyes."

"Yes, you saw something in the dark. But a fly bit my toe just like one bit the owner's son. That happens all the time down there. But the bat is hearsay from a superstitious maid. Wasn't she the one who drank beer all the time?"

"I *told* you, Sean. She found it in the trash! It was still alive. Charlie interviewed her and put it all together. It explains everything."

"It only explains that Joe found a bat in his room and thought he'd killed it. Most people down there kill vampire bats in their rooms, Seliah. They're vermin and they carry disease. All we can do is be rational, here, Sel. Reason is the only thing that can get us through this."

"But Eduardo had taken Joe to see the bats—Joe *wanted* to see them. Eduardo took Charlie to the same cave. And that bat in Joe's trash gave you the rabies and you gave it to me. But we have a *chance*, honey. We have the protocol. Look, I have all these articles about the girl. Please come look at them. She lived, honey. Look, here's a picture of her! A bat bit her in church and she *lived*, and we can, too."

Ozburn stood behind his wife and placed his hands on the back of her neck and gently kneaded the muscles. He looked down at the screen. It showed a smiling girl with braces on her teeth. The headline said: "Rabies Survivor Off to College." He remembered the story from a few years back. The young teenager began having headaches and blurry vision and couldn't walk straight. The doctors could find nothing and she got worse and worse. Finally her mother remembered she had been bitten by a bat while attending church months earlier. Ozburn had always been bothered by that detail: *bitten by a bat in a church*. But, armed with this new information, the doctors had quickly tested her for the rabies antibody, which was rampant inside her. Her prognosis was death. They gave her a few days, maybe a week or two. She had not been vaccinated against the virus and she was heavily symptomatic. No unvaccinated person had ever survived the virus after the appearance of symptoms.

Seliah scrolled down and pointed to the screen. "See, Sean? Right here, now, listen—this doctor, Rodney Willoughby, after Jeanna got diagnosed, he thought up this experimental way to treat her. She was going to die, right, so he had to come up with something fast. He knew that rabies viruses get into your nerve cells and go straight up the body into the brain. They crave the brain. The virus is shaped like a bullet and each one has four hundred spikes that help them penetrate the host cells. They go cell to cell. It's called 'viral budding.' They force their way up the central nervous system and into the brain; then they replicate like crazy. The virus causes paralysis that leads to asphyxiation. That's what kills you. The paralysis starts in your feet and works its way up until you can't breathe. But guess what? Dr. Willoughby also knew that autopsies of human rabies victims showed hardly any brain damage—the whole viral brain invasion didn't really damage the brain cells themselves; it simply caused them to give off fatal commands to paralyze. So he thought, what if you could protect the body against the viral paralysis by knocking the brain unconscious? Would an unconscious victim be less susceptible to the deadly commands of the virus? Could the person simply 'sleep through it'? And, if so, and if this allowed the victim to survive for just a few more days, then the immune system could fight the virus off. Because once in the brain, the virus has almost completed its life cycle. If you can just hang on for a few more days, you can beat it. And it worked! It worked for that girl and it can work for us."

Ozburn continued to look at the screen and massage Seliah's neck and shoulders. "We don't have the virus, Sel."

Her muscles tightened and her tone of voice changed. "What the hell *do* we have, then?"

"I've had a nervous breakdown from fifteen months of dealing with the scum of the earth. You've had one from fifteen months of dealing with me."

"Bullshit. Wise up. I *know* about it. We've got the symptoms. The fever and chills. The revulsion to water and light. The aches and pains and throat spasms. The agitation and insomnia and strength. The crazy sex. One guy in the literature went thirty-six hours straight! Biting, growling, anger. Even the aversion to our own reflections—that's a classic symptom. Back in the old days, it was a test for rabies—if you could look at yourself in a mirror, then you didn't have it."

"Then watch this," he said.

Ozburn set his sunglasses on the table, then walked over and pulled open the curtains to let the late-afternoon sun rush through the sliding glass doors. He looked out to the bright Pacific and though his eyes ached at the brightness of it he did not look away. In the living room he pulled the beach towel off the mirror. The mirror was framed in stamped aluminum that caught the onrushing sunlight. Ozburn stood before the glass and looked at himself. The light scorched his eyes but he willed them to stay open and to stay focused on himself. In his reflection he saw almost nothing he understood or even recognized but he kept staring hard and true into his own vast absence. It was like being burned alive.

"I'm doing it," he said.

"Oh, baby. Look at your tears."

"I'm looking at my reflection."

"You sure are."

He was aware of her getting up from the dinette table, felt the thump of her bare heels on the pavers. In the mirror he watched her wedge between his body and one arm. Her platinum hair shone against his black vest and she faced the glass bravely. She squinted, her eyes almost shut, her fair face wrinkled with the effort and the pain.

"Me, too!"

"You, too, Sel. See? We don't have no stinking rabies. Look at us. We can do it. We're going to be okay."

Their faces were wet ghosts in the glass. He watched Seliah reach up with her hand and wipe her mouth.

"We've got it and I know it. I'm going back, Sean. I'm going to get the protocol. You have to come with me or you'll die down here. I didn't come here for me. I came here to get you."

"I'm here because this is where I'm needed."

"Because some drunk priest tells you so?"

"Joe has nothing to do with this. No more than he caused what's ailing us. See? We're looking at our reflections."

"I can't look anymore. My eyes are on fire."

Ozburn moved between Seliah and the mirror and gathered her close in his arms. Her body was hot through the cobalt satin and he could feel her strength. Their mouths found each other and Ozburn untied her robe and pushed it away and it dropped in a soft rush. He lifted her up firmly so as not to break the kiss and carried her into the bedroom.

He laid her on the bed and straddled her and whispered into her ear. "If I make love to you long enough, you won't have the strength to leave."

"I'm ready. I'm eager. Then I'm leaving."

Twenty hours and eleven orgasms later Ozburn lay exhausted, watching Seliah pack the last of her things. She was just out of the shower and she moved with grim purpose.

Ozburn worked himself out of bed and slipped on his jeans. It was noon. Almost an entire day had gone by and they had barely left the bed. His feet were numb and his legs were weak and his cock ached and was filling with blood again. Out in the living room he dug into his duffel and pulled out the cash and counted out ten grand. This he folded neatly and stuffed down into Seliah's purse.

Daisy trotted from the bedroom like an impresario, followed by Seliah, rolling the suitcase behind her.

She let go of the handle and walked up to her husband and took his hands in hers. "I love you more than anything on earth. In the name of that love, come with me. You'll be dead in a week if you don't."

"I can't."

"You're choosing loneliness and death over life and me."

"They'll lock me up, Sel. You know that. It would be worse than being dead, sitting in a cell and wondering where you were and what you were doing. Don't ask me to do that."

"Charlie says maybe we can work something out."

"Charlie says whatever you want to hear."

"Father Joe Leftwich is not your friend."

No matter how hard Ozburn tried, he still could not see one reason why Joe Leftwich of Dublin, Ireland, would do such a thing. No reason at all. But Seliah had until now been a wise and loyal wife and he owed her allegiance and respect even when they saw things differently.

"I'll get to the bottom of little Joe," he said.

"It will be too late."

"It must be done, Seliah."

She put her face up to his ear and whispered, "Forget him. All you have to do is get dressed, pack that duffel and get in the car. I'll drive. Daisy can have the whole backseat. We'll be in the hospital in Orange by midafternoon. But maybe we can stop off home for a not-so-quickie. Leave Daisy and get one of the neighbors to feed and walk her."

"I love you and I'm sorry. I'm very sorry for everything, Sel. I don't know how to even begin an explanation."

"Good-bye, then."

"Good-bye."

"I didn't think they could ever bring us down."

"Who's they?"

"I don't know," said Seliah. "The whole world? ATF? Father Joe? Charlie? I know there's more to this than you and me. You and I were just fine, weren't we?"

"More than."

"We were good. We were golden. We were the best of them. Write. Call. Pray."

"I'll write and call," Ozburn said. "And I'll come to you when I'm finished. I promise."

"We're never going to see each other again. Do you understand, Sean?"

"I don't believe that. I can't believe it and live."

She put her arms around him and rested her head on his chest. Ozburn felt the weight of it with each beat of his heart. He held her gently and the minutes went by.

He rolled her suitcase to the car and put it in the trunk. He put her laptop and the bouquet of paper flowers on the passenger seat of her car. He was still having trouble feeling his feet and his legs felt heavy as iron.

Ozburn stood in the parking lot watching her drive away. Daisy sat beside him. He watched the Mustang as it slowed, then swung out of the lot and onto the road. It was a red car and it looked optimistic against the gray asphalt but it picked up speed and headed for a rise and she was gone. Ozburn's heart finally broke. He stood there for a long while, dazed by the new silence, waiting for the feeling to come back into his feet so he could walk back into the room.

He ate the leftovers and guzzled some vitamins and packed as quickly as he could. His feet felt better. He found one of Seliah's earrings wrapped up in the bedsheet and for a beat the breath in him stopped. *I am alone*, he thought, *and it is now up to me and I will see you again. I will see you again.*

He swallowed the earring then called Daisy and paid cash for his nights at the Estero and drove Father Joe's loaner to the airstrip where *Betty* waited, yellow and freshly washed, eager to take to the sky.

29

Four hours later Hood was parked outside the Ozburn home waiting for Seliah to come out. In the time it had taken her to get here from Ensenada, Hood had called in a favor with his old LASD patrol sergeant and was now at the wheel of a white slickback Interceptor with screened-in backseats for transportees and a short bar of interior running lights and bulletproof windows. The sergeant had offered a backup unit and two uniforms but Hood had declined. He was afraid they'd set her off and she'd change her mind. He was afraid she might change it anyway. She said it would take a few minutes to pack up some things.

He pulled the buzzing cell phone off his belt.

"Charlie Hood, this is Mike Finnegan. Erin told me you wanted to talk. I was so truly happy to hear that."

Hood looked up at the Ozburn front door. No sign of Seliah. He felt the same uneasy suspicion he'd always felt when talking to Finnegan, a suspicion that the man was somehow outside of his own understanding and experience. Mike's companion, Owens, had once told Hood that the only way to comprehend Mike was to understand that he was insane. But Hood had wondered if it was more than that. As a boy, Hood had seen a tiger walking down a Bakersfield sidewalk—escaped from a private collection, he later learned—and Hood had realized that nothing in his life had prepared him to understand such a being. He had the same feeling now.

"How have you been, Mike?"

"I'm no longer in bathroom fixtures."

"Where are you living now?"

"I can't seem to leave L.A. Owens and I share some nice quarters here. She's getting lots of work."

"And you?"

"Well, the family sold off part of the old Napa County estate. My share was, well, not insubstantial. You wouldn't believe what a few thousand acres of grapes is worth. Of course, the new owners will build embarrassing mansions on it and probably let root rot kill the grapes, but that's progress, American style."

Hood thought back to the first and last time he'd actually seen Mike Finnegan's face. It was a year and a half ago and it was the day Mike had suddenly checked himself out of Imperial Mercy Hospital. His body cast lay in pieces on the floor of his ICU room. He'd been caught on security video, dressed in new street clothes, leaving the hospital with Owens.

Hood found his L.A. apartment abandoned and his phone number no longer good. No forwarding information. Neighbors knew nothing. Ditto Owens. Hood made inquiries but got nowhere. Hood suspected that Mike had tipped Bradley Jones and Ron Pace about ATF's surveillence of the Pace Arms gunmaking facility in Costa Mesa. But he could prove nothing.

"Why did you leave Imperial Mercy like that, Mike? What was the hurry?"

"I just can't sit still sometimes."

"You tore the cast apart with your bare hands?"

"What else could I have used?"

Hood glanced up at the Ozburns' front door. "Of course you know that Pace and Bradley smuggled the guns out of the Costa Mesa manufacturing plant, got them down into the hands of cartel shooters. A thousand of them. They're being used to kill people on both sides of the border."

"How sad. The chaos down there is bound to get worse before it gets better. But Charlie, this was a year and a half ago—ancient history. So, catch me up with your world. Who is this fascinating Sean Gravas character?"

Hood felt his scalp crawl. "You and I both know who Sean Gravas is."

"Yes. Few people do. We're all strange bed partners, aren't we— ATF and the North Baja Cartel and little old me?"

Hood looked up to the Ozburn home. No Seliah. Had she changed her mind? He checked his watch.

"Mike, a few days ago I stood in the Mexican desert where a rabid man had chained himself to a post so he wouldn't hurt anyone else. That's where he died. The post was still there. And his grave. I thought of you."

"Juan Batista! I love that part of the West. From the cerveza to the *curanderas*."

"You know everything, don't you, Mike."

"I absorb your flattery."

"So, what do you know about the Arenal Volcano and Father Joe Leftwich and his vampire bats?"

Silence.

Then: "Charles, I told you once that if there was something you wanted very badly, something I could help you get, that we might form a relationship."

"I don't want a relationship."

"Then what do you want? To make me your informant?"

"Call it that."

"What do I get in return? A lighter sentence when my day in court arrives? Perhaps some cold hard cash? An ATF windbreaker?"

"You can have any or all."

"I don't want any of that. I want like for like, Charlie. That's all I'll ever want from you."

"Okay."

"*Okay?* Just like that?"

"I said okay. I'll play by that rule. Like for like."

Hood expected Mike to laugh but he didn't. When he'd seen the tiger in Bakersfield, the huge svelte beast had lit a spark of panic in him but Hood had kept on walking toward school anyway. What else could he do? His destination was the only answer to his fear and he knew exactly how to put one foot in front of the other. And again. The tiger had faded into a stand of oaks, stripes blending into the shadows.

So now, too, Hood kept walking, toward what, he wasn't sure, but he was walking and his legs were strong. His eardrums buzzed but his eyes saw far and clearly as he looked out over the silver Pacific. He felt cold in his heart and knew this coldness was right.

"Charlie, who murdered the three young assassins in the Buenavista safe house? And the two others in San Ysidro?"

"We don't know yet. We suspect the Gulf Cartel but we don't have good evidence. We do know they're trying to move into the North Baja Cartel's turf in Southern California. The Zetas are going their own way so Armenta needs firepower. Now you, Mike, like for like—Arenal, Costa Rica. Speak to me."

"Where to start? Central America is literally *crawling* with us. The heat, the beauty of the land and the ocean and the proximity to

Caribbean culture. But most of all, the generations of colonial exploitation and craven, power-mad governance. Dictatorships both private and military! Rampant corruption, rampant lust. From Papa Doc to Trujillo to Noriega—it's difficult to find a more fertile place to work. And factor in a widespread belief in magic—they *believe*! García Márquez can bring tears to my eyes, even though I've never been to the Caribbean. I'd so love to meet him. The whole region is brimming with rich potential for us."

"Who is us?"

"I led you to that water once."

"You denied it later."

"We can be whatever you want us to be, Charlie. It has always worked best that way."

"Damn whoever you are. Tell the truth."

"I am trying to provide some context for you. Now, I say this with some embarrassment—all of Central America and the Caribbean is rife with our internecine squabbles. There are jurisdictional overlaps, petty procedural disputes, chasms of noncommunication, turf wars. Pity the human beings down there. You need to understand the history. But Charlie? Back to my question. My guess is Ozburn killed them. Too much pressure working undercover. Too much frustration. Surrounded by too many bad men. Takes it out on the handiest target he can find—the young *sicarios*. He either overrode the surveillence system or, better yet, he didn't. Which means you have him on video. Which means you have proof of a rogue ATF agent running wild along the border."

"He's AWOL as Gravas. We both know that much."

"Yes, but what is he doing? Is he on the run or part of some crafty ATF operation? His apparent madness isn't simply deeper cover?"

"No. It isn't."

"But would you be telling me ATF secrets if they were true, Charlie? Or do you only give me the lies?"

"Only the lies for you, Mike."

"How is Seliah?"

"Fine so far as I know."

"So, you are in her kitchen, so to speak. I mean ATF is, not you personally. You wouldn't personally go into Seliah's kitchen, now, would you?"

Hood looked back up to the Ozburn porch. No Seliah. What if she changed her mind and ran out the back door? "She's uncooperative, Mike. We're keeping her at arm's length."

"Do they communicate, the Ozburns? E-mail, video perhaps?"

"Perhaps."

Mike was quiet for a beat. "You're not quite as rule-whipped as I thought you were, Charlie. You're actually talking instead of interrogating. What if you slip up and let a truth drop?"

"Keep me talking and maybe I will. Now—an alleged priest at Arenal, Father Joe Leftwich."

"I've heard of him, of course, but we've never met. Different region, obviously. Reputation as a hardnose. Drinker, big temper when it blows. Not afraid to be hands-on. Speaks all of the Caribbean languages, even the unusual ones—Papiamento, Taki-Taki, Hindi, Urdu. Helped the Spanish find gold in Costa Rica—first gold on the American continent. Good move on his part. Nothing like an explosion of wealth to challenge an oppressive religious climate and to finance the chaos that ensues. I remember that Leftwich set back his career by consorting with cutthroats on the Spanish Main. They were small-time men, cruel but ultimately useless to us. Leftwich enjoyed the bloodshed, I heard. Later he upgraded, if you can call it that. Had the ears of Pinochet and Somoza. He's been using the priest costume off and on for centuries, Charlie. Apparently, it works."

Hood watched Seliah walk out to her front porch. She was dressed in a black tee, black jeans, the red sneaks. She wore a black bandana pirate style as her husband sometimes did. She had an overnight bag slung over one shoulder and a canvas book bag in each hand. One of them looked heavy.

"Next time we'll talk vampire bats."

"I'd be delighted."

"I've got your number now," Hood said, and punched off.

He got out of the car and trotted up the steps to the porch. He smiled and approached Seliah and hoped she didn't just run up and bite him. Instead she smiled weakly, her face very pale and mostly hidden behind big Jackie O sunglasses.

"Woof," she said.

"Seliah. Lemme take those."

She let him take the book bags and they walked toward the car.

"I tried, Charlie."

"I know you did."

"He wouldn't come. I couldn't make him do it."

"Let's get you fixed up, Seliah. We'll work on Sean next."

"I will not betray him to you."

"I'm not asking you to. How are you feeling?"

"I didn't think I could feel this bad." She stopped. "Holy crap. I gotta ride in the back of *that*?"

"Now you know how the bad guys feel."

"That ought to be funny. The fact that I have to ride back there isn't funny at all."

"Maybe it's best for both of us." He opened a rear door for her but left it for her to close. Then he went around to the other side and slung in the canvas bags.

"I wouldn't try to seduce you in a . . . Never mind. Never mind. I'm sorry for all that. The virus causes it. Dr. Brennan said he's waiting for me. I like him. And drive fast, Charlie. Because when I left Ensenada I took some pills to keep me calm but you know something? I can feel them wearing off. I feel like Lucy Westenra, changing into a killer vampire slut one cell at a time. You ever read *Dracula*?"

"Never."

"It's all told in letters and diaries. It hypnotizes you. None of the movies are as good. Francis Coppola got closest. When this first started happening I wondered if I was turning into a vampire. Then I wondered if all the vampire movies and TV and books were turning me into one. Then, well, it just turned out to be a drunk priest with a fucking bat. What did Sean and I do to deserve all this special treatment?"

Hood got in and turned to see Seliah through the screen. She looked like a captured mutineer. She reached out and grabbed the strap on the handleless door and Hood knew she knew she could not open it again.

"You and Sean didn't do anything to deserve it."

"Now's the time if I'm going to run for it," she said. "Every time I run I get faster. I bet I can outrun you, Hood. I could give you the slip."

"Close the door, Seliah. We've got places to go and people to see."

She sighed and pulled the door closed.

Hood took I-5 North for UCI Medical Center in Orange. He adjusted the rearview so he could see her. She looked out the window at the tan hills of Camp Pendleton Marine Base.

"What they do is pump me full of knockout drugs," she said. "Out I go. It's called a therapeutic coma and they keep the ketamine coming so I stay down deep. Then they give me antiviral drugs and antibiotics and immune system boosters. They pump me full of food and fluids. My unconsciousness allows respiration instead of paralysis. They monitor my blood and saliva to see if the protocol is working. They knock out some people just for a few days, and some they've left KO'd for almost two months. If it looks like I'm going to survive the rabies, they wake me up. Or at least they try."

She checked her watch, then turned her gaze to the bright silver Pacific. Hood tried to imagine what was going through her mind.

"Of course, if I wake up, I'll have some brain damage. They can't predict how much. Jeanna Giese had some, and she spent two months in the ICU. But she worked hard at physical therapy and learned to do most of what she could do before. She still has some difficulty enunciating words and her left foot is weak so she runs funny. She can't play sports anymore. But she can go to school and drive a car. A bright future, that girl . . ."

Hood watched Seliah as her voice trailed off. The sunlight stenciled her face through the security screen. She took off the black bandana and wiped her forehead and cheeks with it. She hugged herself and pressed up closer to the door to get away from the sun. For a long while she hung her head, her swaying platinum hair walling off her face from the light and the world. Hood's heart sank and burst with the clear presence of her peril.

"So, Itixa the maid found a live bat," she said.

"In the trash in Father Joe's room."

"She should have said something."

"She told the owner and he told his son to stay away from the priest. But neither of them told you or Sean."

"But you know, if she had told me personally that morning that she'd found a bat in Father Joe's room, I might not have connected it with the blood on Sean's toe. Down there you could wake up with a howler monkey in your room. Or a boa constrictor in your shower."

"It was your description that made me connect the bat to Father

Joe and Sean. *Something small and heavy wrapped in something loose, like a golf ball wrapped in a washcloth.*"

"I like the way you put it together, Charlie. You and Sean have minds like that. You're naturally suspicious of just about everything. Me? I was always a face-value kind of person. Whatever it said on the label, I believed. I loved that way of looking at things. If it said 'new and improved' I believed it truly was new and improved."

Hood caught the past tense.

"So have you found Father Joe?" she asked.

"I'm working on him. Nobody I talked to in Costa Rica had any idea where he'd gone. Back home, I went online and found mentions of two Father Joe Leftwiches but only one is Irish Catholic. And neither of them were in Costa Rica in July. I've talked to the Irish Embassy, their West Coast consulate, the Catholic Church in Dublin, the Catholic Diocese in L.A. and the Vatican. They don't just give out information on priests like you think they would. Too many scandals. I've checked all the law enforcement databases just in case he's got a warrant or a record. Nada. I suspect he's a complete fraud, not a priest at all. Don't you?"

She turned her gaze to him. "He looked realistic in the getup, Charlie, in that little black shirt with the round white collar. But there I go again, believing the surface of things. He never mentioned what his plans were."

Hood looked back at her reflection in the mirror. "Before I left the Volcano View I got one last look at the registration book. I wrote down the names and addresses of ten of the guests who were there when you were. I've written letters to two and e-mails to eight of them, asking if they remember him, and if he said anything about where he was going. I asked them to e-mail any picture that might have him in it. When I was there, everybody had at least two cameras."

"I took a picture of him. Joe said, 'No, don't do that, I don't need my fat little face on film,' but I shot it anyway. He really didn't seem to mind very much."

"I'd like to see it, Sel."

"When we got home it wasn't on the camera."

"Did you ever see it?"

"Oh, yeah, I know it was there. It was the night we partied. I took Sean's camera and shot them with their arms around each other and their glasses raised. Father Joe didn't quite come to Sean's shoulders. I clearly remember looking at the image to see if I should take another but it was a good enough shot. So I gave the camera back to Sean and he put it in the case on his belt. I shot more pictures the next day. No more of Leftwich. Then we came home. And when I was picking out ones to put on disc, I noticed that the Joe picture was gone. I suppose I could have deleted it by accident."

Hood pictured Father Joe's room at the Volcano View, the screens for windows, the cool tile floor, the bed. And he pictured his own digital camera and the three time-consuming steps it took to delete a picture. "Or, Father Joe could have deleted that picture while Sean was asleep."

"Yes, easily. What's the charge against him if he actually gave us rabies and we die from it?"

"Neither of you is going to die from it."

"Now you sound like Father Joe, telling us how special we are and how we're headed for great things. How come everyone seems to know my future except for me?"

"Murder one," said Hood.

"I'll bet there's never been a murder by rabies. Except when one of us bit someone, or maybe raped or even kissed someone. But it wouldn't be murder unless you knew you had it, right?"

"No. It would be something else."

"You could never convict Father Joe based on what we know."

"No, you couldn't."

Hood watched as Seliah brought one of the book bags to her lap and looked down into it. She held up a Colt Model 1911 .45 semi-automatic and waved it at him.

"Yours from Sean," she said.

"Careful, now."

"Not loaded."

"I can't take that. It's his."

"Not if doesn't get back here in a hurry. He'd want you to have it."

She set the .45 back in the bag and brought out a Smith & Wesson .357 K frame, then a Glock .40-caliber. "These, too. I don't need them. Sorry; I didn't bring any ammo. I don't know where he kept it. This is from me."

She held up a bottle of wine. "It's ten years old. I've been saving it for a special occasion."

"Then keep it for one, Seliah."

"If I live to drink another glass of wine, maybe you can be the one to pour it for me."

"You can beat this thing."

"They've used the protocol eighteen times since Jeanna," she said. "They all died but five. Five, Charlie."

His eardrums started ringing. Brennan had said nothing of this and now Hood's soul felt fooled and helpless and angry. "Five?"

"Yes. Now, I want you to hang on to these medals and give them to my mom and dad if I don't wake up. If Sean and I both go, then everything goes to the families. We have a will on file and I left a few numbers for you at home, on the kitchen counter. But I want these medals to come to Mom and Dad personally, and I want you to say thank you for me. These are mostly from college but some from high school. Mom and Dad drove me to every practice and meet you could think of, paid my way across the country and to Canada and Europe, helped me go to a college where I could swim. I was too wrapped up in myself to appreciate it at the time. But I know these trinkets would mean a lot to them. You can have one if you want but not one of the Pan Am games, okay?"

She held up a handful of them for him to see and dropped them back into the bag and lifted out another batch. In the rearview Hood could see the tears running down her face. Her voice was high and girlish and forced. "Now, I want to have my ashes scattered at sea, of course. So in this other bag I've got some stuff I want to be tossed overboard, too. I'm sure there's a law against that so you just make sure to do it yourself, Charlie. Here's Daisy, a ceramic horse with a broken tail that I loved, and Sean named the dog after. And here's a doll named Betty, which is what Sean named the Piper after, and here's my dried-leaf collection from when I was a girl . . . Just pull out the leaves and throw them in. And this little wooden chest? There's a lock of Sean's hair and I'd like you to throw that into the sea, too. I want the hair to float for a while, then sink down with the ashes. In scatterings at sea, if the sunlight is right, you can see down deep into the water and the ashes get suspended in a big swirl where the boat has traveled. It's a pale streak left by the person, their last track on earth. It widens and lengthens and slowly fades. And that's where I want the hair to be, mixed in with me."

"Okay."

"Now, I don't think this is likely to happen, but if Sean lives through this thing, and you ever see him again, these are for him." She reached into the bag and lifted in succession a stack of envelopes, two small ring boxes, a thick black book. "Love letters and poems from when we were dating. His and mine. And my engagement and wedding rings are in the boxes. They'll make me take them off anyway. If I die, you give them to Sean. There's also a journal I've been keeping for eleven years now. Nobody should read it but him."

She pushed the book back into the bag and yanked off her sunglasses and dabbed at her eyes with the black bandana. Her pupils were tiny and the whites were hot red and the irises faint blue. His eyes met hers in the mirror. She stared at him in between dabs, then growled at him and laughed and growled again louder. She pushed the sunglasses back on and stuffed the bandana into one of the bags. She was shivering and he could see the throb of her pulse in her carotid.

They were halfway there by now. Hood called Brennan on the cell and told him where they were. He told him to have people ready who could handle her in case she was violent. She listened and watched him in the glass. "I can't do this, Charlie."

"You're doing really well, Sel."

"I've changed my mind."

"You have no choice."

"You do not offer or deny me choices."

"You can beat it."

"Pull over. I want out. Now."

"I won't do that."

"I demand that you do it."

"I won't."

"As a friend."

"A friend would not pull over."

"You're a weak man. It's all you are or ever were."

"Jeanna beat it. You can beat it. There are your parents and friends and Sean and all those things you have in the bags. They're all more reasons for you to be strong."

"Oh, what shit you pretend to believe, Hood. What pathetic,

insulting garbage. You know what you are? You're play money. You're a boy. Grow some. You ever use that cock of yours to do anything but pee? Pull over and let me out of here!"

She hit the mesh hard with one fist, then the other. Hood heard the terrific crunch of flesh and bone on steel and when she hit the screen again he saw the blood on her knuckles and the dent in the mesh. She watched him in the glass as she licked her hands; then she wrenched her torso violently and uncoiled her right elbow against the bulletproof window. The impact was heavy. Hood wondered if it would hold. Then again, and again. She flew across the seat and battered the other window and Hood heard her grunting and growling and by the time he got the rearview trained to where he could see her, there were blood smears across the glass.

Hood hit the lights and gunned the Interceptor up tight onto the SUV ahead of him, whose driver quickly signaled and pulled over to let him pass.

30

In the paltry light of an underground security entrance usually re-
served for shackled prisoners, five specially trained orderlies in
bulky protective suits and visored helmets extracted Seliah from the
slickback with long-handled nooses and a large padded blanket.
Another stood by with a stun gun. A small gathering of curious
doctors and nurses watched. Seliah thrashed and growled, saliva
swinging from her chin as she bit at the noose and cursed Hood and
her circle of trained tormentors.

It took them almost ten minutes to get her strapped onto a gur-
ney. Not much of her was visible outside the blanket, only one pale
arm, the red canvas sneakers at one end, and a flowing platinum
cascade of hair at the other. She continued to struggle and spit out
muffled curses from inside. A nurse stepped forward with a syringe
and two of the orderlies pinned down Seliah's arm. Into the crook
of her elbow drove the needle.

Hood watched in shame. A clean-shaven young man in a white
coat and athletic shoes hurried over and offered his hand. "I'm Dr.
Witt. Did she bite or scratch or injure you in any way?"

Hood identified himself and said no.

"Any transference of body fluids from her to you? Blood, saliva . . ."

"None."

"Make sure to clean out your car with a strong bleach and water solution. I'll have the custodial staff make up a bucket for you. If you have any wounds or open sores, I can get them to clean the car for you."

"I'll do that."

"We'll do everything in our power to save her life. We're ready."

Hood sat in the waiting area of the security floor for half an hour. He checked messages and e-mail but couldn't concentrate. Half an hour after that, Dr. Witt came out and told him they'd stabilized Seliah and were prepping her for the first stage of the protocol, the inducement of therapeutic coma.

"Can I see her?"

The room was spacious and had a freeway view through Plexiglas windows. Three doctors talked quietly in one corner as a nurse injected something into the drip system. Seliah was elaborately strapped to the bed frame but Hood saw that she was sedated and her fight was gone. Her knuckles were bandaged. He stood by the bed and touched the fingers of the hand without the IV needle taped into it. "Hey."

She smiled slightly. "Hey, Charlie."

"Quite the tantrum."

"I was always an extrovert."

"I'll bet you were. You've got even more to show them, Seliah. Go blow their minds."

"You bet I will."

"I hope we can bring Sean in, set him up right here beside you."

"You know he won't let you."

"I know he loves you more than anything in the world."

She looked at him and sighed softly. "Yes. That's a splendid notion. You are such a good man."

"Thank you."

Dr. Wong, the anesthesiologist, was short and pleasant-faced. He came to the other side of the bed and said he was going to administer the first dose of ketamine. Later would come infusions of ketamine, midazolam and "propofol *not* titrated to burst-suppression pattern on the electroencephalogram." Ribavirin, a rabies antiviral drug, would not be administered, because of delayed and depressed immunological responses noted in previous protocol patients. Dr. Willoughby himself had strongly advised against the ribavirin. Seliah would be intubated for metabolic supplementation as well. She would go into a deep sleep almost immediately. It would be a peaceful sleep. She would not dream and she would not worry. While she slept her immune system would fight the virus with all its strength. The doctor squeezed the powerful drug into the IV feed.

"Mrs. Ozburn," he said. "Can you count backward for me, from one hundred? Start at a hundred, Mrs. Ozburn."

"Later, Charlie."

"We'll all be here waiting for you."

Seliah tapped Hood's hand with a finger and started counting at one hundred. She stopped at eighty-one and Hood watched her eyelids close.

Dr. Wong glanced at his watch, then at the vitals monitor. "No one makes it past ninety-two. Not three-hundred-pound men or professional athletes."

"She's an amazing woman."

He looked at Hood askance. "There's nothing more you can

do now, Mr. Ozburn. Go home. Try to rest. She'll be here a long time."

Hood stopped at the nurses' station and introduced himself to the three on-duty nurses. He told them that Seliah's husband, Sean Ozburn, might surprise them with a visit. He described him. Hood told them he could be intimidating but not to be afraid of him. Do as he asked. Hood told them to call nine-one-one immediately if he showed up here, and to call him as soon as they reasonably could. He gave each one a card with his cell number on it, and left two more to be taped up on the station message board.

Nurse Marliss Sharer took the card and looked through the glass at Seliah, then back to Hood. She was young and pretty and Hood wondered how Marliss would stack up against the mad power replicating in Seliah's body.

"We'll take good care of her, Mr. Hood. We're the best around when it comes to therapeutic comas."

Hood drove the Interceptor up the ramp from the half-light of the underground entrance into the bright October afternoon. He took the freeway south for Buenavista. He thought about Seliah and how advanced the virus in her was, and he figured if Sean had given it to her, then he must be worse off. Would Sean be more resistant because he outweighed her by more than a hundred pounds? He couldn't get the image of noosed and thrashing Seliah out of his mind. What could possibly lead someone to give one of humankind's most horrific diseases to another human, knowing that he would in turn give it to his wife? Who was the real target? What black motive could underwrite such an act?

The traffic was light and he was through El Centro by early evening. It was cool and clear and the barley and milo and cotton rolled out for miles around him. Then he climbed a few feet in elevation, all it took to bring him into the unforgiving and beautiful desert that would lead him to Buenavista.

A call came through on his cell and he touched the earpiece control.

"Marshal Hood, this is Don August. I'm one of the Desert Flyers. We talked a few days back."

"You've got the strip outside Yuma." Hood's heart jumped. If this went where he thought it might go, then his luck was changing.

"Good memory. Out in Ogilby, right next door to Yuma. Look, I won't take up much of your time but you asked about Ozburn and he, well, he called about a minute ago and asked if he could use the landing strip. I said okay. He said he'd be coming in soon. I said what's soon and he said he wasn't sure. I don't know if there's any problem, but I know you work with him."

Hood wondered if Ozburn was headed to the Yuma ATF safe house to complete a hat trick. With two of three houses already hit, Hood thought the chances were good. But the North Baja Cartel had moved its young stars out of the Yuma safe house shortly after Ozburn had hit San Ysidro. Hood had watched them pack up and leave on a live feed to the Buenavista field station. Ozburn couldn't know this for certain, but he'd certainly suspect it. And he'd certainly suspect a Blowdown trap.

"Tell me exactly where the strip is."

"Before I do, I want you to know that the Ozburn I know is a good man."

"You're right about that, Don. Now, tell me where the airstrip is."

Hood scribbled notes on one of Seliah's canvas book bags. He checked his watch—forty minutes from Ogilby if he drove fast. He voice-dialed Janet Bly. She was in the Buenavista field office, half an hour from the Yuma safe house, on her way, over and out. Now feeling solidly in luck, Hood caught Dyman Morris and Robert Velasquez en route to a Quartz gun store, which meant they were about twenty minutes from the Ogilby landing strip. Morris said they'd be there in more like fifteen minutes; then Hood heard the whine of their engine and Velasquez calling *Who let the dogs out*. Frank Soriana in the San Diego field office ordered Hood to join Bly at the Yuma safe house *as fast as humanly possible*. If Ozburn was there, detain him. If he wasn't, park their cars at Smucker Park, two blocks south, then walk back, let themselves into the house, and wait for him. Janet had a key.

Hood figured he was thirty-five minutes from the safe house if he drove hard. He hit his lights and brights and launched the Interceptor south.

Velasquez called him twenty minutes later: no aircraft on or around the Ogilby landing strip. He and Morris had their vehicle tucked out of sight under a stand of greasewood and would hold tight.

Janet called as soon as Hood rang off: She'd cruised the safe house once and it looked unoccupied. She was parked across the street and three houses down, with a good view of it. "There are cars parked all up and down the street," she said. "Any one of them could be Sean's. But I've been here two minutes and he hasn't come out. How long would it take him to see that no one's home—half of that?"

Eleven minutes later Hood exited the interstate, turned off his lights and headed for the Magnolia Street safe house. He drove slowly, irrationally looking into the western sky across which Ozburn would come from Ogilby, as if Ozburn might descend and land *Betty* right on the street.

Hood passed the safe house and saw nothing unusual and no signs of life inside. He remembered the last time he had been there. He was with Sean, helping Velasquez and Bly wire in the surveillence system—three long, hot days of running cable, placing relays, arguing over the best places to hide the cameras and the mikes, building a fake circuit breaker panel to house the controls. Soriana had directed mainly by loitering. Mars had brooded and never lifted a tool. *The good old days*, thought Hood.

Bly stepped from her Jeep as Hood pulled up beside her. She shrugged, shook her head, threw out her hands in frustration before he could even get out of the car. When she stepped back he swung open the door.

"Seliah okay?" she asked.

"She's in a world of hurt, Janet."

"But is she in the coma?"

"She's in the coma."

"What do the doctors say?"

"They're not saying much."

Hood checked the caller and hit the "receive" button.

"Charlie, Dyman here. Sean just buzzed the strip. Yellow Piper Cub, writing under the fuselage, no doubt it's him. He's not in our sight now."

"Ozburn," Hood said to Bly, pushing the speaker icon so she could hear. "How good is your cover?" he asked Morris.

"It's good. We got the black Ford tucked up behind the trees on the east side of the strip. But I don't know what he sees from up there. I can't know that."

"If he's not back in five minutes, he's seen you," said Hood.

"Then he must not have seen us."

"Dyman?"

"Coming back the other way now! There he is, Charlie, yellow as a school bus."

"From the east?"

"Yeah. East. East this time. And what do I got? I got the ass end of the Ford shining in the sun. Here he comes, Charlie, right at us. Man, he's low. Wings are steady. I can hear him now. Coming at us. Coming right directly at us. Sonofa*bitch*ass Ford hanging out of the trees. Oh, man, he's barely a hundred feet up now. Less! Here he comes. He's tilting his wings, Charlie. He's tilting his wings at *us*! Can you hear him? Can you hear that?"

Hood listened to the wail of the Piper as it shot over Morris and Velasquez and roared west.

Hood stared out at the western sky. He opened the door of the Interceptor and let Janet in, then got behind the wheel and shut the door. They sat for a few minutes, eyes up like stargazers.

Hood saw a small aircraft coming in from the west. It was a speck at first, a bird or a child's glider. He tapped the window with his finger and Bly nodded. The speck grew into a plane. It was still too far out for Hood to register color but the flat, one-story city around them gave him all the distance his eyes could handle. He had twenty-ten uncorrected vision as a twelve-year-old and still had it. Then the plane was yellow and it was coming on a line for the safe house, and for Hood and Bly.

"It's him," said Bly. "Is he going to strafe it or something?"

Betty came in at a steady clip and Hood thought of the World War Two movies his father loved. Ozburn buzzed across the sky not much higher than the power poles. Hood pushed his head back against the rest and looked up through the windshield as *Betty* zoomed over them in one roaring pass. The noise of her engine halved when she went over Hood's car, and he heard it diminishing as he looked through his window and saw *Betty* growing smaller in the blue Arizona sky.

"Think he saw us?" asked Bly.

"No. Plenty of other cars in this lot. But he saw Dyman—that was enough."

Betty shrunk, then vanished. Hood swung open his door and stood looking into the sky. Bly talked with Velasquez on her cell. A few minutes later Morris guided the Explorer into the parking lot.

"The guy who called in this tip wanted me to know that Ozburn is a good man," Hood said softly.

"He was, Charlie; then he cracked."

"I feel like we should have seen it coming. Should have done something. We just let him wander off."

"Hey, we didn't put him up to killing five men in six days. Or make him sick. Or make him do crazy stuff."

"But we built the stage and put him on it. We thought we could write the story our way."

"That's too philosophical. You overcomplicate. We're just law enforcers. It's all we are."

Hood had figured on this from Bly but he was already wondering what he would be doing right now if he were Ozburn, if, like Sean, he had worked himself half-crazy during fifteen months undercover among some of the most dangerous people in the world, been purposely infected with a fatal disease, but still felt, truly and deeply in his heart, that there was good he could do on earth and evil he could defeat. And Hood wondered what he'd do if he had a plane and a dog and some guns and a wife to whom he'd innocently given his deadly virus during an act of love, a wife who'd gone into a deep sleep because of it and might not wake up again. If life was a fairy tale, he could just slay a few more dragons and kiss her. That would be enough to bring her out of sleep and they could live happily ever after. Hood wondered when people started telling themselves such stories, and why. The people must have been desperate. The stories were the opposite of helpful. Instead they were flagrantly immaterial and misleading and finally false.

"I want to write a new story," he said.

"You want a happy ending."

"It doesn't have to be happy. Just one where the characters get what they deserve."

"We don't live in fairy tales, Charlie."

31

Ozburn watched the safe house blur and disappear under *Betty*'s nose. His eyes had started doing funny things to him—bright green tracers and extreme perspectives—but he could still make out the red-tile roof of the safe house and the red gravel yard in front. *Later, little amigos*, he thought, *if you haven't all run away yet.*

He eased the aircraft into a gentle climb as he pictured the black Ford ATF Explorer parked under the row of greasewood trees back behind him, shiny as a mirror. He thought bitterly of their foolishness and the treachery of Don August. There was probably more ATF near the house itself, he guessed, waiting to intercept the madman Ozburn. A curse on them all.

An hour later he was circling the strip near Jacumba for the third time, seeing nothing but the red pickup truck he'd been told to look for. A few minutes after that Ozburn was touching down *Betty* to the flat, hard runway.

It was an old smuggler's strip, not a hundred yards from the unfenced border, and he remembered the night, just a couple of years ago, when he and his Blowdown brethren had nailed two gringos with a Beechcraft filled with cash and thirty guns with the serial numbers gouged roughly from their frames. The smugglers were sitting around a small fire on a freezing windy night, smoking dope and waiting for their partners to cross the border with the shipment. Armed with a tip from a good informant, Ozburn and his team had run their vehicles hard through the darkness and rough desert like beings launched from hell, toward the flames of that little fire. The smugglers had simply stood and raised their hands like bad guys in a Western, plumes of breath hanging on their faces. And later Ozburn had entered the strip coordinates on his GPS, for the day when he or one of the Desert Flyers might want to visit Jacumba without paying airport fees or suffering FAA supervision. *Good days*, thought Ozburn. *Days when I believed and acted well. Will there be any more like that?*

He taxied in a wide circle that brought *Betty* to a stop downwind near the red Dodge Ram king cab. He shut down the engine and climbed out and stood unsteadily. It was like his feet were only half there, like the toes had frozen and fallen off. He marshalled his strength and lifted Daisy from her seat to the ground.

She ran to Father Joe Leftwich, who sat on the lowered tailgate of the pickup truck, his priest's clothes traded out for Wranglers and a red yoked cowboy shirt with mother-of-pearl snaps. His cowboy hat was black and broad. He sat with one boot up on the gate while the other dangled well short of the ground, and he leaned an arm on the upraised knee. He had a toothpick in his mouth. He reached into his pocket and tossed Daisy a small biscuit shaped like a bone.

"You just see *Brokeback Mountain*?" asked Ozburn.

"You try wearing the same clothes every day for thirty years."

Leftwich helped Ozburn tie down *Betty* and he stowed Ozburn's heavy duffel across the backseats of the extended truck cab. Ozburn squeezed into the driver's seat and found the control and slid it back. He remembered one of the hundreds of ways in and out of Jacumba, a onetime smuggler's Mecca. DEA pressure had slowed it down for now, but Ozburn knew Jacumba would get hot again just as soon as law enforcement focused on someplace else.

Daisy sat in back, upright and alert. Leftwich offered Ozburn a nip from his ancient battered flask, then took one for himself. Ozburn was pleased as always by its flavor and cool temperature. It hit him hard and fast. It wasn't like other drinks, Ozburn thought. It brought energy and clear thinking and confidence.

"Nice truck," said Ozburn.

"I'm happy to help. And I have a table for us at Amigos, just as you asked. How is Seliah?"

Ozburn looked over Daisy's snout at Father Joe. The priest's face gave off green tracers. "We'll talk about that later."

"But is everything okay?"

"Why wouldn't it be?"

"I don't like the sound of this, Sean."

They sat in a booth at the back of the restaurant, Daisy allowed to join them after Ozburn growled at the manager and Father Joe gave him a fifty-dollar bill. She lay under the table, next to Ozburn's duffel.

Ozburn ordered a Tecate and two shots of *reposado*, Leftwich the same. The waitress brought the drinks and a bowl of water for Daisy. They ordered dinner and when she was gone they toasted with the tequila shots. Ozburn dug two vitamin packs and five aspirin from his pocket and washed them down with beer. Anything to keep the feeling in his feet and the pain from his joints.

Leftwich watched him. "So you visited the Yuma safe house, did you?"

"Not quite. They were expecting me."

Father Joe regarded Ozburn with his usual optimistic expression.

He looked ridiculous in the cowboy hat. "You must have expected that, after your visits to the other two."

Ozburn said nothing.

"Exactly who was expecting you—ATF or the baby assassins?"

Ozburn sipped the tequila and thought about Seliah. He felt his anger stir. His body was aching more now and he wondered if he should increase his vitamins and supplements again. "It was probably Hood. He's the most durable of them."

"Be very cautious if you try again, Sean. Blowdown will be expecting you, and the *sicarios* will either be gone or very jittery."

"I didn't ask you here for advice about Yuma."

"No, of course not," said Father Joe. "Just trying to catch up with your busy life, Sean."

Ozburn waited until the food came and the waitress had left. He looked across the dining room through the bright green tracers at the scattered guests. Even with the sunglasses his eyes stung and watered. His fingertips tingled. He couldn't feel his feet and he wondered if he could stand up right now. He was thirsty but just the sight of the red plastic tumbler of ice water made him nauseous. For the first time in all of this he was feeling the scouts of defeat, stealing up on him for a look into his empty soul. He finished the tequila.

"Father Joe, Seliah is sick and I am, too."

"Sick?"

"Body and soul. Deeply."

"But you look young and strong, Sean."

"Tell me about the bat in your room at the Volcano View, Joe. Tell me the truth or I will become very angry."

Father's Joe's face went stone serious. He lifted off his hat and set it on the padded leather bench beside him. He ran a hand through his short dark hair.

"I don't know what you're talking about."

"The maid found a bat in your room the morning after I fell asleep in your bed. In the bathroom wastebasket. It was a vampire bat and it was alive."

"A maid claimed this?"

"Itixa, the head of housekeeping. Hood went down there. He talked to her."

"There was no bat in my wastebasket unless she herself put it there. I know what I put into my own wastebasket, Sean. Don't you? Rest assured, there was no bat. And I can tell you that Itixa has a passion for beer. She swills the stuff. I saw her unable to walk because of it. And she's widely known around Arenal as a storyteller and a gossip and a woman who has visions."

Ozburn looked at Leftwich, thinking how easy it would be to snap his neck. The priest's face dissolved in a shower of green tracers. "Seliah saw the bat, too."

Leftwich cut into his steak, looking at Ozburn with a questioning expression. "Oh?"

"Yeah, *oh*. She looked through your window screen and you were sitting at the foot of the bed. When I was conked out. You were leaning forward, doing something to my feet with your hands."

"And she's certainly right about that, Sean. But good gracious, I was simply fanning a fly off your toes. Remember what happened to Eduardo? I explained this to Seliah that night. It was an almost absentminded reflex to the bothersome fly. My larger concern was how to wake you up and get you back to your own room so I could get some sleep."

"And when she came into the room you stood up and something dropped into the bedspread that was on the floor. You saw it, too. Remember? You saw it, Father Leftwich. Seliah said you both looked but couldn't find it."

Father Joe swallowed a bite of his steak, nodding, pointing his fork at Ozburn. "I do remember. That part of Seliah's story is accurate also. We found nothing in the bedspread. Nothing under the bed. Nothing at all." Apparently satisfied with this conclusion, Leftwich cut another piece of meat.

"Seliah says that what dropped from your hands was a bat," said Ozburn.

"That's strange, because she said nothing at all about a bat that night. While we searched, we speculated what it could have been and where it could have gone. But it's absolutely impossible that it was a bat. I'll tell you why—because I would never touch a bat with my bare hands. Not in a million years. I fear them."

"Seliah thinks you trapped it in the bedspread, probably crushed it right then and there, and hid it from her."

"But *why*? *For what reason?*"

"Just a little sleight of hand is all it would have taken—late, poor light, Seliah still half-drunk."

Father Joe's face flushed and Ozburn saw the anger in his eyes. The priest set down his knife and fork on the plate and looked at Ozburn. "What does she imagine I did with this alleged bat?"

"She believes you used it to give me rabies. She believes I gave it to her a few weeks later when we made love."

"*Rabies?* You two have rabies, and I caused it? Sean. Sean, what have I ever done to Seliah to give her such a low opinion of me? What have I done to you? Ever?"

"She tested positive for it, Joe. She's in a hospital right now, in a therapeutic coma. They knocked her out and they're hoping she can outlive the virus. She's got just a very small chance of waking up again."

Leftwich leaned back into the booth. His ruddy face went pale. A moment later a tear ran down his face. "This is all wrong. It's terribly and hugely wrong. There was no bat in my room. Did you hear me? *No bat.* Thus, there is *no rabies.*"

Leftwich stared at Ozburn as the tears came. "Sean. You don't know this about me—how could you—but I studied medicine at Trinity College in Dublin before I decided on the priesthood. I did not graduate, but I came close. So I must ask you—who are these doctors? Did you know that very few doctors have even *seen* a case of human rabies? Now, look at you, Sean. You don't look to me like a man with rabies. Rabies tests are complicated and best done postmortem. The presence of antigens is not always conclusive. What if this is just a simple misdiagnosis by inexperienced physicians? Down through the centuries rabies has been one of the most misdiagnosed of human diseases."

Ozburn looked at the priest's face, suspended in a pool of bright green light. Ozburn's legs were numb to his knees and he wondered if it was his posture. With great effort he was able to move his feet apart and he felt a tingle of feeling down in his toes. He felt Daisy next through his boot. What a feeling to have feeling.

"These last seven weeks have been a living hell for us," said Ozburn. "Pain. Anger. Agitation. Fear of water, fear of light. Insane thoughts, insane sensation. How do you diagnose that, Father Joe?"

"Well, let's think it through. I can surmise by your vitamins and aspirins that you're not feeling well. You wear your sunglasses even at night, so I know that you're sensitive to light. What if you and Seliah contracted an unusual strain of influenza down there in the cloud forest? A strain that, as Americans, your immune systems were unprepared to fight off? A good strong influenza infection could certainly explain those symptoms, right? In this country alone flu kills scores of thousands of people every year. And certainly you could have given it to Seliah with something as innocent as a goodnight kiss. Yes?"

Ozburn looked at the priest and resisted the urge to bite him.

"Or, what if . . ." Leftwich sat forward, looked hard at Ozburn and lowered his voice. "What if this rabies tale was *invented* by Hood and Blowdown, to lure you to Seliah's bedside? Remember, Sean, you and Seliah never talked to this maid. Hood claims to have talked to her. And it was Hood who also forced Seliah to the hospital, correct? Where a doctor sympathetic to ATF could easily have manipulated and convinced her. As she has convinced you. Which was easy because you love her."

Ozburn thought he recognized the tapping of truth on the door of his heart. "But Eduardo said you wanted to see the vampire bats."

"That's a lie from Charlie Hood, Sean. I swear to the god of your choosing that I have never seen a vampire bat. I feel faintly amused at hearing myself deliver that line."

Ozburn thought that the rabies story really did sound like something Hood would come up with. "Eduardo took you to a cave to see them."

"That's another lie from Charlie Hood. And again I will swear that I was not shown a cave."

"You could have captured one in the cave and brought it back to the Volcano View."

"Except that I am too cowardly—and too prudent—a man, to ever dream of touching a vampire bat with my bare flesh. Except that I love you and Seliah and I still believe now what I believed in Costa Rica. I believe you two will do great and wonderful deeds on earth."

"*No!*" Ozburn swept his arm across the table, knocking the plates and glasses and silverware to the floor in a clattering, shattering symphony. Daisy bolted from under the table, then stopped and watched her master from a distance. Everyone was looking over. The bartender stood with his hands on his hips and the wait-ress looked up from her order pad and one of the busboys ducked into the kitchen and came right back out with a rolling rack of bus trays.

Ozburn saw all of this outlined in green light. The broken dishes glowed like emeralds. The room began rotating clockwise, slowly, like a great kaleidoscopic mural. He leaned close to Leftwich and hissed into his face. "I don't believe in our God in heaven anymore. I tore him to bits and scattered him to the Mexican wind. Seliah is gone and I am alone. I don't want to do great and wonderful deeds. Shove them up your ass and up the ass of your gutless God."

Ozburn felt his heart break again, like the feeling he'd had when Seliah drove away in her red Mustang. He looked into Father Joe's eyes. Green embers. Ozburn felt the priest's hand on his wrist.

"No words can make me sadder than those, my son. None. You have crushed my heart and I am in anguish for you."

Ozburn rose and leaned over the table and clamped a hand on Father Joe's cowboy shirt. He lifted him up and threw him against the wall behind the booth. Leftwich hit with a loud huff and fell to the booth bench like something suddenly deflated. A painting of calla lilies slid off the wall and crashed to the floor. Father Joe came to rest approximately where he had been seated before. His eyes were wide and welling and he fought to catch his breath. It took a moment. Then he wiped the cuff of his Western shirt across his eyes.

"You're a strong one, Oz."

"You've ruined us. All of you."

"No bat. No virus. This is not a time for superstition and specu-lation. It is time for the cold light of reason. It is up to you to carry on, Sean, despite your wild fears. Rise to your task or you will be destroyed."

Ozburn stared down at Father Joe for a long moment. He was a little surprised that he could still do something like this. He felt his feet going numb on him again. Then Ozburn looked up at the busboy who would not approach, and at the bartender still glaring at him, and into the faces of the guests, men and women amazed at what they were seeing, at the cooks peering over from the kitchen, at the waitress whose face was filled with fear and sympathy.

Ozburn pulled out his wallet and took out five hundreds and dropped them on the table. He picked up Father Joe's cowboy hat and slapped it back onto the priest's head. "I'll still need your help on Monday."

"You shall have it. You're a good man, Sean Ozburn. I wish you would believe it, as I so strongly believe."

Ozburn pulled the duffel from under the table and slung it over one big shoulder. Snapping his fingers for Daisy, he strode across the dining room and into the entryway. He stumbled on his unfeeling feet and nearly knocked over a woman who had just entered the building. She was dark-haired and singularly pretty and wore a red dress with white polka dots that looked to be from another era. She had a black coat folded over one arm.

"Madam," Ozburn managed, dizzied by her scent.

"Excuse me," she answered without slowing down.

The Amigos manager stood behind the counter at the cash register with a look of indignation on his face.

"I left five hundred to cover the dinner and the damage," said Ozburn.

"I hope that covers it. Do not come back here."

"I'm sorry for the spectacle. I didn't want it to happen."

"This is a family restaurant."

Ozburn leaned over the counter and he saw, even in his green vision, a blush of fear on the man's face. Ozburn bared his teeth at him.

He swung open the door and looked back across the dining room at Leftwich, who was holding the black coat belonging to the pretty woman as she waited for the busboy to ready the booth. They looked like a pair from central casting: the dude ranch cowboy and a forties femme fatale. The woman was speaking to Joe, sharply it looked, and the small cowboy-priest had the coat over his arm and a hapless expression on his face.

In the parking lot Ozburn hit the Ram key fob and swung open the truck door. Daisy sprang into the driver's seat, then hopped over the center console to the passenger side. Ozburn threw open the half door and climbed into the rear part of the cab and set the duffel out across the bench.

"Back here, girl," he said. Daisy obeyed, curling into the floor space between the seats.

From his duffel Ozburn took both of his Love 32s, loaded with full magazines, and set them on the front passenger seat. He took two extra full magazines and set them up front next to the weapons. He tossed a windbreaker over them all. He zipped and yanked the duffel back down to the floor, which gave Daisy plenty of room to stretch out on the rear bench. She did so, thumping her tail.

"Just in case, sweetie. You never know who you'll run into on the road."

At the sound of his voice Daisy's tail thumped harder and faster. Ozburn shut the rear door and climbed up front and started the engine. He roared out of the parking lot for Interstate 8, his foot with little feeling in it and heavy on the accelerator.

32

Hood sat in his dining room with the American League division series muted on TV, reading online stories about bats, rabies and the Milwaukee Protocol. An October wind bent the white sagebrush outside and rattled the paloverde and his windows. He was tired from the day but very much looking forward to a visit from Beth Petty, who was coming over after her four-to-midnight ER shift. He hadn't seen her since the Buenavista safe house massacre twelve days ago. He had bought good wine and a light dinner to prepare.

Hood was fascinated to learn that the vampire legends originating in eighteenth-century Eastern Europe followed a major rabies outbreak there in 1720. The author, Spanish neurologist Juan Gomez-Alonso, pointed out that rabies victims have symptoms very similar to the traits often attributed to vampires. He wrote that because the virus attacks the limbic system, which is a part of the brain that influences aggression and sexual behavior, rabies victims—like vampires—are prone to biting and to hypersexuality. And because rabies also affects the hypothalamus, which controls sleep, people with rabies suffer—as do vampires—from insomnia and become energized and agitated late at night. The doctor pointed out that rabies causes hypersensitivy to strong stimuli such as light, bright reflection and strong odors—including garlic—all of which appeared early in the vampire legends. He pointed out that rabies victims commonly vomit blood, and of course, an over-full vampire could be expected to do the same. Most obviously, Gomez-Alonso pointed out, both rabies and vampirism are most commonly spread by biting.

Hood took a sip of beer and checked his watch. A gust of wind rose outside, and in the island of light cast by his security floods he saw the desert sand stand up and take a human shape and travel a few feet toward the house before collapsing. As a child, he had been more frightened by vampire movies than by other horror movies. They had seemed more possible, and a vampire could appear to be normal—a threat that could walk unrecognized among us.

Tapping at his keyboard now, Hood brought up the picture that he had e-mailed to Sean just minutes after Seliah had gone into the coma. In the picture she looked fresh and lovely and relaxed but Hood knew she'd been blasted into unconsciousness by drugs. He'd hoped that the picture might help persuade Sean to surrender himself. He'd promised Ozburn that if he did surrender, their first stop would be UCI Medical Center. Hood had also told Ozburn that Seliah had given him some things she wanted Sean to have. Again, a lure. But there was only silence from Ozburn. Hood wondered if Oz might be shamed or infuriated by the picture and by Hood's proximity to her. Who could know?

He called the nurses' station at the ICU and got Marliss. She told him there was no change; Seliah's vitals were all good.

"The doctor will let you know when she'll be brought out of it," she said. "It will be days, Mr. Hood. They will taper her off of the sedatives when the rabies is over. And she will come back. Very slowly."

He asked if she could hear what was going on around her, down in a sleep that deep.

"No," said Marliss. "She's not aware of anything at all. Nothing. Are you in law enforcement?"

"Yes."

"Her husband called a few minutes ago. He sounded very agitated and angry. He said if she dies, terrible things will happen. We reported it to hospital security as we were told."

"Is the marshal still there?"

"Oh, yes. There is supposed to be a marshal twenty-four/seven. He looks bored to tears."

Hood called Soriana at home and told him about Ozburn's threat and asked him to put another U.S. Marshal outside Seliah's room. Soriana was quiet for a beat, then said he would.

Back on his computer Hood looked at a pictorial of vampire bats in the wild. A camera crew had gotten video and stills of a cave filled with them. The scientists all looked happy to be there but the local guides looked spooked and guilty. One of them held out a vampire bat by its wingtips while the animal bared its teeth and hissed. One ran along the bottom of the cave floor upright on its feet, wings half-out for balance, its tiny chest strangely human, its face piggish. *Vampire bats almost always approach their prey on the ground*, Hood read. *They are nimble runners.*

Hood pictured the priest leaning forward over Sean's feet and Seliah at the window screen with the moths and beetles and flies seething around her. He pictured the priest standing when he became aware of her, and Hood saw the small dark thing drop from his hands as he turned to open the door for her. He pictured Sean asleep through all of this, ignorant that the seeds of his and Seliah's destruction had just been introduced to his innocent blood. Again, Hood heard the voice of skepticism commenting on these images and this story. *A priest with a vampire bat in his hands? Come on, Charlie, could this have happened? Isn't there a simpler explanation for what had fallen to the floor and what had happened to Sean and Seliah? How truthful was superstitious, heavy-drinking Itixa?*

He checked his e-mail and found another communication from one of the German bird-watchers who had stayed at the Volcano View back in July, at the same time as the Ozburns. So far, six of them had responded to his inquiries about Father Joe Leftwich, specifically, pictures of the man, but none had taken a picture of him and none knew anything at all about where he might have gone.

Dear Mr. Hood,

I am sorry to report that I did not speak often with Father Joe Leftwich. He was a talkative man and often engaged in conversation. He was provocative in subtle ways and made some people angry. But he had a great curiosity about birds and bird-watching. Being Irish he knew that the English call birders 'twitchers.' I have gone through my many digital images of that trip and I have some unforgettable pictures of the trogons, but no pictures of this man. I am sorry I am not able to help.

Sincerely,
Heinz Tossey

Hood looked outside to see another dirt devil spinning through the security lights. He wrote a thank-you e-mail to Heinz, then lay his head back on the couch top and looked up at the beam ceiling of the old home and listened to the wind outside; then he closed his eyes.

When he opened them the baseball game was over and his beer was warm and his screen saver had long since engaged. The wind had gotten stronger. The telephone vibrated against his hip at eleven forty-five—Beth saying she'd be an hour late at least, so sorry, an extra-busy night again, an attempted suicide and a burn victim. She sounded upset and Hood took the phone into the kitchen, which was better protected against the wind.

"I was really looking forward to you," she said.

"I miss you a lot. You hang in there, Beth. I'm going have some dinner and wine ready for you."

"I want you first."

"I won't argue that, Beth." Hood liked saying her name out loud. She was easy to imagine—lovely, tall, dirty-blond, chocolate-eyed. She was goofy and self-unimpressed. Hood leaned against the big butcher block and looked through the window over the sink, out to the silver-rimmed mountains in the east. There in the lee side of the house grew a grapefruit tree and Hood could see the big yellow orbs swaying in the wind.

"I hate this job sometimes," she said. "I mean, I love-hate it. If I went to days, I could see my guy more than once in a while, but then you'd get sick of me."

"Fat chance of that, Doc. But your guy has been plenty busy, too, so don't blame everything on you. Just get here when you can."

"I'm there. I'm so there, Charlie."

Suddenly, behind him and out of sight, the front door blew open. It was a heavy mahogany-and-iron affair and Hood heard it whack into the wrought-iron hat rack, then heard the hat rack crash to the entryway tile with a metallic twang. It was not the first time this had happened.

"What was that, Charlie?"

"Hold on."

Hood went to the kitchen pass-through and looked out. The wind hurled a blast of sand through the open door and blew the hats that had spilled off the rack across the foyer and into the living room. Some slid and some tumbled end over end.

"Just the wind." He came around and out of the kitchen, walking across the living room for the front door. He could feel the cold wind hit him. He hooked a Stetson with one boot toe and flung it up into the cold front and caught it midair.

"You get wind," said Beth. "I get paramedics on a code three with a gunshot suicide attempt. Gotta go."

"Okay, Beth."

Hood put the Stetson on his head and held the cell phone in one hand and pushed the door closed with the other. He was surprised how strong the wind was and when he looked out at the vast desert before him he saw the ocotillo swaying and the cholla quivering like lambs' tails in the moonlight and the blink of stars in the wind, as if they were squinting into it.

He slid the dead bolt home and put his phone back in its hip case, then tilted the hat rack upright. He looked where the rack had hit the wall and there was a new impression there, and not the first. The old bevel and latch plate were worn smooth and the heavy door was prone to this. *Another fix*, he thought. The old adobe was full of them.

Hood set out collecting the hats. He put on his favorite Borsalino fedora over the Stetson, then a nice Panama on top of that; then he got his Dodgers, Angels and Padres ball caps in one hand and a canvas breezer in the other and carried them back into the foyer for the rack. He set them back one at a time, thinking of Beth.

When he walked back into the living room Sean Ozburn was

standing back in the darkness in the far corner, two Love 32s slung over his shoulders and aimed in Hood's direction.

"I was standing on your porch and the door opened," he said. "I took it as an invitation."

"Sean."

"Slide your Colt across the floor to me."

"The whole rig is in the kitchen, by the coffee machine."

"Then the AirLite on your ankle."

Hood took a knee and slid the revolver slowly from the holster on his left ankle, backhanding it across the tile to Ozburn like a shuffleboard puck. It clattered and spun to a stop. Hood failed to mention the two-shot .40-caliber derringer he carried in a tiny canvas holster on his right calf, just above the sock. He packed the ankle cannon on days he thought he might need it, and he had carried it twelve days running now. It was passably accurate within ten feet but would stop a man cold.

He opened his hands to Ozburn and stood. "How do they fire, the Loves?"

"Extremely well. The sound suppressors are ingenious—Ron Pace uses steel wool and aerosol foam inside the fiberglass tube, so they're sponges acoustically, and super light. You can hardly hear these things, just the shells feeding in and spitting out. They clack like a child's plastic machine gun."

"Where's Daisy?"

"Out in the truck watching our stuff."

Hood studied him. Ozburn let go one of the guns and pushed his sunglasses up onto his head. He studied Hood back, swaying slightly like a man just off a boat. "Good to see you, Charlie."

Ozburn looked leaner and paler than the biker-surfer-snowboarder who had essentially vanished undercover fifteen months ago. His hair was longer and his gunslinger's mustache was trimmed. His well-muscled body had always filled out his clothes, which he had worn snug in admitted vanity, but now the leather vest had some slack in the chest and his badass leather pants looked a size too big. Back from the crags of Ozburn's face his eyes stared, blue and cool, and in them, even at this distance, Hood saw something haunted. Ozburn growled softly, then rolled one big shoulder up and wiped his mouth on the leather vest.

"That was a shitty thing, sending me a picture of Seliah like that," he said.

"I hoped you'd see it and just give yourself up."

"Well, I'm not. And it was shitty of you tricking her into the hospital that first time, too. I've thought of punishing you for it. I should."

"You wouldn't if you'd seen her that night. She was mean and crazy. She was dangerous to herself. She scared the hell out of me, Sean."

"So you say. Maybe you did the right thing. But maybe you staged this whole thing to get me to surrender. The whole thing, start to finish."

"That's not rational."

"Rational means nothing after the things I've done and seen."

"I didn't stage Arenal or Father Joe or the wound to your toe. I didn't stage Seliah's symptoms, or yours. I didn't stage the tests they gave her. It's all real, Sean—everything she told you. Nothing has been faked or staged. You just spent three days with her—was she the woman you used to know? Answer me. Was she?"

Ozburn lowered the machine pistols and walked across the living room toward Hood. Gone was his easy athletic grace, replaced by a heavier, more conscious gait. He sat in a faux cowhide swivel chair, one of two that had come with the rental. He let one of the weapons dangle to his side on its sling and the other he rested across his lap, hand still on the grip, finger still inside the trigger guard. He nodded toward the other chair, which sat opposite across a big, tattered Navajo rug that looked two hundred years old. Hood walked to the chair and sat.

"No," said Ozburn. "She's not the woman I knew. I'll admit there's something wrong with both of us. Big wrong. The list of ailments goes on and on. The latest is, I can't feel my feet sometimes. And sometimes, I can't feel anything below my knees. Can't walk or even stand when that happens. Don't get any big ideas, Hood, because they feel just fine right now. And everything I see is green. You're green right now. The whole house, the whole world."

"Well, no shit, Oz—your nervous system is filled with the rabies virus. So is hers."

Ozburn wiped his face with his free hand, and when his hand passed over his eyes they were still fixed on Hood. "Okay. Okay. I've thought this through, Charlie. Whether what you say is true or not, Seliah is where she belongs right now. She can make it. She's strong and good."

"And you?"

"I'm right where I belong, too. I chose this path and I'm staying on it. I'm going to deliver ninety of these Loves to Blowdown. And you're going to take down some nasty Mara Salvatruchas in L.A. and a hundred and fifty-seven grand in cash. It'll be the best bust I've ever made. It's the proof of my training and my skill and my value. It's the reward for the last fifteen months. It justifies what I've become. After that? Well, I'm not spending the rest of my life in prison for taking out a few of our enemies. You wouldn't. Which brings me to a proposal."

"Propose, Sean."

"Why should I surrender? ATF needs me now more than ever. I do things you regular agents won't do. I've crossed every line that can be crossed except for one—I've stayed loyal to my cause and my people. If I know Soriana, he hasn't gone upstairs with those videos of me in action. He can't afford the fact that one of his best special agents has gone upriver and taken out some bad guys. If that got public, it would damage ATF. Badly. Soriana knows this. So, tell him to destroy the videos and fire me. They'll have to put me on a cash payroll but they'll never see me again. You'll be my contact. We'll talk in the ether. I can nurse Seliah back to health. For ATF, I'll be the guy who does what it takes for you to win. I'll be the black agent. When you need to cut a deal with the devil, you send in Oz. Makes sense, doesn't it? Doesn't it, Charlie?"

Hood considered. The wind rushed the house and the sand ticked at the windows. He looked at Ozburn in the lamplight of the living room and saw a dead man. "It makes no sense that I can see."

"Tell Soriana."

"I'll tell him."

"I've got some interesting news. Herredia wants to deliver the guns to me in California."

Hood thought about this. "Why?"

"El Tigre says the U.S. is safer than Mexico. He'll use his drug supply lines to move the weapons. He must feel solid in California."

"After two safe houses get blitzed?"

"I'm not complaining," said Ozburn. "Saves me a run from south to north with ninety new machine guns in my truck. I'm taking it as good luck."

Hood was caught short at the blunt irony of this: guns going not south, but north. Guns made in Mexico by an American businessman. Was the union now complete? Were they one now, the United States and Mexico, joined and made identical by drugs, money and guns?

"When?"

Ozburn stared into his face for a long beat. "None of your concern, Charlie. I'll deliver the guns to the Gulf people sometime after. That's when Blowdown sweeps in. That's when I give myself up to you. If that's what ATF wants."

"I'm supposed to believe that?"

Ozburn looked at Hood for a long moment. "A deal's a deal, Charlie. Don't you forget that. I'll e-mail or call you when I've got the units."

Hood heard the wind rise up outside and saw the ocotillo shivering in the moonlight.

"Why did you come here, Sean?"

"I want my things from Seliah."

"There are two bags in the extra bedroom. Foot of the bed."

Ozburn stood. "Let's get them. You go first. Move slow, Charlie. I'm feeling kind of hyped up right now and I'd hate to have an accident."

"Roger."

Hood led the way to the hall, flicked on the light, and walked to the first bedroom. He turned on a light there, too, and stepped in. There was a loaded revolver under the bed pillow but the pillow was a long way away and Hood wasn't sure what he'd do with it. He went to the foot of the bed and took a bag in each hand, then turned to face Ozburn.

"Good, Charlie. Back out slow now and we'll go back in the living room."

Ozburn stepped aside and let Hood go back down the hallway ahead of him. Hood held up a heavy reusable shopping bag and set it next to Ozburn's chair. "Here are your guns."

"Excellent."

"Then, also . . ."

Hood took a knee and brought out the items one at a time and set them on the floor: the ring boxes first, then the bundle of love letters, the journal. He hesitated on the items that Seliah had given to him to keep, but only for a moment, then set them out, too. "And here's a bottle of wine she was saving for a special occasion, and Daisy the horse and Betty the doll, and the pressed leaves in this book, and a lock of your hair. She wanted those last things scattered with her ashes if she doesn't come through this."

Ozburn stared at the things for a long moment. "Okay. Well. I never thought . . . this."

"I can have you up to UCI Medical Center in a little over two hours, Oz. They'll knock you out, too, and try to let you fight off the virus. You'll be with her."

"And if I'm lucky enough to live through that, it's off to prison for this fine agent. No, thanks, Charlie. I won't do that. And I've got a job to finish."

"I hope you're clear on this, Oz. You've got a lethal virus multiplying itself in your brain. You're going to die very soon if you don't let those doctors treat you."

"Clear."

Ozburn waved Hood away with one of the guns, then picked up the two ring boxes. He opened them both, then closed them and tossed them one at a time to Hood. "If Seliah doesn't make it, make sure these rings go with her ashes. I've got no use for them without her to wear them."

Outside the wind lashed the house. In between gusts coyotes yipped from the dark distance. Ozburn knelt and swept Seliah's offerings into the bag with his big hands, going strictly by feel as he stared at Hood. When he was done he swung one of the machine pistols to his side and picked up both bags with one hand. He lifted the back of his gun hand to his face and wiped a rope of saliva from his chin. He bared his teeth at Hood and growled. Hood looked at

Ozburn's horrific face. Then movement outside caught his eye and he saw the lights of Beth Petty's car coming up the rough gravel road.

"Company," said Ozburn. "You didn't hit a panic button, did you?"

"It's Beth."

"That right? I'd like to meet her, Charlie."

"Gotta stay on your good behavior, Oz."

"Never lecture a man with two machine guns."

"She's innocent of all this."

"So was Seliah. God, I miss her. You wouldn't believe how much good old-fashioned lust builds up when you got whatever in hell I have."

"I read that."

"Seliah tell you about it?"

"No."

"I thought she might have been coming on to you the night you put her in handcuffs."

"She put herself in them, Sean."

"Like Juan Batista."

"Like him, yes."

"The sex is like nothing you ever felt. It goes from pleasure to pain to something much bigger and stronger. You can't get enough. There isn't any word for that feeling. I can't even describe it."

Hood watched the headlight beams swing across the window glass and go out. He saw Beth, wrapped in her long knit sweater coat, a brown bag in the crook of one arm, coming up the walkway toward the front door.

"She's pretty," said Ozburn. He turned to watch her, gun in one hand and the bags in the other. His breathing got faster and in a smooth, quick motion Hood raised his right knee and slipped the derringer from its home, then quietly set his right foot down again.

"I'm going walk past you to the door and open it for her," said Hood. "I'll make the introduction."

Ozburn continued to stare out the window and Hood heard the rattling wet inhale of his breath as he passed behind the man. Ozburn swung around, the silenced machine gun pointed at Hood's middle.

"Hold your fire, Sean," said Hood. "I'm a friend, remember?"

Hood stepped to the door. He was between Beth and Ozburn now, the derringer cupped in his right hand and held firm by his thumb. He let her knock, then swung open the door with his free hand and cocked the hammer into the gust.

"Finally!" Beth stepped in and threw an arm around Hood's neck and kissed him. He broke it off quickly and put his mouth to her fragrant ear.

"Beth. There's someone behind me. Don't be afraid. But if anything happens, run outside into the darkness and don't stop. I'll come to you."

"*What?*"

He felt her body tense and he drew her by her hand into the foyer and pushed shut the door, then turned and presented Beth Petty to Sean Ozburn.

"Pleased to meet you," she said cheerfully. "Nice guns!"

Ozburn stared at her. "You are an unbearable pleasure to my eyes."

"That's the nicest thing I've heard all day." She glanced at Hood and offered her hand to Ozburn. Hood's heart was pounding.

Ozburn set down the bag, took Beth's hand lightly, bowed and kissed it. Then he let go of the gun and closed his other hand over hers and smiled at her. "You're mine now and I'll never let you go."

"Well, don't tell *him*, but I'm kind of Charlie's for the time being."

"I was the best of them once."

"Oh?"

Ozburn pulled her closer and leaned into her, head tilted, nose to her temple, then her ear, then her neck. A thick ribbon of saliva swayed from his chin.

Beth looked at Hood, the fear bright in her eyes. Then she made a graceful tangolike turn that left her sweater coat half-on and half-off and Ozburn no gentleman's choice at all. He took the brown bag from her and held the coat so she could slide out of it.

Palming the derringer, Hood stepped between them and accepted the coat from Ozburn, which left the concealed weapon pointed roughly at Ozburn's heart.

"It was good seeing you, Sean. You're a true and good friend. We need to talk again. Soon, but not now."

"*Unbearable.*" Ozburn wiped his chin on the back of a fist and looked ashamedly at Beth, then Hood. "I am sorry."

"Here are the treasures from Seliah."

Ozburn took up the bag. "Thank you. Remember to talk to Soriana about my proposal."

Hood stood in the doorway and watched him walk into the wind. Ozburn stopped and turned and Hood knew that at this range he was defenseless against Ozburn's weapons. Ozburn saluted him, then lowered his sunglasses and continued on, looking back once, then continuing down the driveway to the road. Hood saw the glint of glass and metal in the distance. Beth came up next to him. Hood watched Ozburn make his way down the gravel road. He stopped once and waited, then walked on. A moment later the interior lights of a vehicle came on and Hood could make out a red pickup truck. A dark shape moved back and forth inside the cab.

Ozburn opened the door and climbed in. The interior lights went out and the brights shot to life. A moment later Ozburn hooked a U-turn and sped down the road and out of sight, his dust a faint contrail rising in the darkness.

"I'm not sure what we just avoided," said Beth. "But I think it could have been very, very bad." She held his arm in both hands and Hood could feel her trembling.

"We can't stay here," said Hood. "But I'll take you to the very finest motel in Buenavista."

"How about my place?"

"Better."

"You've got a story to tell me."

"Do I ever."

While Beth packed up the dinner provisions from the refrigerator Hood called Soriana, Bly, Morris and Velasquez.

He drove them to Beth's home in his vehicle, his Colt unholstered and secure between his thigh and the seat. He didn't think Ozburn would change his mind and try something, but Hood wanted Beth Petty in his sight. He watched the rearview attentively and took an elaborate route before rolling to a stop inside her garage and waiting for the garage door to close behind them. When it clunked into silence Hood felt a flutter of relief.

Hood hugged her but did not close his eyes as he wanted to, and he kept his ears tuned to the sounds of the night around him.

"It's okay, Charlie. He's gone."

33

Ozburn woke up in a motel room with disjointed memories of how he got there. He remembered Hood's house. Wind and a pretty woman. Flying *Betty* through the cool, clear night. A young Mexican man who would watch over *Betty* for a modest price. A beaten, once-silver Mercury courtesy of Father Joe. Meeting Paco in a bar and collecting the remaining eighty-seven thousand, five hundred dollars for final payment on the Love 32s and later giving him the first ten guns right here in this motel room. *No wonder I'm exhausted*, he thought. He propped himself up against the headboard and took stock.

Daisy was curled up at the foot of his bed, eyes on him, tail thumping against the spread. His duffel was on the floor, brimming with money, right where he had put it. His vision was clear and not colored with green. He showered and put on clean clothes and left a disappointed Daisy to guard the fort.

He stepped out of the lobby and into the tourist zone of Nogales, Mexico. He recognized it immediately. Just across the border from Arizona, the narrow streets jammed with cars and pedestrians, bars and restaurants, curio vendors presiding over acres of wood carvings and colorful pottery and leather purses and boots and belts and blankets hanging brightly in the sunlight.

He took some video on his Flip, then had the proprietor shoot him as he picked out a dozen wooden flutes painted in scintillant pinks and yellows and purples, twelve leather purses, twelve pairs of huaraches with soles made of old car tires, like numbers of assorted earrings and necklaces possibly containing turquoise, and a dozen tooled leather wallets. He examined the many small wooden crucifixes arranged neatly in a display case, remembering the surge of strength he used to feel at such a sight and comparing it with the blankness he now felt. But he bought twelve anyway, each with its leather necklace. He overpaid the woman and thanked her effusively for taking the video.

He bought breakfast burritos and *sopadillas* from a street cart and ate them standing up outside an art gallery, looking through the window at the paintings inside—Madonnas and calla lilies and peasants done in the style of Rivera. His feet began to tingle then lose feeling so he ate faster. When he was done he hoisted up his plastic bags and walked back across to the cart and got Daisy *carnitas* wrapped to go in tinfoil.

An hour later they set off in the old Mercury heading south on Highway 15. Near Cibuta he pulled off the road where a group of schoolchildren waited for their bus. He covered the machine guns on his front seat with the bags of curios, then got out and gave the children the flutes. They accepted the gifts happily and Ozburn tried to say a prayer for them but he couldn't think of anything to say and they seemed puzzled by his words. When he pulled away he heard musical notes and laughter rising up behind the car in spirited chaos and he believed he had touched the children in some good way.

He drove through the rough country, his mind fixed on Seliah, trying to find her in the depths of her unconsciousness. Was she thinking? Did she feel? He imagined her in the hospital bed, nurses and doctors hovering above her, her pale beauty arrested in sleep, Seliah an object to them, a hope, a possibility given certain odds. What could he do?

In Imuris he stopped and approached the group of old men who were sitting in the meager shade offered by the eaves of the mini-super that stood adjacent to the dirt town square. They squinted wordlessly at him but when Ozburn struck up a conversation in decent Spanish they were happy to tell him that no, they knew of no airstrip; no, they had not seen any *narco* activity at all lately; no, there was almost no rain last season but the government said maybe more this year. He said he might go check the airstrip himself, the one they didn't know of. They laughed. He gave them the huaraches and wallets and they smiled, some toothlessly, others with the great white teeth that seemed to follow so many Mexican men into old age.

At the bakery he found some women and girls but they were suspicious of him and hardly answered his Spanish. He bought some pastries and bottled water and gave them some of the purses and jewelry and some of the crucifixes.

Outside of Imuris he turned east on a dirt road. He had driven it six months before on an undercover meth buy that had strengthened his standing with some low-level players in Carlos Herredia's North Baja Cartel. Ozburn had been treated disrespectfully by a gigantic one-eared cartel enforcer and it was last night's dream of this man that brought him here now. The road was rough and narrow but firm enough to buoy the heavy, low-slung car. Rounding a curve he could see the airstrip and the cinder-block building with the tin roof and the window frames with the glass long smashed out and the smugglers' trailers baking in the sun. There were no vehicles in sight and Ozburn scanned the rocky peaks of the hills for lookouts but he saw no movement except for three vultures circling in the thermals high above.

He kicked in the door of the cinder-block building and lowered both Love 32s but the place was empty. There were old sofas and folding chairs and a television with rabbit ears tipped in tinfoil. The fireplace was black and there were food cans tossed on the floor among the mattresses and old blankets and mouse turds. Daisy investigated. Ozburn stood approximately where he had been searched by the enforcer's men and he remembered the roughness of it and their insults and the terrible serrated edge of flesh where the man's ear had been detached. He looked over at the slouching plywood countertop where he had laid out five thousand dollars in ATF buy money to cover the methamphetamine. He stood in the doorway and watched the road and the rocky hills for approaching *narcos* but saw none. He hoped that his dangerous questions to the old men would result in a quick phone call as soon as he left them, so he sat with his machine guns crossed on his lap on a rickety wooden chair outside in the shade and waited.

By midafternoon no one had arrived so Ozburn drove south, then west to Atil where he found a two-track that he had also once traveled on a quad vehicle with a college buddy, ostensibly on a quest for a hot spring they had been told attracted beautiful Mexican girls who bathed naked and were sexually loose. They never found the hot spring or any girls at all, but Ozburn did remember an oasis where clear, cool water flowed up from the rocks and formed a pool beneath a cluster of greasewood trees and fan palms.

Here he spread a blanket in the shade and sat with Daisy beside him. He faced away from the pool because the sight of water would cause his muscles to cramp as if hit with an electrical charge. He began to get hungry and with the hunger came the aches in his body and the cursed green tint to his vision and the frightening numbness to his feet. He ate some of the pastries, oddly flavorless, then removed his bandana and dipped it in the cold water without looking at the pool and lay back on the blanket and covered his eyes, sunglasses and all.

He listened to the thumping of his heart and felt the downward pull of sleep and when he awakened and peeled off the almost-dry bandana, three men stood across from him on the other side of the small pool. A green sun hovered behind them. They wore jeans and hoodies and he couldn't see their faces. Daisy growled and Ozburn growled, too. He found the Love 32 with one hand and swung it up and at them. The tallest one, in the middle, raised a hand, as if calming Ozburn.

"Can I help you?" Ozburn asked. His voice sounded to him like a croak.

The middle man nodded to the west. Then he turned and walked away in that direction, one fellow on either side.

Ozburn clambered around the pool after them, his feet dead and clumsy. He dropped the machine pistol and it landed hard on the rocks but he picked it up and slung the strap over his shoulder. Daisy easily caught them, touching her sensitive black nose to their legs, tail down and not wagging. They stopped and let Ozburn approach. He came to within a few yards and studied them. The sun was still at their backs and their faces were lost in the folds of the hoods and he couldn't tell who they were—Mexicans, Americans— they might have been Inuits or Swedes for all he could see.

"If you repent, Seliah will live," said the tallest one.

Ozburn felt his anger spike. He was long past trying to suppress it. He felt the trigger against his finger. "Repent for what?"

"The faith you have abandoned. The lives you have taken."

"How can you find faith where there is none?"

"In your heart."

"It's empty. And what can my repentance do for the lives I have taken?"

"It can save your wife."

"You know nothing of Seliah."

"She is in the hospital in California. Don't doubt us. Don't make yourself smaller to us. You spit on the face of God. His mercies are small and easily withdrawn. Ours are even smaller."

"Who are you?"

"Representatives."

"What guarantee do I have that Seliah will survive?"

"There is no power higher than the word."

"Pull down the hoods. All three of you."

"If you repent, Seliah will live."

"Let me see your faces!" None of the three moved so Ozburn pulled the trigger and swept the Love 32 across them but only one shot fired. He heard the round spit and felt the recoil and saw the quick dimple form on the sweatshirt of the man on the left. A stomach shot. The man didn't so much as flinch. Rather he tilted his head down as if for a look at it, then turned his face back up at Ozburn. Ozburn felt for the extended fifty-shot magazine but it was gone. He looked back to where he had dropped the gun and saw the magazine, faintly green and luminescent, shining upon the rocks.

When he turned back the men were gone and Daisy was crisscrossing the ground where they had stood, nose lowered for scent, tail wagging hopefully. Ozburn labored up the nearest rise and from here he looked out on the vast, barren desert, unpeopled and motionless. He folded to his knees and sat slumped amidst the rocks and asked God to return his faith but he felt no return of it, just the ocean of dark urges moving inside him. And he repented to God his several murders but even as he did this there was a voice inside him, speaking more quietly than the voice with which he called to God, and it said, *The brutes deserved it, the brutes deserved it, they deserved to be exterminated.*

Backtracking to the Imuris airstrip, Ozburn parked short of a hillock and left Daisy in the car and climbed to the top. In the wavering green distance he could see the airstrip and the building and the black SUV parked nearby and the huge one-eared enforcer sitting in the shade just has he had done. Teodoro, Ozburn remembered. Teodoro "El Gigante" Caborca. Another *sicario* stood beside him, eyeing the landscape, a weapon slung over one shoulder. The door that Ozburn had kicked in swung in and out with the breeze. Ozburn slid down the hillside to his car and made sure the two Love 32s had full magazines; then he locked the car and hiked around to the south side of the cinder-block building, which was tucked against the rocky hills.

It took almost an hour. The feeling in his legs came and went. The numbness was climbing him now, almost to his hips. He was sweating hard. Daisy panted and stayed a few yards behind, never venturing ahead. She seemed to know the difference between playing and working, and Ozburn was impressed by her intuitions.

When Ozburn finally settled behind a boulder for a concealed look he could see that the enforcer's SUV was still parked where it had been. He could hear music spilling out from the building, then laughter. When he had caught his breath Ozburn picked his way down the hill on a game trail and soon he was pressed up against the back of the building, Daisy at his feet, a machine pistol ready in each hand.

He quietly picked his way along the perimeter. The music was a *narcocorrido* and the voices were of three men. He heard a beer can spit open. When he came to a window he motioned Daisy to stay, then ducked beneath it and sidled past. Rising to a crouch he hustled around the corner, then snuck beneath another window and stopped just short of the open front doorway. Laughter and an accordion. Laughter and profanities. Another can popping open. Daisy had broken her stay and now came crawling around the corner on her stomach, ears down in penance and an apologetic look on her face. *Repentance*, thought Ozburn. *You want repentance— watch this.*

Ozburn motioned her again to stay; then, guns up, he burst through the door for the second time that day.

All three men stared at him in disbelief. Two had beers in their hands instead of weapons. El Gigante sat hugely on one of the battered old couches and Ozburn knew that he could shoot both of the beer-drinking bad guys before their leader could get off the couch, and he saw that Teodoro knew it, too.

He ordered the two men to their knees and they took their positions with doomed expressions on their faces. One bowed his head and prayed. Ozburn ordered Teodoro to join them and he tracked the big man's slow movements with one of the Love 32s. Teodoro finally righted himself and lumbered toward Ozburn. When the big man came abreast of his comrades he did not kneel but instead lunged forward at Ozburn. Ozburn stepped aside deftly and let the gun in his right hand swing free on the shoulder sling. He hit Teodoro's jaw with an uppercut so hard the big man stopped and straightened, then dropped to the floor. When Teodoro managed to get to his knees Ozburn leveled a machine pistol at his forehead.

Daisy sat in the doorway wagging her tail.

—Do you repent, Ozburn asked in Spanish.

—I repent.

—I repent.

—I'll find you in hell and kill you, said Teodoro.

Ozburn looked down at the big man's quivering face, the dark, searching eyes, the jagged edge where the ear had been.

—Who has the vehicle keys?

Teodoro nodded toward the TV and Ozburn saw the fob and keys sitting beside the rabbit-ear antenna. He retrieved the keys and stuffed them into a vest pocket without taking his eyes off the men.

—Touch your faces to the floor, all of you.

ATF training was to never get on the ground on orders from an armed opponent: You will almost certainly be executed. Stay on your feet. Stay on your feet. Ozburn knew that trained or not, the cartel men understood this. The two smaller men lowered their heads to the concrete. One began to sob. He offered five thousand U.S. dollars for his life. Then ten thousand. Then ten million. Teodoro stared down at the floor muttering words that Ozburn couldn't understand. He caught the word *Malverde*, patron saint of the *narcos*, and that was all.

—I've bet the life of my wife on this moment. Her name is Seliah.

With that, Ozburn let go of the left gun and brought the last three crucifixes from his vest pocket. He moved from man to man, left to right, working the leather necklaces over their heads with his left hand and the barrel of the machine pistol he held in his right. Teodoro's head was too big so Ozburn dropped the crucifix to the floor in front of him where it landed with a clear tap.

—The god I no longer know has asked me to spare your lives. He says he can save Seliah. We'll see about that, won't we? Stay where you are until I'm safely away or I'll certainly kill you all.

. . .

Ozburn drove back to his car and shot flat the tires of the SUV, then took the Mercury to the spring near Atil and stayed in the wilderness three days. He ate the bread and pastries and forced himself to drink the water he'd bought at the *panadería*. There was a blanket and a heavy jacket in his duffel on top of the bricks of tightly wrapped cash. He had enough kibble in the bag for Daisy, who seemed perfectly content to sleep under the stars, her back to him for warmth. Ozburn's body was alternatingly numb or pain-riddled. Hours were minutes and seconds stretched to days. He hallucinated and wailed and sobbed when the pain was upon him, and he slept through the numbness. He slept for what seemed like a lifetime. He awakened to music, terrifying music so loud his eardrums pounded in pain. His visions were of violence and beasts that he knew did not exist, then of Seliah, whose beauty burst away the ugliness but when he could no longer hold her image the terrors returned and were worse.

The evening of his second day he lit a fire against the chill and just before dusk he saw the black SUV roll to a stop in the distance and Teodoro and his two associates climb out of it. Ozburn and Daisy sat side by side on a hillock and watched them come across the desert toward them. They carried weapons and made no effort to conceal themselves. When they were a few hundred yards away Ozburn saw the three men in the hooded sweatshirts walking across the moraine toward them. Ozburn watched the Mexicans slow down their steady march and the hooded men approach. Teodoro and his *narcos* stopped uncertainly but the men continued toward them. When they were a hundred feet apart Ozburn heard the distant boom of Teodoro's voice and the softer reply of the tall man in the middle. The conversation lasted a full minute but Ozburn couldn't make out the words. Then the gunmen unleashed a fusillade of fire. Ozburn saw the bullets lifting little wisps of rock dust all around him like raindrops and then he heard the reports. A bullet whined overhead in ricochet, trailing off with diminishing volume. Daisy stood and wagged her tail. Ten seconds later the shooting was over and the hooded men had not moved and the Mexican men were running back toward their vehicle with all the speed they could muster. Ozburn saw Teodoro look back and fall down and when Ozburn looked again at the three hooded strangers, they had disappeared, but Teodoro was up and running just the same. Then Ozburn was lying on his back near the spring, his mind blank, his body sweating and his heart pounding as if from a dream he couldn't remember.

Early on Monday Ozburn drove the Mercury into the Mexican side of Buenavista and took a room at the Gran Sueño Hotel. Mateo called him on the room phone just after three o'clock and told him where he was to go. Ozburn knew that part of L.A. County so he didn't have to marshal his trembling hands to write down the address.

—I hope you are rested and feeling well, *pendejo*. You will have to leave Buenavista soon or you will have no deal.

—I'll be there on time, old man.

Mateo gave him a number to call for last-minute instructions. Ozburn shaved, then showered with the duffel propped against the outside of the shower door. Daisy lay on the thin floor rug and licked the water off his ankles when he got out. Ozburn swallowed a handful of vitamins and fed the dog and changed into clean clothes and looked at himself in the mirror. His face was green and his pupils were just dots in the iris. He slipped his sunglasses on and carried his duffel into the clean light of the border afternoon.

Ten minutes later he was speeding east on Interstate 8 in Father Joe Leftwich's beater Mercury. Daisy sat upright in the passenger seat and looked out the window.

34

Bradley Jones walked briskly across the barnyard toward his Cayenne. Mateo had just called and Gravas was on his way north. The afternoon was warm and the huge oak tree was filled with doves that whimpered and flitted and cooed. Jones wore cowboy boots and old dungarees and an oversize Nat Nast shirt. He sported a brown Stetson that Erin had given him on his eighteenth birthday and a matching suede vest he'd stolen from a saddlery in Calabasas the very next day. Tonight she was playing the Halloween party at the Troubadour, sold out of course. The nightclub was a small venue with a history of great music, and she'd driven up earlier in the day for an interview and photo shoot with the *Los Angeles Times*.

He set his holstered Glock .40-caliber on the seat next to him, then drove down the long compound driveway toward the road. His dogs bounded along with him, twelve in all. Bradley looked out the side window and smiled. The dogs might eat him out of house and home but watching them run alongside his vehicles was worth it. He reached up and pressed the controller button. Erin had strung the gate with cardboard witches that flew along as the gate rolled open. Bradley barreled through with a nod to Call, as the dogs skidded and eddied and howled at this, the received boundary of their world. In the rearview he saw the gate slide shut and Divot, the small Jack Russell terrier, leaping straight up and down and barking with the utter abandon of being abandoned.

Bradley drove through the hills of Valley Center, enjoying as always the native oaks and the riotous bougainvillea and the liquidambars and sycamores and flame trees all blushing with reds and oranges and yellows. He followed Interstate 15 north of L.A. and into the desert toward Lancaster. This was unincorporated L.A. County desert, Bradley knew, patrolled by his brethren LASD out of the Lancaster substation, formerly Charlie Hood's turf.

Bradley thought about Hood and the strange convolutions of will and circumstance that had brought together his mother and Hood and himself. He remembered clearly the day that Hood had walked into their lives. Bradley was sixteen and had disliked him on sight. He had disliked the way his mother looked at the detective and the small change of inflection in her voice. He had disliked Hood's clean-cut good looks, the odd combination of hope and skepticism on his face, his unhurried eyes. He had disliked Hood's pride in being LASD and his questioning of his mother. True, Hood had encouraged Bradley to consider law enforcement one day, and told Bradley that LASD pay was "fair" and it was a good place to work. Bradley had bragged about being good with a handgun, which he now remembered had brought a look of concern to Charlie Hood's annoying, freshly shaven face. The only thing that Bradley had liked about Hood was his IROC Camaro, beautifully maintained. But Suzanne had liked the whole package, or fallen for it, or fallen for her version of what he was. Back then Bradley had believed that Hood was her cause of death, and he still believed it now. For this he could not forgive him. He could respect him. He could admire him. He could even see something of what his mother had seen in him—decency, strength, humility. He could befriend him. He could use him. But not forgive.

Bradley continued west now on Highway 138. Mateo had given him an address and a time and Bradley had called Commander Dez immediately. Dez would have her undercover team in place and some cruiser teams ready for backup and a helo in the air but out of sight and earshot. Gravas and Herredia's low-level couriers, whom Bradley had told Dez were in the employ of the Gulf Cartel, wouldn't have a chance.

For the deal, El Tigre had chosen a busy avenue in a newly developed part of Lancaster. Bradley was familiar enough with it—a shopping center anchored by a Ralph's and a Target, ringed by every fast-food franchise in the West and the usual corporate suspects: Blockbuster, CVS, Verizon, Baskin-Robbins, Hallmark Gifts, Supercuts, Mobil Gas and Wash, and a huge parking lot shared by all of the stores. It was a busy place, Bradley knew. Hide in plain sight, he thought: Ninety neat little machine pistols and seventy-five grand in cash wouldn't be noticed in the consumer chaos. The Mobil Gas and Wash was ground zero, in the back, where the condensed air and radiator water were dispensed.

By his own design Bradley himself would not participate in the bust. Too much suspicion would come his way. He told nobody of the intel he gave to Dez that Sunday and he was confident that Dez had kept his name far removed from her operation. But naturally he couldn't resist watching it all go down, thus this voyeur's journey to the desert to watch crazy Sean Gravas and Herredia's lambs be sacrificed to the beautiful and courageous Commander Miranda Dez. She had called him into her office just yesterday to ask about his life, his job, his wife—and to thank him again for bringing the Gravas bust to her. She couldn't wait to take down the Flying-Fabio–Hell's Angel–Jesus Wannabe. At the bust of Gravas and the Gulf men, she would have an undercover deputy get video and stills for the department and of course the media. One of her sergeants had been in touch with Theresa Brewer at FOX, and Dez had thanked Bradley for that contact, too.

The magic hour was to be eight o'clock, and by then Bradley was sitting in his Cayenne in the parking lot, right up close to the Mobil Gas and Wash. He had a good view of the rear part of the station, where the deal was set to go down. He also had a good view of the fourteen pumps, the mini-mart and the drive-through wash. Even at eight P.M. the station was busy, though the wash was being only lightly used. A van disgorged a band of vampires and goblins and a tiny Darth Vader who were led toward the restrooms by a woman while a man swiped his card at the pump. The shopping center and the parking lot were all overrun with customers, Antelope Valley having no antelopes and far more people than services.

He could see Miranda Dez, dressed in jeans and athletic shoes and a black thigh-length leather jacket, leaning against her red Corvette while the gas pumped in, a wireless headset on her ear, her head tilted to one side as if in casual conversation. He saw two scruffy undercover deputies posing as customers in the mini-mart, an older pickup truck with two more UCs getting gas from pump eleven, a Ford 500 freshly out of the wash with two more plainclothes deputies—a man and an attractive woman—wiping it down. Bradley watched a uniformed gas station attendant slip an OUT OF ORDER cover over the car wash control panel, then stand in the middle of the wash entrance with his arms crossed, as if daring anyone to defy the sign. *Strange,* Bradley thought. *Unless . . .*

A silver Mercury sedan bounced into the station and Bradley caught a glimpse of Sean Gravas's blond mane and pale face and the dark insect lenses of his sunglasses. Gravas proceeded across the station as if headed to an empty pump but he drove past the pumps and back onto the avenue and Bradley watched the Mercury join the traffic. Darth and company were marched from the mini-mart back toward the van. Then Gravas was back, entering where he'd exited this time, and crossing the lot again before driving back to where the air and water were dispensed.

A moment later came the vehicle that Mateo had told him to watch for, a white, late-model Denali XL, the four men inside just barely visible behind the smoked windows. Bradley noted the California plates and the BAJA JOE'S decal on the back bumper, just over the trailer hitch. Just as Gravas had done, the Denali crossed the station and exited on the boulevard, only to reappear a few minutes later.

But instead of heading for the darkened back portion of the lot where Gravas now waited, the Denali proceeded to the car-wash entry, where the attendant stepped aside and waved it into the wash. Suddenly the Mercury reversed in a nifty highway-patrol turn and shot forward to the car-wash entry and followed the Denali inside.

Not bad, thought Bradley—a little cave of privacy in the middle of this public place. They could transfer the guns and weigh out the money in less than five minutes, while the "attendant" kept any innocent bystanders from joining the party.

He saw Dez get into her Corvette and pull toward the car-wash entry. The attendant waved his arms and shook his head and Dez began arguing with him. She got out and left her lights aimed into the car-wash tunnel and she must have called in the cavalry, too, because as Bradley watched, the two undercover deputies in the mini-mart and the couple polishing up their 500 and the two more

UC men gassing the pickup truck all drew their weapons and broke for the car wash.

Bradley felt an incredible surge of adrenaline hit him. *There's nothing like this feeling*, he thought, *and no worse torture than having to sit here and just watch.*

Dez waited for the first two deputies to reach her and together they charged into the wash, guns up. Bradley heard one of them yelling at Gravas to *Get down, get down, this is L.A. County Sheriffs and you are under arrest!* Two more plainclothes charged into the entrance, one brandishing a gun in one hand and a video recorder in the other. The last two ran around to cover the exit. A dog began barking inside.

Everyone down! Everyone DOWN!

The first four gunshots rang from inside the tunnel in amplified roars. A woman screamed but another volley of gunfire drowned her out. Curses in Spanish, a man screaming with pain. Then the strange rapid sound of metal being pierced but no sound of gunfire and Bradley knew that Gravas had unleashed a silenced Love 32. Bullets whined and shrieked in ricochet, some of them finding the exits and howling off into the night. One of the plainclothes men staggered out of the entrance and collapsed. The car-wash attendant ran across the avenue. The dog barked faster.

Gravas, down!

Then another long, pounding volley of handgun fire, each blast echoing sharply in the tunnel, and Bradley Jones could control himself no longer.

He ran toward the car-wash exit. He had just rounded the building when the Denali headlights came on and the big vehicle jumped toward him and Bradley saw Gravas and his dog bearing down on him. Bradley raised his gun but even then he saw he was too late.

Gravas reached through the driver's side window with a big tattooed arm and a gleaming machine pistol and sent a silent burst of
fire into Bradley's chest. The fusillade knocked him over to the slick
concrete and the Denali would have crushed him if Bradley hadn't
rolled over and out of the way, the tires squealing past his ear. By
the time he got up and into shooting position the Denali was well
into the boulevard traffic and there was no shot he could safely
take. He dropped his gun and curled into himself and felt the wild
pain in his torso and ran his hands across his chest. But nothing
liquid, nothing warm. Deputies ran past him for the avenue and he
looked up to see Dez's red Corvette scream off in pursuit.

Finally he rose to his knees and looked down at his shirt. No
blood. He felt through the tattered Nat Nast shirt and looked at his
fingers and there was no blood on them, either.

He picked up his gun and stood and stepped into the car wash. In
the semidarkness he could see the big rubber roof brushes tucked up
against the ceiling and the side brushes waiting on their assemblies
and the six bodies heaped on the slick concrete floor like old rags.
Herredia's couriers, he saw, and two of the undercover deputies—
the man and woman who had been detailing their beloved Ford.
One of the couriers groaned and Bradley walked over to him on
wobbly legs. The man stared up at him while his hand walked a few
inches across the wet car-wash floor in search of his weapon.

"We're fools," said Bradley, kicking away the gun.

He staggered outside and leaned against the wall and watched as
three LASD radio cars flew into the gas station from three different
entrances, followed by the paramedics and two more plainwraps.
Traffic was heavy and stalled with spectators, most of them out of
their cars with their cell cameras pointed toward the wash. The helo
hovered overhead. He stuck his gun in his waistband and walked

not slowly and not quickly to his car and got into it and drove away in the opposite direction that Gravas had gone.

He made West Hollywood in less than an hour. On a darkened side street near the Troubadour he stepped from the Cayenne and stripped off his suede vest and shirt, then painfully wriggled out of a heavy steel mesh vest concealed beneath his shirt. The vest had been a wedding gift. The accompanying card was signed, "Your Mother." Bradley had found the joke infuriating but intriguing, given that she was a year dead on his wedding day. According to the jokester, the vest had been custom-forged by a Bakersfield blacksmith of French descent for Joaquin Murrieta, his great-great-great-great-great-great-great grandfather, in 1851.

He opened the hatchback and heaved the vest in. In the vehicle's interior light he could see the buttons that ran down one side of the vest—silver 1851 eight-*reales* coins, drilled on-center and attached to the mail with leather ties. And he could see the old marks and dings and dimples that the vest and someone—El Famoso?—had endured. Bradley looked at the newer dings and divots that had just been added by Sean Gravas and his Love 32. These had a different patina—smoother, cleaner and deeper than those that his great ancestor had survived—and Bradley knew that his luck was holding, that if he'd been shot with a high-caliber handgun or a magnum load, he would be lying back in that car wash with the rest of the luckless dead.

He lifted his undershirt and looked down at his chest. The welts were raised and red with white tops and painful as burns but the skin was unbroken. It looked like he'd been stung by hornets. He got back into the bullet-shredded shirt, then found the old denim jacket he always carried in his vehicle and bundled up against the sudden cold.

He walked around the block, stopped at a liquor store and

bought a pack of smokes and a bouquet of flowers. He stood out-side the Troubadour and lit up and waited for his body to stop trembling and his breathing to slow. It took a while. When he was ready he stepped inside, where the doorman recognized him and gave him a brief nod of acceptance.

35

Ozburn dropped the last of the nine wooden gun boxes into the trunk of the Corolla, then set his duffel over them, grabbed both Love 32s and closed the lid.

He got into the passenger seat and set the guns on the floor and Daisy licked the back of his neck as he cinched up the restraints. Father Joe signaled and looked over his shoulder before slowly pulling onto Floral Street.

"Pick up the pace a little, Padre," said Ozburn. "You don't want to get pulled over for going too slow."

Leftwich smiled and goosed the accelerator and the little four-cylinder hummed obligingly.

"I take it there was a problem," said the priest. He was dressed in his clerical uniform again—black shirt with a stiff white collar, black pants.

"Five men and a woman down and probably dead. I think I killed three of the men and maybe a fourth on the way out. There were so many people and so much shooting, I could hardly tell what was going on."

"But there was no killing in the plan, was there?" Leftwich handed Ozburn his ancient flask and Ozburn took a big drink.

"Just a straight-up, money-for-guns buy. I don't know what happened. Four of Herredia's errand boys had the guns. The others screamed they were deputies but by then they were shooting at me. Anybody can yell cop. Gulf Cartel gunmen came to mind. But two were women so I'm thinking LASD. Seven in all. Fuckin' chaos, Father. When I saw them coming at me from both ends of that tunnel I just did what I had to do. Thanks for being here."

"I told you I'd be here."

Ozburn hit the flask again and gave it back. Leftwich signaled and turned onto Avenue L and accelerated slowly down the wide street. "We'll take the back roads for a while. Stay off the interstate. Maybe use the Pearblossom Highway. Love that drive. Have you seen Hockney's painting of it?"

"Move it, Joe."

"It's only a four-banger."

"Here we go!" said Ozburn.

He released the lap harness and jackknifed his body and scrunched into the leg space as far as he could, his back buckling and his legs aching while the LASD cruisers whined past them with their lights flashing.

"Looks like two more coming up," said Leftwich. "And one has a headlight out. That's amusing."

Ozburn felt the top of his head pressing against the glove box and his back rippling with pain and he stared down at the floor mat. Balled tightly as he was, his sunglasses steamed up as two more sirens shrieked and two more sets of lights flashed by overhead. He growled. He felt Father Joe's small hand on his back, rocking him gently, and heard his soothing voice: *Be still, my son. You have performed good acts and defeated evil.*

"I feel like my body is being eaten," said Ozburn.

"You are overtired. Delia was like that as a child. You need rest. They're gone, Sean. You can come up."

Ozburn flung himself upright against the seat and again fumbled for the lap harness and again Daisy licked the back of his neck with great enthusiasm.

"Delia?"

"My sister. The woman you saw that night in the restaurant."

"She's pretty."

"She's a very bright person, too. Troubled, at times. Now, tonight you should stay at my place. I've got a very nice little double-wide right up here in Phelan. On half an acre and neat as a pin. And I'll be busy elsewhere for the next few days, so you'll have the run of the place. I'll be gettable by phone. Oh, and there's a rather old Chevy Malibu in the carport but it runs well and you're welcome to it."

Ozburn groaned and leaned his head against the rest and squinted through his sunglasses at the oncoming headlights, bright and merciless.

They rode in silence for a long while, looping around the regional airport in Palmdale and picking up the Pearblossom Highway toward Phelan.

"Sean, you've done some very fine work these last few weeks. There have been some unexpected setbacks, but a man's character is revealed when he's challenged more than when he's triumphant. I'm honored to have helped you in my own small way. You know what I'd like? I'd like to for you to tell me what you're planning to do with those guns in the trunk."

Ozburn rolled his head to the left and took a long look at the priest. "My job."

"Your job? Oh, you're going to sell them to bad men and let ATF swoop in?"

"Roger."

"You are a delight to know and a delight to work with."

"Step on it, Padre."

"We're almost there."

Later that night after Leftwich had driven off, Ozburn sat on the couch in the trailer with Daisy at his feet and listened to the wind skid across the high desert and nudge the trailer. He thought it was like a lion nosing a mouse. He drank Father Joe's Irish whiskey. For a long while he sat with his head back looking up at the ceiling and he could feel nothing at all in his body. Not one sensation, not the awareness of a limb or a pulse or the taking of a breath. He willed his feet to move and they did not. He willed his head to lift off the couch back but it did not lift. In this state, emptied of the physical, he thought of Seliah, imprisoned by sleep like a butterfly in amber. Where did her mind go? Somewhere pleasant? Surely she dreamed. He thought of the first time he'd seen her in the winter quarter freshman comp class at the U of A in Tucson, walking in with one of her swim team friends, both of them tall, pretty girls wrapped up against the desert cold in Wildcats Swimming sweatshirts, their hair greened by the hours of chlorine, faces tan and lovely. The friend had caught his eye first, but then he looked at Seliah and she smiled back and he elbowed the dive-team buddy beside him and said: *Look!* He thought of the swimmer-diver parties they'd had and a long hike they took up Sabino Canyon in the spring where he'd plucked her a handful of wildflowers and this had moved her far more than he'd thought it would, and later, when he took her arm and stopped her as a big Western diamondback inched across the trail in front of them he had felt her shiver; then she pulled him back down the trail and clamped her body onto his and kissed him hungrily for what seemed like an hour. Ozburn thought of watching Seliah get third in the women's freestyle at the Pan Am Games, of the wild grad party, and of meeting her folks in Boulder, their wedding day and honeymoon and the day he got his acceptance notification from ATF. He thought of the good years, then the undercover assignment, his disillusionment, his rebirth near the volcano, his acceptance of the mission that he himself never really understood. The terrible good acts. Defeating evil. Monstrous desire. The loss of faith in everything he had ever been faithful to. The sickness and the madness and the killing. *What happened*, he wondered. *What?*

Later he felt his body return and he got up for another whiskey and retrieved his laptop from the duffel and he wrote an e-mail to Seliah even though he knew it might be a while before she could read it.

From: Sean Gravas [sGravas23@zephyr.net]
Sent: Monday, October 31, 2011 11:49 p.m.
To: Gravas, Seliah
Subject: for when you wake up

Dear Seliah,

Welcome back to the land of the LIVING, sweet woman! You must be exhausted! The important things are to rest and eat right and get up and move around as SOON as you can. You might want to do it in the water. If you're right about that virus, then your aversion to water would be attributable to it, and now that you've awakened and BEATEN BACK that virus, you can return to the water that you always loved. Three alleged wise men PROMISED me that you would live if I repented and I did repent though the whole thing seemed pretty much beside the point. When you've done and seen what I have, does your contrition really matter? To who, and why?

I don't know what happened. I know they can take me but they CAN'T take away my love for you. It will live until the last beat of my heart. And if, as some people say, what we do in life can reach beyond our deaths, then my love WILL touch you someday when you least expect it! I wish it could have been through a daughter or a son. I'll try to get Daisy back to you, though a dog isn't much of a substitute for a child. So listen for me in the silences and I'll be there, standing off to the side, waiting in the shadows, TOUCHING you like the wind, invisible but present. You're young enough to START again and to have it ALL. I want you to have it ALL. Remember me fondly and keep open a comfortable room in your heart for me. I'll be there and I won't be a bother. Live well. Love well. Multiply. The world needs more of you. I'd be honored if you named your first son after me.

With Love Everlasting,
Sean

A few minutes later Ozburn called Paco's number and gave the time and place to him.

"Bring Silvia or there is no deal, Paco."

"But if there's no deal, we will kill Silvia."

"Paco, *evolve*. Bring Silvia or you'll never get the guns. I'll take her from there. I'll get her home."

After a long silence Paco agreed.

Next Ozburn called Hood and gave him the same place but an earlier time.

"I heard about Lancaster," he said.

"What a mess, Charlie. LASD?"

"Yes. Two of them died. And three of Herredia's couriers. The other one is critical."

"They tried to take me out, Charlie. I figured someone had tipped the deal to the Gulf Cartel. So I did what I had to do to survive. But I've got your guns. And I've got the Gulf Cartel's money. All I need is a ribbon to tie it all up with. Day after tomorrow, Charlie. Will you be there?"

"I'll be there."

"They'll have a girl named Silvia with them. I saved her from death and she lives in Agua Blanca. Promise me you'll get her home."

"I promise."

"It's been a good run. I'm tired."

"I can see Seliah right now," Hood said.

"What is she doing? How does she look?"

"Sleeping. She looks far away."

"When will they bring her out of it?"

"Soon. The antibody counts are almost there. She's almost fought it off."

Ozburn felt his throat constrict and the tears come to his eyes. They burned hot and spilled over. "It's hard to talk right now."

"Sean, the real test is what's she's got left. There will some brain damage. It might be severe. It might be . . . not so bad."

Ozburn said nothing. He pictured his wife again, fair and frozen deep within the coma.

"Oz, we still have a deal? You're going to help us take down these creeps day after tomorrow. Then we're going to see Seliah. Is that right?"

"Soriana didn't like my idea."

"No."

Silence. "I didn't think he would. So, I'm yours, Charlie. The guns and money and I will be in a white Chevy Malibu."

He hung up.

36

Two evenings later Hood sat on the roof of a Vernon warehouse with his knees up and the night-vision binoculars in his hands. He was partially hidden by a ventilation housing in which a canister fan spiraled patiently beside him. He had a good sight line to the parking lot behind the warehouse, where Ozburn would deliver the ninety remaining Love 32s.

Overhead the stars shimmered meekly, their vigor blanched by the lights of L.A. The night was crisp and cool. Vernon was an industrial city with an actual full-time population of ninety-one, making it the smallest city in Los Angeles County. But its dozens of factories and processing and rendering plants employed some fifty-thousand workers. Hood was a fan of Vernon's best-known product—the oversize hot dogs sold at Dodger Stadium. And he knew that this portion of the city had been carved out by MS-13 gangsters tied to Benjamin Armenta's Gulf Cartel.

He looked out at Pacific Avenue, where agent Robert Velasquez sat astride his Kawasaki at the curb. Velasquez was wrapped in black leathers and a black full-face helmet. Bly was in her gray Jeep, parked at the far end of the dark lot. Morris was on the sidewalk just outside the wrought-iron security fence that surrounded the parking lot and the warehouse, wearing a dark hoodie and sweats and beat-up running shoes. Hood could see him limbering up for his run, folding into his hamstring stretches now that his jumping jacks were done. Six more ATF agents in three vehicles were obscured in the darkness within a two-hundred-foot radius from the parking lot, and these would form the second wave. All ten were armed and linked by wireless radio headsets. Blowdown would make the first contact; the six others would do what needed to be done.

Hood watched the white Malibu turn from the avenue into the lot and in the wash of light from the streetlamp he caught the flash of Sean Ozburn's hair and pale face and the dark lenses of his sunglasses. The car prowled the fenced perimeter, past Velasquez on the avenue and Bly in the lot, and finally Ozburn pulled diagonally across two parking places directly below Hood. The engine stopped and the lights went off.

Ozburn sat without moving. Hood watched him through his night-vision binoculars. Oz looked exhausted, his face tilted down as if he were studying something on the steering wheel. He wore a bulky coat with the collar turned up against the chill and his usual sunglasses and a black bandana across his forehead. Hood remembered the Ozburn he had known just a few short months ago, the Ozburn who was alert and brave and strongly made and beautifully trained, and now Hood felt only an angry sadness for the man. Hood wanted to fly down the fire escape ladder and run out and tackle him. Then drag him to UCI Medical where they could try to beat back his disease. So he could see his wife again. And after that? Even with two miracle cures, *was* there an after that? Hood couldn't picture Ozburn spending the rest of his life in prison. He scanned the interior of the car for signs of Daisy but saw none. *Not like Sean to be without her*, he thought.

A shiny black Tahoe swung into the lot, blacked-out windows and custom wheels. It followed the same route that Ozburn had, then parked three stalls away from the Malibu. All four doors opened at once and four men stepped out. The driver was tall and slender and the others were short and thick. They looked young, and a lot like the safe house assassins Sean had rubbed out. *Like spirits come to take their vengeance*, thought Hood.

He saw Dyman Morris jog into his field of view, coming slowly down the sidewalk. Velasquez sat his bike. Bly was not visible but Hood knew she was scrunched down in the seat, watching the deal in her mirrors, using the adjustment toggle to follow the action.

"Oz isn't moving," whispered Hood. By the playbook, Blowdown wouldn't make their move until everyone was out of their vehicles—always the chance somebody would spook and try to speed off. "Four couriers are out. I don't see any guns. Sean's taking his time."

Then Ozburn turned and looked through the driver's side window. A faint smear of condensation spread on the glass, and Oz used a fingertip to draw two eyes and a happy smile. Then the smear and the face faded to nothing. Hood saw that Oz had shaved off his mustache and started a full beard—it looked like he hadn't shaved since Hood saw him last. Ozburn watched as two of the men approached. Then he swung open the door and grasped the car body and pulled himself out, the car wobbling with his weight. Two beer cans spilled out and clinked to the asphalt. He stood uneasily and raised his hands and Hood saw what he had feared.

"It's not Sean! *Not Ozburn!* Let's move!"

Hood dropped the binoculars and sprinted to the fire ladder and flung himself down the rungs fast as he could go. He sprung off early, hit the ground hard and drew his sidearm. He rounded the building in time to see Velasquez on his Kawasaki bounce into the parking lot, and Bly's Jeep screech into a highway-patrol turn. Morris cleared the spires of the fence top and landed with his gun up.

Then Hood heard the screaming:

"United States agents! Drop to the ground! I'm ordering you to—"

Fuck, man! Don't shoot! Don't shoot!

"Police! On the ground! *Now!*"

I'm on the ground! I want a lawyer!

Then the squealing of tires as two more SUVs stormed through the gate into the lot. Hood saw that all four of the gangsters and Ozburn's stand-in were proned out now and Velasquez and Bly had already cuffed the tall driver and were working on another. Morris alone was cinching another. Hood ran to the fourth, a skinny kid who glanced up at him, then popped upright and ran for the building. Hood ran, jamming his gun into his waist holster. He caught up and crashed into the boy and they rolled once and Hood came up on top with a knee on the kid's back and one of his arms pulled back from the shoulder and up at the elbow, on the brink of outrageous pain.

"Be cool, man. *Be. Cool.*"

"Fuck your—"

Hood held the kid's face against the asphalt and Morris kicked away the gangsta's loose gun. The blued steel pistol skidded away with a clatter. Morris lashed the ties, then jumped off the kid and circled one hand over his head like a victorious calf roper, grinning at Hood.

"We're *good*," said Morris. "God, we're good."

Hood helped Bly cuff the Ozburn double and stand him up. He was tall and overweight and his hair and clothes were filthy and he reeked of alcohol and old sweat. Hood pulled off the man's scratched sunglasses and looked into his face.

"What's your name?"

"Billy."

"Billy what?"

"I'm innocent, man. Guy paid me five hundred to drive up here and do this. I wasn't supposed to drink until it was over but I had the five hundred. You know? It was some dude who looked like me if I didn't drink so much beer. He said FATE would understand. Or was it ATF? One of them. I'm innocent. Those handcuffs are tight."

Hood slid the sunglasses back onto Billy's face and walked to the black Tahoe. He swung open the rear liftgate and saw the terrified girl looking back at him, her eyes dark and wide and her mouth plastered with duct tape. Her ankles and wrists were bound with rope. He spoke to her in Spanish.

—No one is going to hurt you, Silvia. You are going home to Agua Blanca soon. Don't be afraid of us and don't cry.

He touched her hand gently, then cut the rope from her wrists and ankles with his pocket knife.

He waved Bly over, then strode toward the warehouse, lifting his vibrating phone from his hip.

"Mr. Hood, this is Nurse Marliss Sharer at UCI Med Center. He showed up, the husband, like you said he might. He had all these guns and he looked deranged. I thought everybody was going to die. We all thought we were going to die. Some were praying out loud. He growled at us. He just now walked out. I called security and police and you. He held his wife's hand and spoke into her ear and kissed her once; then he left. I'm still shaking. Really hard."

37

Ozburn drove the minivan south at the speed limit. He'd bought it for two grand cash the day before at a used car lot in Victorville, just after he'd picked up the big, long-haired man standing near the highway entrance with a WILL WORK FOR BEER sign. Ozburn had taken the man's cursory resemblance to himself as an omen, though he wasn't positive that Billy would be able to stay sober long enough to get the Malibu, money and guns to Vernon.

Ozburn now figured three hours max to Buenavista, then another five to Nogales. At a convenience store in Corona he got gas and provisions and two hot dogs each for himself and Daisy. He was famished. He would not let Seliah's pale sleeping form leave him: He saw the road and the cars and the sky before him through her ethereal, dreamlike face.

The next thing he knew he was pulling up to Charlie Hood's home in the foothills outside Buenavista. No cars anywhere, lights on over the garage and the porch and inside the kitchen. He jimmied the side door to the garage and when he and Daisy were inside he laid his shoulder into the door that led to the house and it burst open without much fight. He carried Daisy's kibble and bowls into Hood's house and filled a bowl with food and the other with water.

Ozburn knelt down and opened his arms and Daisy, sensing catastrophe, very slowly walked over, tail low, head down, ears relaxed. He hugged her and told her Hood was a good guy, *take care of him and of yourself.*

He petted her for a moment, then stood and swung the splintered door shut behind him and made sure the garage door was closed tight. Daisy started howling. He got back into the van and lifted his sunglasses to empty the tears that had built up behind them, then headed down the dirt road toward the interstate.

Yuma. Tucson. Nogales. Ozburn crossed the border easily and followed Mexico 15 south from town to a wide dirt road that took him into the hills. He came to *Betty* and the nice little landing patch. He rousted Miguel from his trailer. The young man was happy to get his money though Ozburn noted that he kept his distance and seemed eager for Ozburn to be on his way. He gave Miguel twice what he'd promised.

—Where is your dog?

—She's with a friend.

—She will not fly again?

—Unless she grows wings.

Ozburn stowed his duffel but stashed a freshly loaded Love 32 up in the cockpit. Miguel had filled the tank. He offered to man the prop but Ozburn waved him away and threw the big propeller himself, thrilled as always at the way his minor strength was magnified by *Betty*, turned into something that could roar and fly. It took him a few tries. When he walked back around the wing to the cockpit he felt nothing in his feet and little in his legs.

He settled into the rear seat using his hands to arrange his numb legs, nodded at Miguel in the darkness and taxied out to the flat, groomed swatch of desert. Seconds later he was airborne and climbing, the sound of *Betty*'s engine right there in front of him like a steady old friend leading the way. He headed west along the invisible border, just sprinkles of lights separated by chasms of darkness. San Miguel was a flicker, Sonoyta a bigger flicker. Then the black bulk of the Agua Dulce Mountains, and the Cabeza Prietas and the Gilas. Later the sprawl of Yuma far ahead and he saw that the dawn was chasing him now, a frail phantom of light gaining from the eastern sky behind him. The needle on his fuel gauge was just above empty.

He followed the California–Mexico border as the sun rose. The towns became cities and the cities grew and he veered north until he could see San Diego, a panoramic, sun-blasted tangle of buildings and freeways already dense with cars in the clean morning light. He looked down on the graceful blue Coronado Bridge and the flat shimmer of Glorieta Bay, and when Point Loma had scrolled away beneath *Betty*, there was the vast silver Pacific stretching as far as Ozburn could see and beyond. The engine sputtered and caught.

His legs and feet were without feeling and even his arms were heavy and dull and slow to obey him. To the north a commercial airbus out of Lindbergh Field began its big U-turn over the water. Far to the south Ozburn saw a small Cessna heading for Catalina Island.

He called up the image of Seliah asleep in her hospital bed. And although her beauty had long ago burned into his memory, it still caught him by surprise as it so often did—Seliah, the girl with the green hair walking into the lecture hall, Seliah cutting through the water at the Pan Am Games, Seliah on their wedding day, Seliah on their honeymoon beach on Moorea, Seliah combing out her hair or making coffee or polishing her car or fussing with a bouquet of flowers. Even sleeping she had the power to move him.

Betty coughed and sputtered and started up again but then she fell silent. Ozburn heard the wind whistling past the fuselage and the hiss of air on the wings. The night was immense beyond all his comprehension.

He felt *Betty's* nose turn toward earth but he couldn't move his arms to correct her course. He looked down at his hands and ordered them into action but they refused. The altimeter reading plummeted and the compass needle circled crazily. He tried to move his feet and raise his knees but they had forsaken him, too. Instead he imagined his first real date with Seliah, breakfast at the Congress Hotel in Tucson, and they ate and sat and drank coffee for two full hours and at the end of it Ozburn knew his life had changed and she was to be the biggest part of it. That was in February and they'd run through a pouring rain to Ozburn's beat-up Dodge, and halfway back to her place the Dodge stalled at a light and they had to get out and push the thing to the roadside. They were drenched and half-frozen and the gutter was a torrent of brown water that pushed at the car like a big hand. Then their first kiss, both of them trembling with cold with the heater on full blast and the windows fogged and the rain belting the roof of the car. Now Ozburn could feel nothing of his body except the vertigo of that kiss, the warmth and softness of it so startling and right in a cold, hard world. He held his eyes open and steady and watched the spangled Pacific rising up to claim him.

38

Ten days later Dr. Jason Witt of UCI Medical Center decided to suspend Seliah's sedatives and wait for her to awaken from the coma. She had been under heavy sedation for sixteen days, metabolically sustained with infusions. She had been bathed daily, and moved several times each day and night to promote circulation and prevent bedsores.

Witt wore a linen suit and white court shoes, and his tone of voice was more neutral than hopeful. "We've been monitoring regional cerebral perfusion using Doppler ultrasonography. Her serum, saliva and cerebrospinal fluid samples have been tested every other day for immune response and viral clearance. Her rabies-specific IgM and IgG and viral excretions in the saliva have fallen dramatically. The nuchal biopsy shows only very weak rabies virus antigen and the polymerase chain reaction was negative. What all that means is she's beaten back the virus. It's almost totally absent now. It has done its damage. If she awakens, she will be insensate to pain and touch, and paralyzed. But she'll be electrically viable. Her brain is functioning and it should continue to function. She'll have to learn many things again. She's going to have to boot up from scratch. So to speak."

Witt explained this to Seliah's parents and two brothers, Sean's parents and two sisters, and to Charlie Hood, allowed by the families to loiter around the edges of the tense inner sanctum. There had been some long and painful hours. Hood felt spent. But the families had shown strength and deep feelings for Sean, and Hood had not detected any blame for what Seliah was now going through. Not of Sean. Not of ATF. Ozburn had been found by fishermen in the wreckage of *Betty*, twelve miles west of San Diego, eight days ago.

"We do know," the doctor said solemnly, "that only a very few unvaccinated people have survived rabies after symptom onset. Very, very few."

"Five," said Seliah's father, Glen.

"Yes," said Witt. "We embarked on this protocol with both hope and awareness of risk. It has worked in the past. Sometimes it has failed. We've hoped and prayed it will work for Seliah. She is obviously loved very much and that is a great help. Now it's time."

There was an uneasy silence during which eyes did not meet. "How long?" asked Seliah's mother, Shivaun. "If she's going to wake up, when will it be?"

"In the best scenario, she should be able to blink or cough within twenty-four hours. After that, the chances of her waking go down significantly. We hope that she will respond to rehabilitation. You've been through a lot. So please stay. Wait together. Talk to her. Talk to each other. Pray. We'll wait for Seliah to come back."

Deep into the first night they took turns sitting with her, waiting for her to cough, or maybe even open her eyes briefly. Sixteen hours came and went and she did not move except to breathe. Her pulse, respiration and blood pressure all registered low normal. The flesh of her face looked somewhat slack, as did her arms. Hood saw that she was pale now, beyond just fair, and with her platinum blond hair spilled back on the pillow, she was a ghostly sleeping beauty. *And your prince came to kiss you*, Hood thought. He heard Janet Bly's voice: *We don't live in fairy tales, Charlie.* She was right. But what did they live in?

Hour twenty arrived with sunrise at its back and Hood looked out at the gray morning light. Beyond a knot of freeways he could see Arrowhead Pond and Edison Field and to Hood these temples of man seemed vain and superfluous. To the northeast the purple flanks of the Santa Ana Mountains sat heavily against the lightening November sky.

Hood closed his eyes and listened to the thrum and mew of the intensive care unit. Sean's two sisters sat to his left and Seliah's two brothers on his right. He thought of his own brothers and sisters and his mother and father. They were spread across the map but they were still a family. For Hood there was some consolation in this.

When he looked at her again he saw the glimmer of Seliah's open eyes.

A week later she still could not move anything but her eyes. She tracked her visitors and gave no sign of recognizing anyone except her mother, whose little finger she was able to squeeze. The others she regarded with mute but unmistakable fear.

Over the next eight days she slept in four-hour cycles and cried for hours in between. Witt said she was frustrated with her paralysis. He said she was like a baby, having to learn things again but she was in a hurry because she remembered how she used to be. She would learn patience. She would have to.

Gradually Seliah began crying less.

By the end of another week she moved her head, then her hands and feet. Her respiration tube was removed and she breathed on her own.

She began looking at people with diminished fear, except for her mother, who held her hand and brushed her hair and rubbed the lotion on her body. Seliah stared at her with love unconditional.

She whispered, then talked very softly, gibberish at first, then words, then sentences.

She sipped water and broth.

She appeared to remember some of the deep past but little of the recent.

She was sleeping less. Slowly she could concentrate on a conversation—ten seconds, then twenty.

What happened?

Why am I here?

I love you, Mom. Is that you, Dad?

It's very loud in this place.

Late one night Hood handed her a plastic cup of ice and water.

She took it and looked at him with an expression of wonder.

"Sean," she whispered.

"I'm Charlie."

She sipped and handed him back the cup and smiled very slightly. Then her eyes closed and she was gone again.

39

Bradley Jones met Mike Finnegan at the Bordello after his night patrol shift. Bradley had changed out of his uniform because he was welcome in this bar but his uniform was not. It was one in the morning.

"I like it better here when Erin plays that stage," said Finnegan.

"She can't play every night."

"Of course, I liked it better here when it was a real bordello, too. Fantastic city, Los Angeles in the eighteen hundreds."

Bradley looked at him and shook his head. "What can I do for you, Mike?"

"I just wanted to hear more about the Lancaster shoot-out. The headlines and pictures and news footage have all been very thorough but I wanted your insider's story. What a mess that must have been."

"It's all old news by now. And I wasn't there."

"But surely you've heard a thousand stories. Share some with me!" Finnegan smiled and his face flushed. To Bradley, Mike looked every one of his fifty-two years, except when he smiled. Then he looked like an eighth grader who'd just gotten away with something—delighted and eager to try it again. Bradley realized that Mike's delight was what made him so easy to talk to. It made you want to help keep that smile on his face.

So Bradley told him what he'd heard: An informant had told an unnamed LASD deputy that a gunrunner was unloading a hundred new machine pistols to L.A. Mara Salvatruchas working for the Gulf Cartel. The deputy had told his boss and his boss had put together a seven-member take-down team and a cover team of four radio cars and a helicopter.

"This must have been Commander Dez," said Mike. "She's the most quoted LASD officer in the papers and on TV—except for the PR people, of course. Attractive. Ambition written all over her pretty little face."

Bradley nodded. "None of that's a secret."

"But who was this mystery deputy, I wonder. The one with the very good information."

Bradley shrugged and drank his bourbon.

"Guess, Bradley. Offer up a guess."

"We're the biggest sheriff's department in the country, Mike. What good would a guess do?"

"Just tell me if you know him." Mike beamed and drank his scotch. He looked like a boy who had just gotten exactly what he wanted for Christmas.

"I don't know him."

"Well, his informant turned out to have the right stuff, didn't he?"

Bradley nodded and smiled. "It was one hundred percent accurate, Mike."

Finnegan rubbed his hands together and smiled up at the ceiling, then took another drink. "Two couriers shot dead by Gravas, and another by your people. And two very fine sheriff's deputies fallen in the line of duty. Five deaths. Five."

"Vicky Sunderland and Bob Dunn," Bradley said, his voice lowered in respect.

"What a terrible shame. And, to add to it, the precious cargo of machine pistols vanishes with Gravas, only to be intercepted by Charlie Hood and his ATF team two days later. With quite a bit of money, also. I couldn't help but feel that the glory should have belonged to LASD."

Bradley sipped again but said nothing. It rankled him that Hood and ATF had gotten the guns, money and glory. He could live with the rankle. But Dez had quickly handed him over to Internal Affairs for the intel that had led to two dead deputies, and IA had landed hard. IA could exonerate him, or they could discipline him, or they could take his job. Bradley understood that they had power over him even the U.S. Constitution couldn't deflect. He couldn't plead the Fifth; he couldn't hire a lawyer. Larry King could not help now. The IA discussions were secret, their findings not subject to appeal. IA was clearly suspicious of Bradley's good luck in the Stevie Carrasco kidnapping. They wanted his car-wash shoot-out informant, and they wanted him now. So far Bradley had wriggled out of it by saying his man was back down in Mexico again. He promised to produce him as soon as he returned. He'd have to produce someone. He hoped that Herredia would be able to hook him up with a convincing actor, but Bradley hadn't seen El Tigre in two weeks, the weekly run to El Dorado now impossible to make with IA shadowing him to and from work and home and anywhere else he went. He worked his patrols diligently, wondering if a departmental suspension was on its way. He felt like a rat being tormented by terriers. All he wanted was to put this suspicion behind him and make his cash runs to Mexico again, bust some of the Gulf Cartel's L.A. soldiers, love his wife and prepare their lives for the baby to come.

"Is the wounded courier going to make it?"

"They say so."

"I heard his name is Octavio."

Bradley nodded.

Mike leaned toward him and spoke softly. "Do you feel a division of loyalty?"

"Division? Between what and what?"

"Your department and your working relationships south of the border."

Bradley shook his head and smiled but he couldn't stop the jolt of adrenaline that went through him. "Mike, you're an idiot."

"Oh, but I did manage to help you and Ron get that product south last year, now, didn't I? In fact, without me, our friend Charlie would have found you out. Without a doubt. So instead of being a deputy right now, you'd be an inmate somewhere—and I don't mean in your wife's band. It's totally different on the other side of those bars, I can assure you. So don't call me names, Bradley. It makes you look shortsighted and mean-spirited. The sooner we can become totally honest with each other, the greater things we can do."

Bradley said nothing. *Rat*, he thought. *Terriers*. He sipped his drink and glanced out at the singer, then looked at Finnegan. Mike's mouth was tight and concern lined his forehead.

"Mike, I've been wondering about something. I don't think we met for the first time at the Viper Room last year. I'd never seen Owens before then. But I'd seen you. I'm sure of it now."

Finnegan's blue eyes twinkled. "Well, now that you bring it up, I'd like to let you in on something—you and I first laid eyes on each other when you were less than a year old. I was acquainted with your mother. But I kept my distance as you grew up."

Another shot of adrenaline ran through Bradley, this one cold and sharp. "How come you never told me that?"

"A time for everything and everything in its time."

"Talk to me."

"I introduced your mother to your father."

"Why?"

"To give you a chance at magnificence."

"What shit."

"Really? I'm extremely proud of the way you came out."

"My father is selfish and unaccomplished. The only skill he ever developed was the seduction of women. Then he exploits them."

"But he was also strong and smart and charming and utterly without morals. The perfect partner for a"—Mike cupped his hand to Bradley's ear and whispered—"*Murrieta!*"

"Then let me be perfectly honest with you, Mike. All the Murrieta stuff I told you in the Viper Room that night was bullshit. Like I've got an outlaw's head in a jar. Like I'd tell you, a complete stranger, if I did. Well, I don't have his head. I don't know what got into me."

"I do. That night you were overstimulated by your proximity to Erin. You were throwing off sparks. I mean that literally—your thoughts were sparking and dying, sparking and dying. Like fireworks in the sky. Now, Bradley, if I'm within thirty feet of a person having clear, strong thoughts, well, I can hear them. And I can see what that person is imagining. It's a gift, most of the time. But things can get a little cacophonous sometimes, if I'm in a crowded bar for instance. I've learned to isolate the thoughts and concentrate on what I need to know. But anyway, Bradley, you were not in control of your own thinking. You were only capable of reaction to her. I've seen that before, young man. It's love with obsession in it. It's the grandest love of all. And one of the most entertaining qualities a man or woman can have."

Bradley stared at Mike, thinking, *Fuck you, Mike. You hear me now?*

Finnegan sighed and looked out toward the stage.

"Okay, Mike, you must be right. I was not in control of my own thoughts. Why else would I make up a story about having the head of an outlaw in a jar?"

"You are proud of the head, as well you should be."

"All lies."

"Oh?"

"Made the whole thing up."

"Bradley? Can I tell you something?"

"Anything you want."

"The head you have is not Joaquin's. It belonged to Chappo, who rode with Joaquin's horse-gang. Harry Love killed five of Joaquin's gang that day at Cantua Creek, including Chappo. Harry chose the most frightening and dramatic head and collected it as evidence of his own heroism. Joaquin was fair-skinned and blue-eyed and his hair was light brown. This is not an uncommon combination in his native Sonora, where the Spanish influence is strong. He wore his hair long. He had a lined and soulful face for a man so young. He stood six feet three inches. He was a charming and even-tempered man until his wife, Rosa, was raped. Joaquin's English was very good, having grown up near the border and working his early life in gringo company. El Famoso was struck by two bullets that day at Cantua Creek—one bounced off the vest that Owens delivered to you as a wedding gift."

Bradley felt his breath shorten. He looked long and hard at the little man.

"From you?"

"And Owens, of course."

"I'm running out of things to feel about you, Mike."

"Then stop feeling and listen—the other bullet went through the back of his thigh. We used kerosene to clean it out. It was not fatal."

"You must take me for a complete fool."

"I'm trying not to."

"You don't know anything. You make it all up."

"I rode with Murrieta. Briefly."

Bradley started a smile but he couldn't finish it. "Then when did he die?"

"Twenty-two years later, in eighteen seventy-five. He was fifty-five years old. I was privileged to attend the funeral."

"Where did he die?"

"In El Salado, where he was born. He lived out his life quietly, adored and protected by the villagers. He was well-off from his robbing and horse thievery. I was able to visit him there."

"Why didn't you tell my mother about the head not being his? There was nothing about this in her journals. She wrote hundreds of pages about herself and about Joaquin, but there was nothing about him living out his life in Mexico. Nothing about his blue eyes and fair skin and light brown hair."

Mike reached into his blazer pocket and handed Bradley a leather-bound book. Jones opened it and recognized his mother's beautiful handwriting. The date on the first entry was July 14, 1991, and on the last entry March 23, 1992.

"I eventually told her, of course," said Finnegan. "We must operate on the basis of truth. It's all in the journal. She was delighted that Joaquin turned out to be even more mysterious than his legend made him out to be. She was fried with excitement, to be blunt. Later I took this book from her. I apologize to you for the theft. Though I have to chuckle when I say this: She was changing your diaper when I bagged it. Your unrepentantly useless father and I were killing off a bottle of vodka. He went to get a fresh lime and I just dropped that little book into my pocket."

"Why?"

"Something told me that I would need to make an impression on you someday."

"I'm not impressed. You just gave her the same bullshit you're giving me. *Riding with Murrieta.* Only she believed it."

"She came to believe it."

"You weren't at Cantua Creek, *Mike.* That would make you a hundred and eighty years old."

"Your math is good but your context is faulty. This is like trying to prove the existence of a forest to a man who denies the existence of trees."

"More bullshit." Bradley listened to his own voice and even he had trouble hearing the conviction in it.

Finnegan drank and smiled very slightly. "Your great-great-great-great-great-great-great-grandfather was an imaginative man. He imagined his legend before he began to create it. He saw no difference between what he could imagine and what he could accomplish. He was prone to superstition, prone to gesture and romance, prone to *belief.* Your mother was the same way. They were both obsessive lovers, like you. You'll be more like them someday. It will just take you longer to get there. In many ways human beings grow up much more slowly than they used to. I've seen this in just a few short generations. Evolution can't be hurried. When you are ready to see, you will see, and when you're ready to believe, you will believe."

Bradley felt surrounded by invisible terriers, unable to find a target. *When you are ready to see, you will see.* He tried to go cool instead. "Well, if I'm supposed to weep or something, I'm just not."

"I love your youth. Dearly. The journal is yours to keep with the others. Now your collection is complete. In the back of that volume are a couple of letters Suzanne wrote to me. Illuminating, perhaps. They're yours, too."

Mike finished his drink and pushed away from the table. "Well."

"Where are you going?"

"Out. November is my absolute favorite month."

"Hold on. Let's get a bottle. We'll talk about imagination and belief and El Famoso."

"Maybe another time, Bradley. I just want to spend some hours outdoors now, walking my city on an autumn night."

"Tell me more about him. I want to know."

"When you're ready. You'll be very busy soon. Hearty congratulations on Erin's pregnancy. I'm very happy for both of you."

"Who told you?"

"You did. You've spent the last hour telling me about your wife and your child to come—more of the mental sparks that you let off when you think of Erin. Just like in the Viper Room."

"But I didn't tell you. I absolutely and purposely did not because she . . ."

"She what, Bradley? She neither likes nor trusts me?"

"Go to hell, Mike. Whoever you think you are I'm not impressed."

"You have such strong and beautiful names in your family— Joaquin, Rosa, Suzanne. Even Bradley. I wonder who will come next. He or she will be yours to name, young man. And Erin's, of course. Consider carefully. Names have different polarities. Different weights. Different histories."

40

Monday morning Hood and his Blowdown brethren began packing the ninety Love 32s back into their wooden boxes. By special order from the assistant director, the guns would be heading back to headquarters in Washington, D.C., soon, some to be saved but most to be destroyed. HQ had allowed them to keep four for study. The DOJ van was there and the driver was waiting to take the contraband to the airport for the flight to D.C.

Hood held up one of the gleaming little handguns. The sound suppressor was screwed on, and the telescoping butt rod was extended, and the graceful, forward-curving fifty-shot magazine was in place. He tilted the gun to the brittle fluorescent light of the indoor range and looked at the name, LOVE 32, on the slide.

"I admire Ron Pace's craftsmanship," he said.

"You can compliment him on it personally when we shut down his TJ factory," said Bly.

"All we have to do is find it," said Hood.

"Octavio says he knows," said Velasquez.

"Octavio says he knows a lot of things," said Morris. "Still, he may be the best thing to come out of this mess."

Hood set the gun down with the others. "Sean delivered. Like he said he would."

A moment of silence. Then Morris: "I'd take this whole deal back if I could."

"Amen," said Bly.

"I'm taking this deal," said Velasquez. "For Oz. And for us. It's ninety machine pistols off the street. And a cartel man in jail with tales to tell."

"For Oz," said Hood.

He wrapped the gun in newspaper and set it into the wooden box and he thought of Sean Ozburn in his own.

At home that night he hovered around his kitchen trying to help Beth make dinner. Mainly he watched. She was a tall woman with an aerobic approach to kitchen work—moving across the pavers in big fast strides, stepping over Daisy with a boiling saucepan in her hands, banging pots and pans while talking on without a comma. She could spin a yarn. And another. As an ER physician in Buenavista's Imperial Mercy Hospital, she was rarely without compelling material.

For instance, she had seen her first case of flesh-eating bacteria just last night. Just as ugly as it sounds. This segued into an account of still another stateside victim of the drug wars along the Iron River, a young courier shot to death outside one of Buenavista's rougher saloons. In the last year Hood had grown accustomed to her peaks of energy and high spirits, and the valleys of quiet that separated them. He enjoyed the fact that between a cop and a doctor there wasn't a lot that couldn't be talked about. There wasn't a queasy fiber between them and sometimes the grisly had its own forbidden but delicious humor.

". . . and I said, sure, there's that and about a hundred *other* things it could be, too. I wish I was more like House on TV. Where's the cumin up here? Didn't I bring some over not too long ago? What's on the computer, Charlie? Are you even listening?"

"I can't help you with the diagnosis but a cane would just get in your way. The cumin's behind the steak seasoning. I'm just checking e-mail. Beth, it's hard to assist a hurricane-like person in the kitchen."

"Can you mash potatoes?"

With Daisy sitting next to him Hood mashed and looked out the window at the vast desert. There was a wash just beyond the back patio and he had seen wild pigs and coyotes and feral dogs and even wild horses passing through. And humans, of course—scores of the Mexican poor shuffling slowly north through the sand and rocks and cacti, the infernal heat and stunning cold.

Beth started in on the asparagus, telling Hood that her father had called today to say he'd shot par for the first time on his club course. She said she was toying with the idea of taking up the game so they could do something together.

Hood thought of his own father, almost gone now, no real perception of who he was. Douglas had been a generous and patient man but the dementia had turned him mean. They assigned him the biggest nurses to intimidate him. Every once in a while, on his visits to the home, Hood would see that old warm smile come to his father's face and then he'd say something like, *So, what's your name, young man?* Or, *Fish come in all sizes but when your shorts ride up there's no fixing the tractor.*

He wished his father would have taken up golf, or anything else he could love enough to brighten his days. He pictured his own life at seventy-nine. Golf? Tennis? Tinkering with cars? He'd read once of someone who had a "diminishing portfolio of enthusiasms" and he thought this applied to his father and, for all he knew, could someday apply to himself.

"I was thinking of getting back into tennis," he said.

"You should. You don't have enough recreation in your life."

"Neither do you."

"I'll learn, too. We can play together, Charlie. Are you competitive and sullen if you lose?"

"Usually."

"They say couples don't make good doubles partners."

"I'd try to make an exception for you, Beth."

"Who knows? Maybe we'd be winners."

Hood reached across the counter and pulled the laptop screen to face him. He hit the "send/receive" tab and watched the new message drop into place as he slapped away at the potatoes.

Instead of sitting down to eat when the food was ready they surrendered their pretenses of self-control and Hood led her by the hand to the bedroom in happy anticipation. The lovemaking was heartfelt and strong and to Hood well worth the cold dinner. He put the plates in the microwave and as it roared along noisily he looked at Beth in the candlelight pouring wine, her thick dirty-blond hair piled and pinned up and her white satin bathrobe open high at the leg and deep at the chest.

"What are you looking at?" she asked, smiling.

"You take my breath away."

"A girl could get self-conscious."

"I'll avert my eyes."

"Please don't."

They managed to clear the dishes before heading back to the bed again. There were stars beyond the windows and a moon still low. Hood looked up at her, facing away from him with eyes closed and lips parted and the loose strands of her hair swaying with their rhythm. His hands were free and he ran them down her face and neck and arms and over her breasts and rested them on her thigh tops, smooth and taut with strength. He watched her and felt the tides of pleasure pushing through him and when her breath caught and she began to shake he loosed them into her.

They raided the refrigerator as lovers do. Beth poured chocolate syrup on the ice cream and Hood finally opened the lone message on his laptop. He didn't recognize the sender.

But he was pleased to read that one of the German birders at the Volcano View on Arenal had written back to him.

Dear Charlie Hood,

I received your e-mail of two weeks ago and was not able to find a picture of Father Joe Leftwich. I did find many superior images of birds and flora. Then Gretchen remembered that she had used her cell phone one day because she had allowed her camera battery to become uncharged. And to my satisfaction I found this picture of Father Joe, here attached. It didn't turn out very well but you can tell who it is. We were all in the Volcano View bar and we were having Schnapps. I hope you are well. We are now making plans for a return visit. We have trogons and quetzals in our dreams!

Hood was eager to see a picture of the man who had tortured and destroyed the Ozburns. He opened the attachment and looked at Father Joe Leftwich. His heart was beating hard and his breath came fast. "Oh."

"What's wrong, Hood?"

"Father Joe Leftwich, the priest."

She came around the counter and stood next to Hood. "I'll

be . . . He's gained weight and dyed his hair black since he graced my ICU. But look. He's got the Catholic priest's shirt and collar but it's still Mike Finnegan. No doubt. *He's* Leftwich? What do you mean? When I treated him he was selling bathroom fixtures in L.A. What's going on?"

41

Finnegan walked down South Olive Street downtown and ducked into the J Lounge. He sat alone and had a quick drink and looked out at the downtown L.A. skyline. *My city*, he thought. *Would love to have been born here.*

Then over to West Eighth for another drink at the Golden Gopher. He talked to some people he knew there, bought a round, then excused himself and left. He hit the Broadway Bar and enjoyed his chat with another patron, a young guy named Marcus, wife had just passed on, had a brother in prison—interesting what strangers would tell you if you just asked the right questions and listened to the answers. But he didn't stay long.

The night was cool and there was a breeze and he loved being out of doors in the autumn. He hit the Edison on West Second, then La Cite on Hill Street, very much enjoying the ranchero music and the bartender, a handsome woman of Chilean-German extraction who held a degree in history from UCLA. She stood him a beer and they talked about the river-laced countryside of southern Chile, well below Puerto Montt, near the village of Coyhaique where Gisela had visited as a tourist and Finnegan said he had fly-fished. Chile was still struggling after the big oh-ten quake, she said. The worst thing was the looting. He told her about his daughter's growing career in commercials and of course Gisela had an agent but not many calls so Mike said he'd pass along her number to Owens, and Gisela wrote it on a bar napkin and gave it to him.

He looked in at the Redwood but the crowd was small. He decided against the Bordello, not wanting to wear out his welcome there or run into Bradley Jones, who was clearly hot to jump into Mike's world. Bradley would keep. Bradley would be a father. Bradley would improve with age, like a good red wine.

At Bar 107 he stood outside and listened to the murmur of the drinkers each time the door opened. *The music of humankind*, thought Mike. It was late but the bar was busy with people coming and going. He looked up at the sky and saw the stars faint above L.A. and when the door was held open for his date by a big man in a black leather jacket, Mike took hold of the handle and stepped aside, smiling, so they both could pass. The big man nodded and the woman said thank you.

Mike held the door and looked into the bar. It was filled with people. *My music*, he thought. Some of them he knew, while the others, as with everyone else on earth, he would like to know.

ACKNOWLEDGMENTS

I offer sincere thanks to the following people for their generosity and patience in answering my endless questions.

David Bagley, for his spirited descriptions of the Piper J-3 Cub and of the pleasures of flying in general.

Michael Dee, retired curator of the Los Angeles Zoo, for his expertise on bats and snakes.

Dr. Doug Lyle, a physician and fine writer, for his very intuitive guidance on how a doctor would approach a medical mystery.

John Torres, of Alcohol, Tobacco, Firearms and Explosives in Los Angeles, for his street-smart stories and good-humored enthusiasm.

Larry Ford, Steve K. Martin, Tim Carroll, Scot Thomasson, Drew Wade and Donna Sellers of ATF headquarters in Washington, D.C., for their insights into undercover work.

Sherry Merryman, aka Supersleuth, for her wide-ranging and always enriching research on topics too many to name. Thanks so much.

Last but not least, thanks to Dr. Rodney Willoughby and his fine colleagues at the Medical College of Wisconsin, for leading the charge against the most terrifying disease in the world.

Thank you all for being my lights for this journey. You took me to some wondrous places.

ABOUT THE AUTHOR

T. Jefferson Parker is the author of seventeen previous novels, including the Charlie Hood thrillers *L.A. Outlaws*, *The Renegades*, and *Iron River* and the Edgar Award winners *Silent Joe* and *California Girl*. In 2009 Parker won his third Edgar, his first in the short story category. He lives with his family in Southern California.